THE COINERS' QUARREL

THE COINERS' QUARREL

Simon Beaufort

This first world edition published in Great Britain 2004 by
SEVERN HOUSE PUBLISHERS LTD of
9–15 High Street, Sutton, Surrey SM1 1DF.
This first world edition published in the USA 2004 by
SEVERN HOUSE PUBLISHERS INC of
595 Madison Avenue, New York, N.Y. 10022.

British Library Cataloguing in Publication Data

Beaufort, Simon
    The coiners' quarrel. - (A Sir Geoffrey Mappestone mystery)
    1. Mappestone, Geoffrey, Sir (Fictitious character) - Fiction
    2. Great Britain - History - Norman period, 1066-1154 - Fiction
    3. Detective and mystery stories
    I. Title
    823.9'14 [F]

ISBN 0-7278-6109-3

Typeset by Palimpsest Book Production Ltd.,
Polmont, Stirlingshire, Scotland.
Printed and bound in Great Britain by
MPG Books Ltd., Bodmin, Cornwall.

In loving memory of my father

One

Sir Geoffrey Mappestone was furious. He stood on the wharf that ran along the banks of the great River Thames with his dog at his side, and scowled at the flotilla of boats that tugged at their moorings, trying to bring his temper under control before his audience with the King. His friend, Sir Roger of Durham, watched him with a troubled expression, not sure what to say to calm him, but aware that for Geoffrey to stalk into the King's presence and accuse him of false dealing would be unwise to say the least. Roger glanced at the sky, and saw dark clouds massing overhead, heralding the start of another autumn storm. They matched Geoffrey's thunderous mood, and Roger muttered a fervent prayer that both tempests would blow over before any damage was done.

Behind the two knights was Westminster, comprising the mighty Benedictine abbey with its cloisters, dormitories and refectories, and the stunning hall commissioned by the previous king. Conveniently close to the teeming metropolis of London, the hall was large enough to accommodate King Henry's army of scribes and clerks, and he regularly convened his great councils in it. It was to this handsome palace on the banks of the River Thames that Geoffrey had been summoned, arriving cold, wet and resentful that blustery October morning.

'I will tell the King you are indisposed,' offered Roger, when he grew tired of waiting for Geoffrey to speak. 'I will say you cannot meet him today.'

Geoffrey continued to glare at the ships. 'Why would you do that?'

'Because *I* have no wish to be hanged because *you* quarrel with him,' replied Roger tartly. 'If you tell him what you think, he will kill you. Then someone will mention that you did not come here alone, and he will hunt out the rest of us – me, Helbye, Ulfrith and Durand – and have us dispatched, too, just to show what happens to men who associate with traitors.'

'I am not a traitor,' snapped Geoffrey. 'You cannot betray a man you do not serve, and I do not serve King Henry. My lord is Prince Tancred, and it is he who has my vow of loyalty.'

'And Tancred has released you from it,' Roger pointed out, nodding to the letter in Geoffrey's hand that was the cause of his friend's fury. 'He has dismissed you from his service and urges you to take an oath of fealty to Henry instead. His instructions are quite clear.'

Geoffrey waved the document in Roger's face and the dog whined in alarm; Geoffrey was not a man given to rages, and it was rare to see him in such a temper. 'Tancred did not send this; Henry did.'

Roger scratched his head. Like Geoffrey, he eschewed the current fashion for flowing locks and plaited beards, and was clean-shaven with hair cut to a practical shortness. Geoffrey was tall and well built, but he appeared slight next to Roger, who was huge.

'But it carries Tancred's seal,' objected Roger. 'How can it not be from him?'

'Henry forged it,' replied Geoffrey, trying to be patient. Roger was inclined to take matters at face value – a rash assumption when men like Henry were concerned. 'Tancred wrote to him demanding my return a few months ago, and he copied the style of writing and the seal from that.'

'No,' said Roger stubbornly. 'I accept you are more useful to kings than me – you write and speak several languages – but you are not *that* valuable. Henry's Court is full of clever men, and you are deluding yourself if you think he would commit forgery to secure you.'

Geoffrey did not reply, but reluctantly conceded that Roger might be right. Henry, who had seized the English throne when his brother William Rufus had been shot in a hunting accident two years before, had indeed surrounded himself with intelligent and able courtiers. Also, he set great store by loyalty, which would not be forthcoming from those forced to serve him against their will.

'Besides,' Roger went on, 'other than a small manor on the Welsh border, all you own is armour and a warhorse. You have wits and education, but you overrate the importance of those.'

Geoffrey was well aware of what the illiterate Roger thought of his clerical skills. As a fourth son with scant hope of inheritance, Geoffrey had been destined for the Church, but he had proved himself unsuitable for a life of chastity and obedience, so had been sent to Normandy to train as a knight instead, to make his own fortune and not be a burden to his family. As a mark of the strategy's success, it had been more than two decades before he had returned to England.

'It is the timing that bothers me,' he mumbled, some of his irritation dissipating when he saw Roger might be right. 'We were on the ship at Southampton, on the verge of leaving England, when the King's men arrived and ordered us here.'

'Ordered *you* here,' corrected Roger. 'My father is the Bishop of Durham, Henry's sworn enemy. He is quite happy for me to leave his kingdom. It was you he summoned back.'

'"Summoned back",' mused Geoffrey. 'That is a polite way of putting it! They pounced on us with drawn swords, and we were brought here like prisoners. And then, as soon as we arrive, I am given this.' He brandished the letter again.

'That was delivered here *after* Henry had dispatched men to fetch you back,' said Roger patiently. 'The messenger explained all this when he gave it to you.'

Geoffrey regarded the parchment with contempt, and wondered how Roger could be so naïve. As far as Roger was concerned, the missive was exactly what it seemed: a recommendation from Tancred that Geoffrey should now serve Henry, delivered to Westminster because that was where Tancred thought Geoffrey might be. But Geoffrey was inclined to be suspicious, and suspected the royal clerks had needed more time to perfect their forgery – the letter had not been ready when Henry had ordered his soldiers to prevent him from leaving England.

'I can think of worse men to serve,' Roger continued. 'He has plenty of gold to pay you, and an abundance of enemies to fight. What more can you want?'

'I do not trust him,' said Geoffrey, feeling his temper flare again. 'And I want to return to Tancred.'

'But Tancred does not want you,' said Roger, brutally blunt as he nodded to the letter.

The wind was sharp, and it was cold at the edge of the river, but Geoffrey did not feel like asking for an audience with the King just yet. The royal summons had nothing to do with Tancred's letter – or it should not, if the missive really had arrived after Geoffrey had been ordered back – so Henry obviously had something else in mind. Geoffrey was not sure he was ready to know what.

He walked along the riverbank to where a pier jutted into the grey, murky Thames, wanting time to think about the letter, the summons and the implications of both. The tide was out, so only the far end of the jetty was in the water. Geoffrey's black and white dog trotted off the path, and headed for the structure's barnacle-clad legs and the dark spaces between them. Then there was a flurry of activity. It began to bark furiously and a man broke cover and raced away, tossing something into the reeds as he went. The dog did not follow, but sniffed and worried at something that lay on the beach.

Grateful for any excuse to delay speaking to the King, Geoffrey picked his way across the sticky, rock-strewn shore and ducked under the pier. The dog liked nothing more than a moving target to harry, and the knight was curious to know what it considered more interesting than a chase. He stopped short when he saw. A man lay there, his face covered with blood and his eyes staring sightlessly upward.

When Roger realized a corpse had been abandoned under the jetty, he tore after the fleeing man, although Geoffrey knew he would not catch him. A Norman knight was heavy in his armour, and could only manage shorts bursts of speed. Roger's quarry had too great a start, and was soon lost to sight, leaving Roger to return breathless and frustrated.

'He threw this away,' he said, dropping a bloodstained stone at Geoffrey's feet.

'His murder weapon,' mused Geoffrey. 'He used it to stove in his victim's head.'

'They were both Saxons,' said Roger, noting the corpse's flaxen locks and home-sewn woollen tunic. 'Would you recognize the man I chased, if you saw him again?'

Geoffrey shook his head. 'I did not see his face.'

'I saw yellow hair under his hat. He and his victim are probably here to petition the King. But we cannot leave this corpse here, or the tide will carry it away. Stay here, while I fetch help.'

It began to rain after Roger had gone, spiteful little needles that stung, carried by a wind that was growing fierce. Trees swayed and bent, and the surface of the Thames was ruffled into scum-topped waves. While he waited, Geoffrey reread Tancred's letter, trying to be objective.

The writing was identical to that in missives he had received in the past, with distinctive embellishments on the letter T and, if the seal was not Tancred's own, then it was an excellent imitation. But why would Tancred suddenly decide he could do without Geoffrey? Was it because his knight had recently spent too much time on personal business, and other men had taken his place as trusted advisers? Was it because he had not returned the moment he had been summoned, and Tancred did not want officers who disobeyed his orders? Or was it because Tancred had not sent the letter at all? Geoffrey did not know what to think, although he was aware that if the message *were* a forgery, and he followed its instructions to serve Henry, then Tancred would be furious. And being caught between Tancred's temper and Henry's scheming was not an attractive proposition for any man.

Roger soon returned with four soldiers. Two began a futile search for the killer, while the others wrapped the body in a blanket, chatting to Roger as they worked.

'The victim's name was Fardin,' said one in Norman-French. 'He is one of a party of Saxons who are here to accuse each other of dishonest dealings. There are two factions, and they are bitter enemies. As far as I am concerned, we should

5

leave them to kill each other. I am tired of hearing about downtrodden Saxons and Norman usurpers.'

'Aye,' agreed Roger fervently. 'It is time the Saxons learnt to live with their lot.'

'These men have been here a week now,' the soldier went on. 'They were polite at first, but the King has kept them waiting too long, and now they are rude and resentful. They are moneyers.'

'Moneyers?' queried Roger, confused. 'You mean they own money?'

'I mean they *make* money. They own mints in a place called Bristol, and Master Sendi has accused Master Barcwit of making underweight pennies. They detest each other, and it looks as though Barcwit's men have just murdered one of Sendi's.'

'It is a pity I did not see the killer's face, but he should not be too hard to find,' said Roger. 'You cannot smash a man's head with a stone and not be covered in blood.'

The soldier promised to inspect Barcwit's party for tell-tale stains, then he and his companion carried Fardin away. When they had gone, Roger gave Geoffrey the news that the King was currently out hunting, but that he intended to see them that afternoon. Geoffrey was startled. It was far sooner than he had expected – as the squabbling Saxons had evidently discovered, people could be kept waiting a long time before the King deigned to grant them an audience.

'Tancred probably prefers life without you,' said Roger, seeing his friend turn his attention back to the letter. 'Like me, he enjoys honest slaughter, and does not want someone preaching mercy all the time: he has more fun when you are not there.'

'Perhaps.' Geoffrey had indeed urged Tancred to clemency when the Prince would have killed his enemies, but sparing them had reaped its own rewards in terms of returned favours, and he did not think Tancred should resent him for what had proved to be sound counsel.

A jangle of bells announced that a meal was about to be served, and Roger brightened. It had been a long time since the pottage they had eaten before dawn, and he was hungry.

But Geoffrey was still too angry for food. He stared moodily across the river, to where the ships at anchor shifted and strained in the gusting wind. He wondered whether they were in for a storm, and thought it might be a good thing if Westminster Palace was torn apart by a gale, preferably while the King was inside it. Then Henry's older brother, the Duke of Normandy – whom many people thought was England's rightful monarch anyway – could claim the throne.

But would England be a better place under the Duke? Geoffrey reluctantly conceded that it would not. For all his faults, Henry was a good ruler, and had already exiled several greedy and corrupt barons – men like Roger's father and Bellême, the Earl of Shrewsbury, popularly regarded as two of the most wicked men in Christendom. These selfish, profligate nobles would no doubt prosper again if the amiable, but lenient, Duke came to power.

'Hurry, or there will be nothing left,' said Roger, glancing to where people were beginning to converge on the hall. 'These clerks eat far more than—'

'There they are!' came a shout. 'They have not even left the scene of their crime. Come on!'

Geoffrey watched in astonishment as half-a-dozen men formed a tight little knot and began to charge towards him, wielding daggers and cudgels. He knew by their clothes that they were Saxons, and the one in the lead was a particularly large specimen, with flowing yellow locks and criss-cross leg bandages of a type never worn by the fashion-conscious Norman. They looked intent on mischief, so he drew his sword, but indicated to Roger that they should not fight if it could be avoided. It was obvious they were not warriors, and he did not want to begin his interview with Henry by trying to explain why he had massacred six of his subjects.

He parried the leader's clumsy, hacking blow, and sent him staggering back among his companions, amazed that the man would dare to attack fully armed knights. Both he and Roger wore mail under their Crusader's surcoats, and helmets protected their heads. They carried heavy swords and daggers, and were formidable opponents to men armed only with knives and sticks.

'You murdered Fardin!' the leader yelled, struggling to regain his balance. His companions, quickly seeing they had picked a fight they could not win, prudently held back, weapons wavering uncertainly.

'That soldier told us two Norman knights "found" him,' spat another, who seemed angry enough not to care about the odds of victory. He was a small man, who wore peculiarly shaped shoes: the heels were higher than the soles, and were evidently designed to make him appear taller. 'But my father taught me that the man who "finds" a murdered corpse is nearly always its killer.'

'He was right,' replied Geoffrey evenly. 'Fardin's attacker *was* with him when we stumbled across the body. My friend did his best to catch him, but he escaped.'

'Fardin was my best coin-maker,' snarled the leader. 'How much did they pay you to kill him?'

'No one pays *me* to kill,' objected Roger indignantly, ignoring the fact that he often sold his martial skills to wealthy men. 'I do it because I like it.'

'But not in this case,' interjected Geoffrey hastily. 'We did not harm Fardin.'

The short man was unconvinced, and appealed to his companions. 'He is just trying to make our feud with Barcwit worse than it is already. Do we let Norman scum—?'

'Lifwine!' came a sharp voice from the path. Geoffrey turned and saw a woman hurrying towards them. She wore a blue kirtle with pendant cuffs, and a belt accentuated her tiny waist. She was in her thirties and, in defiance of the Norman custom for women to conceal their hair with veils, she wore hers in two long plaits, so fair they were almost white.

'Adelise,' said the leader, clearly not pleased to see her. 'I told you to let me deal with this.'

When Adelise spoke, her voice was sharp. 'I would not be a good wife to you, Sendi, if I let you fight two knights who will chop you into pieces.'

Sendi was dismissive. 'We are six, and they are only two.'

'But they are experienced warriors,' replied Adelise coolly. 'And you are not.'

The soldier had mentioned a moneyer called Sendi, and

8

Geoffrey studied the Saxon carefully, noting that although his clothes were of a design that had been popular before the conquest, they were well made. There was silver thread in his tunic, and the brooch on his cloak was gold. Sendi was a man of some substance. The small man whom Adelise had called Lifwine was not so finely attired, although his shoes were clearly expensive. The rest of the Saxons were more plainly dressed, indicating they were Sendi's supporters, rather than his equals.

Adelise continued to address her husband. 'It is obvious what has happened here: Barcwit's men killed Fardin. They want to intimidate us into dropping the case against them.'

'But Lifwine told me these Normans were alone with Fardin's body,' objected Sendi. 'And—'

Adelise rounded on Lifwine. 'You should have listened more carefully. They *also* said that whoever killed Fardin will be drenched in blood.' She indicated the knights were not, then turned to Geoffrey. 'No harm has been done here. My husband and his colleagues made a simple mistake, that is all.'

She nodded that her followers were to leave. Most went willingly, relieved to be away from what they knew was a dangerous confrontation. Soon, only she and Sendi were left. Sendi was unhappy.

'But we watched Barcwit's minions all morning,' he said, perturbed. 'Alwold escaped briefly, but I later heard him telling Rodbert he had been in the latrines – Norman food distresses his bowels.'

'You watched Barcwit's men, but not Barcwit himself?' asked Geoffrey. 'Perhaps he is the culprit.'

'Barcwit is not here,' replied Adelise shortly. 'He sent his wife Maude and his deputy Rodbert to plead his case, because he believes the King will dismiss our accusations as soon as he hears them. He said leaving Bristol was a waste of his time.'

'Perhaps he is right,' said Roger coldly. 'You accused *us* without evidence, so perhaps you have done the same to him.'

'We have an excellent case,' she snapped. 'It will see him discredited and his mint dismantled.'

Sendi waved his knife, unwilling to leave without having the final word. 'I will let you go this time, but if I discover you had anything to do with this murder, I *will* kill you.'

'You could try,' said Roger, bristling.

Adelise spoke soothingly to her husband. 'It is horrible waiting for the King to hear our case, but if we want him to believe us, we *must* show ourselves to be law-abiding citizens. It would be a pity if he decided in Barcwit's favour, just because you start a fight with strangers. It is probably what Rodbert and Maude hope will happen, and is why they murdered Fardin. Do not let their tactics work.'

They walked away, and Geoffrey exchanged a weary grin with Roger. He supposed such accusations were commonplace in the King's Court, where folk with grievances were forced close together, and hoped he would be able to leave it as soon as possible.

'We should get some food,' said Roger. 'And after, you will meet the King. Perhaps he will ask something you can decline, and we can start back for Jerusalem today.'

Geoffrey doubted it would be so easy, and felt the anger begin to bubble inside him again.

'You should eat,' advised Roger, when his friend made no move to leave. 'It may calm your temper. Henry will not like it if you are hostile towards him, and you do not want to begin the interview with both of you in a temper.'

The palace at Westminster was a grand affair. It was dominated by its hall – the largest secular structure of stone in Europe – which was cathedral-like in its proportions. However, here any resemblance to a church ended. Its internal walls were covered with hunting-scene murals, and there was not a religious motif in sight. Its builder, William Rufus, had argued bitterly with the Church, and wanted none of it in his home.

The hall opened on to a yard that thronged with people. Monks hurried from their devotions; grooms and cooks in the King's livery flitted here and there; petitioners waited for royal audiences; and courtiers chatted in small groups. Despite his anger, Geoffrey looked around with interest, astonished by the vast number of folk who had gathered. He saw Sendi, Adelise, Lifwine and their companions huddled together, speaking in low voices. He followed the direction of their accusing scowls, and saw another cluster of Saxons. Unlike Sendi's rabble, these were less defiantly Saxon, and two – a dark-featured knight, whose functional armour suggested he was a competent fighter, and an elegant woman with hair decorously concealed under a wimple – wore clothes that made them indistinguishable from high-ranking Normans. The woman sensed Geoffrey's eyes on her and turned to stare back. Her expression was one of amused disdain, as if he was just one of many men who found her worthy of scrutiny and she was bored with it.

Also among the crowd were Geoffrey's travelling companions. Old Will Helbye, who had been with him for more than two decades, hurried forward with the two squires at his heels. Roger's man was a burly Saxon called Ulfrith, who strode through life with a cheerful innocence that was sometimes irritating; Geoffrey's own squire was called Durand.

Geoffrey knew he would never make Durand a soldier, no matter how much effort was invested in his training. Durand had been destined for the Church, but had behaved badly and been dismissed. When his father had begged Tancred to make him a warrior, Tancred had promptly foisted him on Geoffrey. Durand was small and delicate, with a head of golden curls and a mincing walk. He was devious and sly, and Geoffrey longed to return him to Tancred and have no more to do with him. The fact that the King's summons was prolonging time spent in Durand's company was another reason to be annoyed.

'Well?' Durand asked insolently. 'Have you calmed yourself? Or would you prefer *me* to meet the King and find out what he wants? It might be safer. He likes me.'

Geoffrey grimaced, aware that Henry probably did like Durand, because he doubtless detected a kindred spirit. He also suspected that Henry had paid Durand to spy on him over the previous summer, although he had no proof.

'Go to the stables after you have eaten,' he said to Roger. 'Saddle the horses and be ready to leave at a moment's notice. Keep my dog, too. It has a habit of biting people it does not like, and I have a feeling we may meet a good many of those this afternoon.'

'I am coming with you,' said Roger, surprised Geoffrey should think otherwise. He fingered the hilt of his sword meaningfully. 'You may need me.'

'No,' said Geoffrey, suspecting that Roger's response to courtly threats would see them both killed.

'You should take his advice,' said Durand. 'He is still not in charge of his temper, and the King will kill him if he says anything rude. You do not want to die, just because *he* cannot control his tongue.'

Geoffrey ignored him and continued to address Roger. 'Helbye and Ulfrith can stay, too, and Durand will come to warn you if anything goes wrong.'

Durand stared at him. 'But that means I will be in the hall with you. Where it might be dangerous.'

'Yes,' agreed Geoffrey. 'That is what squires are for – to be at their masters' sides.'

Durand blanched. 'But what if you end up in a fight? Then what shall I do?'

'Stand with me.'

'But I am a man of God!' cried Durand. 'I cannot take up arms – especially under conditions where I might be hurt or killed.'

Even Geoffrey, used to Durand's feeble ways, was startled by the brazen cowardice. 'You gave up the privilege of non-aggression when you tampered with that butcher's son. But I do not think there is cause for concern: Henry would not bring us here just to kill us.'

'It is not *him* I am worried about,' protested Durand. 'It is you. You have no idea how to be a proper courtier, and it may get us into trouble.'

'And you do know, I suppose?' asked Roger in disgust. He did not like Durand.

'Of course. It is no different from a monastery. You must agree with whatever the King says, no matter how inane. Never answer back, and never lose your temper. Sir Geoffrey is normally slow to anger, but this letter from Tancred has incensed him.'

'It is a forgery,' said Geoffrey tightly. 'Of course I am angry.'

Durand took it from him and inspected it closely. 'I am as good at my letters as you are – better, even, with my monastic training – and this writing definitely belongs to Tancred's scribe. And this *is* his seal. It is genuine – there is no question about it.'

'What was in the other letter waiting for you when we arrived?' asked Roger, to change the subject. He did not want Geoffrey and Durand to begin a long and tedious debate about counterfeiting.

'Was it from your sister Joan?' asked Helbye fondly. 'She is a good lady.'

'She is a *persistent* lady,' corrected Durand. 'She writes to him every month, although most of her missives go astray because we travel a lot and the messengers cannot find us.'

'It does not matter whether he gets them or not,' said Roger. 'He has been reading them to me for years now, and all they do is tell him which ram has mated with which ewe, or how much grain is stored in which barn. I do not know why he wastes his time with them.'

Geoffrey sighed. It was not the first time this particular topic had been aired, and he was tired of Roger's dismissive contempt and Durand's mockery. Ulfrith and Helbye were more understanding – Helbye because Joan often included a message from his wife, and Ulfrith because, as a farm lad himself, he was interested in sheep and granaries. Although Joan and Geoffrey invariably quarrelled when they were together, her letters were a mark of affection and, other than an estranged brother called Henry, she was his only family and therefore important to him.

'Did she mention my pig?' asked Helbye eagerly. 'Or my wife?' he added as an afterthought.

Geoffrey ignored Durand's snort of derision. 'Your sow had a litter of nine.'

'Nine!' exclaimed Helbye, pleased. 'And Goodrich's estates are still thriving?'

Geoffrey nodded, fighting the urge to knock Roger and Durand's heads together for their smirks. 'Joan struggled for years to keep them working, but over the past few months they have become prosperous. She has bought new cattle, repaired the castle roof, and even plans to rebuild the chapel.'

'She has probably been raiding her neighbours,' said Roger, thinking about what he would do to improve his income. 'How else would she suddenly become so rich?'

'From a series of successful harvests,' replied Geoffrey, although he was sceptical. Joan had been uncharacteristically vague when she had described the manor's sudden upturn in fortune, and he suspected she had tapped into a source of wealth she intended to keep to herself. It was not something he wanted to discuss with Roger, however. 'Her prosperity comes from hard work and kind weather.'

'But the weather has not been kind,' argued Roger. 'It was damned hot in August, and crops withered in the fields.'

'And there was the war with Bellême,' added Ulfrith. 'Many folk were too frightened to gather their grain – or he burned it.'

'I have never met Joan,' said Roger, when Geoffrey did not reply, 'so I cannot say whether she is the kind to work miracles, but . . . Here comes the King's clerk. What does he want?'

'The King will see you *now*,' said the young man as he approached. 'It is windy, so he returned early from the hunt. When he heard you were here, he sent me to fetch you. You had better hurry; he does not like to be kept waiting.'

With no choice but to comply, Geoffrey and Durand followed the clerk across the yard to the hall. As they climbed the flight of steps that led to the door, the wind gusted sharply, whipping dust into Geoffrey's face. Instinctively, he closed his eyes, and immediately collided with someone who was coming down. He opened his mouth to apologize, but the man had already taken offence.

'Clumsy oaf!' he snapped. 'Did you not see me?'

'No,' replied Geoffrey. He started to step around him, but the fellow refused to let him pass.

'Will you slink away after almost knocking me to the ground, you unmannerly lout?'

Geoffrey regarded him appraisingly. He was plump, with

an oddly boyish face surrounded by fair curls. There were gold buckles on his shoes, while a huge silver brooch fastened his cloak around his shoulders. A sword dangled from his belt, and Geoffrey made the determination that, for all his lard, the man was probably an able fighter.

'Hurry,' urged the clerk. 'The King is waiting.'

'The King can wait,' snapped the man. 'I demand an apology.'

'Apologize, Sir Geoffrey,' recommended Durand. 'And then come with us before the King accuses you of unnecessary dallying.'

Geoffrey was about to oblige – not because he was cowed by the man or worried about offending the King, but because he had no desire to become enmeshed in a squabble that might interfere with his plans to leave – when others joined the altercation. The group Sendi had been glowering at was suddenly behind him, and he supposed the fat man was one of their number. He saw he should have guessed as much, because the fellow looked Saxon for all his Norman finery, and his handsome clothes indicated he held a lucrative post, such as moneyer.

'What is going on?' demanded the dark-haired knight, who, unlike his companions, was Norman. He looked strong and competent, and his well-maintained armour and weapons led Geoffrey to suppose he was a mercenary. 'Do you need me, Rodbert?'

The large man gave a derisive snort. 'I need no help to teach this villain a lesson.'

'The King,' hissed Durand to Geoffrey. 'You can thrust your sword into this fellow's gizzard later, but now you should attend Henry.'

'He will not be thrusting weapons into anyone while *I* am here,' said the knight. 'He may be a *Jerosolimitanus*, but I fought at Constantinople before I left the Crusade. He is no match for *me*.'

'He is a what?' asked one of the followers, bemused.

The knight laughed mirthlessly. '*Jerosolimitanus* is a title afforded to those who were at the Fall of Jerusalem, although many claim it falsely. Are you one of those, sir?'

His tone was insulting, but Geoffrey declined to be baited by the likes of a man who had abandoned the Crusade as early as Constantinople. He tried to step around Rodbert again, not surprised the moneyers were such bitter rivals when none seemed able to speak without saying something nasty.

'He has lost his tongue,' said Rodbert with a sneer, still preventing Geoffrey from passing. 'What do you think, Tasso?'

'Terrified into silence,' agreed the knight. 'Let him go. He is not worth our notice.'

Durand heaved a sigh of relief. 'Good. We should—'

'No,' said Rodbert firmly. 'He must apologize. I will not be jostled by peasants.'

'I am not a peasant,' said Geoffrey mildly. 'So you can rest assured you have not been jostled by one. But we both have better things to do than dance from side to side all day, so step aside.'

Rodbert was angry. 'What if I refuse? You have only your squire to stand with you, whereas I have Sir Tasso and several strong men. Look behind you. My friends are armed and ready to fight.'

'The King will not approve of that,' said Durand in a fearful squeak. 'Not in his own hall.'

'We are not *in* his hall,' said Rodbert smoothly. 'We are outside.'

'God's teeth!' muttered Geoffrey, wondering why so many people seemed intent on quarrelling with him that day. He glanced back, and saw five or six Saxons clutching daggers. They posed little threat to him in his armour, but he did not want to brawl in the King's palace, and he certainly did not want Henry angry with him just because Rodbert fancied a diversion from the tedium of waiting for a royal audience. He moved quickly.

He feinted to his left, so Rodbert dodged that way to prevent him from passing and, while the fat man was off balance, Geoffrey grabbed his cloak and swung him around, so he crashed into Tasso. Saxon and knight toppled backwards, falling on to the men behind them; all tumbled down the steps in a melee of arms and legs. Howls of laughter came from around the yard, most notably from Sendi and his rabble.

Without a word, Geoffrey turned and marched inside the hall.

'You are too late,' snapped the waiting clerk. 'I have just been informed that the King grew tired of waiting for you, and is seeing someone else. I told you to come at once.'

The hall was busy when Geoffrey entered it to wait until Henry deigned to see him. At one end, a multitude of scribes laboured over desks, some writing, some dictating and others copying completed deeds on the great sheets of parchment that comprised the Court Rolls. The King was literate, and always ensured records were kept of his various transactions – or at least, records good enough to be used to his advantage later, if required.

At the opposite end of the hall, near the door, were tables loaded with food for those who had been hunting. Men stood around them, helping themselves to bread and roasted meat, and Geoffrey recognized one or two. Most prominent, by virtue of his enormous size, was Maurice, Bishop of London, who was famous for raising a cathedral in London dedicated to St Paul. He was chatting to a lean, grim-faced man who wore a hair shirt under his habit. William Giffard, Bishop of Winchester, was a sober, unsmiling cleric fanatically loyal to Henry.

'Sir Geoffrey!' exclaimed Maurice in pleasure. Geoffrey recalled his adventures that summer, when he had not known which of the various men who surrounded Henry had been loyal. Maurice had been among his suspects, and so had Giffard. 'I thought you would be in Jerusalem by now.'

'I wish I were,' muttered Geoffrey.

Maurice did not seem to notice his lack of enthusiasm. He turned to Giffard and laughed, reminding Geoffrey that he had an attractive face when he smiled – which was just as well, given that, while he was famous for his cathedral, he was infamous for seducing large numbers of women on a daily basis. He claimed they were necessary to maintain a healthy balance of humours, and believed that if he did not satisfy himself regularly and often, he would become mortally ill. The austere Giffard suffered from no such vices, however, and remained uncompromisingly celibate.

17

'Do you remember Geoffrey?' asked Maurice. 'He helped the King with that spot of bother involving Bellême earlier this year.'

Geoffrey regarded him warily, recalling that the 'spot of bother' had involved several sieges, a campaign of guerrilla warfare, and the exile of several vengeful barons and their families.

'I do,' said Giffard. 'He proved himself useful, which is why Henry is loath to let him leave. He should not have performed his duties so efficiently.'

'I had no choice,' replied Geoffrey curtly. 'The King threatened to leave my sister exposed to a Welsh invasion if I did not succeed.'

'Hush, man!' said Maurice, glancing around in alarm. 'This is no place to bray about the King's penchant for blackmail! Let us talk of more pleasant matters before you have us arrested. Have you seen my cathedral? You will find the work advanced significantly since you saw it in March.'

'I did not think you would come,' said Giffard before Geoffrey could reply. 'You were so keen to return to the Holy Land that I assumed you would decline the King's invitation.'

'It was not an invitation. It was an arrest – carried out by twenty men with drawn swords.'

'Is your woman with you?' asked Maurice hopefully. 'The glorious angel who came to my tent that night when we were besieging Bridgnorth Castle?'

'My squire,' said Geoffrey, who had forgotten that Durand had convinced the lecherous bishop he was a woman and charged him a considerable sum for the privilege. Normally, Geoffrey would not have cared – Maurice was a grown man and should have been able to tell the difference – but the penalties for 'unnatural acts' were severe, and he did not want to be accused of ordering his squire to corrupt a prelate. Durand had not been forgiven for the deception, as evidenced by the fact that he had made himself scarce: when Geoffrey looked behind him, the squire was nowhere to be seen.

'Angel Locks,' breathed Maurice wistfully. 'If you plan to be here for any length of time, perhaps you might persuade her to oblige me a second time? I pay well.'

'I leave today,' replied Geoffrey firmly. 'I intend to tell the King to go to the Devil and ride south as fast as my horse will take me.'

Giffard's voice was sharp. 'Guard your tongue! Maurice is right: a court is no place to speak your mind. If anyone else asks, tell them you came willingly, because you are eager to serve your King.'

'But I am not—'

'So I see, but there is no need to tell the world. You are a good man, Geoffrey, and I do not want to see you hanged for making imprudent remarks to men who are not worth half of you. Westminster is full of them. I saw you shove a couple into the mud just moments ago.'

'Rodbert and Tasso,' said Maurice. 'I shall be glad when their case is heard and they leave Westminster. They are nothing but trouble. I imagine boredom led them to quarrel with you. They are restless and want to go home.'

'Sendi and his louts are no better,' said Giffard. 'They are all bad-tempered and argumentative.'

'So, why does the King not hear their case and get rid of them?' asked Geoffrey.

'We do not know,' replied Maurice. 'But squabbling Saxons are not our concern, and we should not waste time discussing them. Why did the King ask you here, Geoffrey? Has he told you?'

'I thought *you* might know,' said Geoffrey. But he could see from Maurice's open, cheerful face that he did not, although Giffard's was inscrutable. Geoffrey studied him hard, but the Bishop of Winchester was far too clever for a mere knight to read. Seeing he would have no answers from staring, he pulled 'Tancred's letter from his scrip and showed it to them.

Giffard scanned it, then handed it to Maurice. 'It arrived two days ago, and we have been waiting to give it to you.'

'I am sorry,' said Maurice, laying a chubby paw on Geoffrey's shoulder. 'I did not know it contained a dismissal. You must be upset, and I understand now why you are surly. It is unlike you to be rude to old friends.'

'Arrived from where?' asked Geoffrey. He liked Maurice and Giffard, but they were the King's servants, and he did not consider them 'friends'. He glanced towards the scribes. 'From them?'

Giffard regarded him in astonishment, while Maurice gasped. Geoffrey did not care. He had had enough of Henry and his scheming, and was not concerned whom his words might offend.

'It came from Tancred,' said Giffard firmly. 'You can see it carries his seal. And I warn you again: keep your thoughts to yourself if you want to remain a free man. The King does not tolerate traitors.'

'I am not—' began Geoffrey.

Giffard overrode him. 'Do not say you cannot be a traitor because Henry is not your king. He *is* your king. You have estates in England, which means you owe him your fealty.'

'Estates?' echoed Geoffrey. 'A tiny manor with a few houses and a derelict hall? Henry can have it. All I ask is that he leaves me alone.'

'Henry does not want Rwirdin.' Giffard nodded at the letter, which Maurice had stuffed back into Geoffrey's hand. 'But you are not in a position to be choosy over your masters. You tarried here too long, and your own lord is tired of waiting for you. He does not want you, so Henry is all you have.'

The thin lid Geoffrey had put on his temper was beginning to come apart. First, there was the letter, which he was still sure Henry had forged. Then there was the incident with Fardin and the accusation of murder levied by Sendi. Next came the altercation with Tasso and Rodbert. And finally, he was being told by two bishops that he had no choice but to enter the King's service.

'Henry promised to let me leave after I helped him this summer,' he snapped. 'He broke his word.'

Giffard's stern expression softened. 'When the King explains, you will appreciate – and be grateful for – him ordering you back.'

The wind blew in a hard, violent gust, so one of the great wooden doors slammed shut with a resounding crash. There was a shocked silence, then people started to laugh at the fright it had given them. Giffard had jumped slightly, but Maurice had almost leapt out of his skin.

20

'Lord!' he muttered, fanning himself vigorously. 'My humours have been unbalanced by listening to your treasonous ranting, Sir Geoffrey. If I do not have a woman within the hour, I shall have a fatal seizure.' He moved away, looking for a suitable candidate.

'Not Adelise,' Giffard called after him. 'She did not appreciate your advances yesterday, and I doubt I can mollify her a second time. These Saxon ladies are fiercely virtuous.'

'Adelise?' asked Geoffrey. 'Sendi's wife?'

Giffard sighed as the Bishop of London weaved through the crowd. 'I hope he heeds my counsel. Sendi said he would kill Maurice if he spoke to Adelise again. But the world is full of men who ignore my wisdom, including you. However, I shall offer it again, since I dislike bloodshed: Henry has a good reason for asking you here, so feign loyalty, even if you do not feel it. You will be glad you did.'

Geoffrey did not like the sound of that at all, and felt his anger turn into something far less comfortable: an uneasy sense of foreboding.

Two

A mused, Geoffrey watched the Bishop of London frantically search Westminster's grand hall for a lady to oblige
him, while Giffard pursed his lips. Maurice grabbed one
woman's arm and whispered something in her ear. She recoiled
in shock at whatever he had muttered, then started to laugh.

Geoffrey could see why Maurice had picked her. She wore
a yellow kirtle under a dark-blue super-tunic and a wimple
covered her hair; an escaping strand showed her tresses were
auburn, the same colour as her arresting eyes. She was not beautiful, because her mouth was too big and her chin too long, but
there was something captivating about her. She was the woman
who had been with Rodbert in the yard, who had turned to stare
at Geoffrey when she had sensed him watching her earlier.

Giffard made a sound of disgust at the back of his throat.
'Maurice is a fool! When I told him to avoid Adelise, I did
not mean he should prey on Maude.'

'She is just the first one who happened to cross his path,'
said Geoffrey. He saw her break away from Maurice. 'What
is wrong with her, anyway? She looks all right to me.'

'I am sure she does,' replied Giffard frostily. 'She seems
to have caught the eye of most men since she arrived, and it
will not be long before there is trouble. But she is the wife
of Barcwit the moneyer.'

Geoffrey saw him about to launch into further detail, and
raised his hand. 'I have already met people from both sides
of the coiners' dispute; they are rash, argumentative and stupid.
I do not want to hear about them or their quarrels.'

'Never decline freely offered information,' advised Giffard.
'You never know when it might come in useful. Barcwit is
the richest coin-maker in Bristol, and is said to be one of the

22

most feared men in the county. His fellow moneyers are here to complain about him to the King.'

'Because he steals their trade?' asked Geoffrey, forcing himself to be polite and listen.

'They accuse him of making underweight coins – too much tin in the silver. No king wants his currency debased.'

'Why is that?' asked Geoffrey absently. His attention was on Durand, who was talking animatedly to a red-haired man with a prominent nose, blithely unaware that Maurice was moving in his direction. Even a bishop blinded by lust could not fail to see Durand was no woman in the cold light of day, and Geoffrey braced himself for trouble.

'Use your wits!' said Giffard impatiently. 'If word gets out that some pennies are worth more than others, confidence in the currency will falter. People will decline to accept it, and the country's economy will flounder.'

Geoffrey was relieved when Durand glanced up, saw Maurice closing on him and beat a hasty retreat. Thwarted, Maurice rubbed an agitated hand over his chins and cast around for another victim. Maude was still nearby, and the prelate regarded her appraisingly. He evidently liked what he saw enough to give her a second chance, because he moved towards her again. Meanwhile, Giffard was still lecturing on the tedious subject of money.

'Any country that wants to trade must have a sound and stable coinage, based on a metallic standard. England has a centralized system that controls the size and number of all coins produced in our seventy or so mints, but it is not difficult for moneyers to be dishonest. If Sendi is right, then Barcwit is committing a serious crime.'

'Not so serious,' said Geoffrey, watching Maurice sidle up to Maude. 'Or Henry would have heard the case immediately.'

Giffard also became aware that Maurice was making a second play for Maude, and sighed gustily. 'Barcwit is powerful and dangerous, and Maurice is a fool to seduce his wife. You see that fellow over there? That is Alwold, Barcwit's steward. He follows her everywhere, and reports her movements to Barcwit's henchmen – Tasso and Rodbert. They are the two you just threw down the steps.'

23

'Maurice must be used to dealing with such situations,' said Geoffrey, recalling that it was Alwold who had been accused of murdering the man by the river. He studied the steward carefully, but could not tell whether he had been the one running away. All the moneyers wore dark clothing, and Fardin's killer could have been any of Barcwit's people, even Maude. 'He will charm Barcwit's louts.'

'But he plays a dangerous game nonetheless. Tasso is an experienced mercenary, while Rodbert is a skilled swordsman. I shall be glad when the lot of them are gone. It is only a matter of time before someone takes offence at something they do or say, and we have a fight on our hands. They are bored, and resentful for being kept waiting.'

Before Geoffrey could reply, there was a rumble that grew louder until it was almost deafening. The drizzle had become a downpour, hammering on the roof. Through the door he could see hail forming a white carpet on the ground. The wind gusted, hurling a curtain of rain inside the hall, and several folk shrieked and darted out of the way. Two barons, who had effected an undignified sprint across the yard, arrived to clapping and laughter, and one made a show of removing a shoe and pouring out a considerable volume of water.

Maude was near the door, with Alwold at one side and Maurice on the other, joining others to watch the unusually strong shower. Maurice eased forward, looking up at the sky to gauge when the rain might stop, so he could escape and be about taking his medicine. He frowned, then stepped into the downpour to squint heavenward, oblivious to the fact that he was instantly drenched. Others strained to see what had attracted his attention, then began shouting and pointing. Maurice dropped to his knees. Intrigued, Geoffrey and Giffard went to see what was causing such consternation.

Hanging in the sky, and blazing through a gap in the black clouds, was the sun. And just below the sun was a second orb, burning in a pale imitation of the first. But, even as people stared, the clouds merged together, and the phenomenon was lost to sight. Immediately, whispers began that it was an omen.

'What *was* it?' asked Sendi in an awed voice. His wife and men gathered around him, as if they thought there might be safety in numbers. Tasso and Rodbert stood nearby, all signs of their rivalry temporarily suspended in the face of the celestial spectacle.

'It was a sign from God,' announced Durand confidently, drawing a gasp of wonder from the crowd. He considered himself an expert on such matters, because of his former vocation, and spoke with such authority that no one doubted him.

'It was natural,' contradicted Geoffrey. He had read an account by Arab astronomers about heavenly manifestations, and was inclined to believe it had something to do with the way sunlight filtered through heavy clouds and rain. 'It was caused by the storm.'

'No, your squire was right,' said Giffard softly. When Geoffrey looked for him, he saw that he, too, was on his knees. 'It was most definitely a sign from God. It is a warning that we must mend our sinful ways, particularly regarding fornication.' He glared meaningfully at Maurice.

Maurice was gazing dreamily upwards. 'It is a sign of God's love. Perhaps He likes my cathedral. After all, I was the first to spot the Two Suns. The message must have been meant for me.'

'Actually, it was meant for me,' came a familiar voice from behind Geoffrey. It was the King, resplendent in an ermine-fringed cloak. 'It is a sign that God looks with favour on His anointed earthly representative. Why would He bother with bishops, when He can commune with a monarch?'

'Or perhaps He is displeased because a murder has just taken place,' said Geoffrey to Giffard. He spoke softly, but his voice carried in the silence of the hall.

'What murder?' demanded Henry immediately. He inspected the knight's travel-stained clothes with disapproval. 'I see you took some trouble with your appearance before meeting your King.'

Geoffrey pointed to where Alwold was huddled in the shadows nearby. A knife protruded from the steward's stomach, and there was an expression of abject shock on his face. From the angle of the dagger, it was clear he had not

25

stabbed himself. Someone bold, rash or desperate had just committed murder in the King's splendid palace.

'God's blood!' exclaimed Henry, regarding the fallen man in shock. 'How did that happen? He was alive a moment ago, because I watched him stalking Maude.'

'Alwold follows me everywhere, sire,' said Maude. Geoffrey wondered whether she had tired of such attention, and had decided to free herself from it. She did not seem shocked or angry by the steward's death, but nor did she seem relieved or pleased. She was impassive.

'Why?' asked Henry. 'Is he enamoured of you?'

'He was following her husband's orders, sire,' replied the fat Rodbert, stepping forward with a bow. 'Barcwit does not trust the amorous men who prowl places such as these.'

'He is doubtless right,' muttered Henry, glancing at Maurice.

'But he will be distressed when he learns about *this*,' added Tasso. He glared at Sendi. 'Alwold has been in our service for many years, and it is shameful that he should be so brutally murdered.'

'And doubly shameful that it should happen in my hall,' said Henry coolly. He turned to Geoffrey. 'You have not answered my question: how did Alwold come to be killed?'

'I do not know, sire,' replied Geoffrey, alarmed the King should think he did, and wishing he had not drawn attention to the murdered man in the first place. 'But someone must have seen something.'

He looked around questioningly, but was not surprised when no one replied. From what Giffard had said about Barcwit, only a fool would become involved with his household, while Henry would not be happy about a murder committed within spitting distance of the Royal Person, either. Besides, the attention of most people – including Geoffrey's own – had been on the Two Suns.

Geoffrey glanced at Sendi and his men. It was not too great a leap in logic to assume that 'justice' had been done, and Fardin's death had been avenged. They gazed at him with expressions ranging from alarm to satisfaction, and any one of them could have been the killer. Lifwine stood nearby, while, next to him, Adelise's pretty features were carefully blank. It took little strength to thrust a knife into a man's belly, and even the smallest two members of Sendi's household could have done it.

Next, Geoffrey looked at Rodbert and his followers. They could have killed Alwold, too, secure in the knowledge that Sendi's mob would be the obvious suspects. Their own steward's murder could only help their cause, because who would believe accusations levelled by men who murdered their opponents in the King's own hall?

Geoffrey was not the only one who thought the moneyers were the most likely candidates for the murder. Other courtiers had also weighed the evidence and found it pointed to the Saxons. They edged away, so that both factions soon stood alone.

'I saw nothing of relevance,' said Giffard in the silence that followed. 'But Geoffrey is wrong: God did not reveal the Two Suns as a sign that He disapproves of murder. Rather, the killer used them as a diversion – they were already in the sky when he committed his wicked sin. Perhaps that is why God did not let us see them for very long.'

If there was a wide berth around the moneyers, then there was an even larger one around Alwold. No one had gone to inspect him or to offer prayers for his soul. Geoffrey moved forward, and was somewhat startled when the man's eyes fluttered open. Alwold was not dead, although the amount of blood and the location of the wound indicated he would not live for long. Geoffrey knelt and pressed one hand over the injury, to stem the bleeding and give him a chance to make a final confession.

Meanwhile, Henry snapped his fingers at the watching crowd. 'Fetch the Court physicians. Clarembald assures me he can cure anything, while the Bishop of Bath claims *his* skills are superior. We shall see whether their boasts are justified.'

But Geoffrey knew a fatal injury when he saw one; physicians, talented or no, could not save Alwold. He leaned close to the dying man, sensing he had something to say. 'Do you want a priest?'

Alwold shook his head and his gaze fell on Maude, Rodbert

27

and Tasso, who were still shooting accusing glances at Sendi. Sendi glowered back, while Adelise was informing Maurice in a strident voice that her people were innocent.

'Do you want Rodbert?' Geoffrey asked. Alwold shook his head, eyes fixed firmly on Barcwit's sensual wife. 'Maude?'

Alwold nodded, so Geoffrey beckoned to her. Careful not to trail her clothes in the growing pool of gore that seeped from the steward, she knelt and took one of his limp hands.

'What is it, Alwold?' she asked softly. 'What did you want to say?'

Tasso and Rodbert stepped closer, too, but when Alwold's mouth clamped shut, she indicated they were to move away. They obliged willingly enough, and went back to their conspiratorial muttering. Geoffrey was under the impression that neither liked Alwold, and were more indignant than grieved by his mortal wounding.

'He must go, too,' breathed Alwold, looking at Geoffrey. 'He may be Sendi's man.'

Geoffrey started to oblige, having no desire to hear whatever deathbed secret Alwold was about to impart, but blood arced from the man's injury and made a lacy pattern on the floor.

'Stay where you are,' ordered Henry, who was watching. 'It would be a pity to have the poor fellow bleed to death, just because you cannot wait a few moments for my physicians to arrive.'

'Speak softly,' said Maude to Alwold. 'This knight will not hear if you whisper.'

Alwold seemed to know he had no time to argue. He began to speak in a low voice that had Maude straining to catch his words. Geoffrey, who cradled the man in his arms, heard him a lot better.

'Tell Barcwit the silver is with Piers,' Alwold breathed.

'What?' asked Maude, suddenly a lot more interested.

The smile that parted Alwold's bloodstained lips was not a pleasant one. 'The silver,' he repeated. 'Give *Barcwit* my message, no one else. He will be angry if you betray him. You do not know what he can be like when he is angry.'

'Who is Piers?' demanded Maude. 'Where can I . . . where can Barcwit find him?'

'Tell Barcwit I am sorry, but I was loyal to the last. His silver is with Piers. He will understand.'

'Who is Piers?' pressed Maude again. 'I know of no one by that name. Where does he live? And why did you leave the silver with him, when you should have brought it to Barcwit? We believed you when you said it had been stolen by outlaws. Are you now saying it was not?'

'No,' whispered Alwold. 'Outlaws.'

'Piers is an outlaw?' Maude spoke urgently. 'Is that what you are saying? Piers is the villain who robbed us? For God's sake, man, tell me! This is important!'

'Tell Barcwit,' insisted Alwold, while Geoffrey thought he was deluded if he believed Maude would be a trustworthy messenger. It was obvious, even to him, that she had plans of her own. 'You must . . .'

'Where does Piers live?' interrupted Maude frantically, seeing Alwold beginning to slip away. 'I cannot help you, if you do not tell me who—'

'Move out of my way,' came an important voice that drowned any reply Alwold might have made. Maude glanced up in surprise.

A portly, fussy man with bristling ginger eyebrows shoved through the crowd and came to crouch at Alwold's side. Maude was almost knocked over, and only a timely lunge by Maurice prevented her from taking a tumble.

'That is Clarembald,' said Henry for her benefit. 'One of my Court physicians.'

'*I* am here, too,' announced a second voice. Geoffrey saw a tall, lean cleric approach. 'I am also a *medicus* – and a better one than Clarembald. My name is John de Villula, Bishop of Bath.'

'This man has been stabbed,' said Henry, while Geoffrey thought that if either physician needed that pointed out to them – the knife was still embedded in the steward's stomach and he was drenched in blood – then Alwold was doomed indeed. 'I want you to save his life.'

'That is not possible,' said Clarembald. 'The wound is fatal, and only God can heal him.'

'Then I shall ask Him to do so,' said John, dropping to his

29

knees. 'He always listens to the supplications of His bishops, although He does not bother much with lay physicians.'

'*I* heal with the gifts God gave me,' retorted Clarembald, displaying his hands as though they were something of significant value. '*I* do more than order Him to make my patients better.'

John opened his mouth to reply, but Henry intervened. 'Yes, yes, we know what you think of each other. But a patient needs you, and I want you to rescue him, because I heard him mention silver.'

'Clarembald will not succeed,' said John disdainfully. 'That man is beyond *his* meagre skills.'

'You do it, then,' invited Clarembald. He stood, and indicated John was to take his place.

But John was no fool; he also knew Alwold was a lost cause. 'I can do nothing *now* – not because the patient is beyond my skills, but because Clarembald has touched him and done his damage.'

Clarembald was aghast. 'Are you accusing me of killing him?' His voice dropped to a furious whisper. 'This is *Barcwit's* steward, man! Do you want Barcwit to murder *me*, because you have made some false and wicked accusation?'

The expression on John's face indicated that he thought it would be a very good idea indeed. 'You should avoid Bristol in the future, then,' he said smoothly.

Henry made an impatient noise and stepped between them, while Geoffrey, thinking it was poor form for healers to squabble when a man lay dying, turned his attention to Alwold. The steward was grey-faced and needed a priest, not physicians.

'The secret lies with the priest at St John's,' Alwold whispered in a voice so low Geoffrey was not sure he had heard him. His eyes were open, but they were glazed, and the knight suspected he thought Maude was still with him. 'The King knows about it, and so do Bloet and William de Warel . . .'

His voice trailed off, and the only sounds came from the quarrelling medics. Then Alwold stopped breathing, and Geoffrey had a sudden uncomfortable sense of something slipping away from the man's body. Alwold was dead.

* * *

When Geoffrey saw he was holding a corpse, he laid Alwold on the floor and stood up. Giffard moved into the spot he had vacated, and began to recite prayers for the man's soul. Maude hovered with Rodbert and Tasso to Bishop Maurice's left, while Sendi and his followers were to his right. Geoffrey suspected the burly prelate had positioned himself deliberately, to prevent the two parties from coming in contact with each other and committing more murders.

'What did Alwold say?' asked Henry of Maude.

'Nothing that made sense,' she replied, while Geoffrey struggled not to gape at the lie. 'He wanted me to pass a message to my husband – something of a personal nature.'

'What?' asked Henry. He regarded her through narrowed eyes: Geoffrey was not the only one who had noticed how eagerly she had leaned forward to catch Alwold's words. 'Nothing in my Court is secret from me. What did he say?'

Maude held his gaze as she replied. 'It was a message about a man called Piers, sire. He must be a friend of my husband's. As I said, it made no sense.'

Geoffrey glanced at her companions. Tasso maintained a professional indifference, but Rodbert's eyes darted between the King and Maude as he listened to the discussion. Geoffrey strongly suspected that Maude intended to keep Alwold's confession from Barcwit, and wondered whether she planned to do the same with Tasso and Rodbert, too.

He recalled Alwold's very last words – which Maude had not heard – about the secret lying with the priest of St John's, the King, Bloet and William de Warel. He supposed he should repeat them, but decided to hold his tongue. The wisest course of action was to forget about the whole business, and have no more to do with the moneyers or their silver – or with the King, whose greedy instincts were already alert.

'Tell me *exactly* what he said,' invited Henry, treating Maude to one of his most winning smiles. '*I* might be able to help you understand what he was trying to communicate.'

'It was of no significance,' replied Maude evasively. 'He said this Piers has something to tell Barcwit. When I return home, I shall suggest that my husband visits the man.'

'I heard Alwold mention silver,' said Henry, and the smile

was gone. He knew Maude was trying to mislead him.

'He was rambling,' objected Maude uneasily. 'He did mention silver, but he was a moneyer's steward, and his whole life revolved around it – we use silver for making coins.'

'Is that all?' asked Henry. His face was expressionless, but his voice oozed danger.

Maude glanced at him and evidently realized she was playing with fire. 'Normally, I would not bother you with our petty troubles, sire, but since you ask, I shall confide. About three weeks ago, on the Feast of St Michael and All Angels, Barcwit had a large amount of silver stolen. I suppose the matter was on Alwold's mind as he died.'

'And why would that be?' asked Henry casually.

Maude relented further, and Geoffrey was under the impression that her story held no surprises for the King: he already knew it. 'Alwold had been escorting that particular consignment from a mine in Devon, but the carts were attacked just outside Bristol and the silver was taken. It was not Alwold's fault, but he doubtless felt guilty about losing such a valuable load.'

'I know about the robbery.' Henry smiled at her surprise. 'Precious metals do not go missing on *my* highways without my knowing.'

'My husband says the roads are safer now *you* are King,' said Maude with an ingratiating smile. 'So, we were surprised when the convoy was attacked.'

'Shocked, too,' added Rodbert. 'There was a lot of silver on those carts, and its loss was a serious blow to our business.' He shot a glance at Sendi, making it clear whom *he* held responsible. Sendi bristled and glowered back, but Adelise was pinching his arm, so he said nothing.

'All this puts a rather different complexion on Alwold's death,' said Giffard, standing as he finished his prayers. 'He may have been killed because of the silver. Did anyone see who stabbed him?'

'I was near Bishop Maurice,' replied Maude, smiling coyly at the fat prelate, 'so I saw nothing.'

'I was aware of very little once I had set eyes on the Two Suns,' said Maurice apologetically. 'I think you were behind me, but I cannot be certain.'

'*I* was next to her,' declared Rodbert loyally. He glared at Maurice. 'Some prelates show too much interest in their flock, and I wanted to ensure she came to no harm. Tasso will attest that we were all together when Alwold was so foully slain.'

Geoffrey was unimpressed; their willingness to give each other alibis meant nothing. Henry turned his gaze from Barcwit's supporters to Sendi's mob. Sendi stepped forward immediately.

'Begging your pardon, sire,' he said, 'but we have nothing to do with Alwold's death, either. We came here for one purpose: to report that Barcwit cheats you. He strikes under-weight coins and—'

Henry waved him to silence. 'I have already told you I will hear your case later. I do not want your grievances aired now.'

'They are lies anyway,' said Rodbert sullenly. 'Sendi is jealous because Barcwit is more successful than him – but that is because we work harder and produce better coins.'

Sendi raised a finger that shook with rage. 'Lies!' He appealed to Henry. 'They murdered Fardin today, and now they have killed Alwold, too. They hope you will see Alwold as a revenge killing – so we will be blamed and our case dismissed.'

Rodbert sneered his disdain. 'Why would we kill our own man? We—'

'Enough!' roared Henry. 'I said I do not want to hear your squabble today. Do you dare defy your monarch? All I am interested in now is Alwold, and in anyone who might have seen his killer.' He glowered at his courtiers in a way that had many of them shuffling uncomfortably.

'We were all looking at the Two Suns,' said the red-headed man with whom Durand had been giggling earlier. His eyes sat too close together at the top of his long nose, lending him a sly expression. 'But none of us courtiers are killers, so you must look to strangers for your culprit.'

'Must I, indeed?' asked Henry archly.

The man included the moneyers and Geoffrey in a wide sweep of his arm. 'These Saxons bear grudges against each other, while I have heard about the kind of men who rallied to the Pope's call for Crusaders. They are a dangerous and unruly brood.'

33

'Is that true, Geoffrey?' asked Henry, amused. 'Are *Jerosolimitani* dangerous and unruly?'

'Yes, sire,' replied Geoffrey, knowing that to claim otherwise would be untrue. Most of the men who had cut a bloody trail through the civilized world to 'liberate' Jerusalem were as far from the popular vision of saintly gentleness as it was possible to be.

'Geoffrey did not kill Alwold, Bloet,' said Giffard irritably. 'He was with me when it happened, and I would have noticed had he taken out his dagger and stuck it in some passer-by.'

'My agents will look into the matter,' said the King, in a way that was vaguely threatening. 'And I *will* find out if anyone has lied to me.'

'*We* have not lied, sire,' said Maude quickly. 'Alwold would not have summoned me to hear his dying words if I had killed him. And no one should set too much store by his ramblings over silver, either. He just felt guilty that he had been in charge of the convoy when it was seized by outlaws.'

'We shall see,' said Henry vaguely. He clapped his hands to indicate the matter was closed, and his gaze settled on Geoffrey. 'I will see you now. In my private chamber.'

Without waiting for a reply, he stalked away. Immediately, an excited babbling broke out, as people began to chatter about the Two Suns and the simultaneous murder. As Geoffrey turned to follow him, he felt his arm caught in a powerful grip. Annoyed, he shrugged it off, prepared to follow it with a punch if the fellow did not let go. His clenched fist relaxed when he saw Maude. Her eyes blazed as she leaned towards him.

'Well?' she hissed. 'What did you hear?'

He was unwilling to admit that he had heard more of Alwold's final testimony than she had done, sensing that to do so would certainly embroil him in the coiners' feud. However, he did not want to arouse her suspicions by saying he had heard nothing at all, when she knew for a fact that he had.

'Why do you want to know?' he asked, side-stepping the question.

'You heard nothing to contradict what I told the King,' she

said, as if teaching him what to say to anyone who asked. 'Besides, Alwold spoke English, which very few Normans understand.'

'Henry does,' Geoffrey pointed out. 'That is why he picked out the word "silver".'

'He probably knows the words "silver", "gold" and "money" in every language under the sun,' retorted Maude caustically. 'But you will say nothing to anyone about Alwold's last words. If you go against my advice, you will put yourself in grave danger.'

'From you?' asked Geoffrey coldly. He disliked being threatened, even by attractive women.

'From the King,' replied Maude, as if surprised he should think otherwise. 'This silver is worth a good deal of money, and Henry seems far more interested in its whereabouts than is appropriate for something that does not belong to him.'

Geoffrey followed the King to a spiral staircase, where two soldiers stood aside to let him pass. When Sendi tried to go too, evidently keen to press his case, their lances blocked his way and a captain stepped out of the shadows with a sword. The Saxon backed away quickly.

At the top of the stairs was a sumptuously furnished room. A servant knelt by the hearth, blowing on a fire to make it burn, while another hurried to close the window shutters. Geoffrey glimpsed trees flailing in the wind outside, while a nasty drizzle swept around them. Inside, wall hangings covered every scrap of masonry and thick rugs lay on the floor, so soft that Geoffrey's feet sank into them, like fresh manure. Brimming wine jugs stood on the window sill, along with dishes containing nuts, imported at considerable expense. Dominating one side of the room was a mattress strewn with furs, and Geoffrey realized he had been invited, not to an office, but to the King's bedchamber. These were private places, open only to his most trusted advisers, and the knight's heart sank: he did not want to be considered an intimate by Henry, or to be seen as such by a palace full of jealous courtiers.

'Nuts?' asked Henry pleasantly. Geoffrey was about to accept – no soldier declined food when he did not know where his next meal might come from – when he noticed they were waterlogged from the rain. He shook his head.

Henry clapped his hands, and the servants left the room at a run. 'Do you still have that dog?' he asked amiably, so Geoffrey began to be worried. The King was not the kind of man who wasted time on idle chatter. 'It was not with you in the hall.'

'I left him in the stables, sire.'

Henry was none too pleased. 'With my horses?'

'My men will not let him bite anything too valuable.'

'You had better be right,' warned Henry. 'I will be angry if I discover teeth marks in my warhorses. They are expensive, and your mongrel is far too free with its fangs.'

'Yes, sire,' agreed Geoffrey, wishing the King would come to the point.

'I expect you wonder why I asked you here,' said Henry, peering into the bowl and deciding he did not want sodden nuts either. He took an apple instead, and ate it as he waited for a reply.

'I already know, sire,' replied Geoffrey, trying not to sound sullen. 'I was handed Tancred's letter – the one urging me to enter your service – as soon as I arrived.'

Henry stared at him. 'You think I brought you here to give you that?'

'Is there another reason?'

Henry had an expressive face. It could be sunny and affable, and it could be dark and cold. It could also be unreadable, and Geoffrey had learnt that, when the monarch's expression went blank it was when he was in his most dangerous moods. When Geoffrey asked his question, the King's friendly manner dropped, and his face became a mask of impassivity.

'There is, as a matter of fact,' he said coolly. 'I summoned you here as a favour – to reward you for helping me this summer.'

Geoffrey was not convinced. 'The letter from Tancred—'

'The letter from Tancred arrived *two* days ago,' snapped Henry. 'I sent for you *five* days ago. How could I have known about Tancred's message when I asked you to come here?'

'I see,' said Geoffrey, not sure what else to say.

36

'You do not believe me!' exclaimed Henry. He shook his head, as if he could not find the words to express himself. 'You think that I, Henry of England, have fabricated an excuse to bring you here, to urge you to carry my banner? I can scarcely credit this! I do a man a favour, and he assumes I have an ulterior motive! Me, a king with an army of good men under my command.'

Geoffrey had never seen him so angry. His face was white, and he almost spat his words. 'You do have good men, sire,' he agreed hurriedly. 'There are Giffard and Maurice, and . . .' But he could not think of any more people he considered trustworthy, so faltered into silence.

'I should not have wasted my time,' Henry went on. 'I have not yet reached the point where I am obliged to force men to serve me. I was more than happy to see you on your way to the Holy Land – I even gave you gold for your journey, if you recall.'

'Yes, sire,' said Geoffrey, not pointing out that it had been very little gold.

'And now you accuse me of fabricating this letter from Tancred.' Henry hurled the apple at the hearth, so it smashed and pieces flew in all directions. 'I should have you executed. No man should accuse his monarch of dishonesty and live.'

'No, sire,' said Geoffrey, becoming irritated by the King's wounded innocence when he felt his conclusions had been justified – particularly given the fact that he had been forced to Westminster under close guard and not given the opportunity to decline the King's 'invitation'. 'But Tancred—'

'Tancred does not care what happens to you,' snapped Henry spitefully. 'I, too, had a letter from him, delivered by the same messenger. He is doing well as Prince of Galilee, surrounded by strong men eager to see him succeed. He does not need you, so has released you from your vow. He recommended you to me, because he knows you were active on my behalf this summer. *I* did not tell him what you were doing here, so I assume you did?'

Geoffrey nodded. 'I wrote to explain why I had not returned immediately, as he had ordered.'

'Then you have only yourself to blame. *I* would not want

a knight who accepted gold from other masters, either.'

'But that was not my choice,' objected Geoffrey. He took a deep breath, and reminded himself he was speaking to a powerful monarch; if he did not want to throw his life away, he would be wise to control his temper.

'You are in an unenviable position,' said Henry unpleasantly. 'I do not want rebellious, resentful knights in my service, just as Tancred does not want them in his. Sooner or later you will realize it is a good thing to serve a king, and will no doubt offer me your sword. But I doubt I shall accept it.'

Geoffrey said nothing, thinking that Henry was dreaming if he thought he would ever own his loyalty. He would sooner sell himself to the highest bidder among the warring Holy Land princes, or go to live on his manor in the Forest at Dene.

'So,' said Henry eventually, after what felt like a long silence. 'We have established that Tancred's letter was genuine, that I do not want you in my household, and that you would not accept an offer from me, even if it were made. I am tempted to send you on your way without telling you the reason I summoned you. But I am not a vengeful man, and I *shall* reward you for what you did for me.'

'I am sorry, sire,' said Geoffrey, trying to sound sincere. He now had no idea whether the King was playing some complex game with him, or whether the summons really had been altruistic.

'It is too late for that. You have insulted me, and if you ever do it again, I will have you hanged.'

'Then I shall try not to, sire,' replied Geoffrey evenly.

Henry sighed. 'But, when all is said and done, you are an honest man, and there are not many of those around these days. Most people would have kept their treasonous thoughts to themselves and sworn any oaths I required – and broken them just as easily. But I am weary of anger between us. Sit by this miserable fire, and I shall show you why I ordered your return.'

Reluctantly, Geoffrey complied, his thoughts in turmoil. He was bemused by the speed at which the King's temper had subsided, because his own certainly had not: he was still seething. He sat on the stool Henry indicated and waited for him to begin.

'You saw those Saxon moneyers?' asked Henry. 'I have kept them here for the last week because I want you to hear the case they bring. Usually, I listen to such complaints immediately, assess the evidence provided by both sides, and make a decision. But I have not done so this time.'

Geoffrey recalled that people were bemused by Henry's tardiness, because the petitioners were making a nuisance of themselves and it was time they were gone. 'I do not know them . . .'

'No,' interrupted Henry. 'You do not. They hail from Bristol. You heard Sendi claim that Barcwit runs a dishonest business? That is a serious allegation, because I accrue considerable revenues from my mints, and there are fierce laws to prevent moneyers from cheating me – anyone caught clipping my coins, or making inferior ones, loses a hand and faces heavy fines.'

Geoffrey knew the laws governing mints were vigorously applied. 'Being appointed Master Coiner is a great honour – and very lucrative. Only a fool would risk mutilation and the loss of all his property for dishonest profit.'

'My kingdom is full of fools, Geoffrey, and Barcwit may be one of them. Besides, you put too much faith in the law. There is a tendency among criminals to think they will not be caught, and therefore will not be punished. There are harsh penalties for stealing sheep, too, but that does not stop people from doing it.'

'If you think Barcwit is guilty, then why not sentence him?' asked Geoffrey, puzzled. 'Why stay your hand?'

'Because of you,' replied Henry. He stopped the knight from responding to this peculiar claim by passing him a scroll. 'Here is a summary of the evidence Sendi intends to present. It says Barcwit's coins weigh less than twenty grains – tin is lighter than silver, and he is using too much of it in his alloys – which means my currency is debased. There is also a list of people who have encouraged him in his deception. You will see Simon Bloet's name there.'

'Bloet,' mused Geoffrey. A man called Bloet – Durand's

red-haired friend – had accused him of killing Alwold, merely on the grounds that he was a stranger to the Court. And Bloet had been one of the names Alwold had muttered before he died, too.

'Bloet is the Bishop of Lincoln's son,' Henry explained. 'He is here in Westminster because he wants to convince me that his name on Sendi's list means nothing.'

'Does it mean nothing?' asked Geoffrey, bewildered by the mess of connections that were beginning to emerge. 'Or has Sendi simply written the names of important men to gain your attention?'

'Bloet denies any illegal involvement, but he is a schemer, and certainly the kind of man to make a quick profit at my expense.'

'How?'

'Sendi claims Bloet and others have invested heavily in Barcwit's business. It is very simple: a moneyer needs cash to buy silver. If he has lots of cash, he can buy lots of silver. If he has lots of silver, he can make lots of coins. And if he makes lots of coins, he can sell them all and make lots more money. *Ergo*, the more cash he has, the more profits he will make. Do you understand?'

'Yes,' said Geoffrey, not liking the King's patronizing tone: he did not need basic economics explained to him in words of one syllable. 'But lending money for mints to buy silver is not illegal.'

'No, it is not,' agreed Henry. 'And, as long as all the coins are made with official stamps – we call them "dies" – it is actually very patriotic to invest in mints. But Sendi tells me Barcwit makes some coins with unofficial dies: forgeries.'

'And forgeries are where large profits will be made,' surmised Geoffrey, to show he was not entirely clueless. 'Because Barcwit will not have to buy the official dies, which are probably expensive.'

'Precisely. The profit from forgeries is huge, so men like Bloet can expect a substantial return on their investments.' Henry gestured to the scroll again. 'Bloet's is not the only name that concerns me. Both my physicians are mentioned – Bishop John and Clarembald. That is why they are here, too.

I never normally summon them at the same time, because they squabble, but I wanted to hear what they had to say for themselves when Sendi puts his case.'

Geoffrey was confused. 'Why would wealthy courtiers and royal physicians invest with a moneyer in a remote place like Bristol?'

Henry gave a grim smile. 'That is what *I* want to know. You are right: there is no reason why they should invest with a Bristol moneyer, as opposed to one in the towns where they live. Perhaps Barcwit promised them huge rewards. Or perhaps there is another reason.'

'Such as . . . ?'

'Such as to make my currency unstable and bring economic hardship to my country. Despite the fact that I have – with your help – rid myself of several rebellious barons, there are still others who believe my crown belongs to the Duke of Normandy.'

Geoffrey was startled. 'I do not see how you can conclude this from coins—'

Henry sighed impatiently. 'It is quite straightforward. Outright revolt against me failed – the episode with Bellême proved there is no point in engaging me in open warfare, because I will win. But there are other ways to attack a monarch. One is to debase his currency to the point where a penny is worthless. The peasants will revolt because they cannot buy bread, and my soldiers – peasants themselves – will not fight for me, because I will pay them with useless coins.'

Geoffrey stared at the parchment. 'Do you believe these accusations? Or is Sendi merely jealous that Barcwit's business is more lucrative than his own?'

'Those are good questions. And I need a man of intelligence and cunning to answer them.'

'Is that why you ordered me here?' asked Geoffrey warily, feeling as though they were finally reaching the crux of the matter. 'To conduct an investigation for you?'

'Actually, I want Bishop Giffard to do it,' said Henry, rather coolly. 'It had not occurred to me that *you* might volunteer. I brought you here to show you that list of investors, so we

41

might talk about the matter before I let Giffard loose on them.'

Geoffrey glanced at the list, struggling to read the untidy writing. Besides Bloet and the two physicians, there was a man named William de Warelwast, and several knights whom Geoffrey had met during his summer of campaigning along the Welsh Marches. However, towards the end of the document was a name that made his blood run cold: Olivier d'Alençon and his wife Joan.

'Olivier d'Alençon,' said Henry, watching the expression on Geoffrey's face. 'And his wife Joan. Your sister and her husband.'

Three

Geoffrey stared at the parchment in disbelief, his thoughts in turmoil. Was it true? Had Joan and Olivier invested money with Barcwit? And if so, why? Was it simply because he offered them a good return, and they were naïve enough to believe it was legitimate? Or had they given the moneyer funds for a more sinister purpose – to attack Henry by corrupting his currency? Joan, like Geoffrey himself, thought the Duke of Normandy should be King of England. Had she decided to support the Duke with more than her voice? She was a strong-minded woman, and she might well involve herself in such a plot if she thought it was the right thing to do.

There was something else, too, which made Geoffrey's thoughts whirl in horrified confusion. Over the last few months, Joan had written about how the family manor of Goodrich on the Welsh Marches had gone from a struggling, impoverished estate to one that was wealthy. She claimed it was due to new breeding stock and a succession of good harvests. But, as Roger had pointed out, the weather had been unseasonably hot in August, and harvests had been poor because of the war with Bellême. It was impossible for Joan's crops to have fared so much better than everyone else's.

So, where had the money come from? An uneasy truce existed between Goodrich and its Welsh neighbours, and it was possible she had broken it with raids. But she often wrote about how important she considered peace, and he thought it unlikely that she would destroy it by wanton looting. So, were her new-found riches the result of investing with Barcwit? Geoffrey knew the only likely explanation for her odd upturn in fortunes was a windfall of some kind – and, to set Goodrich on its feet, it would have to be a very large one. Since he knew no one became rich overnight honestly, the only explanation was that she had done so dishonestly.

But why? Had she become involved with Barcwit purely to set Goodrich on the road to recovery, or did she have a more sinister motive? Regardless, it was not good that she was on Sendi's list. At best, it would mean the loss of her investments – and the figure written by her name was an enormous sum, and one she could not afford to lose – and at worst, it would mean a traitor's death. Geoffrey became aware that the King was watching him.

'There must be some mistake. Joan lives miles away from Bristol.'

Henry shrugged. 'Then explain how Sendi knows her name.'

Geoffrey felt he was clutching at straws. 'Perhaps he passed through her estates at some point, and added her name to make his case more strongly.'

'Why would he do that?'

'She upset him,' suggested Geoffrey. He sounded desperate, but was unable to help himself. 'She argued with him, or gave him a piece of her mind, and he added her name as revenge.'

Henry smiled ruefully. 'I have met your sister, and she does have a sharp tongue. But she must have said some *very* rude things to induce a man to put her on a list of people suspected of treason.'

Geoffrey studied the parchment again. 'Do you suspect Clarembald, John and Bloet of treason, too? If so, then why are they wandering freely around your Court? Why are they not arrested?'

'Because, as you pointed out, Sendi may have made mistakes or added names for vengeance's sake. I asked my physicians and Bloet whether the allegations were true, and they denied them.'

'Of course,' said Geoffrey, thinking no one was going to confess to such heinous crimes on the basis of what sounded like a very casual enquiry. 'But what do you believe, sire?'

Henry smiled at his directness. 'All three are keen to secure my favour, and I find it difficult to imagine them risking it for a few bags of coins. But would they risk it to see the Duke of Normandy on my throne, when the rewards might be very much greater? I cannot say. Loyalty does not grow on trees, and almost everyone in my Court is here for himself, not for love of me. But there are exceptions, and Bloet, Clarembald and John may be among them. As may Joan.'

'Perhaps Joan knows nothing about it,' said Geoffrey, looking at her husband's name. 'Sir Olivier buys horses from a village near Bristol. Perhaps he invested with Barcwit without telling her.'

But was that likely? For reasons wholly beyond Geoffrey's ken, Joan adored her weak, cowardly husband, while Olivier doted on his strong-willed wife. They discussed everything, and Geoffrey could not imagine Olivier investing a penny without her approval – or vice versa.

'Even if he did, she would notice the profits,' Henry pointed out. 'You can see from Sendi's estimates that they are huge. She would demand to know where such large sums had come from.'

'How does Sendi know so much about his rival's business?' asked Geoffrey, unwilling to admit he was right. 'Surely Barcwit did not volunteer this information?'

'Sendi has a spy in Barcwit's mint, and Barcwit is thought to have one in Sendi's. They are business rivals, so such a situation is quite normal. I have agents myself, in all sorts of odd places.'

Geoffrey pinched the bridge of his nose. 'Alwold's murder must be connected to these allegations. He was Barcwit's steward, and so could probably say with certainty who invested with his master, and who did not. Maude, Tasso and Rodbert may also be in danger . . .'

'Alwold was killed to avenge Fardin,' interrupted Henry dismissively. 'I have kept these Saxons in close proximity to each other for too long, and they have reached the point where violence is an attractive way to ease tensions.'

'Why have you waited so long to hear their case?'

Henry sighed. 'I have already answered that: because I wanted to speak to you first.'

Geoffrey only just managed to prevent himself from saying he did not believe him. Sendi had brought to light a serious charge of treason, involving men who were close to the King and a possible plot to damage the financial roots of the country. Geoffrey could not imagine why it would be deferred to await the arrival of a poor knight who served another prince.

Henry poured a cup of wine, which he pushed into Geoffrey's hands. 'Drink this. You are as white as a corpse. I know you are fond of Joan, but I did not expect you to swoon over the matter.'

'I will not swoon,' said Geoffrey, although he was awash with the sense that the situation was not real. He was aware of small things – cinder burns in the rugs, his goblet was dirty, bird droppings on the window shutters. He sipped the wine. It was strong and burned his mouth, and he wondered what sort of brews Henry enjoyed when he was on his own. He set it down, unwilling to drink more.

'Not to your liking?'

'A little sour,' replied Geoffrey carefully, not wanting to tell the King that he would not foist that particular brew on his enemies.

Henry smelled it carefully. 'I wonder if it has been poisoned. It would not be the first time, and my tasters have become lax recently. I shall see what happens to you before I try any. Have some more.'

'No, thank you,' said Geoffrey firmly. He gazed at Sendi's document again. 'I could leave Westminster tonight, and go to warn her – take her away with me.'

'You could,' agreed Henry. 'And I shall not stop you, if you think that is the best thing to do. But what would happen then? Tancred does not want you, and Joan would not like the Holy Land anyway. You could go to Normandy, where the Duke would accept you into his service, but you cannot stay there, either.'

'Why not?'

'Because it is the home of Robert de Bellême, the man you recently helped oust from England. He has long arms and many kin, so you will never be safe in Normandy, and neither will Joan.'

Geoffrey knew he was right. 'You have something else in mind?'

'I cannot allow traitors to go unpunished – imagine the message that would send to anyone thinking of organizing a revolt! Bellême would be back in days, and I do not have funds to fight another war yet. If there is a rebellion in the making, I must quash it decisively and without hesitation.'

'But you have already waited a week,' Geoffrey pointed out.

Henry smiled. 'I am not a vicious ruler, who reacts to the smallest threat. But, at the same time, I must be perceived as strong, or my enemies will move in for the kill. I do not want Joan to hang, but nor can I condone treachery. However, I thought we might reach an arrangement.'

Geoffrey stared at him. 'You are giving me a chance to save Joan and Olivier?'

'And the other people on this list.' Henry sighed and for a fleeting moment, seemed genuinely distressed by the notion of a few dozen minor nobles joining in a plot to overthrow him. His expression was haggard. 'Fools or traitors?'

'I am sorry?'

'I need to know whether the "investors" on Sendi's list are real traitors, or simply fools seduced by the prospect of quick profits. Giffard will "investigate", but his remit will be to arrest everyone for a trial that will be swift and one-sided. He believes it is better to squash a spider before it bites, rather than throw it out of the window. But spiders kill flies, and I dislike flies more than spiders.'

Geoffrey was nonplussed by the monarch's contorted zoological analogy. He cleared his throat. 'When you say flies, you mean . . . ?'

'I mean men who buzz around me and profess false loyalty,' explained Henry, with a touch of impatience. 'So, here is what we must do. I will hear Sendi's case tomorrow morning, and you will be there – although I doubt you will learn more than you know already. Then I will dismiss them, pending further enquiries, and you will travel to Bristol to look into the matter on my behalf.'

Geoffrey had suspected as much. He recalled how Giffard had forced information about the moneyers at him, on the grounds that it might later prove useful. Now he understood why: Giffard knew exactly what Henry intended, and had been trying to help him prepare.

'And if I learn that there is a conspiracy and Joan is involved, then what?' he asked carefully.

'Then you must persuade her to recant and throw herself on my mercy,' replied Henry. 'I am prepared to be lenient to one traitor, so I will seem magnanimous. I will also let her keep Goodrich.'

'What about the others? Will my investigation result in a round of executions?'

'Yes, if you find they are guilty.'

'I am not an inquisitor,' said Geoffrey distastefully. 'I do not want this sort of responsibility.'

'Then your sister will hang, because Giffard's investigation will be short, swift and irreversible. He will not become bogged down with details – he thinks I should crush this nasty little vipers' nest once and for all. But I do not want a mass killing of suspects, because I would rather know the truth.'

'I do not think I can do it,' said Geoffrey unhappily.

Henry ignored him. 'I want honest answers and I trust you to get them. You will ride to Bristol as soon as the moneyers have put their case, and you will assess whether these investors are traitors or fools. After a few days, Giffard will join you. He will listen to the evidence you have procured before passing judgement – and the folk on that list had better hope you have deemed them innocent, or that will be that. Or would you prefer to ride to Goodrich and spirit Joan away?'

There was no choice. Bellême would find out if Geoffrey tried to take Joan to any Norman domains overseas, and would exact revenge for the loss of his English estates. Joan would never be safe, and Geoffrey would be unable to protect her for ever. He nodded reluctant agreement.

Henry immediately became businesslike. 'Good. Then we are finished here. You may go.'

Geoffrey hesitated as he reached for the latch. 'Thank you. For giving me the chance to help Joan.'

'You are welcome,' said Henry. His face wore its expressionless mask again. 'But I was not speaking in jest about your accusations earlier: I *will* hang you if you ever insult me again.'

Geoffrey was sure he would.

Geoffrey was restless and unsettled after his audience with the King. He did not know what to think about the fact that Joan was on Sendi's list, but there was an appalling plausibility about the whole situation that made him suspect the accusation was true. Joan had a rigid sense of right and wrong, and was not afraid to act on her principles. And there was no denying that Goodrich's fortunes had improved at a time when most other manors were in decline. He was lost in thought when he walked through the hall. Absently, he indicated Durand was to accompany him, noting at the same time that he was talking to the long-nosed Bloet. The squire abandoned his new friend reluctantly.

'Actually,' he whispered, 'I am busy at the moment. Are you sure you need me?'

At first, Geoffrey thought he had misheard. No servant should tell his master such a thing. 'Busy?'

Durand had been with Geoffrey long enough to know the limits of the knight's patience. He saw he was close to crossing them, and hastened to explain. 'The man I have befriended is Simon Bloet. He is here because he is accused of investing money with Barcwit, who is rumoured to be a traitor.'

Geoffrey knew this perfectly well. 'What does that have to do with you being busy?'

Durand looked hurt. 'I have been encouraging him to gossip, to tell me more about this dispute between Barcwit and Sendi.'

Since Geoffrey had only just emerged from his discussion with Henry, Durand could not possibly know what the knight had been ordered to do, so had no reason to pump courtiers for information – unless he had learnt of the King's plans in advance. Geoffrey stared at him and wondered whether he had. It would not be the first time the squire had been one step ahead of his master.

Durand hurried on with his explanation. 'Sendi accused you of killing Fardin, and you had an altercation with Rodbert and Tasso that left them rolling in dirt. If you insist on making enemies in a place like this, then it is wise to find out as much about them as possible.'

Geoffrey saw he had jumped to the wrong conclusion. 'True. But do not overlook the fact that Bloet accused me of killing Alwold. Therefore, he may be considered my enemy, too.'

'Everyone here should be considered your enemy,' counselled Durand wisely. 'But my point remains: I have learnt interesting facts about Barcwit and Sendi – and about Bloet, too, for that matter – and I am in the process of gathering more.'

'Such as?'

'Such as that Sendi appears to be a lout overly ready with his fists, but he actually has a clever mind. Such as that even mentioning Barcwit's name strikes fear into the hearts of Bristol's inhabitants. Such as that Bloet is ambitious and will do anything to prove his innocence of Sendi's charges. Such as that Alwold lost a lot of silver, which he was guarding for Barcwit, and that Rodbert and Maude hated him for it.'

'So, Rodbert or Maude might have killed Alwold,' mused Geoffrey. 'And because Fardin was already murdered, they knew it would look as though Sendi had dispatched Alwold in revenge.'

'Precisely,' said Durand, his eyes glittering. 'So, you see, I *have* been working on your behalf. I may not be handy with a sword, like Helbye and Ulfrith, but I am better than them in other ways.'

Geoffrey was about to tell him to see what else he could learn before it became common knowledge that he was investigating and people started to clam up or lie, when someone shoved him so hard he staggered. His dagger was drawn before he had even turned to face his assailant. It was Rodbert, with Tasso behind him and Maude to one side. Durand shrieked in alarm and shot behind a pillar, where he listened to, but took no part in, the discussion that followed.

'I would put that away if I were you,' advised Rodbert, nodding at Geoffrey's knife. 'The King does not like exposed weapons in his palaces, and I am unarmed.'

'We have not forgotten you,' said Tasso icily. He gestured to his cloak, stained with muck from the yard. 'No one pushes *me* in the mud.'

'Enough,' said Maude, moving between Geoffrey and her companions. She smiled, and he was instantly on his guard: she wanted something. 'Did you tell Henry what Alwold said? That he claimed to have left my husband's silver with a man called Piers? I did not tell Henry the complete truth, as I suspect you noticed. I only told him Piers had a message for Barcwit about the stolen ingots.'

'Alwold was raving,' said Tasso, before Geoffrey could reply. 'He lost a consignment of silver to robbers just outside Bristol. It was on his conscience as he died, but that is all. There is no Piers. The "confession" was only the fevered imaginings of a dying man.'

Geoffrey recalled Alwold asking Maude to tell Barcwit he was sorry, and supposed it could have been a crisis of conscience that had led the man to talk about the matter with his last breath. However, Barcwit could not have been too furious with his steward, because he had promptly entrusted him with the care of his wife – the silver had been stolen three weeks before, on the Feast of St Michael and All Angels – but Alwold had been guarding Maude until a few moments before his death.

Maude turned her arresting eyes on Geoffrey. 'When Alwold first started to mutter, I hoped he was going to tell me that his claims about the robbery were untrue – that he had actually put the silver somewhere safe. But it was just wishful thinking.'

'More is the pity,' said Rodbert, glancing around to make sure he was not overheard. 'However, the King is greedy and, if Alwold *had* confessed to stealing the ingots and hiding them, we would not want *him* to know. We would never see the merest glimmer of it if *he* got there first.'

Maude shot him a withering look for such blunt speaking, although Geoffrey thought he was right. If Alwold had secreted a valuable cargo with a friend or a relative, and the King found it first, then its original owners would never see it again.

'Rodbert speaks the truth,' said Tasso to Maude, indignant on the deputy's behalf.

'Perhaps so, but this is not the place to do it,' snapped Maude. 'Nor is it the place to exchange dangerous confidences with a man who is invited to intimate discussions in the King's bedchamber.'

'Geoffrey will not repeat this discussion,' said Tasso, fingering his sword meaningfully. 'Besides, who will believe the word of one man against three? And do not say folk will accept his story because he is Norman and you are Saxons. *I* am Norman, and people know I am honourable.'

'Not here they don't,' said Maude irritably. 'You are just another petitioner, and a lesser man because you are in the pay of a Saxon – regardless of the fact that Barcwit is one of the most upright and decent men in the country.'

'I was under the impression that people are afraid of him,' said Geoffrey, sensing a contradiction between her claim and what Giffard and Durand had told him.

'They are,' said Maude. 'Barcwit hates liars, thieves and dishonesty. But upright men have no cause to fear him. To them, he is just and good.'

'But most people are not good,' elaborated Rodbert. 'So, they see the darker side of his character. He is like God – gentle with those who deserve it, but wrathful to those who do not.'

'So, what did you tell Henry about Alwold's confession, Sir Geoffrey?' asked Maude wheedlingly. 'It would be helpful to know.'

Geoffrey raised his eyebrows. 'Why should I co-operate with you, when your friends have done nothing but insult and threaten me since we met?'

Maude glared at Rodbert until he spoke. 'We hate this place, and we do not know why Henry has kept us waiting so long. We are bored and uneasy, but we should not have quarrelled with you. We apologize.' He stared at the floor and did not sound at all sincere.

'No,' said Tasso firmly, when Maude's gaze shifted to him. 'I will not say I am sorry when I am not. I may not have liberated Jerusalem, but I played my part in God's holy war at Constantinople. Barcwit ordered my return after that, but I would have been a *Jerosolimitanus* had I remained.'

'Tasso is a proud warrior,' said Maude briskly, to shut him up. 'And indispensable to Barcwit. But Rodbert has explained why he argued with you – it is because we are all feeling the strain of the vile accusations laid at our door. Now, since we are friends, you can tell me what you told the King.'

Geoffrey regarded her thoughtfully, and it occurred to him that any investigation of Barcwit and his alleged crimes would not be easy when the man had surrounded himself with people like Maude, Tasso and Rodbert. He began to wish he had not agreed to do Henry's bidding. Joan was not some simpering damsel, but a formidable woman with a sharp mind, who could look after herself.

'I told Henry nothing,' he said eventually. 'I did not understand what Alwold was talking about, and the King wanted to discuss other matters anyway. You told him all I heard Alwold say, and I could have added nothing more even if he had asked me – which he did not.'

He did not mention the last part of Alwold's message, about the King, Bloet and William de Warel knowing some secret shared by a priest of St John's. It all sounded very sinister, and he did not want to become embroiled in the matter without knowing more about it first. He determined to keep the information to himself until he knew whom he could trust.

Maude stared at him, gazing into his face as if she imagined she might be able to read the truth there. Geoffrey was struck again by how attractive she was, with her amber eyes and the intriguing strand of auburn hair that escaped the confines of her veil. He did not blame Bishop Maurice for attempting to inveigle an assignation with her.

'Very well,' she said eventually. 'I believe you.'

'Are you really afraid Henry might send agents to locate Piers, and retrieve this stolen silver before you?' he asked.

'There is no Piers in Bristol,' said Rodbert. He sounded angry about it. 'At least, no Piers of substance. Doubtless there is some river rat of that name, but Alwold is unlikely to have left a hoard of silver in the hands of a pauper who would be tempted to steal it. Tasso was right: Alwold was raving in his delirium.'

'Thank you for being honest,' said Maude, touching Geoffrey's hand. She smiled, the expression simultaneously mocking and sensual, and was about to add something else when Rodbert saw the exchange and pulled her away. Tasso merely touched his sword as he passed, an unmistakable threat.

When they had gone, Durand emerged from behind his pillar and heaved a sigh of relief. 'I thought they were going to fight us,' he said unsteadily. 'And both men give the impression they know how to handle weapons, especially the deputy, Rodbert. The henchman, Tasso, is merely a braggart.'

'No,' argued Geoffrey, who had seen the way Tasso moved in his armour. He was comfortable in it. 'Tasso will be the more able fighter. He has—'

'I have decided not to quiz Bloet after all,' interrupted Durand, never interested in military matters. 'I do not want a knife slipped between my ribs by *that* trio, merely because they think my death may annoy you. I—'

'You went to see the King,' said an accusing voice. 'If you told him about our little misunderstanding down by the river, I will dash *your* brains out with a stone.'

Geoffrey had been watching Adelise and her rabble shoulder their way across the hall towards him, and had been anticipating some hostile remark. Durand had not, and jumped in alarm at the sudden voice so close behind. Adelise and her men had barged across the room, not caring if they trod on toes or trailing clothes, or if they shoved bishops or nobles as they passed. Furious glowers followed them, and it crossed Geoffrey's mind that Alwold and Fardin might have been killed by irate courtiers who were fed up with their shabby manners.

'Lord!' muttered Durand, placing one hand on his chest to indicate he had been given a fright. 'You should not creep up on people like that, madam. My heart is all a-flutter.'

Adelise regarded him uncertainly, disconcerted by his brazen effeminacy, then turned her attention to Geoffrey. 'Well?' she demanded. 'Did you tell the King about our quarrel?'

'Everyone is very interested in my discussion with the King,' replied Geoffrey, amused. 'If he asks to see me again, I shall recommend we meet in the hall, so everyone can hear. It will save a good deal of speculation, and I shall not be obliged to repeat everything.'

She scowled at him. 'You are avoiding my question.'

'Why should I answer?' asked Geoffrey. 'If you do not want the King to know that you hurl false accusations at people, then you should not do it in the first place.'

'It was a mistake,' said Sendi sullenly. 'The soldiers misled us.'

'No,' said Geoffrey, unwilling to let the untruth pass. 'You drew conclusions from their chatter without thinking them through. You cannot blame others for what you did of your own volition.'

'We should have killed you,' said Lifwine, standing as tall as he could on his heeled shoes. 'I am sick of Normans and their condescending attitudes.'

'What do you want?' asked Durand, easing behind Geoffrey for protection. 'We do not know you, and you have no right to charge up to us and make inflammatory remarks. It is not polite.'

'I am sorry we are not *polite*,' said Sendi, almost spitting the word. 'But we came to Westminster because we have evidence of treachery and fraud. We thought Henry would be grateful, but instead he keeps us here, among people we despise. We have lost Fardin, and it is only a matter of time before another of us is taken.'

His men glanced around nervously, as though they anticipated the attack might come there and then – in the hall, in broad daylight and surrounded by people. Of course, that was what had happened to Alwold, and Geoffrey studied Sendi's mob again, wondering which of them had had the courage to commit murder in such a public place. Sendi's temper was hot enough to drive him to rashness, while Lifwine seemed sufficiently bitter. Meanwhile, Adelise was grimly determined, and it required little strength to stab a man.

'We have not made friends here,' said Adelise resentfully, as though the fault lay with everyone else. 'There are many who would love to see us fall from grace. That is why we need to know whether you mentioned the misunderstanding over Fardin. If you did, and Henry thinks we habitually make unfounded accusations, it will weaken our case, and we shall have to reconsider how to present it.'

'This case of yours,' said Geoffrey, thinking that it was a good opportunity to start his investigation. 'What sort of evidence do you have?'

'We have been monitoring Barcwit's antics for three years now,' said Sendi, pleased to find someone willing to listen. 'We watch his mint and record the comings and goings of his customers. Since Christmas, he has encouraged more folk to invest, and his profits have risen accordingly.'

'How do you know?' asked Durand curiously. 'Are his finances public knowledge?'

'We have our ways,' replied Lifwine smugly. 'His scribes can be bribed to make copies of transactions, and we listen at windows.'

'They do the same to us,' said Sendi defensively, when he saw Durand's disapproval. 'But what else can we do? We are loyal subjects, and it would be wrong to let Barcwit cheat the King of vital revenues. We are duty bound to tell Henry what Barcwit is doing.'

'Very honourable,' said Geoffrey dryly. 'And, I suppose, if Barcwit's mint loses its licence to operate, it would mean better trade for you?'

'Yes,' admitted Sendi. 'But that is not why we are here.'

'So, your evidence comprises copies of documents?' asked Geoffrey, wondering whether they would be sufficient to implicate Joan. Documents could be forged.

'And our own observations,' added Adelise. 'Take Bloet, for example. We saw him visit Barcwit on six separate occasions – all the times and dates are in our sworn statement. We also have copies of agreements in which Barcwit paid him more interest than is legal.'

'There are others on your list, too,' said Geoffrey, intending to lead the discussion to Joan. 'The two royal physicians, several knights . . .'

'How do you know?' demanded Adelise immediately. Her eyes narrowed. 'So, we *were* the subject of your discussion with Henry!'

One of her men disagreed. 'He may have heard from bishops

Giffard or Maurice. We have kept nothing secret, and lots of people know about our list.'

'You are too trusting, Edric,' said Lifwine disdainfully.

Edric ignored him and turned to Geoffrey. 'Is there someone particular you are interested in?'

'Olivier d'Alençon,' replied Geoffrey. 'And his wife Joan.'

'They came four times, the first of which was Easter,' replied Edric, promptly. 'She handled the money and deposited several gold coins from Venice. She was paid interest that almost doubled her original investment.'

'And you are sure it was her?' asked Geoffrey. 'Not someone who used her name?'

'A sturdy lass, with the kind of glint in her eye that suggests you would not want her as an enemy,' elaborated Edric. 'But she loves her runt of a husband. Another man was with them on their first visit – called Henry – but he never came again. She hails from a manor called Goodrich in Herefordshire.'

'She and Olivier often visit Bristol,' added Sendi. 'They buy horses from the nearby village of Beiminstre, and stay with Sir Peter de la Mare, constable of Bristol Castle. Why? Do you know her?'

Geoffrey nodded; there was no point in pretending otherwise, when they would soon learn the truth anyway. He felt his hopes for mistaken identity fade. Edric's description of Joan was uncannily accurate, and he and Joan had a brother called Henry.

'She is definitely one of Barcwit's collaborators,' said Adelise. 'She has a liking for silver.'

'Silver,' said Geoffrey thoughtfully. 'Barcwit lost some silver recently.'

'Yes,' said Lifwine gleefully, while his friends nudged each other and sniggered. It was evidently a popular story. 'Alwold was supposed to be looking after it, but robbers stole the lot.'

'It was not you, was it?' asked Geoffrey, thinking the question not unreasonable, given the rivalry between the two mints.

'I wish it had been,' said Sendi fervently. 'It would be a welcome addition to our coffers. But we had nothing to do with it, although it is a delight to see Barcwit trying to track it down.'

'It has disappeared completely?' asked Geoffrey, wondering how the thieves managed to dispose of what sounded like a considerable quantity of metal. The obvious way would be to sell it to a mint, but that would be risky under the circumstances.

'Without a trace,' said Lifwine, snickering. 'I think the robbers were horrified when they realized it was Barcwit's, so just hurled the whole lot into the river. Only a fool would cross Barcwit.'

'But you have,' Geoffrey pointed out. 'You crossed him to no less a person than the King.'

'That is why we came in force,' said Sendi soberly, indicating his men.

'So, you can see why we need to know what you said to Henry,' said Adelise. 'If your tale of wrongful accusations means we are sent home without our case being heard, then Barcwit will wreak revenge and we will lose everything.'

'Perhaps even our lives,' added Edric plaintively.

'I did not mention what happened by the river,' said Geoffrey, to put their minds at rest. 'There was no need, and I doubt Henry would have been interested anyway.'

'I hope he is interested in us tomorrow,' said Edric uneasily. 'Because that is when we have been told he will hear our case.'

'Well?' asked Roger, when Geoffrey and Durand walked into the stables to look for their companions. Several barons were there, inspecting their warhorses and exchanging desultory comments about hounds and hunting, while grooms laboured with shovels and pitchforks as they changed the straw in the animals' stalls. 'What did the King want?'

'He said he would hang me if I offended him again,' replied Geoffrey, thinking about the last thing Henry had said.

Roger groaned. 'You insulted him? Did you listen to nothing I said? I warned you to keep a civil tongue in your head, but you never heed my advice. You think that being able to read makes you better at these courtly games than me, but my father is the Bishop of Durham, and there is nothing you can teach *me* about the ways of places like these!'

'I would not speak so loudly, if I were you,' said Geoffrey, knowing the Court would make mincemeat of a simple and straightforward man like Roger. 'The Bishop of Durham is not popular, and this is no place to declare your kinship.'

'I will kill any man who defames my father's good name,' said Roger, reaching for his sword and immediately on the offensive. 'Ranulf Flambard is noble and honest, not like the folk around here.'

Geoffrey said nothing, but indicated Roger should sheath his weapon before someone saw it and they had a fight on their hands. He caught Durand's eye and smothered a smile. Roger was virtually the only person in England who had even a modicum of respect for the profligate bishop. Even when Flambard had used Roger shamelessly for his own ends, his son had remained doggedly loyal and blind to his many faults.

'What else did Henry want?' asked Helbye. 'I am sure he did not drag us all the way to Westminster to tell you not to be rude to him.'

Geoffrey explained what Henry had asked him to do, knowing exactly how they would react. Roger was pleased; he liked the Holy Land for its looting and ready women, but his heart lay in the country of his birth. Helbye was worried about what might happen to his pigs if Joan were found guilty. Ulfrith was excited about the prospect of a new adventure, while Durand was relieved.

'Good,' said the squire. 'I would not have minded going to Normandy or Anjou, which are civilized places, but the Holy Land is not for me. You plan to dismiss me as soon as we get there, and I may find myself in company with someone worse.'

'We will go there when we have finished helping Joan,' vowed Geoffrey. 'I want to hear from Tancred's own lips that I am no longer needed.'

'You should face up to the truth, Geoff,' said Roger soberly. 'You have been gone so long that Tancred has filled your place with new men and, if you return, he will have nothing for you to do. You will be relegated to scribing letters or guarding some distant outpost.'

Geoffrey did not want to think he was right, although he

had an uncomfortable suspicion that he might be. 'I will not know unless I ask,' he said shortly.

'Did you see the Two Suns?' asked Helbye conversationally in the silence that followed. 'We missed them, which was a pity. I have never seen a divine omen before.'

'We were talking to a fellow named William de Warelwast at the time,' elaborated Roger. 'He knows my father, and is soon to be Bishop of Exeter.'

'William de Warelwast?' asked Geoffrey, thinking about Alwold's last words. One of the men alleged to know 'the secret' was 'William de Warel'; perhaps Alwold had died before he could finish saying the name. Was it significant that the man should be chatting to Roger when his name was breathed by a dying man? Geoffrey recalled that Warelwast was also one of the investors on Sendi's list, and did not like the odd connections that were beginning to form. They reeked of plots and conspiracies, and made him feel there was more to the situation than Henry had led him to believe. 'Did he hunt you out, or did you meet him by chance?'

'His horse was lame, so he returned late from the hunt,' explained Ulfrith. 'I helped him remove a stone from its hoof.'

Chance, then, thought Geoffrey. Probably. 'What did he say?'

'He asked after my father's health,' said Roger. 'And he told us about two royal physicians who argue all the time. John de Villula was made Bishop of Wells by William Rufus, but John did not like Wells, so Rufus sold him Bath, and he moved his see there instead. He likes big wax candles.'

'*Very* big ones,' elaborated Ulfrith. 'He measures a man's height and the size of his waist, and adds the two figures together. His candles are the combined length high.'

'What does he do with them?' asked Geoffrey, bemused.

'He lights them for his patients,' explained Roger. 'Warelwast says it saves him the bother of a consultation, where he might catch something nasty.'

'And what did he say about Clarembald?' asked Geoffrey, in the hope that the indiscreet bishop-elect might have let slip some useful information about another of the men on Sendi's list.

'He lives in Exeter,' said Roger dismissively, suggesting

Warelwast had told him nothing overly scandalous about the ginger-browed *medicus*. 'He has a big house and is Warelwast's physician as well as Henry's. However, while John de Villula prays for his patients, Clarembald uses medicines that contain horse piss and powdered worms. Needless to say, neither is successful with the desperate cases. Where is Villula, by the way?'

'Overseas,' replied Durand helpfully. 'These physicians did not cure Alwold, though, did they? They just stood over him and accused each other of being charlatans.'

'Did *you* see who killed Alwold?' Geoffrey asked him, knowing the squire had been close by when the stabbing had occurred.

Durand shook his head. 'I was otherwise occupied at the time – and do not look so accusing. I was watching the Two Suns, not groping Bloet behind a pillar. I doubt anyone saw the crime, given that the omen was so much more interesting. Did Henry ask you to solve Alwold's murder, too?'

'No,' replied Geoffrey. 'But knowing the culprit may help my investigation.'

'You listened to his dying words,' said Durand. 'Did he not tell you then who stabbed him? If one of the Saxons was his killer – a man he would have known – surely he would have mentioned it?'

Geoffrey was annoyed he had not thought of this himself. It was odd that Alwold had not named his killer – especially if he had known him. 'He only muttered messages for Barcwit about silver.'

'It is a pity so many dying words involve earthly affairs, not the soul,' remarked Durand piously. Geoffrey winced at the hypocrisy: Durand was just as interested in worldly goods as the next man.

'If Alwold was so worried that he spent his last breath on the silver, it must be important,' declared Helbye. 'It is certainly relevant to your investigation – Barcwit makes coins with too little silver in them; now you have a dying steward sending messages about silver that has gone missing. Perhaps the theft left Barcwit short, so he was forced to use more tin – that would explain the underweight pennies.'

'Barcwit's bad coins are alleged to have been circulating for months,' replied Geoffrey. 'But the silver only went missing three weeks ago.'

'Did Alwold steal it himself?' asked Durand. 'And decide he had better put matters right before he died? Is that why he gave Maude that odd message about Piers?'

'She only heard half of what he wanted to say,' said Geoffrey. 'Clarembald pushed her away before he had finished. Barcwit will never know that the King, Bloet, Warelwast and the priest of a church dedicated to St John know "the secret", whatever that might mean.'

'Will you tell Barcwit this?' asked Ulfrith. 'To fulfil a dying man's last wishes?'

'Not when his companions have been to such trouble to convince me they are the ramblings of a deranged mind,' replied Geoffrey. 'Besides, I do not think it would be wise to tell Barcwit – who sounds violent and ruthless – that the King is involved in a secret that may involve his lost silver.'

'So, we travel to Bristol tomorrow?' asked Helbye.

Geoffrey nodded. 'As soon as we have heard the case Sendi presents to the King. You are coming, then? You do not want to go to the Holy Land without me?'

'We do not,' said Durand, before the others could reply. 'This matter in Bristol sounds intriguing, and I am more than happy to pit my wits against dishonest moneyers. We will come.'

Geoffrey smiled, thinking Durand was the one man in the party who had no choice: he would travel west regardless of what the others decided. In some ways, Durand was a good companion, because he was literate and intelligent, and Geoffrey often found it helpful to discuss complex matters with him – far more so than Roger, who tended to dismiss anything he did not understand as the work of the Devil. But mostly, Durand was a menace for his lack of loyalty, flagrant cowardice and selfishness.

'Mints are odd places,' mused Helbye. 'Warelwast said there are about seventy in England. Do you know why there are so many? Because if there are plenty of mints producing plenty of coins, no one can say he cannot lay his hands on the money to pay the King's taxes.'

Roger's face split in an acquisitive grin. 'If there is silver involved in this particular mission, the King might reward us with some when we are successful.'

'He will reward us,' agreed Geoffrey. 'He has agreed to leave Joan alone.'

'Is that all?' asked Roger, disgusted. 'You did not tell him to pay you, too?'

'I did not,' said Geoffrey. Doubtless Henry thought he was generous enough by sparing Joan.

'You should have done,' said Roger admonishingly. 'It costs money to travel, and I do not see why we should have to pay to do the King's bidding. Go back, and ask him for expenses.'

'I will not!' said Geoffrey, laughing. 'That would have us hanged for certain.'

That evening, Geoffrey did not want company, and opted to spend some time alone. In the gathering dusk, he sat on the sea wall that fringed the River Thames, and thought about Joan and Olivier, and the last time he had seen them. He had received regular letters from Goodrich over the past twenty years, and had come to look forward to the banal chatter about his family's estates, the animals, the amount of corn grown and the happenings in the nearby villages. None were subjects that would have interested most knights, but Geoffrey enjoyed the insights into rural life, and considered them a spark of sanity in the violence and bloodshed that so often surrounded him.

He had not always seen eye to eye with Joan, but she was the only surviving member of his family for whom he felt any affection. He was less fond of her cowardly husband, but Olivier was devoted to Joan, which redeemed him somewhat. But what were they thinking of, to make dubious financial deals with a moneyer? Had Olivier done something that had allowed Barcwit to blackmail him, so the investments were made unwillingly? But Joan was not the kind of woman to submit to extortion, so Geoffrey dismissed that particular solution.

Had she made the investments to strike at the King, whom she considered a usurper? Geoffrey assumed she had put

63

politics behind her, after an unpleasant escapade involving Bellême the previous year. But Joan was a woman with brave opinions and the strength of character to act on them. Perhaps she had found it too difficult to remain mute on issues she found morally unacceptable.

He rubbed his eyes and stared into the gloom, knowing he would have to speak to her if he wanted answers. He listened to the slap of water and reeds hissing in the wind, and turned his mind to his investigation. Barcwit was accused of dishonesty, and of encouraging others to break the law with him. His steward had been stabbed. Why and by whom? Was it Sendi, so Alwold would not add his voice to Maude's when she defended her husband against the charges? Was it someone from Maude's clan, in the hope that Sendi would be blamed and the case against Barcwit discredited? Or was it some sensitive soul in the royal household, whom Alwold had offended?

Durand's point had been interesting: Alwold could have spent his dying breath denouncing the man who had killed him, but he had not. He had talked about missing silver, and was desperate that Maude took his message to Barcwit. Was it a guilty conscience – that he had been in charge of the silver when it had been stolen – as Maude claimed? Or was the theft a ruse and he had taken it himself, passing it to his accomplice Piers for safe keeping? And what was 'the secret' the King knew, along with Bloet, Warelwast and the unidentified priest?

The damp late-autumn evening was growing colder, so Geoffrey decided to beg some ale from the kitchens, preferably warmed, before retiring for the night. He stood stiffly; he had been still too long. His left leg was numb from where he had been sitting on it, and when he put his weight on it, it buckled, making him stagger. It was this which saved his life.

The crossbow quarrel clattered harmlessly into the wall next to him. He reacted instinctively, hurling himself to the ground and rolling towards the reeds, where he hoped he would be more difficult to spot. It was a dark night, because clouds covered the moon and the lamplight that blazed from the hall did not reach the beach; the blackness was Geoffrey's friend, because it made it difficult for his attackers to see him. His manoeuvre did not deceive them for long, however, because another missile smacked into the mud near his hand. He clambered to his knees, and scrambled deeper into the rushes. He heard voices, low and angry, which told him he had more than one assailant to worry about.

He edged through the undergrowth and strained his eyes, looking for moving shadows. Then his dagger clanked against a stone, and he heard someone move towards him. The reeds near his head shivered and there was a swishing sound. Someone was scything through them with a sword, blindly slashing in an attempt to hit something. Geoffrey launched himself forward, aiming to knock the person from his feet. But his dead leg let him down, and he did not dive as far as he had anticipated. He succeeded in bowling into the man, but not in pushing him over.

He deflected the blow aimed at his head, then countered it with one of his own. He heard his assailant grunt, and knew from the way the swipe was parried that he was fighting a poor swordsman. He went on the offensive, striking out with clean, controlled swings until he felt the blade connect with something soft. There was a gasp of shock.

'Put up your weapon,' he ordered. 'Or I will kill you.'

There was no reply, so he lunged again, but encountered nothing but air. He stood still and listened. He could hear ragged breathing coming from his right, and a sound to his left, too. Then something struck his chest. Someone was throwing stones. Another missile followed the first, but they made little impact through his armour and surcoat. He charged at the stone-thrower, and heard the satisfying sound of someone running for his life.

'Come on,' shouted a voice to his right. 'We have done all we can. Leave him!'

Two more sets of footsteps followed the first, but Geoffrey did not feel like running through the night in pursuit. He was unlikely to catch them, and did not want the inconvenience of strained or broken limbs if he fell. They were not worth the effort. He sat on the wall again, this time with his back to the river, and wondered who would want to kill him before his investigation had properly begun.

Four

None of Geoffrey's companions were particularly concerned the following morning when he told them he had been attacked. Roger and Ulfrith were unimpressed, because he had no wounds to show and no corpse to prove his story. Helbye was a little worried, but the damp weather was making his hip ache, and the tale did not keep his attention for long. Durand merely pointed out that was what happened when one paraded around palaces wearing the insignia of *Jerosolimitani*; other knights saw it as a challenge, and Geoffrey should anticipate such attacks and be ready for them.

Even Henry's soldiers were not bothered by the fact that a royal guest had been assaulted, and claimed their job was to protect the King; everyone else could fend for himself. Bishop Maurice was more interested in explaining how he had entertained some hapless wench in his bedchamber from dusk to dawn, while Giffard listened politely, then began a diatribe against courtiers who ate too much.

Geoffrey looked in vain for men who limped or were bloodstained, but everyone seemed hale and hearty. He paid particular attention to the Saxons, but none sported injuries, nor did they regard him with the kind of nervous resentment he would have expected, had they been the culprits. Rodbert looked tired and out of sorts, but he imagined the Saxon would be a better fighter than the three of the previous night, while Tasso would have been formidable.

Eventually, with no suspects to question, he decided he was reading too much into the attack, and there was no more to it than an opportunistic ambush. They had tried to rob him and had failed, and their leader had ordered their retreat when he saw they would not succeed. Geoffrey comforted himself with the knowledge that they would think twice before attacking anyone else.

Geoffrey had hoped Henry would hear Sendi's case that morning, so they could start the journey to Bristol immediately, but dawn was gloriously clear and Henry wanted to hunt, so it was well into the afternoon before a messenger came to announce that the Court was getting ready to sit. Geoffrey and Durand walked to the hall, while Roger, Helbye and Ulfrith claimed they had no interest in tedious legal proceedings, and elected to remain outside.

Sendi's hearing took place in a quiet aisle away from the main hall, where a wooden chair had been set for the King, and stools and tables prepared for the scribes who would take notes. Only a small group was present, comprising the rival moneyers and a few of the King's advisers. Bishop Maurice was among them, and as soon as Durand caught sight of the portly prelate, he hid behind a pillar. Geoffrey noticed he was immediately joined by the friend he had made the previous day: Bloet, who furnished him with gossip. Bloet looked uneasy, and Geoffrey did not blame him. He would have been uneasy himself, had he been accused of treason, regardless of whether he was innocent.

Also present were the squabbling physicians. Clarembald's ginger eyebrows twitched and trembled anxiously, while John's face was pale and impassive. Geoffrey was not sure whether he would trust either with his own health, and was thankful he was never ill. And finally, there was Giffard, muttering to the scribes in a low voice. It told Geoffrey that he had already been warned of his impending visit to Bristol, and was making his own record of the proceedings.

'Who is that near Clarembald?' Geoffrey asked of Maurice, pointing to a haughty Norman with flowing black hair and piercing blue eyes. His clothes were plain, but they were well made and fashioned from the finest cloth.

'William de Warelwast, soon to be Bishop of Exeter,' Maurice replied. 'I am not sure it is a good appointment, personally. He is rather worldly.'

'Unlike you,' said Geoffrey. There were few men more interested in pleasures of the flesh than Maurice.

'I have a medical condition that obliges me to relieve myself with ladies,' said Maurice stiffly. 'Warelwast, however, chooses to be secular.'

Before Geoffrey could respond, the King arrived and began the hearing without further ado. Henry ordered Sendi and his supporters to stand on one side, while Maude waited on the other with Rodbert and Tasso. It was clear she intended to argue Barcwit's case, which Geoffrey thought was wise: Tasso was not sufficiently eloquent, while Rodbert was inclined to lose his temper. There was an expectant hush, and Henry began to speak.

'Before we start, we express our sympathy to Mistress Maude for Alwold's untimely death, and to Master Sendi for the demise of Fardin.'

Rodbert glared at Sendi. 'Alwold's murder means there is one fewer voice to protest Barcwit's innocence, but justice will be done, and—'

'Barcwit is not innocent,' shouted Sendi, incensed. 'He is a bullying, evil—'

'Silence!' roared Henry. The vast building went so quiet that Geoffrey could hear Maurice's soft breathing next to him. 'This is an official legal proceeding with rules – which means you do *not* yell across me and contradict each other. You will each have an opportunity to present your case, then you will go home and await my decision. Do I make myself clear?' Everyone nodded. 'Good. First we shall hear Sendi, Master Coiner of Bristol – and do be brief. I am hungry.'

Sendi was wearing his best clothes for the occasion, flaunting his non-Norman ancestry. His golden mane was tied in a tail at the back of his head, and he was covered in jewellery that bore Saxon motifs. When he spoke, his voice was confident, and he immediately transcended the status of uncultured, argumentative petitioner and looked more the part of the wealthy and influential merchant.

'I own a mint near St John the Baptist's Church in Bristol. This is my wife Adelise, and my silversmith Edric. Lifwine is our "exchange" or *cambium* – the independent agent who assesses each coin to ensure it is the correct size, weight and quality.'

Each stepped forward to make his obeisance to the King, and Geoffrey thought Lifwine was a long way from being independent. The diminutive *cambium* was most definitely Sendi's man, and the knight wondered to what lengths he would go to see Sendi win his case. Would he lie about the quality of Barcwit's pennies, or turn a blind eye to inferior coins produced by Sendi?

Sendi continued. 'Barcwit is also a moneyer. His mint is next to the Church of St Ewen.'

'We do not need to know the names of churches,' said Henry impatiently. 'They are not relevant.'

Sendi inclined his head, although Geoffrey saw he was angry at the rebuke. 'Barcwit has been minting coins longer than me. He also owns the best site – which was my point in telling you its location. It stands in the centre of the town.'

It was beginning to sound like sour grapes. Sendi was jealous of Barcwit's long-established business and good position. Geoffrey began to feel more hopeful about Joan's predicament, but Adelise quickly realized her husband was not making a good impression, and began to speak herself.

'You know that every English mint is monitored by a *cambium* and you have met Lifwine. But Barcwit's *cambium* is a drunk who has not assayed a coin in three years. That is our first complaint: we ask that Barcwit's *cambium* be replaced by a sober, trustworthy man who will not cheat Your Majesty of the revenues rightfully his.'

Clever Adelise, thought Geoffrey. She had gone straight for Henry's weakness: the possibility that he might be losing money. He saw she had the King's complete attention.

'I can suggest some suitable candidates,' offered Lifwine. Geoffrey grinned, seeing Henry turn sceptical again. Lifwine's 'helpful' proposal had just lost any advantage Adelise might have won.

'Our second complaint,' she said quickly, 'is that Barcwit makes more than the requisite two hundred and forty coins per pound of silver. Also, his silver is less than the required ninety-two per cent pure. We brought samples.'

Sendi handed Henry a small bag. The King opened it and

passed a penny to Giffard, who gave it the most disinterested of glances before tossing it to Geoffrey. It looked much like the ones in the knight's own purse. It bore the King's head on the front, and a cross and Barcwit's name on the back. If it was lighter or contained too much tin, then the difference was invisible to Geoffrey.

When the coins had been inspected – and Geoffrey noticed Henry did not give them back – the King indicated that Adelise was to continue.

'Our third complaint is that a large number of people have been investing funds with Barcwit of late. This is not unusual: silver pennies are a stable commodity, and men like to know where they stand with their finances. The price of silver has been set for some years now, and people would rather invest in it than in wool or grain, which is dependent on demand, weather and so on.'

'Why do these people choose Barcwit over you?' asked Henry.

Adelise stepped closer, clasping her hands. Geoffrey was reminded of a nun, and saw that was exactly the image she intended to project. Nuns were honest and upright, and that was how Adelise wanted to appear before the King.

'That is what concerns us, sire. We offer the same returns on investments, so there is no reason for anyone to select Barcwit over us. But we have evidence that he offers some of them a better rate.'

'What is wrong with that?' asked Maurice, who was captivated by Adelise. His eyes glistened, and he ran a red-tipped tongue around his lips to moisten them.

Henry raised his eyes heavenward that the prelate should ask such a question, while Giffard started to explain, presumably to demonstrate that not all bishops were so blinded by lust that they did not understand their country's fiscal policies.

'It is illegal,' he said dryly. 'And probably means the King is getting less profit than he should. Let me explain: if you had a hundred pennies and you invested them with me at an annual rate of ten per cent, you would have a hundred *and ten* pennies after a year.'

'But you must make a profit, too,' said Maurice, his eyes

fixed on Adelise's chest. 'Or messing around with my money would not be worth the bother.'

'Your investment would allow me to buy more silver and dies, which I would use to make more coins,' agreed Giffard patiently. 'And, at the rates currently set by the treasury, my profit would also be ten pennies – five for me and five for the King. *But*, if I offered you twelve per cent, instead of ten, your profit would be an additional two pennies. Those two pence must come from somewhere, and no moneyer is going to give up his own share.'

Adelise smiled at Maurice, who made a peculiar noise at the back of his throat. 'Bishop Giffard understands perfectly: the two pence will be taken from the revenue that should go to the treasury.'

'But what advantage is this to the moneyer?' asked Maurice, not using the sharp wits Geoffrey knew he had while the distraction of Adelise paraded before him.

Henry sighed. 'Think! Your hundred pennies will allow him to earn twenty pennies more. But if he offers you twelve pennies instead of ten, it only leaves eight, and he will not be content with taking three while I have five. He will keep all eight for himself. That is why we set interest rates – to remove such temptation.'

'But it is not unknown for some moneyers to make private arrangements, and so cheat the treasury of its dues,' said Giffard. He looked at Adelise. 'And this is what you accuse Barcwit of doing?'

She nodded. 'We have compiled a list of those we suspect of helping him. Some are here today.'

'We shall ask them for their defence later,' said Henry. 'Continue.'

'Our fourth and final complaint relates to Barcwit's behaviour,' said Sendi. 'The whole town of Bristol is under his control. It is not fair and it should be stopped.'

Henry was not very interested in this particular charge, because it did not impact on the far more important issue of money. He turned to Maude, who had listened to the accusations with a dignified silence. 'Well, madam? Here is your chance to respond.'

*   *   *

Taking a leaf from Adelise's book, Maude stepped towards the King and turned the full force of her personality on him. Compared to her, Adelise was a novice in the art of allurement, and Henry was immediately captivated by her grace and eyes full of mysterious promise. Poor Maurice was almost beside himself, and repeatedly wiped his face with a piece of linen. Rodbert was none too impressed, however, and Geoffrey noticed Tasso gripping his friend's arm, silently encouraging him to let her deploy her magic for their cause.

'These charges are wicked lies, intended to harm one of your most loyal subjects,' she proclaimed in a low, husky voice. She walked closer, fingering a cross that hung around her neck and thus drawing Henry's attention to the vicinity of her bosom. 'My husband would lay down his life for his King, and would never deprive him of funds.'

'I am glad to hear it,' said Henry with a faint smile.

'I shall refute these four charges one by one, sire,' she went on. 'I am here with my husband's deputy, Rodbert, and Sir Tasso de Taranto, who sees to our protection against thieves. My husband considers Sendi's charges too ludicrous to answer, and refused to come himself.'

'Yet they take up the time of his monarch,' Henry pointed out dryly.

'Something he considers a grave crime,' replied Maude, gazing at Sendi in a way that indicated the King should hold *him* responsible and punish him accordingly.

'You oversee the security of Barcwit's mint, Sir Tasso?' asked Henry. Tasso stepped forward and nodded in a military kind of way. 'Then how did this silver get stolen three weeks ago?'

'We buy from several different mines, sire,' explained Tasso. 'I was escorting a load from Somerset when Alwold lost the shipment from Devon.'

'Have you heard rumours about where this silver might be?' pressed Henry. 'I understand it is worth a great deal of money.'

Maude's eyes were still fixed on Sendi when she replied. 'We have our suspicions, sire.'

Sendi was immediately on the defensive. 'Do not blame

us! You should have transported it in smaller loads, not hauled mountains of the stuff halfway across England. It was asking for trouble.'

Maude turned to Henry. 'The load was worth a fortune,' she admitted. 'And my husband is distressed over its disappearance. It was well guarded, and we had no reason to think it was in danger. However, we have heard no rumours about its whereabouts. I only wish we had.'

Henry looked equally disappointed. 'Well, it cannot stay hidden for ever. Thieves are greedy by nature, and will not wait too long before they are overcome by the urge to sell their ill-gotten gains.'

'He should know,' Durand murmured imprudently, easing from his hiding place now Maurice's attention was taken with Maude. 'He is more greedy than the rest of us put together – except maybe those two physicians. Clarembald sold Bloet a remedy for his blocked nose that cost six pence. When it did not cure him, Bishop John lit one of his big candles and demanded a shilling. Bloet's nose still does not work, and he is down eighteen pence.'

Geoffrey turned his attention to Henry, who had moved on from the issue of the missing silver. The King asked again if Maude would like to refute the charges Sendi had levelled, then looked meaningfully at the tables being readied in the hall. She did not have long before he went to his dinner.

'First, we are accused of having a drunken *cambium*,' she said. 'Send someone to meet him, sire. Your representative will find him sober and diligent.'

'Assuming the representative is introduced to the right *cambium*,' Durand whispered. 'Bloet tells me he is always in his cups.'

'Then I shall,' said Henry, which had Tasso and Rodbert glancing at each other in alarm.

Maude smiled, to indicate she was pleased by Henry's decision. Geoffrey supposed Durand was right: she intended to impose an impostor on the King's agent. 'Second, we are accused of making bad coins. But the coins you inspected just now are *not* from our mint.'

Henry raised his eyebrows. 'They bear Barcwit's name.'

73

'They are forgeries.' She gazed coolly at Sendi. 'Anyone can see they are mules.'

'They are what?' asked Maurice, simpering at her.

'Mules,' repeated Maude. 'It means the side bearing the King's head is genuine, but the reverse – which carries the name of mint and moneyer – has been struck using an old or a corrupted die. We call such coins mules, and they are illegal. I can assure you that no mules ever emerge from *our* mint, so someone made the ones you hold in your hand, for the express purpose of discrediting us.'

'Lies!' spat Sendi. He turned to the King. 'Sire! She is accusing us—'

'Silence!' snapped Henry. 'You have had your say; now it is her turn. Pray continue, madam.'

Maude edged closer still, stroking the cross that lay at her throat. Maurice's glittering eyes were fixed firmly on the creamy skin of her chest, while Henry leaned back in his chair and met her gaze with an unreadable one of his own. Geoffrey wondered whether she would be entertained in the royal bedchamber that night; he was sure she would be delighted to put her case a little more intimately.

'Thirdly, Sendi objects to the number of our investors,' she said. 'But Barcwit has been a moneyer for a long time, and people trust him. He works hard – and even sent an additional payment to the treasury at Easter, when he knew funds would be needed to fight the evil Bellême.'

'That is true, sire,' confirmed Giffard. 'Barcwit did send more money than required, and he included a letter saying he hoped it would help you against the rebels.'

Geoffrey was impressed. If Barcwit was indeed plotting to harm Henry, then it was clever to make a donation to disguise his true intentions.

Maude pressed her point. 'People invest with us because they know us. Ask Sendi what happened when Abbot Serlo gave *him* ten pounds last year. Serlo lost twenty per cent of it, because the dies broke and it took a month to acquire new ones. Word spreads quickly about that sort of thing.'

Adelise flushed deep red. 'We *were* only able to give Serlo eight pounds when he asked for his ten, *but* we returned the rest – with interest – before Easter. She has twisted the truth!'

'Not really,' mused Henry, scratching his chin. 'The bald fact is that when the abbot needed his money, you were only able to give part of it back.'

'It was Barcwit's fault!' shouted Sendi. '*He* damaged our dies, then arranged for our couriers to be ambushed so the new ones were late in arriving. And he encouraged Serlo to make a withdrawal.'

'No yelling,' said Henry sharply. 'If you howl at me again, I shall have you fined.'

Adelise stepped forward to speak, but Henry raised his hand. It remained in the air until she backed away, and only then did he gesture that Maude was to continue.

'If you do not believe us, then study the list Sendi has fabricated,' said Maude softly. 'On it are men he claims cheat you by accepting higher rates of interest. But some of these men are here today, and you know they are honourable. For example, Simon Bloet is the Bishop of Lincoln's son. With an ecclesiastical father, his character is beyond reproach.'

Bloet cleared his throat nervously, aware that not all bishop's sons were paragons of virtue – and neither were all bishops. When he spoke, his voice was oddly nasal, as though the physicians' remedies had done more harm than good. 'My father has always been proud of my achievements, sire. He thinks I will be of great value to you—'

'Yes, yes,' said Henry. 'We know you are keen to enter my service. But I want to know about these investments you made with Barcwit.'

'I have never done – nor will I ever do – anything to harm Your Majesty,' declared Bloet fervently.

'You deny making investments with Barcwit?' asked Giffard.

'I deny making *dishonest* investments. I have a glittering future ahead of me, and will not risk it for a few illicit pennies. It is not worth it.'

'Well, that is honest, I suppose,' said Henry, amused.

'Your physicians, Clarembald and the Bishop of Bath, are also on Sendi's list,' Maude went on.

'My Lord Bishop,' said Henry, gesturing to John de Villula. 'What do you say to these charges?'

'I have done nothing wrong!' cried John. 'I invest with Barcwit, because he owns an old and established business and I trust him. The same cannot be said for every moneyer in England.'

'There is a mint in Bath,' said Henry, watching him carefully. 'You own it yourself. Why do you not invest with that moneyer?'

John began to gabble. 'Because Bristol is just fifteen miles from my home in Bath, and investing with Barcwit provides me with an opportunity to visit the place. I like it: it is vibrant and busy, and one can buy all manner of exotic spices not available elsewhere, while its leather goods are unsurpassable. I bought these shoes there.' He raised the hem of his habit to reveal some very handsome footwear.

'Nice,' said Henry, leaning forward to inspect them. 'Bristol is good for shops, then?'

'Excellent, sire. And purchasing attractive items is good for the health. I always feel so much better after a visit to Bristol's traders. You should try it. You will find yourself a new man.'

'Find myself a new man!' breathed Durand in Geoffrey's ear. 'I am beginning to like the sound of Bristol more and more.'

'Master Clarembald,' asked Henry, 'do you invest with Barcwit because it provides you with an opportunity to spend money on fripperies?'

Clarembald's impressive eyebrows waved disdainfully. 'I do not demean myself with trivialities, sire. I invest with Barcwit because the roads to Exeter – where I live – are spangled with outlaws, and I have been robbed twice. It is safer to leave my money in Bristol, and Barcwit provides as good a place as any. I am certainly not involved in anything corrupt.'

'The last of Sendi's claims – that Barcwit frightens people – is arrant nonsense,' Maude concluded coolly when the courtiers had finished protesting their innocence. 'Barcwit has no patience with liars and cheats, so his wrath descends on corrupt men like Sendi. But good citizens have nothing to fear.'

'I would like to visit Bristol and assess this situation,' said

Henry. 'And perhaps even go shopping for the good of my health. But other matters require my attention. However, I shall do as you suggest and send a representative to meet Barcwit's *cambium* and ask a few questions on my behalf.'

'Who, sire?' asked Sendi nervously. His unease was reflected in the faces of Maude's companions: neither side wanted a King's agent poking too deeply into their affairs, giving the impression that both engaged in practices that might be construed as murky by a diligent inspector.

'I think Giffard, the Bishop of Winchester,' replied Henry, as if the name had just popped into his head. Everyone turned to look at Giffard, who acknowledged with a nod.

'Lord!' muttered Sendi, regarding the austere bishop with trepidation. 'He will have us all paupers.'

'He only persecutes criminals,' said Henry, which did little to soothe their fears. 'However, I need him here for the next few days, so, Sir Geoffrey Mappestone of Goodrich will conduct a preliminary investigation. He will travel with you to Bristol tomorrow; Giffard will come later.'

'Why do you need two investigators?' demanded Rodbert, alarmed by the prospect.

'Giffard has no time to chase witnesses and collect detailed information,' replied Henry tartly, not pleased to have his decisions questioned. 'So, Geoffrey will do that; Giffard will review his findings.'

'Geoffrey comes from Goodrich?' asked Adelise, eyes narrowed. 'But that means he is related to Joan of Goodrich, who is on our list of corrupt investors. So, *that* explains why he asked about her last night. Well, we will not have him!'

'For once, I agree,' said Rodbert. 'Geoffrey has already insulted me and I do not want him poking into my affairs. Tasso shoved him in the mud, and he will want to avenge himself for the humiliation.'

'He tried to fight *us*, too,' added Lifwine in a petulant voice. 'He is not the kind of man you should appoint, sire. Choose someone else.'

Henry's face was angry as he stood, and Lifwine tottered backwards in alarm. 'Very little happens in my Court that I do not hear about,' he said, his voice softly menacing. 'I know exactly who pushed whom in the mud, and I know who charged along the riverbank intent on slaughter, when they only had half the facts.' His gaze raked across the assembled Saxons.

'But what about his connection to Joan?' persisted Edric, not clever enough to know the battle was lost. 'He will find Barcwit innocent, regardless of any evidence he uncovers to the contrary.'

'He knows better than to deceive me,' said Henry, his voice still dangerously low. This time, it was sibilant and unsettling enough to silence even the outraged Edric. 'He would not dare to present me with anything other than the truth – and if you have any sense, you will follow his example. All you moneyers will travel to Bristol together, and he will accompany you.'

'The hearing is over,' announced Giffard in the silence that followed. 'Sir Geoffrey is appointed as King's agent, and I shall come later, to assess his evidence. You are dismissed.'

'You knew!' snarled Sendi at Geoffrey, as soon as the King and his bishops had left. 'You *knew* he planned to appoint you, so you encouraged us to argue with you, just to weasel information from us.'

'Not so,' replied Geoffrey calmly. 'You accused me of killing Fardin yesterday morning, but my audience with the King was in the afternoon. Ask anyone.'

'I cannot imagine why Henry wants *you* as his agent,' said Rodbert in disgust. 'You are dirty, quick to take offence and have a bad temper.'

'I was irritable yesterday,' admitted Geoffrey. 'But that was due in part to Saxons picking fights with me.'

'But you are still dirty,' said Lifwine, looking Geoffrey up and down in distaste. 'And it will not be pleasant to travel with you.'

Geoffrey glanced at his surcoat and acknowledged that it might benefit from a wash. The rest of his clothes were hidden under his armour, so no one could know they were full of holes and more grimy than was decent. He usually considered himself presentable if he was cleaner than Roger, but it occurred to him that his friend was not a good measure of respectability, and that he might have allowed his standards to slip over the years.

'We do not want to travel with *you*, either,' Sendi was saying to Maude.

'The feeling is mutual,' replied Maude icily. 'But it is safer in large groups, and a second knight might come in useful.' She smiled at Geoffrey in a way that suggested the usefulness had nothing to do with his skills as a warrior.

Rodbert saw the look and was furious, but Tasso spoke before he could begin a tirade. 'If we ignore the King and travel separately, his creature here is sure to report us. We have no choice but to go with him to Bristol.'

'If he lives that long,' hissed Sendi. 'It is a long way, and the roads are notorious for outlaws.'

'True,' agreed Geoffrey, refusing to be goaded. 'But none of us are free to do what we want, so I suggest we make the best of the situation and at least be civil to each other.'

'It is too late for that,' growled Rodbert. 'Men who push others in mud are not the civil kind.' He shouldered his way out of the hall, with Tasso at his heels. Maude shot Geoffrey another of her suggestive smiles and followed, with the rest of her companions trailing behind.

Sendi pushed close to Geoffrey and waved a finger in his face. 'I do not like the fact that Henry has appointed the kin of one of Barcwit's investors. It stinks of corruption. But I was right in what I said: the roads to Bristol *are* dangerous, so you had better be on your guard.'

He stalked from the hall. Lifwine lingered long enough to follow his master's example and wag a finger at Geoffrey, but scurried away when the knight took a step towards him. Adelise did not deign to speak at all, while Edric spat on the floor at Geoffrey's feet. When they had gone, Geoffrey blew out his cheeks in a sigh and wondered how he was going to conduct an investigation when everyone was hostile and unhelpful. He had the feeling he might have nothing to show Giffard when he arrived, and worse, that he would not have enough to persuade Henry to keep his promise and spare Joan.

'Not good,' said Durand, breaking into his thoughts. 'This is not a good start.'

That evening, Geoffrey sat in the hall and considered all that had happened, while, outside, a gale raged, rattling the window shutters and gusting down the chimney. Roger, Helbye and Ulfrith were playing dice in a quiet corner, declining the requests of others who wanted to join their game, on the grounds that Roger would not be able to resist cheating them, and Geoffrey had warned him not to start a fight.

Durand was with Bloet. They sat in a window seat, whispering and giggling like a pair of virgins, but when Durand released one of his piercing girlish laughs, it drew the attention of the Bishop of London. Maurice was in a terrible state after his brush with Adelise and Maude, and was determined to have a woman at all costs. Fortunately, Durand saw him coming and fled, dragging Bloet with him.

'Damn!' muttered Maurice angrily, seeing Geoffrey alone nearby and coming to talk to him. 'Why does she always run when she sees me coming? And why does she insist on wearing the clothes of a man? It is a sin for her to disguise her womanly curves, which—'

'He has already secured himself a partner for tonight,' interrupted Geoffrey hastily, wanting to hear no more of that particular description.

'She will be gone tomorrow,' said Maurice, declining, as always, to take issue with him over Angel Locks' sex. He sighed wistfully. 'I shall never forget that night at Bridgnorth. She certainly knows how to please a man! There are many things the lasses in Henry's Court could learn from her!'

Geoffrey felt the matter had gone quite far enough. 'Durand really is my squire, you know. He—'

Maurice gave a weary smile and patted his arm. 'You are trying to make me feel better, because she will not have me. It is a kindly thing to do, but I shall survive without her. Look, there is Maude. Perhaps she will deign to spend a few quiet moments with a needy bishop.'

'Giffard warned you not—'

Maurice cut him off. 'That was when Alwold was alive to tell tales to Barcwit. But he is dead and she wants me badly. You must have seen the way she looked at me today during that hearing.'

'I think you will find she was directing her attentions towards

Henry. He has more to offer her at the moment.'

'She is a woman ready to seize any opportunity and turn it to her advantage,' said Maurice astutely. 'I imagine she will try the same with you, on your way to Bristol. She will want to ensnare you with her charms, so you will believe her husband's innocence. But you must be ready to separate business from pleasure – enjoy what she offers, but do not let it turn your head.'

Geoffrey was amused. 'Is that what you would do?'

'Of course. To do anything else would be insupportable.' He shivered when a particularly ferocious gust of wind shook the windows. 'This storm is getting nastier. Folk are saying it is another omen.'

'An omen of what?'

Maurice shrugged. 'It may presage disaster, or it may portend something good. Let us hope the latter. But I had better speak to Maude, before Rodbert appears. He seems to have taken up where Alwold left off. God's speed, Geoffrey.'

He sketched a benediction and was gone, weaving in and out of the crowd as he stalked his prey. Geoffrey looked for Sendi and his followers, and spotted them near the door. They looked unhappy, dismayed by the outcome of the hearing, and he saw they had genuinely anticipated that Henry would accept their claims without question and send troops to Bristol to arrest Barcwit.

It was not long before someone else came to disturb Geoffrey's solitude. Clarembald's eyebrows were particularly orange that evening, because they caught the red glow from a nearby brazier.

'I have come to ask whether I might travel with you,' the *medicus* said, after they had exchanged the formal pleasantries of two men who knew of each other, but who had never met. 'My practice is in Exeter, and I always travel there by way of Bristol.'

'If you like,' said Geoffrey. 'As long as your rival, John de Villula, does not want to come, too.'

· 'Actually, I suspect he will,' admitted Clarembald. 'He lives in Bath, which is near Bristol, and he would be a fool not to take advantage of your protection.'

'Then no,' said Geoffrey. 'You will argue, and I shall have enough trouble with the Saxons.'

'We will quarrel,' acknowledged Clarembald. 'But we do not fight with weapons. You may need the services of a physician, anyway. Sendi believes you will find against him in your investigation, so he may try to disable you and force Henry to appoint someone else. You have also made enemies of Tasso and Rodbert. The only one who likes you is Maude, but that will only be for as long as you do not displease her in the bedchamber.'

Geoffrey was amused by his bluntness. 'Then let us hope I do not.'

'Henry ordered me here to answer Sendi's accusations,' Clarembald went on, annoyed. 'But then he barely gave me the chance to speak. I cannot decide whether he thinks me guilty or innocent. Bristol is a convenient place to deposit money safely – and earn a little extra in the process. It is a mercantile town, so of course they know how to conduct good business. But I have never been offered an illegally high interest rate, by Barcwit or anyone else.'

'Barcwit,' mused Geoffrey. 'Maude claims he is a good man repelled by wickedness, while Sendi maintains he is a terrifying despot who holds an entire town under his sway. Which is true?'

'The people of Bristol *are* frightened of Barcwit, although he has never coerced me. I invest with him willingly, because he is scrupulous about his repayments.'

'What does he look like?'

'I am not sure.' Clarembald sounded surprised at the answer himself. 'I usually deal with Rodbert or Maude. I glimpsed him once, though, when I was visiting his mint after dark. He is a huge man who favours dark clothing. Even bold knights like Tasso hold him in awe. He is a *presence*.'

'A presence?'

'You know,' said Clarembald impatiently. 'One of those people you always notice when they are there. He has a personality that blazes. The King is the same.'

'Charismatic?' suggested Geoffrey.

'Yes, charismatic. Even though I have never met Barcwit

in person, he exudes confidence, which is why I choose him over Sendi or the moneyers in Exeter. However, while *I* have never been offered an illegal rate of interest, I cannot say the same for Bishop John.'

'You think he is dishonest?' Geoffrey was not surprised when Clarembald nodded.

'Very. He was a great admirer of King William Rufus – it was Rufus who sold him Bath – and he has not done as well under Henry. I think he plans to undermine Henry financially, and usher the Duke of Normandy on to the throne instead.'

'All alone?' asked Geoffrey innocently, to encourage him to gossip. 'Or with help?'

'With help.' Clarembald waved his eyebrows for emphasis. 'Young Bloet is also not proceeding as quickly through the ranks as he would like, and he is another of these investors. I anticipate you will uncover a veritable vipers' nest once you look more deeply into this unsavoury affair.'

'Yes,' said Geoffrey with a sigh. 'I thought I might.'

'Good,' said Clarembald, rubbing his hands together, as if something had been decided. 'I shall travel with you, and you shall have my professional services if the likes of Tasso, Rodbert or Sendi break through your defences. John will offer the same, but I strongly advise against accepting them. All he will do is pray and light candles.'

He bustled away, and Geoffrey was about to sit again, when another shadow loomed. This time it was the man with the flowing hair and piercing eyes, whom Giffard had identified as William de Warelwast, Bishop-Elect of Exeter.

'I am here to beg a favour,' Warelwast said with a pleasant smile when he had introduced himself.

'You want to come with us to Bristol?' predicted Geoffrey.

Warelwast laughed. 'Sir Roger said you were a clever fellow. He and I have known each other for years, through his father. I am a great admirer of the Bishop of Durham.'

'Are you? That cannot make you popular here.'

'Popularity is like spring blossom. It comes and goes.'

'Clarembald has asked to join us, and he says John de Villula will come, too. With Sendi's horde and Barcwit's disciples, we shall number about thirty people. Such a large group will not travel very fast, so if you need to be in your see with any urgency, I recommend you make your own way.'

Warelwast shrugged. 'It is not my see yet. The present incumbent still lives, and I cannot take office until he dies – which I hope will not be for many years yet. However, as a nephew of the Conqueror and a cousin of the King, I have plenty to occupy me until I am invested.'

Far from impressing Geoffrey with his family connections, Warelwast made him wary. Such men, with royal blood in their veins but a long way from real power, were apt to be dangerously ambitious. Warelwast seemed amiable enough, but it was not difficult to feign cordiality and charm. Geoffrey listened politely as Warelwast chatted in a friendly way about life at Court and the new cathedral he planned to build in Exeter, but was relieved when he left. He watched the man glide across the hall, where he bumped into Maude. She turned one of her smouldering looks on him, and Geoffrey saw him begin to vie with Maurice for her attention.

'You will need to protect her on your journey, Geoffrey,' said a voice at his side. This time, it was Henry, with Giffard in tow. 'Sendi's rabble are argumentative ruffians, and she is too vital a beauty to lose to a stray dagger. I may visit Bristol one day; it would be a pity if she were not there to greet me.'

'She will not be greeting anyone if her husband is guilty of debasing your currency, sire,' said Geoffrey, predicting that Joan might not be the only woman to enjoy Henry's clemency. The King had a soft spot for females he intended to seduce.

'True,' admitted Henry. He was silent for a while, then spoke again. 'I meant what I said yesterday about you uncovering the truth. It may be uncomfortable, and you may think it is not what I want to hear, but I trust you to tell me anyway.'

Geoffrey nodded, thinking that truth was a many faceted thing, and that Henry might as well ask for the moon. He turned to watch Maude again, and was astonished to see Maurice the victor in the competition with Warelwast. Warelwast was younger, more handsome and a good deal thinner than the bishop, but it was Maurice's arm that Maude selected to escort her away. Geoffrey did not understand why women did not run for their lives when Maurice approached, but they seldom did; and even if they did not comply with his lustful requests, they at least listened to what he had to say. Geoffrey decided to study the prelate's technique, so he could try it himself.

Giffard snorted in disgust. 'The man is insatiable! He has had three serving wenches since dinner, and claims his humours are still unbalanced. It is a pity poppy juice does not work for his condition.'

'It probably would,' said Geoffrey, 'if you made it strong enough.'

'No,' said Henry sharply, when Giffard began to consider the suggestion. 'I do not want him perpetually drowsy; I need him awake and working on my behalf. But enough of Maurice. What did you think of the hearing today? Were you more convinced by Sendi or by Maude?'

'I do not know, sire,' replied Geoffrey honestly. 'I would like to say Maude, because I want Joan exonerated of any wrongdoing. But it would be a lie.'

Henry nodded. 'Maude is more convincing than Sendi, but that means nothing other than that she is a more experienced orator. However, if Sendi is right, then he has done me a great service by coming here and exposing Barcwit. If the man is as dangerous as everyone claims, then he has done so at considerable risk to himself.'

'But it has taken him a long time to act,' Giffard pointed out disparagingly. 'Possibly years. Imagine how much money has been lost to the royal coffers in that time.'

'I have,' said Henry dryly. 'But I shall have it back one way or another. If Barcwit is guilty, I shall have his mint and his property. If Barcwit is innocent, then I shall fine Sendi for wasting my time.'

'Either would be lucrative,' mused Giffard, doing the calculations in his head.

'The truth,' said Henry, fixing Geoffrey with his penetrating stare. 'Any fool can look into this and declare Barcwit guilty or innocent, but I want the *truth*. I want to know *why* Barcwit is cheating me or *why* Sendi wrongfully accused him. The truth is more important than the solution in this case. But be careful. I sense you are about to swim through some very turbulent waters, and I would like to see you emerge from them unscathed.'

He walked away, nodding lordly greetings to his subjects as he went. Giffard lingered for a moment. 'The King is right,' he said softly. 'I do not know what to make of this business myself, but I wish you well, and I hope to find you alive when I come to Bristol.'

Geoffrey was used to travelling fast. He, Roger and their men started moving the moment it was light enough to see, and only stopped when it became dark. Then they wrapped themselves in their cloaks and slept wherever they happened to be – sometimes enjoying the luxury of a tavern, but more often bivouacking under a tree. But the journey from Westminster to Bristol was different.

The party was huge, and included not only Maude, Sendi and their respective retainers, but the two physicians, Warelwast and an army of servants. Clarembald and Warelwast had asked whether anyone objected to their company, but Bloet and Bishop John had simply appeared and announced they were coming, too. Their presumption caused ill feeling in an assembly that was already fraught with bitter rifts. The first trouble started the morning after the hearing, when the travellers began gathering in the pre-dawn gloom and Sendi discovered he was missing a horse.

'You have seventeen,' said Geoffrey, itching to be away. It was a long way to Bristol, and he did not want to spend the next three months getting there. 'Surely, you cannot need more?'

'You do not understand,' said Adelise. 'That horse carries our dies. We cannot leave until it is found.' She glared in Maude's direction, to make it clear she knew who might have stolen the animal.

'Dyes?' asked Roger, also irritated by the delay. 'Surely you can buy some more along the way? A bit of colouring is no reason to dally here.'

'Dies!' shouted Edric, as if volume would help Roger understand. 'The engraved punches we use for making coins. They are our most important pieces of equipment, and certainly the most expensive. Tasso must have stolen them. I saw him lurking around the stables last night.'

Tasso bristled. 'I am a knight,' he declared through clenched teeth. 'I do not steal. And you are lucky you are a peasant and not a warrior, or I would kill you for impudence.'

Sendi drew his dagger, perfectly willing to pit his skills against Tasso's. Geoffrey tensed to intervene, anticipating a bloodbath, and not wanting to have to report to Henry that there was no need to investigate the moneyers, because the main protagonists were all slaughtered outside his stables. He glanced at Roger, and saw his friend was ready to join any affray, although he doubted the big knight would do much to calm troubled waters – and might well double the casualties.

'Tasso was checking our horses,' said Maude quietly. 'And I am sure you did not leave anything as valuable as dies in the stable overnight. They could not have been with this missing horse when Tasso was here yesterday.'

Edric said nothing, but the expression on his face suggested her assumptions were correct. 'Well, someone has them,' he persisted. 'And who else would bother, other than a rival moneyer?'

'What does this horse look like?' asked Geoffrey.

'Brown,' snapped Sendi, not very helpfully. 'This could ruin me.'

'Why?' asked Roger, puzzled. 'You are a wealthy man, so why not buy some more?'

Sendi gazed at him in disbelief. 'You do not wander into a market stall and pick these things up, you know! Their issue is carefully controlled by the Crown, and they can only be bought from one place: Otto the Goldsmith in London. No one else in the country has the right to make dies, and any coins manufactured with stamps not produced by Otto are designated forgeries.'

'He is right,' said Bishop John. 'It is one of the ways the Crown keeps control over the currency – the dies wear out after producing a certain number of coins, forcing moneyers to buy new ones. Each time this happens, the King is paid a commission. He can also control the amount of coins circulating, because he knows how many dies are being used at any one time.'

'How do you know all this?' demanded Rodbert. 'You are just a physician.'

'I am also Bishop of Bath,' replied John grandly. 'I own my own mint, and I know a great deal about the business – or, at least, about the profits.'

Geoffrey recalled Henry asking at the hearing why John had chosen to invest with Barcwit, rather than with his own moneyer. Was it significant that the lofty physician–bishop, who had just admitted to knowing a good deal about coin-making, was on Sendi's list of corrupt investors? His explanation had been that he liked to visit Bristol for shopping. Was it true? Did he really relish trailing around stalls and haggling with merchants for goods his servants could purchase on his behalf? Geoffrey hated such activities, and found it hard to believe anyone would enjoy them.

'I will not leave until I have my dies,' declared Sendi hotly. 'I demand to search everyone's bags.'

'You can go to Hell,' snarled Rodbert. 'I will not permit my possessions to be pawed by you or your filthy rabble.'

'Do you call *me* filthy?' demanded Sendi, brandishing a knife. 'You, who are corrupt scum, and who will hang when the King discovers you have been cheating him all these years?'

'We have not cheated anyone,' countered Tasso, drawing his sword. 'The accusations that dragged us here are pure fabrication. Why do you think the King appointed an agent to look into the matter? Because he saw *we* are innocent, but *you* are not. He said as much.'

'He did not,' argued Adelise. 'He said he wanted more evidence – which we shall provide. Even Geoffrey will be unable to twist the truth once he sees what your vile investors have done.'

'We are not "vile investors", madam,' said Clarembald sharply. 'We are businessmen who made financial arrangements in good faith. We have done nothing wrong, so do not sully our good names.'

'*My* good name,' corrected John argumentatively. 'You do not have one.'

'Now, just a moment!' shouted Clarembald, rising to the bait like a hungry fish. John cut across his angry words, and then they were both yelling at the same time.

'What "truth"?' sneered Rodbert, ignoring the two physicians as he addressed Adelise. 'You have nothing but unfounded speculation. If you had real evidence, you would have brought it with you and shown it to Henry already.'

'Is that the missing horse?' asked Geoffrey, pointing to where a brown nag was happily devouring the special feed that had been put aside for Henry's best mounts. No one took any notice.

'I will kill you where you stand!' Sendi howled, advancing on Tasso. Tasso was delighted, and Geoffrey saw he intended to hack his less-experienced opponent into pieces – there was no earthly way a merchant like Sendi could best a knight, and Saxon bloodshed was inevitable. Meanwhile, Rodbert beckoned Lifwine towards him with an insulting gesture, and the *cambium* responded by urging his friends to meet the challenge on his behalf. Several obliged. Adelise ordered Sendi to show Tasso what Saxon men were made of, while Maude muttered encouragement in Rodbert's ear.

'You cannot remove a splinter without saying a dozen masses,' Clarembald yelled at John.

'I pray, because God gives me inspiration,' retorted John piously. 'And because my patients prefer Him to be involved in their cures rather than powdered worms. At least *I* do not poison my clients.'

'How dare you!' snapped Warelwast. Geoffrey recalled that Warelwast was Bishop-Elect of Exeter, and Clarembald had his home in the same city. 'Clarembald is the best physician in the country. Why else do you think I recommended him to my cousin the King?'

The sound of raised voices was deafening. Geoffrey's dog, excited by the clamour and the threat of violence, began to bark, while the horses pranced and shifted in alarm, unsettled by the racket.

'God's blood!' muttered Roger, looking around in disbelief. His sword was drawn, but there were so many quarrels that he did not know which one to join. 'Are you sure Henry ordered us to travel with these people? It will not be pleasant.'

'They will kill each other long before we reach Bristol,' said Geoffrey, watching the spectacle in disgust. 'Still, at least it will make our task simple: we will only have Barcwit alive to question.'

'There are more than thirty people here,' said Roger. 'And the only ones without drawn weapons are Bloet and Durand.'

Geoffrey glanced to where the pair stood with linked arms. Durand's satisfied grin indicated that they had spent the night together, but Bloet's expression was less ecstatic, and Geoffrey suspected the attraction might not be entirely mutual. Had Bloet seduced Durand in order to obtain inside information about the investigation Geoffrey was about to begin? Durand had certainly prised a lot of chatter from Bloet, and Geoffrey was not so naïve as to think the exchange was all one way. He realized he would have to be careful when Durand was near.

The clamour grew louder, and there was a clang as Sendi's blade met Tasso's. The knight deflected the blow with single-handed ease, and urged him to try again. Rodbert had cornered Lifwine and several of his friends, and was poking them with his dagger, laughing when they tried to defend themselves against his superior skills. Adelise pummelled him with her balled fists, so Maude grabbed her by one of her thick golden plaits. Geoffrey's dog snapped at Warelwast, then scurried away when the bishop-elect tried to kick it. It bit John instead, who immediately started to shriek about the damage to his fine boots.

Geoffrey had had enough. There was a manger outside one of the stables, piled high with the pots that were used for feeding and watering the horses. He shoved it as hard as he could, so it toppled on to its side. It landed with an almighty crash. Jugs and bowls smashed out of it, bouncing across the cobbles with ringing clatters. When the last vessel had finished rolling, everyone was silent, and even the dog had stopped barking.

'What did you do that for?' asked John indignantly. 'Look at the mess you have made.'

'If there is a repetition of this spectacle, I shall tell the King you are *all* traitors eager to cheat him,' said Geoffrey, gazing sternly at the astonished gathering. 'We have already lost an hour because of your bickering, so gather your possessions and let us make a start before someone is killed.'

'I am not leaving without my dies,' said Sendi firmly.

Geoffrey pointed. 'Your pony is there, eating the mash prepared for the King's favourite warhorse. You are too quick with your accusations, and one day it will land you in trouble.'

'It has done that already,' said Rodbert spitefully. 'The King saw straight through his lies.'

Geoffrey rounded on him. 'The next person who makes an inflammatory remark can travel alone.'

'But that would be dangerous,' objected Rodbert.

'Then behave,' snapped Geoffrey. 'You can resume these childish quarrels tonight, if you like. But we are leaving now, and if someone is not ready, then that is just too bad.'

He climbed on to his horse, and headed for the road that led west, while the others scrambled to follow. Roger caught up with him and rode at his side.

'And you accuse *me* of being impolitic,' he murmured. 'Those people already loathe you, and you have just given them cause to detest you more. What were you thinking?'

Geoffrey was disgusted enough that he did not care.

Five

The caravan of moneyers, physicians and courtiers was so ungainly that progress to Bristol from Westminster was frustratingly slow. They travelled along roads that had been built by ancient conquerors, with raised centres of gravel or stone and ditches on either side to keep them drained. Nevertheless, so many people used them that even the ingenuity of the long-dead engineers was hard-pressed to cope with the volume. In parts, the track degenerated into morasses, which earlier travellers had skirted around. In time, the secondary tracks had become mud-logged, too, so another path was made, and another, with the result that the highway was so wide in places that it was difficult to find.

The rain did not help. It fell in a steady drizzle that penetrated even the most carefully oiled cloaks. Geoffrey was used to being cold and wet, but the physicians, Warelwast and Bloet complained vigorously, and even suggested finding a tavern in which to wait until the weather cleared. The Saxons regarded them as if they were insane, and scornfully asked if they intended to arrive in Bristol the following summer.

They followed the River Thames west through fields that were ploughed and ready for winter frosts to break up the clods. Everywhere, granaries were empty or only partly full, and Geoffrey wondered how many people would starve that winter, unable to pay the high prices that would be demanded for bread. He turned his thoughts to Joan and her inexplicable turn of fortunes when others had been broken by weather and war.

After London, the country became hilly, and overlain with woods. Geoffrey urged his companions to move faster, knowing the longer they took to amble through them, the greater were their chances of being ambushed by robbers. Bloet maintained that only a fool would attack such a large party, while Tasso declared he would kill any outlaw who so much as looked at him. Sendi asked what he would do if the thief shot him with a crossbow first, which began yet another row.

Warelwast contrived to ride next to Geoffrey as often as possible. The bishop-elect seemed to sense Geoffrey's distrust of him, so sought to win him around by discussing architecture – a subject the knight found fascinating. However, Geoffrey was obliged to listen to more lectures on ecclesiastical construction than even he wanted, because the journey was taking so long.

Bloet and John owned several mules that had to be loaded each morning. The process invariably took longer than it should have done. Clarembald only had one packhorse, but he was fussy about it, claiming it carried expensive medicines from distant lands, and hinted that John would stop at nothing to steal them; John always reacted to the accusation. Meanwhile, Bloet and Durand made a habit of disappearing into churches, ostensibly to pray, and everyone was obliged to wait until they had finished. Geoffrey suggested leaving them once but, in a rare consensus, everyone agreed that prayers were important, and no one wanted God irked over the abandonment of two such fervent petitioners.

'I was not pleased when I heard we were to travel with women,' Roger muttered one morning. 'But Maude and Adelise are always on time. It is the men who give us trouble. It was almost noon before Bloet was ready yesterday, then Tasso's horse went lame. We only covered five miles. At this rate, we will be old men before we reach Bristol, and Barcwit will have died from senility.'

'We will arrive tomorrow, thank God,' said Geoffrey. 'Bath tonight, and Bristol the next day.'

'The physicians are a nuisance with their bickering,' said Ulfrith. 'If I fall ill, I do not want them near me. They let Alwold die, when timely intervention could have saved him.'

Geoffrey disagreed. 'There was nothing they could have done. His wound was fatal.'

'But the Two Suns had just appeared,' argued Helbye, crossing himself. '*Anyone* could have been saved from *any* wound after that had happened.'

'And that powerful gale the next night showed God was none too pleased about it, either,' added Roger. 'He sent the physicians a sign, and they ignored it by failing to bring someone back from the dead. I know about these things, because my father is a bishop.'

Geoffrey said nothing; there was no point. Roger and Helbye were superstitious, and there was no changing their minds once they were made up about religious matters. He went to urge the others to hurry, because he wanted to be certain of reaching Bath that evening. They had been on the road for more than three weeks, and he was keen for the journey to end and begin his investigation in earnest.

'Tonight will be our last chance,' whispered Maude, when he went to help her on to her horse. She regarded him reproachfully, declining to put her knee in his hand until she had had her say. 'You do not know what you have missed by declining my offers.'

'I do,' he replied. 'The anger of Rodbert and Tasso – not to mention the wrath of Barcwit.'

'Are you implying a dalliance would not be worth the risk?' she asked, amusement in her voice.

'I am sure it would be memorable,' he replied carefully. She was virtually the only Saxon who had not threatened – or actually tried – to harm him over the last twenty-three days, and he felt he owed her some courtesy in return.

'It would.' She reached out to touch his cheek in an intimate gesture that drew the immediate hostile attention of Rodbert. 'And I am sorry for us both. I wanted to hear tales of the Holy Land, but you spend all your nights with Roger. Or with women you barely know.'

He saw she was laughing at him, referring to the occasions when prostitutes had inveigled themselves into his company. None had compared to Maude's alluring sensuality, but, on the other hand, nor did they come with vengeful husbands or play a part in a case involving treason. However, he wondered whether he should have allowed her to seduce him after all.

It certainly would have livened up what had been a tedious journey.

She seemed to read his mind. 'It would have passed the time pleasantly. It might also have deterred some people from trying to murder you as you slept.'

There was no arguing with that point. He had woken at least three times when his dog had begun to growl. Once Rodbert appeared with a dagger, and once it was Sendi, although both claimed they were only taking the night air. Then Lifwine jabbed at him with a knife. The *cambium* proclaimed himself appalled when he recognized Geoffrey, saying he had seen a thief enter the room. A few moments later, there was a howl of pain and a would-be robber hobbled out with the dog attached to his leg, leaving Lifwine vindicated and Geoffrey not sure what to think. On yet another occasion, Adelise was keen for him to try some wine. Recalling the incident in the King's chamber with the bitter brew that may have been poisoned, Geoffrey declined, and later saw her pouring it away. When he challenged her about it, she claimed it was sour.

'I have survived,' he replied, thinking that being a royal agent was far more risky than a crusade. 'And we shall be in Bristol tomorrow. I am sure you are keen to see your husband after so long.'

'Of course. It is always a pleasure to see Barcwit. He is a lovely man.'

'Many people are frightened of him – even Clarembald, who does not live in Bristol. Lifwine told me he bites the heads off the pigeons that raid his currant bushes, and Bloet says he kills *people*, too. He has the reputation of a bully, and it seems Sendi was right about one of his accusations.'

'Rumours and gossip,' she said dismissively. 'You will not find a shred of evidence that he has killed anyone.'

It did not escape his attention that she failed to deny the charge, only stating that he would not be able to prove it. He frowned thoughtfully as he lifted her into her saddle, wondering what sort of stories he would hear about Barcwit when he reached Bristol. He was surprised that Tasso, who claimed to be honourable, should be willing to serve such a man.

'What a filthy place,' said Adelise in disgust, wiping her feet as she came out of the inn. 'And full of whores, too.' She glared at Geoffrey. 'But I am sure you do not need me to tell *you* that.'

'I had an early night,' said Geoffrey. He saw her jump to the wrong conclusion. 'Alone.'

'This has been a wretched journey,' she continued. 'I hope I never leave Bristol again. The beds in every hostelry are crawling with vermin – I shared with a rat last night . . .'

'Yes,' murmured Maude. 'His name is Sendi.'

Adelise ignored her. 'The food is disgusting, the weather dismal, and the water provided for washing stinks of sewage.' She looked Geoffrey up and down. 'Although I doubt cleansing water ever touches any part of *you*, so you probably do not care.' She flounced away.

Maude chuckled. 'She is right, Geoffrey. A scrub would not go amiss with you. But dirt does not show in the dark, and I am not fussy. Come to me tonight, and perhaps I will make you a donation of some of my lavender oil. It masks all manner of stenches.'

'I have been travelling,' said Geoffrey shortly. 'Roads are muddy, so what do you expect?'

'We have all been travelling,' said Maude, laughing. 'But not all of us are as grimy as you.'

Geoffrey stared indignantly after both women, sorely tempted to seize a handful of the ankle-thick muck in which he stood and hurl it at their retreating backs.

They had been following the dark green ribbon of the River Avon for some time before Warelwast had his accident. The Avon was a smooth, mysterious channel with a deceptively calm surface. Its banks were steep and lined with bare-branched trees that curled over it like skeletal hands. When the party stopped to allow Tasso to catch up – his horse was lame again – Warelwast claimed he was thirsty and went to the river to drink. Recent rain had rendered the bank treacherously slippery, and he was not halfway down it before he lost his footing. He disappeared from sight, and when his head finally broke the surface, it was some distance away. The flooded river had a powerful undertow.

'Damn the man!' muttered Geoffrey, snatching a rope from his saddle.

Warelwast was being carried almost as fast as Geoffrey could move, and the knight could see his terrified face as he tried to break free of the current. Geoffrey ran harder, so he was in front, then hurled the rope. It was a good throw, but Warelwast failed to catch it nonetheless. As quickly as he could, Geoffrey gathered it in and tried again. This time, the rope was too short, because Warelwast had been drawn to the other side of the water. Geoffrey raced ahead again, suspecting that if his third attempt failed, Warelwast would drown, because the man could not keep himself afloat much longer. He threw the rope as hard as he could and saw Warelwast splash towards it.

Then it was over. Roger arrived and added his brawn to the operation, so Warelwast was soon out of the water and gasping for breath in a patch of grass. Geoffrey covered him with his cloak, rain-sodden though it was, while Roger tried to take the rope from him. But Warelwast gripped it tightly and Roger sat back on his heels, perplexed.

'It is all right now,' said Geoffrey kindly. 'You can let go.'

'I thought I was going to drown,' gasped Warelwast, 'and I have not yet been invested.'

'Stand up and move around before you take a chill,' advised Geoffrey practically. 'But give me the rope first.' A rope often came in useful, and he did not like to be without one when he travelled.

Warelwast's expression was alarmed. 'I cannot! My fingers will not unfold. Lord help me! I am doomed to carry it for the rest of my life as a reminder of what passed today. It is a sign from God!'

'It is a sign of fright,' corrected Geoffrey, sawing off the end of the cord with his dagger, so the bishop-elect was left with a piece the length of his forearm. 'Your fingers will unlock in time.'

'I have seen men after battles, with their fists set rigid around their swords,' said Roger conversationally. 'Of course, they were all dead.'

'Are you saying I *did* drown, and that I am a corpse?' asked Warelwast uneasily.

'You could be,' replied Roger helpfully. 'It would explain the clenched fingers, the white face, the wide and staring eyes, the—'

'Corpses do not shiver,' said Geoffrey firmly, before the discussion could go any further. He did not want the others to rebel at the prospect of travelling with a cadaver and insist the King's cousin was left behind. Or worse, knowing how superstitious many folk were, that they dig a grave and bury the 'corpse' in it. 'And you are shivering now.'

'Thank God!' said Warelwast. 'I do not like the notion of being dead and still able to walk and talk. I doubt the Archbishop of Canterbury would anoint a corpse as Bishop of Exeter.'

'I would not be so sure about that,' said Roger prissily. 'He has consecrated some very odd people in the past. Just ask my father.'

Geoffrey saw some of the others hurrying towards them, too late to help. Clarembald arrived first, while Helbye, Durand and Bloet were behind him. Of the Saxons there was no sign, and Geoffrey supposed the drowning of a Norman cleric was not deemed sufficiently important to warrant their attention. He was surprised and disappointed, since he had always believed that people forgot their differences and pulled together in a crisis.

When Bloet saw the rope and was told Warelwast could not release it, he started to laugh, considering it a fine joke. Durand crossed himself, and added his voice to Helbye's in claiming that it was a sign from God, while Clarembald fussed in what seemed genuine concern and offered to make a poultice of snakes' eyes when they reached Bath. Snakes' eyes, he assured the dubious bishop-elect, worked wonders on stiff muscles.

'What did you pay him?' asked Bloet, when he had brought his mirth under control. He was, Geoffrey decided, the kind of man who found humour in old ladies slipping on ice, or buckets of water cunningly placed over doors.

'Pay him?' Warelwast was bemused.

'For saving you,' said Bloet. 'Your life has a price, surely? Ask the King for some of that silver he believes is hidden in

98

Bristol. You are a favourite cousin, so I am sure he will oblige, and you can discharge your debt.' His tone was acidic, and Geoffrey saw he was jealous of Warelwast's kinship with Henry. He sighed, seeing there was yet another rift in the group.

'What silver?' asked Roger, immediately interested. He was fond of silver himself. 'Do you mean the load that was stolen from Alwold? I thought outlaws took it.'

'That is the rumour,' said Bloet. 'But the King has doubts.'

'How do you know?' asked Geoffrey. 'Did he talk to you about it?'

Bloet nodded. 'He thinks it odd that such a large consignment should disappear so completely, and believes it must be hidden.'

'Why did he confide in you?' asked Clarembald, voicing what Geoffrey wanted to know. Bloet did not seem the kind of man whom Henry would choose as an intimate.

'I happened to meet him just after Alwold died, and it was on his mind, I suppose. The Saxons had been hurling accusations back and forth ever since they arrived at Westminster, and everyone knows the tale: Alwold, escorting ingots from Lideforda in Devon, was nearing Bristol when he learnt that Sendi had gone to report Barcwit to the King. Eager to be at his master's side in his time of trouble, Alwold rode ahead, trusting the silver would manage the last mile unmolested. It did not.'

'He left it unguarded?' asked Roger. 'That was stupid.'

'He left it with three soldiers,' corrected Warelwast, who was also familiar with the tale. 'The story goes that he intended to return to it once he had established that Barcwit did not need him. But Barcwit *did* need him: Alwold was the only man he trusted to guard Maude on her way to London.'

'What about Rodbert and Tasso?' asked Geoffrey, thinking that both were good swordsmen and better able to protect her than the grubby Saxon.

Bloet gave a leering wink. 'Barcwit considers Rodbert part of the danger. You must have noticed the way he growls when Maude flutters her eyelashes in your direction? But now, with Alwold gone, Maude is free to take any man she chooses.'

Geoffrey frowned. 'Are you suggesting Rodbert killed Alwold to get at Maude? It had nothing to do with having Sendi blamed for a murder – to discredit him?'

Bloet shrugged. 'Who knows? These Saxons are cunning, and I would not put any criminal act past them. The tale *I* heard was that Rodbert grabbed the opportunity to kill Alwold, because everyone would immediately assume Sendi had done it – to avenge Fardin. And Rodbert was certainly not sorry to see Alwold dead. He made his move on Maude that very night.'

'Did she accept him?' asked Geoffrey, thinking that murder was an extreme measure to take, just to seduce a woman.

'An hour after Bishop Maurice,' said Bloet salaciously.

'It is true,' said Durand. 'We both saw Rodbert and Maude *déshabillé* in a quiet corner the night following the Two Suns and Alwold's death.' He saw Geoffrey's irritation that he had not been told sooner, and became defensive. 'You cannot be angry with me for not mentioning it, when you have always made it clear you dislike gossip of this nature. Besides, I did try, but you told me to keep my "womanly tales" for Bloet.'

Geoffrey recalled the exchange and knew Durand was telling the truth. He did not like the nasty chatter that intrigued courtiers, and rarely listened when Durand tried to share it with him. 'So, Alwold's death had nothing to do with Sendi, nothing to do with the missing silver, but a good deal to do with Maude?' he asked.

'Possibly,' drawled Bloet. 'But possibly not. Who knows? However, one thing is clear: Alwold certainly caused trouble by muttering about silver as he died.'

Geoffrey rubbed his chin, thinking there were a lot of un-answered questions over Bloet's interpretation of the evidence. 'Why did Barcwit not send someone else to escort the silver that last mile? And what happened to the three guards who were left with it?'

'According to Sendi *and* Tasso – so it must be true if they agree – they were discovered dead with arrow wounds,' replied Warelwast. 'The silver was nowhere to be found, although everyone looked.'

'What did Barcwit say?' asked Geoffrey, surprised that Alwold had been spared his life, given Barcwit's reputation, let alone be trusted to look after the man's spouse.

'I cannot imagine he was pleased,' said Clarembald. 'However, he did not blame Alwold, or the man would have been dead long before he reached Westminster. Regardless, I imagine it was some deep-rooted fear that saw Alwold muttering about the incident on his deathbed.'

Geoffrey thought about Alwold's very last words, which only he had heard: that the King, Bloet, Warelwast and a priest were party to some secret. Both Bloet and Warelwast seemed very well acquainted with the details surrounding the lost silver, and he regarded them appraisingly.

'Do you know anything else about this missing hoard?' he asked, trying to sound casual. There were already too many people determined to prevent him from carrying out his duties, and it would be unwise to tell two more he had information connecting them to hidden treasure.

'That is all any of us know,' replied Bloet. He sounded bitter. 'Details gleaned from Alwold and the other Saxons. Anything else is speculation, not fact.'

'You spoke to Alwold?' asked Geoffrey, wondering if Barcwit's steward had confessed 'the secret' to Bloet and Warelwast, just because they were interested enough to ask him about it.

Both nodded and Bloet answered. 'A vast quantity of silver stolen a mile from its intended destination amid claims of treachery and corruption? It is exactly the kind of tale us courtiers love, so of course I spoke to him. But he told me nothing I did not already know. He was very secretive.'

'Guilt,' elaborated Warelwast. 'His secretiveness was guilt, because he lost something so valuable.'

'Do you think Sendi took it?' asked Geoffrey.

'No,' said Bloet with absolute conviction. 'I think outlaws took it, and Alwold would have been killed, too, had he not ridden ahead. Looking for it is a waste of time.'

'I see,' said Geoffrey in sudden understanding. '*That* is why you are on this journey. You are here to find this silver for the King! It explains why you know so much more about the theft than anyone else, and why you have been listening to gossip about it.'

Bloet looked distinctly shifty. 'Maybe I am, and maybe I am not.'

'He means yes,' said Warelwast. 'To locate the silver is exactly why he is here. The King has offered him a pardon from any wrongdoing if he can get it. Henry did not want to burden you with finding the hoard as well as investigating charges of corruption, so he charged Bloet to do it instead.'

'It is a wretched waste of time,' said Bloet sullenly, scowling at Warelwast for his loose tongue. 'The silver will not be in Bristol, no matter how hard I look. Henry has set me an impossible task.'

'And you?' Geoffrey asked of Warelwast. 'Is that why you are here?'

'No,' replied Warelwast. 'I am just a loyal servant of the King.'

He glanced at Bloet, and Geoffrey thought he understood what the bishop-elect was trying to say. Bloet was fickle and crafty, and Warelwast had been ordered to make sure he did not run off with any treasure he happened to find. He wondered whether Warelwast was instructed to watch *him*, too, to make sure he was unbiased when it came to the crimes in which his own sister was implicated.

When they returned to the place where the Saxons waited, Tasso and Rodbert did not so much as glance in their direction to see whether Warelwast had survived, while Adelise merely glowered at the hapless cleric for causing a delay. Geoffrey supposed he should not be surprised by such attitudes towards a Norman courtier, but he found their disinterest callous nonetheless.

'You saved me,' said Warelwast when they reached their horses. 'You could have let me drown – these others would have done – but you rescued me and I shall not forget that. Bloet is right: I should reward you for your kindness. Name your price, and I shall pay it.'

'I do not want anything,' said Geoffrey, although he would not have refused an instant pardon for Joan and a berth on a fast ship bound for the East.

Warelwast smiled. 'Then you shall have my friendship instead, which is worth a good deal more than gold or manors. Any time you need me, Geoffrey, I shall do all in my power to help you.'

'Lord!' muttered Geoffrey to Roger as Warelwast ran away, flapping his arms and raising his knees high as he tried to pump warmth into his chilled limbs. 'I am not sure I want the friendship of a man like him. I should have asked for gold.'

'You should,' agreed Roger. 'But you gave him your reply before I could decide on an appropriate sum. The next time this happens, let me do the talking.'

'Let us hope there will not be a next time,' said Geoffrey fervently.

Bath lay snugly in a bend of the River Avon. It comprised a settlement surrounded by a wall that encircled an abbey, several churches, buildings that encased hot springs, and smelly streets lined with houses. Warelwast, who rode next to Geoffrey, explained that the walls had been strengthened by Saxons more than a century before, to repel raids from violent pirates who came from the north.

'Bath is a fine place,' he went on. 'Its springs have healing powers, which is why Bishop John chooses to live here, rather than Wells. As a physician, such fountains are useful. Clarembald says they are just water, though. They argue their cases strongly, and it is difficult to assess who is right.'

'Dip your hand in one and see what happens,' suggested Roger, nodding at the rope still gripped in Warelwast's fist. 'That will give you your answer.'

Geoffrey was interested in buildings, and had seen many glorious edifices on his travels, but Saxon architecture had never impressed him as anything special. Bath was different, though. Its abbey was made of gold-coloured stone, so it appeared mellow and sunny, even in the fading light of a wet November afternoon. It was reminiscent of Westminster, with sturdy walls and round-headed arches, and it possessed a set of tuneful bells that chimed sweetly across the meadows as the monks were called to prayer. With Warelwast chattering beside him, he touched his heels gently to his horse's sides, and entered the city through one of its three main gates.

Bath's streets followed the grid pattern favoured by Saxon burghs. Land was being cleared in its southeast corner for a new abbey, and the foundations already laid indicated it would be even more impressive than its predecessor. By contrast, the buildings over its springs were ancient and crumbling, although groups of people gathered at them to bathe in or drink the salt-laden waters. Geoffrey glimpsed an emerald pool inside one. The odour of sulphur was powerful, but not strong enough to mask the eye-watering stench of urine, rotting meat and discarded fish heads from the street itself. Bath was a very dirty place.

'My humble home is near the market,' said John as they rode. 'And you are all welcome to avail yourselves of my hospitality – everyone except Clarembald.'

'I would not demean myself by staying with a man who tells his patients that *water* has healing powers,' retorted Clarembald disdainfully. 'It would be insupportable.'

'But it will be cheaper,' said Roger, who was tired of paying for his accommodation. 'Where is it? I am in sore need of a jug of warmed ale.'

While Clarembald stalked away to find an inn, John led the others along a wide street thick with manure that had been churned into a sticky morass by carts, hoofs, feet and rain. Eventually, they reached John's home, a substantial building with a thatched roof that stood between a bath house and a church called St Mary de Stall. The house was anything but 'humble', being a palace worthy of a wealthy prelate. It boasted two floors, a central hearth that kept all the rooms warm, and a range of outbuildings that included stables, kitchens, store-rooms and a consulting chamber for patients.

Servants rushed to greet their master, and it was not long before the party was relieved of wet cloaks, hats and mud-caked boots, and shown into the hall. At first, the travellers were too relieved to be out of the rain and in front of a fire to think of anything more than sipping their wine, but, as their spirits and energy returned, they turned their attention to each other again, and it was not long before a quarrel broke out.

It was Warelwast who started it, albeit unwittingly. He held his hand in the air, so all could see the rope gripped there.

'God touched me today,' he declared. 'This winter is a time for omens. First, there were the Two Suns and the terrible winds that followed, and now there is this.'

'The Two Suns appeared because God was angry when Sendi murdered Alwold,' said Tasso in a matter-of-fact voice.

Sendi was on his feet. 'How do you know they did not appear because justice was done when someone thrust the knife into Alwold's belly – and God was pleased?'

'Is that a confession?' demanded Tasso. Meanwhile, Geoffrey looked at Rodbert. Was the deputy guilty of Alwold's murder, as Bloet had suggested, simply in order to secure Maude's affections? And if so, was Tasso unaware of what his colleague had done? Then Geoffrey looked at Maude, only to find her staring at him. Her gaze flicked to the door, then back again, passing him an unmistakable invitation. Geoffrey ignored it, and refilled his goblet.

'I cannot confess to something I did not do,' said Sendi coldly. He drew his dagger. 'But I will fight you willingly to prove my innocence. I challenge—'

'No,' said Geoffrey. Innocent or not, Sendi stood no chance against Tasso, and the fight would certainly end in his death.

'What?' demanded Sendi furiously, turning on him. 'Do you, the King's creature, dare to tell *me* what I can and cannot do in my own home?'

'It is John's home,' Geoffrey pointed out. 'Put away your weapon before someone is hurt. Tasso, sit down.'

'I will not,' said Tasso angrily. 'I take orders from no man.'

'What about Barcwit?' asked Adelise spitefully. 'You are frightened of him. You know we are right to complain to the King about his tyranny, but you are too much of a coward to stand with us and fight for what is right. You claim you are a man of honour, but I have more strength in my little finger than you have in your whole body. I have the courage to stand against Barcwit, and you do not.'

Tasso was incensed. 'But I do not want to stand against him! Besides, he only strikes terror into the hearts of evil men, so I have no need to fear. And if you ever call me a coward again, I shall . . .' He spluttered into silence. He could hardly challenge a woman to a duel.

'What?' she sneered. 'Run to Barcwit?'

'Barcwit will have too much else to occupy him,' said Lifwine, who was carefully drying his heeled shoes in front of the fire. 'He will want to know why Rodbert made a cuckold of him, and why Tasso did not bribe the King, so that the case against him could be dropped.'

Tasso glowered furiously at him. 'Rodbert would never lie with—'

'Nor did we need to resort to bribery,' interrupted Rodbert hastily, before the discussion could go too far in that particular direction. 'Although, *you* may have tried.'

'Why should we?' asked Sendi disdainfully. His temper had faded as quickly as it had flared, and his dagger was back in its sheath. 'We have an excellent case.'

'Then why did the King demand an official investigation?' asked Rodbert. 'Why did he not pass sentence in Westminster? It is because he did not trust you or your "evidence".'

'It is because Geoffrey offered to pry further,' snapped Adelise. 'His sister is one of your investors, so it is in his interests to twist the truth. Why do you think the King would not hear our case until he arrived? It was because *he* paid Henry to wait.'

Maude laughed at that notion. 'You only need to look at him to see he does not have the kind of funds to bribe kings.'

'That is true,' agreed John. 'He could do with an afternoon in one of my baths.'

'Besides, he has no real power,' Maude continued, while Geoffrey gazed at John in speechless astonishment. 'Bishop Giffard will make the important decisions. Geoffrey is nothing.'

'I am not so sure,' said Sendi nastily. 'He is Henry's—'

'Music,' announced Roger loudly. 'I would like music. Do you have players, My Lord Bishop?'

John clapped his hands obligingly and, within moments, servants appeared with stringed instruments, horns and a drum. The horns were loud enough to make conversation difficult, and Roger turned to Geoffrey and winked, indicating that his ruse to end the argument had worked. But although Roger tapped his feet and bobbed his head enthusiastically, more or less in time with the rhythm, the musicians were mediocre, and Geoffrey did not want to spend his evening listening to them. He left, intending to find a quiet corner where he could read a book that Warelwast had lent him.

The text was an interesting one, containing part of Aristotle's *De Caelo* that Geoffrey had never encountered before. He lay on a straw mattress in an upper chamber, and struggled to make out the words as the daylight faded outside. The philosopher talked about the permanence of the heavens, and his belief that they did not – and could not – change through time. It reminded him of the Two Suns, and the fact that he seemed to be the only one who thought the phenomenon was natural.

'You are staring into space,' said a low voice that made him jump. It was Maude.

'It is becoming difficult to see,' he said, closing the book and standing to leave. He did not want Rodbert to find him alone with the woman he may have committed murder to get. But she had locked the door and was advancing with purpose in her eyes. However, he could hear both Rodbert and Tasso talking in the chamber below, and supposed he was safe enough for the time being.

'Do not worry,' she said mischievously. 'No one can come in. Besides, you can always jump out of the window if we are invaded. It is not far to the ground.'

Geoffrey had no intention of hiding from anyone, but Rodbert and Tasso seemed settled in the hall, and it seemed churlish to reject her company under such conditions. He assumed she would not bray about her infidelity to her husband, and the chamber was quiet and private. She gave him one of her smiles, and pulled off her veil, releasing a sheet of shining hair that fell almost to her waist, then shrugged out of her kirtle, revealing voluptuous curves under a gauze-like undergarment.

Once their passions were spent, they lay together, exchanging silent caresses by the light of a single candle, before Maude decided they were pushing their luck, and that people might soon try to enter the chamber to sleep. She slipped away from him and donned her clothes with a speed that indicated she was highly experienced at whipping them on and off at short notice.

'You see?' she said in a low voice, the first words either of them had uttered for an hour or more. They were both too worldly to bother with empty endearments. 'You should not have waited so long. We could have pleasured each other on many long nights.'

'Not if Rodbert was there.' Geoffrey lay back to watch her dress.

She smiled. 'Rodbert is a very dear man, but he knows I like a little adventure now and again. Now I can include a *Jerosolimitanus* among my conquests.'

'Conquests?' asked Geoffrey, startled and amused at the same time.

'Well, yes. It was hardly the other way around. Left to you, we would never have taken our friendship to a new level.'

'Are we friends?' Geoffrey was dubious.

She laughed, her voice low and husky, and came towards him, leaning close so he could smell her musky scent. Then her hand moved fast, and he glimpsed the glitter of metal in the candlelight.

Maude was not quick enough to fool Geoffrey, and he caught her hand long before the dagger was anywhere near his chest. It was a tiny thing, but sharp, and it made a tinny clatter as it fell from her fingers to the floor.

'Well, there is one question answered,' he said dryly, pushing her away from him and bounding off the mattress to don his armour. 'We are not friends.'

'You cannot blame me for trying,' she said, not at all discomfited that her murderous attack had been thwarted. 'Everyone else had a go. Besides, I did not try very hard, or you would be dead.'

'Is that so?'

'I could have killed you at any point,' she insisted casually. 'My dagger was close to hand the whole time, but we were both enjoying ourselves, and it seemed a pity to bring it to an early end.'

'You delayed stabbing me only as long as I was doing what you wanted?'

She grinned. 'I am a practical woman. I hope this misunderstanding will not prevent us from meeting on future occasions.'

'We shall see,' replied Geoffrey, thinking she was deluding herself if she imagined him to be the kind of man to overlook an attempt on his life. He knew some men thrived on that sort of uncertainty, but he was not one of them. He raised his finger to his lips when he saw the latch begin to rise on the door. Then he became aware that he could no longer hear voices from the hall.

'Damn!' she whispered. 'The musicians are still playing and I did not think Rodbert would leave as long as they were performing. You had better go out through the window, before he catches you.'

'The door is locked. He can only come in if you let him.'

'You do not know him,' she murmured. 'He is fiercely jealous and will sit outside all night if it means catching me with a lover.'

Geoffrey indicated the mattress with his hand. 'I can think of ways to pass the time.'

'You do not understand,' she said sharply. 'I care for Rodbert, and I do not want him hurt. Jump out of the window, and I will tell him I have been here alone.'

'No,' said Geoffrey unchivalrously. '*You* jump out of the window, and I will tell him *I* have been here alone. You are the one who wants to avoid him.'

She sighed crossly, but went to the window and peered out. 'I see you still have that rope you used to save Warelwast this afternoon. You can put it to use again, and lower me down. I trust you will not let me fall, to avenge yourself for the dagger incident.'

'Probably not,' he replied, gratified to see her regard him uncertainly. 'Hurry, or he will suspect something amiss, no matter who he finds in here.'

The latch jiggled, and someone started to knock. 'Are you there?' came Rodbert's voice. 'Maude?'

She tied the rope around her waist and slipped through the

109

window, pausing only to plant a kiss on Geoffrey's lips. It was not far to the ground, and she was down in moments. He tossed the rope after her and went to answer what had become a furious hammering. When he opened the door, Rodbert shot inside like an arrow loosed from a bow, looking around him wildly.

'What have you been doing?' he demanded. 'Where is she?'

'As you can see,' said Geoffrey, gesturing around him. 'I am alone.'

'Then why did you take so long to answer?' asked Rodbert suspiciously.

'I was washing,' said Geoffrey, saying the first thing that came into his head.

'You have not done a very good job,' said Rodbert, looking him up and down. 'Unless you have concentrated on the parts that do not show. Most people do it the other way around.'

'Rodbert,' said Maude from behind him, breathless and slightly dishevelled. 'I have been looking everywhere for you. Where have you been?'

Rodbert jumped in surprise, and Geoffrey was impressed by what had been a serious burst of speed. It was a long way through the garden to the front of John's house, across the hall and up the stairs.

'There you are,' said Rodbert, aggrieved. 'I thought Geoffrey might have imprisoned you here against your will. I was coming to rescue you.'

'He would not dare,' said Maude. 'But let us retire to bed. I am weary and we have another long day of travelling tomorrow.'

'Unfortunately, we do not,' said Rodbert. 'That is why I was looking for you – to give you the news. Clarembald came to tell us that the River Avon is flooded near Sanford, and the road will be closed until the waters recede. There has been too much rain recently.'

'Damn!' said Maude, echoing Geoffrey's own thoughts. 'I thought we would be home tomorrow.'

'So did we all,' said Rodbert. 'But John has offered us his house for as long as we need it, and says he will travel with us when we leave – to visit the shops and make an investment with Barcwit.' He shot Geoffrey a challenging stare. 'And he would hardly do *that* in front of the King's agent if there was anything untoward going on, would he?'

Geoffrey did not bother to point out that the Bishop of Bath might be staging an honest public transaction in an attempt to disguise previous ones that were less straightforward. Maude took Rodbert's arm and led him to another chamber, whispering in his ear as she went. He could tell from the expression on the man's face that she was making promises about the evening to come, and he admired her stamina.

He went back to the mattress and lay down, trying to resume his study of the Aristotle by the flickering light of a candle. Durand arrived a few moments later, and informed him that he would go blind if he read in the dark, claiming to know several monastics who had done just that. The squire sat on the end of the mattress and started to remove his boots.

'Bloet went to investigate the swollen river,' he burbled. 'He does not believe Clarembald's witnesses who say the road is closed. He is not back yet, but I am too tired to stay up for him.'

'You are not concerned?' asked Geoffrey, surprised the squire's affection for his new lover should be so shallow. 'It is dark, and he is out on a road he does not know.'

'Sendi, Tasso and several others are with him,' replied Durand. 'They will be safe enough together – only a very foolish outlaw would attack that quarrelsome rabble. But I am surprised you do not know all this. What have you been doing all evening?'

Geoffrey waved the Aristotle at him, then changed the subject when Durand inspected the rumpled covers on the bed and raised meaningful eyebrows. 'I learnt today that the King has charged Bloet to find the missing silver. Has he mentioned it to you?'

Durand's expression became thoughtful. 'I wondered why he is so interested in it. He has interrogated every one of the Saxons – Sendi's men as well as Barcwit's – since we left Westminster. He started the journey in high spirits, but he has grown increasingly despondent. I assumed it was because our arrival in Bristol means he will spend less time with me, but I see there may be another reason for his gloom.'

'I do not understand what you are saying. He will be better placed to hunt out the silver once he reaches Bristol. Surely, he will be keen to make a proper start?'

'But therein lies his problem. He does not *know* where to start. He has already questioned his most promising witnesses, because they are all here. But he has uncovered nothing that will help him locate the silver – only a lot of rumours and speculation. I also heard him tell Warelwast that he thinks the hoard is no longer in England.'

'What is his reasoning?'

'Bristol is a port with sea connections to Ireland. He believes that any sensible thief would have loaded his loot on a ship and transported it out of the country.'

'And you?' asked Geoffrey. Whatever he might think of his squire's unappealing nature, Geoffrey respected his opinions on matters like missing treasure. 'What do you think?'

Durand shrugged. 'I cannot say,' he replied unhelpfully.

'You can,' replied Geoffrey. 'Unless you want to muck out horses until we reach the Holy Land.'

Durand regarded him with dislike. 'I have deduced nothing, if you must know. There is simply not enough information to allow *anyone* to make even the most tentative of guesses. If I were in Bloet's position, I would be worried, too. His hopes for advancement in the Court are about to experience a serious setback, because I do not think he – or anyone else – will be able to solve the mystery.'

Geoffrey supposed he was telling the truth, although it was difficult to tell with Durand. They were silent for a while, and Geoffrey was grateful the King had not ordered him to locate the ingots as well as investigating the moneyers. The fact that the consignment seemed to have disappeared so completely indicated the thieves had been well organized, and he thought Bloet's pessimism might well be justified: the hoard might indeed have been smuggled out of England on the first available ship.

Durand brushed mud from his cloak and boots, then did the same for Geoffrey's, although all the grooming in the world could not disguise the fact that the knight's clothes had seen better days. While he worked, Durand said Warelwast was still unable to release the rope, despite dunking the afflicted limb three times in Bishop John's holiest waters. Clarembald's paste of snakes' eyes was currently being administered, and was expected to work by morning – by everyone except John.

Geoffrey lay with his arms behind his head, and thought about Maude. He had thwarted her attack on him with ease, so had it been half-hearted, as she had claimed, so she would not be in the invidious position of being the only traveller not to have tried to dispatch him? Or was she just not very good at stabbing her lovers? He found he could not answer, no matter how many times he replayed the incident in his mind.

Six

When Warelwast awoke the following day to find the rope on the floor by the side of his bed, there were several opinions as to what had happened. Clarembald, who had arrived uninvited that morning, claimed his potion had eased the rigid muscles, while John maintained his holy waters had worked their magic. Durand asserted that God had intervened, and Geoffrey believed the relaxing effects of sleep were responsible. However, no one was surprised when the bishop-elect opted for a religious explanation. Uttering plenty of prayers, he took the rope and fastened it to a chain that he placed around his neck, vowing to wear it until God told him otherwise.

'It looks like a doll,' mused Durand. 'It is frayed in two places, which gives it arms, and the knot at the top is a head. Meanwhile, the bottom splays out like skirts.'

'No,' breathed Warelwast as he inspected it more closely. 'It looks like a monk in a habit! God is telling me it is time to abandon my secular attire and take the cowl.'

'The head has a face, too,' said John. 'These two impurities are eyes, here is a nose, and this line is a mouth. The squire is right: it *does* look like a doll.'

'Do not give it to a child, though,' said Geoffrey, regarding the twisted, rather malevolent features with amusement. 'It will give him nightmares.'

'You are all wrong,' said Clarembald archly. 'It looks exactly what it is: a piece of frayed rope. There are no human features that *I* can see.'

'That does not surprise me,' said John. 'You cannot tell one end of a patient from another, either.'

Bloet and the moneyers slept until they were awoken by

114

the ensuing squabble, then came to the hall for a late break-fast. They had not arrived back in Bath until well past nine o'clock the previous night, wet from their foray to the swollen river. They reported that the waters were receding slowly, and that the road should be clear by the next day, as long as there were no more persistent downpours.

'The worst rain is said to be over,' said Clarembald, helping himself to ale, uncaring of the fact that John had ordered him to leave his house at least three times. 'And if you had listened to me, you would have saved yourselves that unpleasant expedition.'

'We needed to see it first-hand,' said Tasso. 'Barcwit would not be pleased if we tarried here when we could have been home. Now we know for certain that the delay is unavoidable.'

'And we would not want to upset poor, kindly Barcwit, would we?' asked Adelise in a sneer.

'No,' said Rodbert abruptly. 'It would be rude, and Barcwit does not appreciate poor manners.'

'It seems to me that Barcwit does not approve of very much,' Geoffrey muttered to Maude, who had come to sit next to him. 'Including, I imagine, his wife frolicking with his deputy.'

'Not nearly as much as he would object to me lying with the King's agent,' she replied laconically. 'So, if you tell him about Rodbert, I shall claim you seduced me.'

'Would he believe you?' Geoffrey saw doubt flicker across her face. 'Do not worry. I am not the kind of man to inform husbands that I cavort with their wives, although you should tell Rodbert to learn discretion. He is watching you in a very proprietorial way, and Barcwit would have to be blind not to guess the meaning behind such an expression.'

She sighed, but took his advice and went to speak to Rodbert, while the others began to discuss how they would pass their free day. Roger, Helbye and Ulfrith were keen to sample the taverns, while John offered to show any interested parties Bath's best shops. Bloet, who was depressed and listless, accepted gloomily, and Durand went with him. Warelwast wanted to pray in the abbey, to give thanks for his deliverance from drowning. But the Saxons declared themselves uninterested in any of the diversions John suggested and finally, in a desperate attempt to make them abandon their quarrels for at least some of the day, the Bishop recommended a visit to his mint.

'It is operated by a man called Osmaer,' he said. 'I have employed him there since—'

'I will go,' interrupted Sendi. There was a determined gleam in his eye. 'Osmaer is a good friend, and will speak on my behalf at any trial Bishop Giffard might—'

'Osmaer is *Barcwit's* friend,' argued Rodbert. 'I will not let you see him alone to spread your vicious lies. He will speak for us, not you.'

Then another row was underway, and it was not long before every Saxon had decided to descend on the hapless Bath moneyer.

'What, *all* of you?' asked Geoffrey, startled. 'Will this poor man mind such a large deputation?'

'He will not object,' said Sendi curtly. 'Not to me, at least.'

'Do not stay long,' said John, before Rodbert could argue about who would be the more welcome. 'I do not want my profits affected because you distract Osmaer from his work.'

With a day to spare, and thinking it would be a good opportunity to learn about coin-making from an independent source, Geoffrey decided to go with them. The Saxons were still bickering when they arrived at the mint, and did not stop until Lifwine called out to warn Osmaer that he was about to be invaded by guests.

Osmaer, a tall man with long dark hair, seemed young to hold such a responsible post, but as soon as he started to speak, it was clear he was a man of intelligence and integrity – which explained why both Sendi and Rodbert wanted his support. He was too sensible to take sides, and was adept at side-stepping most of their attempts to trap him into making a choice.

Geoffrey had never been inside a mint – sightseeing was not encouraged in such places, on the grounds that they were full of money – but Osmaer agreed to show him around. He led the way to a large stone-built chamber that was full of noise, and began to describe his craft, while the others jostled and pushed at each other to stand close to him. Sendi was keen to demonstrate that he knew more than Osmaer, to prove he was worthy of the man's approval, while Maude seemed determined to get Osmaer on his own and practise her own methods of persuasion.

'First, we take an ingot, melt it and pour it into moulds,' said Osmaer. 'Once it has cooled, we tip the silver – now in little buttons – out of the moulds and hammer them to a uniform flatness.'

'You have fine ingots,' said Maude, standing closer to the Bath moneyer than was proper or necessary. Rodbert bristled, and Adelise gave a snort of disgust. 'The silver must be very pure.'

'*Silver*,' said Lifwine meaningfully to Geoffrey. 'Not gold.'

'Yes,' said Geoffrey, wondering if the man thought he was stupid. 'The only English coin in circulation is the silver penny. Foreign ones – of any metal – are melted down or re-stamped.'

Rodbert affected boredom. 'Lifwine thinks he is a cut above the rest of us, because his ancestors made coins in the reign of King Aethelred.'

'*Gold* ones.' Lifwine was clearly proud. 'My ancestor, Wulfric of Warwick, was famous for his *gold* pennies.'

'Rubbish!' said Tasso. 'That would be a waste of gold. Silver is the only metal for coins.'

Sendi stepped forward. 'Are you questioning the word of my *cambium*?'

'The man is a liar,' said Tasso coolly. 'He lies about his ancestors, just as he lies about the dross you dare to call pennies.'

Sendi's dagger was out of its sheath. 'You filthy-tongued villain! I will—'

'You will fight me?' asked Tasso, sword in his hand. 'Then let us do so! I am tired of bandying insults with you, so let us settle this with blood.'

'No,' said Geoffrey, stepping between them and pushing away Sendi's dagger with his hand. He was not so foolish as to try the same with Tasso's sword, sensing the knight had reached his limit with his argumentative rivals and was close to losing control.

'No?' asked Tasso, his voice dangerously low. 'No, what?'

'No to fighting in a place where you are a guest,' said Geoffrey, pointing to where Osmaer watched with an expression of alarm. 'It would be rude to spill blood on his clean floors.'

'Very rude,' said Osmaer hastily. 'Especially over whether or not some long-dead king issued gold coins. It is irrelevant – no matter whose ancestors made them – because we only use silver nowadays.'

'Where does the silver come from?' asked Geoffrey, hoping to begin a conversation that would give tempers a chance to cool. Tasso's sword was still drawn, but he had lowered it, while Sendi's dagger was back in its sheath. Sendi was like a fighting cock, Geoffrey thought. His temper flared quickly, but it subsided just as fast. Tasso was the brooding type, who would still be furious in an hour.

'Mine comes from Lideforda in Devon,' Osmaer explained, seeing what Geoffrey was trying to do and determined to give him all the help he could. He rattled off more information than was needed, watching with wary eyes as Tasso took a breath to calm himself and eventually shoved his weapon away. 'Lideforda is also favoured by Sewine of Exeter, who produces exceptionally fine coins. We are all admirers of Sewine.'

'We are,' agreed Maude with an ambiguous smile. 'He is quite a man!'

'My silver comes from Lideforda, too,' said Sendi. He smiled at Osmaer, trying to atone for his lapse of manners, desperate to win the man's support. 'So does *some* of Barcwit's.'

'We buy ours from a variety of sources,' explained Maude, declining to rise to the bait. 'You never know when one mine's output might become unpredictable – or simply run out – and it is good practice to have more than one supplier.'

'But different sources lead to irregular qualities,' argued Sendi immediately. 'And—'

'Please!' interrupted Geoffrey, becoming exasperated by their constant sniping. 'I want to hear what Osmaer has to say, and I cannot if you argue over every detail.'

'Perhaps Sendi can answer your questions, while Osmaer and I enjoy a goblet of wine,' suggested Maude. The glance she shot the man smouldered with sensual promise. 'I am very thirsty.'

'I do not take wine when I am working,' said Osmaer, flustered. 'But my wife will give you some.'

Adelise shot her a spiteful smile, so Maude promptly bumped into a table, upsetting an inkpot that splattered its contents over her rival's kirtle. Adelise's smirk turned to dismay.

'So sorry,' said Maude. 'You had better go and soak that before it stains.'

'Ink is permanent,' snapped Adelise. 'As any decent woman knows. This kirtle is ruined!'

'Ask John to help you look for another,' suggested Geoffrey helpfully. 'I am sure he will oblige.'

Osmaer gave a gulp of laughter, more from nervousness than amusement. 'We call him the "Shopping Bishop" in Bath, because he enjoys haggling for trinkets. But, you did not come here to discuss our clerics, Sir Geoffrey. You came to learn about the process of moneying. Now, once we have cast the silver buttons, we hammer them to a predetermined thickness. Each ingot weighs a pound, and we aim to make precisely two hundred and forty discs from it.'

'It is a very skilled part of the process,' added Sendi. 'It is important to get every coin in the realm as alike in size as possible. Or at least, some of us try.' He looked meaningfully at Rodbert.

'Barcwit does not,' Lifwine confided to Geoffrey, lest the knight had not understood Sendi's point. 'His are made from overly thin silver and they are lighter than the legal twenty-two and a half grains. It means he gets an extra thirty pennies from every ingot – and that is a lot of money.'

'It is,' acknowledged Geoffrey. 'Thirty pennies would pay a household servant for a month.'

'You see?' said Rodbert to Tasso. 'He is agreeing with Sendi's men already.'

'I am not,' said Geoffrey impatiently. 'I merely said thirty pennies is a lot of money.' He cut across Rodbert's response and addressed Osmaer. 'What happens after the discs are hammered flat?'

'When they reach a specific standard, we call them blanks,' said Osmaer. 'That means they are ready for coining – but only when my *cambium* is happy that they are the correct size and weight.'

'That is what I do,' supplied Lifwine proudly. 'I am Sendi's *cambium*.'

'But not a very independent one,' Geoffrey heard Osmaer mutter, in the only personal opinion about the Bristol men he was to offer all morning. Osmaer did not approve of a *cambium* who was so thick with his moneyer, but he said no more, and Geoffrey did not ask him to elaborate.

'Then comes the interesting part,' said Sendi, who had not heard the comment. 'With the dies.'

'Every mint must purchase dies from Otto the Goldsmith in London,' said Osmaer. 'They are expensive and last for a limited period of time. When they wear out, we must buy new ones.'

'Some of us do,' said Rodbert unpleasantly. 'But some doctor them, so they can continue to be used after they should be thrown away. This saves the corrupt moneyer a lot of expense.'

'Some mints *do* use their dies more than they should,' said Osmaer, carefully looking at no one. 'But coins made with worn dies are inferior, and since every die is marked with the name of the moneyer, it is easy to see who has been cheating.'

'Mules,' said Geoffrey, recalling the discussion at Westminster. 'Where the two sides of a coin are made from non-matching dies.'

'Exactly,' agreed Osmaer. 'That is one way some mints extend the lives of their dies.'

'And *some* moneyers change the name on the dies, too,' said Rodbert, gazing at Sendi. '*Some* coiners change their own names to someone else's.'

'It happens,' said Osmaer. He hurried on with his explanation when Sendi started to protest his innocence, and picked up two pieces of metal from a table. 'This is a die, and you can see it is in two parts. The "pile" or lower part, has a spike which is driven into the workbench and so is held stable. The silver blank is placed on the pile. The upper part is the "trussel", which is placed over the blank, so the blank is between them. The trussel is held in place by a twisted withe—'

'Then it is struck,' finished Edric enthusiastically. 'That is the fun part.'

'The pile carries the *obverse* of the coin,' said Adelise. She regarded Geoffrey superiorly. 'That is the side with the King's head on it – "heads" to you. The trussel carries the *reverse*, which bears a cross, the name of the moneyer and the place of issue.'

Osmaer handed Geoffrey a bright new coin. 'Here is my name, written around the top in good, clean letters, and BATHAN for Bath is at the bottom.'

'But not all letters are good and clean,' said Sendi. 'And because most people do not read, they will not know some letters are meaningless. Thus the corrupt moneyer ensures he is safe, because his own name is not carried on the coin.'

'We have safeguards against corruption,' said Osmaer to Geoffrey. He nodded at a man who leaned close to his work because his eyes were ruined from working in bad light. 'My *cambium* assays my blanks and coins. Nothing leaves my mint that he has not inspected.'

'Unfortunately, it depends on having a reliable *cambium*,' said Adelise. 'Ones who are perpetually drunk are not good regulators.'

'Nor are ones who lick the—' began Rodbert hotly.

'And that is all I can tell you,' said Osmaer loudly to Geoffrey. 'It is simple, but skilled. There are safeguards to prevent corruption, although the determined cheat will circumvent them.' His gaze encompassed all his visitors. 'But the penalties are dire – severed hands and testicles, heavy fines and the loss of all property. Only a fool would do it.'

'Look out!' shouted someone in the silence that followed Osmaer's none-too-subtle warning.

Only Geoffrey's quick reactions saved him from serious harm as one of the casts of molten silver upended and splattered over the floor. Osmaer's apprentices immediately darted forward with buckets of sand to prevent fire. The cast had been full, and Geoffrey did not like to imagine the injuries he might have sustained had it spilled on him. He glanced at the Saxons, trying to gauge which one had made this latest attempt on his life, but found he could not tell, and there was no point in ordering the culprit to own up. They would only accuse each other and begin another argument.

'Dangerous places, mints,' said Rodbert flatly.

Sendi agreed. 'You should never turn your back on molten metal.'

'Christ's wounds!' breathed Osmaer, ushering his unwelcome guests out of his workshop while his apprentices dealt with the mess. He spoke in a low voice to Geoffrey. 'You may visit me again, if I can be of further help to the King, but please do not bring this rabble with you.'

It was dry that afternoon, although cold and windy. Roger, Helbye and Ulfrith were nowhere to be found, and Geoffrey supposed they had found some cosy and doubtless disreputable tavern where they would spend the rest of the day with their dice. The Saxons were bickering in John's hall, while the Bishop himself was touring the market with a chain of servants to carry his purchases. Warelwast was still at the abbey, and Bloet was drinking himself into a state of even blacker depression, despite Durand's attempts to distract him with wittily spiteful chatter. Geoffrey did not want to be with any of them, so elected to see more of Bath by himself.

He clicked his fingers to his dog as he left, but wind was whistling down the chimney, and the animal gave him the kind of look that indicated it thought he was insane. Geoffrey did not press it. It was not good company, with its penchant for killing chickens and harrying goats, and he was just as happy to leave it behind.

He spent a long time admiring the Saxon abbey, then inspected the foundations that were being laid for its Norman replacement. Dusk approached, but he did not feel like returning to John's house to be insulted – or worse – so set out in search of the hot springs for which the town was famous. The gate of the largest fountain was locked for the night, so he decided to look for some of the smaller ones, in the hope that they would still be open.

He discovered one in the southwest quarter of the town, housed in an unstable structure that was made of the same pale sandstone as the abbey. Its guardian had either forgotten to secure it, or it was not considered worth locking, because its door was ajar. He walked inside and waited for his eyes to become accustomed to the gloom. Finding a lamp near the door, he kindled it to discover walls that were thickly coated in slime, but saw faint splashes of colour underneath: once, when the town was more important, they had been decorated with bright and elaborate paintings.

In front of him was a cistern full of a sulphurous liquid. It was fed and drained by lead-lined conduits, so it would never overflow but always be full, and, although the system was ancient – its stones were worn and its channels furred with salt deposits – it still worked. He knelt to dip a tentative hand in the water, and was pleasantly surprised as the warmth soaked through his chilled skin.

Geoffrey did not take baths – although he had once made an exception in the Holy Land – because only a fool divested himself of clothes and armour and sat in a vat of water. But there was something appealing about the green tank before him, perhaps because it was hot and not topped by a layer of scum from previous users. He thought about the number of people who had recently told him he was dirty, and made his decision.

He closed the door and placed a stave across it. It was not a particularly strong door, and the bar was soft and rotten, but it would serve to keep out casual visitors and afford him some privacy. Then, for the second time in as many days, he divested himself of his clothes. Clad in tunic and baggy braes, he walked across the floor to the bath and stared at the steaming water. The lamplight gave it an emerald sheen, and the spring that provided its fresh water rippled its surface. He could not see the bottom, and was inclined to abandon the whole foolish venture and join Roger in his game of dice. But it had taken him some time to clamber out of his armour, and it seemed a pity to give up now. Not liking the notion of a wet tunic

123

when he dressed again, he shrugged it off and laid it on the floor, although the braes remained in place: only Greeks, heathens and the insane bathed naked, as far as he was aware.

He sat on the side of the bath and lowered one foot. The water was hot and tingling, so he dipped the other one in, too. He remained there for some time, enjoying the sensation of heat bubbling around his legs. Then he took a deep breath and launched himself forward, keeping one hand on the edge in case some hidden current caught him and tried to drag him away, as the Avon had done to Warelwast. But the water only reached his chest, and he discovered underwater benches that allowed bathers to sit. Reclining against the hot stones, with the water flowing around his body, was one of the most pleasurable sensations he had ever experienced. He closed his eyes and relaxed properly for the first time in weeks. The sound of the wind outside made him feel warm and comfortable, and soon he did not even notice the rank smell of sulphur and mould.

He had no idea how long he had been asleep when he woke with a start. The lamp had burned out, and it was dark. He raised one hand, feeling fingers that were tender and wrinkled from being soaked too long. He was overly hot, too, and sweat trickled in his eyes. He listened hard, wondering what had woken him, and wished his dog were there, because it was excellent at warning of lurking menaces. Rain had started to patter on the roof, but the only other sound was the gurgle of water from the spring. He was about to climb out, assuming the heat had roused him from his doze, when he heard something else: the soft tap of a leather-soled shoe on a flagstone.

He tensed. His sword and knives were with his clothes on the opposite side of the chamber, and he cursed himself as a fool for wanting to take a bath when he should have known no good would come from it. He stood slowly, and glanced at the door. It was still closed. Then he scanned the room and saw a dark space where earlier there had been a wall. There was a second way in, which he had not noticed, and he supposed the algae covering the walls had disguised it, along with the fact that he had not bothered to conduct a proper search.

124

He stayed stock still for a long time, feeling the water move around his body as he listened for any indication that someone else was there. There was nothing but silence. He took a step forward, towards the centre of the bath, and then he was underwater. Too late, he realized it was deeper in the middle than around the edges, designed to give bathers the choice of immersing themselves or sitting. He splashed to the surface and made his way to one side, eager to put solid ground under his feet.

Then the attack came. He saw a dark shadow looming over him, and knew from the elongated arm that it held a dagger. He jerked back in time to avoid the blow, but that put him in the path of a second assailant. Strong hands fastened around his throat, immediately tightening, so he could not breathe.

He knew he did not have long to act. He would quickly become light-headed from lack of air, and once he lost his strength it would be an easy matter for the two men to drown, strangle or stab him. He jerked to one side, so the man gripping his throat crashed into the one with the knife. Someone cursed, and there was a plop as the dagger fell in the water. Then he took a firm grip on the arm around his neck, braced his feet on the side of the bath, and pushed forward as hard as he could.

The result was spectacular. The would-be strangler flew over his head, landing with an enormous slap that drove the breath from his body, because he surfaced gasping and choking. Geoffrey took a deep breath and ducked in a desperate attempt to locate the dropped knife. When his groping fingers eventually encountered it, he pushed to the surface, aiming to stab the second assailant. But the man was ready for him and, as Geoffrey broke through the water, he lashed out with his fist. He missed, but the blow was so forceful that he lost his balance. He, too, fell in the water, landing on Geoffrey and forcing him under with the weight of his body. The knife slipped from Geoffrey's hand.

Geoffrey tried to wriggle away, but the first assailant had joined the second and suddenly four hands combined to keep his head under the surface. He kicked with his feet and punched with his hands, but could not break their hold. The sound of churning water roared in his ears, and he was aware that his struggles were becoming more feeble. At first, all he could see was darkness, but then pinpoints of light began to dance before his eyes. He gradually abandoned his attempts to break free, and felt himself floating. At first, he thought he was moving up, to where he would be able to suck air into his protesting lungs. But then something bumped against his face and he knew he had gone down, to the bottom of the bath.

Geoffrey dreamed he was swimming in the Holy Land, where scarlet hills plunged into a warm ocean fringed with amber sands. His dog spoiled the idyllic scene by barking furiously. Tancred was there, too, explaining why he had released his knight from his vow of allegiance and asserting that Henry was a good master, worthy of loyalty. When Geoffrey responded with a disgusted snort, he began to choke. Then the peaceful lapping of waves on a sun-drenched beach receded until only the dog's strident barks remained, along with the splintering of wood.

For an instant, he had no idea where he was, but the air tasted of sulphur and then everything snapped into place. He was hanging on to the side of the bath, and someone was pounding on the door he had barred. He hauled himself out of the water and slapped wet-footed to where his sword lay on his clothes, gripping it with both hands and ready to fight whoever was so determined to enter. The door flew open with a crash and Geoffrey's dog was suddenly at his side, winding around his legs. Then it went to the second door – the one Geoffrey had missed – and shot out of it.

'You should choose your wenches with more care, lad,' said Roger, regarding him disapprovingly. Durand and the others were behind him. 'This one almost drowned you. What happened?'

Geoffrey was not sure. He supposed the dog's racket had driven off the two men who had tried to kill him, and vaguely recalled kicking his way to the surface after they had gone. He opened his mouth to speak, but coughed water instead.

'Your dog went wild when it passed this building,' explained Ulfrith. 'Roger said it could smell a cat, but it only ever turns

126

in those tight little circles for you, so I said we should look inside.'

'This is a bathhouse,' said Helbye. He glanced uneasily at Geoffrey, then gestured at the water. 'You did not get in that, did you?'

'He came with a woman,' said Roger, because it was something he would have done himself. 'But he let her trap him in an awkward position. That would explain the splashing we heard. She must have escaped through the back when she heard us coming. What did she look like?'

'She did not steal anything,' said Ulfrith, casting an eye over Geoffrey's clothes and armour. 'We probably disturbed her before she could try.'

'You were lucky,' said Durand, inspecting Geoffrey in a way that made the knight want to grab his tunic and clutch it to his chest; he felt like a virgin being examined on her wedding night by some lecherous old bridegroom. 'You could have lost everything.'

'It was not a woman,' said Geoffrey, at last managing to break into their discussion. 'It was a man.' He coughed again, wishing he could control the irritating tickle at the back of his throat. 'Two men.'

'Men?' said Durand mischievously. 'I had no idea!'

'They burst in on me,' objected Geoffrey, hauling his tunic over his head. It felt unpleasantly oily and stiff against his clean skin.

'Where was the woman when this happened?' asked Roger, looking around as if he imagined some wench might appear.

'There was no woman,' said Geoffrey. 'I—'

'No woman?' echoed Roger. He looked suspiciously at his friend's undressed state. 'Then what were you doing in here?'

'Taking a bath,' Geoffrey replied, coughing again.

'A *bath*?' said Helbye, appalled. 'Do you not know how *dangerous* those can be?'

'I do now,' spluttered Geoffrey, still trying to catch his breath.

'I thought you disapproved of baths,' said Roger, mystified. 'You have always claimed that men who take them are left prone to chills and fevers. And now you expect me to believe that you took one in here? In the dark, in a strange place and with no clothes on?'

'It seemed like a good idea at the time,' said Geoffrey tiredly. He did not feel like explaining that he had done so because the Saxons had accused him of being unwashed, and that even the King had commented on his unkempt appearance.

'I suppose you *read* about these baths,' said Roger scathingly. 'No good will come of burying your nose in scrolls, Geoff. The knowledge you get from them is unnatural and will lead you to a bad end.' He gestured at the bubbling water and slime-coated walls of the bathhouse to underline his point. Geoffrey found it hard to argue.

'What are you doing here anyway?' he asked, shaking off Durand's attempts to help him get dressed. He did not like the feel of the squire's hot hands on his bare skin.

'Your dog,' said Roger. 'It jumped on to John's dinner table and made off with the suckling pig. It escaped through a window and set off down the street, and the Bishop asked if we would mind fetching it back – the pig, I mean, not the dog.'

'We have been chasing it for ages,' said Helbye, rubbing his hip resentfully. 'Then it dropped the pig outside this house and started doing its funny circles. We could hear lots of splashing from inside.'

'So, Roger battered down the door, while I waited outside until it was safe,' said Durand prissily. 'You cannot be too careful with strange buildings in towns you do not know.'

'Quite,' agreed Roger, fixing Geoffrey with a hard stare. 'I cannot believe you charged into one and ripped off your clothes without a second thought. You should have asked me to keep guard.'

'Or me,' offered Durand with an impish wink.

'I take it you did not see them escaping, then?' Geoffrey asked. Roger had re-lit the lamp, so he took it to examine the place where he had struggled with his attackers. A good deal of water had slopped from the bath and was cooling on the stones around the edge. Meanwhile, the door he had missed earlier led directly outside, but it was too dark to see whether anyone still lingered there.

'I saw no one,' said Roger.

'I heard someone running away, but assumed it was the whore.' Durand frowned, struggling with his memory. 'But there *was* more than one set of footsteps, now that you mention it.'

'Where is my dog?' asked Geoffrey. Its timely intervention had saved him, and he wanted to make sure it was properly rewarded. But the animal was nowhere to be seen, and Helbye and Ulfrith regarded each other in dismay.

'The pig!' yelled Ulfrith, racing outside. 'It has gone after the suckling pig again.'

'Damn the beast!' groaned Helbye. 'I do not want to chase it all night while Bishop John waits for his dinner. He promised to light one of his big candles for me tomorrow, which he says will cure the pain in my hip. I do not want that vile dog to annoy him, so he does not bother.'

'If John fails you, there is always Clarembald,' said Roger kindly. 'He claims his poultice of hog grease and warm coals is far more effective than John's candles. I recommend you take both and hedge your bets. If one does not work, the other might.'

'I shall,' vowed Helbye, wincing as he sat on a bench. 'I would take a cure from the Devil himself, if he promised me relief from this gnawing agony.'

Geoffrey walked along the dark, rain-soaked streets, with Roger on one side and Helbye limping on the other. He glanced at his ageing friend in concern. He had not realized the ache in his bones had reached the point where it was difficult for him to run. Helbye had been with him since he was old enough to raise a sword, and he had assumed the man would be a permanent fixture in his life. But it was clear Helbye's fighting days were at an end, and he wondered how he would tell him it was now time to go home. It would be a wrench for them both.

He coughed, tasting the foul water he had swallowed, then considered the attack. It was obvious why it had happened: they were a day's ride from Bristol, where his investigation would begin in earnest. It was a desperate, last-ditch attempt to prevent him from reaching his destination and starting his work. Of course, anyone with any wits about him would know that Geoffrey's inquiry had started the moment he had received his orders from the King, and that he had been asking questions and making observations every inch along the way. But, he supposed, the attack told him that Bristol was where the real answers lay, and that at least two people were determined that he should not reach it.

So, who had tried to kill him this time? He did not think it was Maude – he imagined she would have learnt from her failure the previous night, and would have done a better job – but it could have been Tasso and Rodbert. It was possible they had decided not to challenge him to open combat, because fatal wounds from a broadsword would tell the King exactly who had dispatched his agent. They may have decided on drowning as a viable alternative once they had seen him jump in the bath.

Or was it Sendi and one of his friends? Or Bloet or Warelwast? Geoffrey was increasingly suspicious of the Bishop-Elect of Exeter, and was not convinced that Henry would use a high-ranking churchman merely to keep an eye on Bloet and his hunt for the missing silver. He suspected Warelwast had a different agenda. Or perhaps the attackers were John and Clarembald, working together in a rare display of unity to prevent their exposure as traitors. They had a good deal to lose if Geoffrey found them guilty, and might well decide that murdering him was an acceptable way to defer matters until they had devised a more permanent solution to their predicament.

He considered the attack on him at Westminster. Could it have been carried out by the same men? He considered carefully, and decided not. There had been three at Westminster, and he had driven them away with ease. The two in Bath had been tougher and more determined. Or had they just seemed that way because he had been armed at Westminster, and defenceless in Bath?

He and his companions reached John's house and knocked at the door. The moment it was opened, Helbye shoved past, aiming for the fire. Geoffrey followed, and was surprised to find the hall empty and the feast abandoned. The only person present was Ulfrith, who had helped himself to a sizeable portion of the rescued pig and was starting on a plate of pastries.

'I found it outside the bathhouse,' he said, gesturing to the pork. 'The dog did not go back for it after all, so he must still be hunting your attackers. If he succeeds, there will be some sore ankles tonight.'

'Where is everyone?' asked Geoffrey, pouring some wine. He had expected to find his fellow travellers embroiled in one of their arguments as they waited for the return of the feast's centrepiece.

'Not here,' replied Ulfrith, stating the obvious. 'Perhaps they decided to look for the pig. You can see why: it is the only thing worth eating. Everything else is either bread or vegetables.' He looked disgusted, being one of those who did not think he had dined unless half a sheep was involved.

'Everyone?' asked Geoffrey. It would be difficult to isolate culprits for the attack if the entire party had scattered around the city. It had started to rain hard, which meant he would not be able to identify his assailants by their wet clothes.

The door opened and John entered with Bloet at his heels. Both were breathless and sodden, and Geoffrey regarded them warily. Were they the ones? He saw the simpering exchange between Bloet and Durand, and found himself wondering whether *they* had perpetrated the attack, so Durand would be free to leave Geoffrey's service and go wherever Bloet was bound. But Durand was a coward, and would never take on Geoffrey, even when he was unarmed. He crossed Durand from his list of suspects, although Bloet – and John – would remain on it until he knew more about them.

'There is no sign of that horrible dog,' said John. He stopped short when he saw the pork on the table. 'Ha! Where did you find it?'

'Outside,' said Ulfrith, prudently declining to mention that it had been hauled halfway around the town's filthy streets in the dog's slathering jaws before he had managed to retrieve it.

John went to sit near the fire. 'It is no night to be out. I

131

am soaked. I swear, if I see that wicked beast again I shall run it through.'

'Not unless you wish to die in the same way,' said Geoffrey, experiencing a rare affection for the dog. It bit, behaved badly and was an inveterate thief, but it had saved his life, and he was not prepared to see it killed by an irate prelate over a piece of meat.

John saw he was in earnest and recanted hastily. 'Forgive me. I did not know you were fond of the thing – I assumed it was some stray that had latched on to you at Westminster. However, I will not have it in my house again. It can sleep in the stable with the servants.'

The door opened a second time, and Warelwast was ushered in. 'I have been visiting Bath's taverns with Clarembald,' he announced. He hurled his cloak to the floor; it was so wet that it made a moist, slapping sound as it landed. 'He knows some excellent inns, and one of them seemed a good place to wait until the suckling pig was retrieved. Is that it?'

'There is not much left,' said Bloet, squelching as he sat. He offered no explanation for where he had been, and merely ripped himself a portion of flesh from the pig's ravaged carcass.

The last to arrive were the Saxons, also trailing sopping clothes and declaring it was no night to be out. Soon, the only people missing were Clarembald, who had not been invited to John's hall, and Maude. Rodbert – also dripping – said she had retired with a headache and should not be disturbed.

'A headache,' said John, rubbing his hands gleefully. 'I am good with headaches.'

'No,' said Rodbert, more sharply than was polite. 'She wants to be alone.'

And why was that? Geoffrey thought. Because she was enjoying the company of some other man, and had fabricated an excuse to keep Rodbert away? Because she was one of the attackers, and had been injured in a way that would be hard to explain? Or was she simply tired of her companions and really did want to be alone? He understood why; he longed to be away from them himself.

'I saw Clarembald walking to his lodgings not long ago,' said Bloet. 'He looked as though he had fallen in the river,

132

he was so wet! It must have been quite a tour of taverns to see him so damp.'

'Please!' said Warelwast with a shudder. 'No talk of falling in rivers, if you do not mind. I have had more than enough of near-drowning recently.'

Geoffrey studied him covertly, but there was nothing in the bishop-elect's expression to allow him to read anything into the comment, just as there had been nothing to read in the demeanour of the others. Analysis was hopeless: no one had any kind of alibi he trusted, and everyone was wet. It was late and he was too tired to think properly, so he allowed his mind to wander as he listened to the desultory discussion that broke out.

'It is good to be in a decent house,' said Warelwast politely. 'One where the roof does not leak.'

'Lord!' muttered John, flummoxed. 'You had better sleep down here tonight, then. We tend to be used to dripping ceilings in this part of the world, where it rains so much.'

Everyone looked up as the door opened yet again. But it was only Geoffrey's dog, which had managed to slip past the bishop's servants and make its own way to the hall. John's eyes narrowed, but he made no attempt to oust it while Geoffrey was there.

'What does it have in its mouth?' he asked, watching it warily.

'Gold,' said Tasso, rashly trying to remove the object from the dog's maw. It snapped, and only the presence of the object between its teeth stopped it from breaking skin. 'It tried to bite me!'

'Like all Normans, it loves treasure,' Geoffrey thought he heard Sendi mutter.

'You will not get it away from him,' warned Roger, as Tasso looked ready to prise the animal's jaws apart with a dagger. 'Not now he knows you want it.'

But Geoffrey knew how to deal with the dog. He took a piece of pork and waved it until the animal agreed to a bloodless exchange. While the animal gulped the meat, Geoffrey inspected its loot. It was a pendant on a chain, comprising a disc with a cross on it. It looked ancient, and its weight indicated it was valuable. There was a thread caught in it, which led him to conclude it had been torn from its owner by force – and that the dog was probably the culprit. Geoffrey regarded it thoughtfully. Did it mean that the dog had caught one of the men who had tried to drown its master? And in that case, if Geoffrey could identify the pendant's owner, would he then know the identity of one of his attackers?

'This should go to its rightful home,' he said, holding it up for all to see. 'My dog must have found it on the street after it dropped from someone's neck.'

But that would have been too easy, and Geoffrey did not really expect the culprit to claim the thing. Blank stares met his enquiring gaze, and he saw he would have to devise more devious means to learn why someone was so determined to prevent him from looking into Bristol's problematic moneyers.

It was several days before Geoffrey was able to leave Bath. Helbye's hip was too painful for him to ride, and he was feverish from his hectic evening of chasing stolen pork. Geoffrey declined to leave him to the tender mercies of Bishop John, preferring to tend him himself, despite Helbye's protests that he did not need mothering. It was the first time Helbye's infirmity had interfered with Geoffrey's plans, and it pained both of them to know it would not be the last.

'It got worse after he consulted those physicians,' said Roger, watching Geoffrey kneel next to Helbye with warmed ale. 'He was all right before that.'

'But John only prayed and lit candles,' said Durand. 'That should have helped. It was Clarembald who did the damage, by slapping that poisonous poultice on him.'

'The paste contained a harmless mixture of bryony root and yew leaves,' said Geoffrey. 'I think the ailment was brought on by the journey from Westminster, in the wet and the cold.'

'I am not some old woman who cannot go out in the winter,' snapped Helbye angrily. 'I am a soldier, and a ride in the rain is nothing to me. I was doing it before any of you were born.'

The Saxons had left as soon as the flood subsided, keen to travel the last fifteen miles to Bristol as soon as possible. They had all been away too long and longed to be back among friends, families and the familiar things of home. Geoffrey had watched them go in the grey light of early dawn. They were arguing as usual, each accusing the others of trying to drown the King's agent. Geoffrey pointed out that Henry had plenty more spies, and the death of one was immaterial; he would send others until he had what he wanted. There had been silence while this information was digested.

Bloet and Clarembald had also elected to travel to Bristol immediately. Bloet was morose, and confided to Durand that he was so pessimistic about finding the silver, he was tempted to buy some and pretend his hunt had been successful. The only problem was that the stolen load had been huge, and he did not have the funds to match it. Meanwhile, Clarembald's parting shot was to incense John by declaring Bath a city of thieves: his saddlebags had been ransacked the previous night and some medicines stolen. He added insultingly that they were of little value anyway, because he had bought them in Bath.

Warelwast declined to leave, though, on the grounds that he was indebted to Geoffrey for pulling him from the river. Geoffrey did not want his company, but the bishop-elect was adamant, and could not be persuaded to go with the others. He said he was in no hurry, and claimed that an extra pair of eyes would not go amiss in a place where someone had already made his murderous intentions known. Geoffrey pointed out that his main suspects were going to Bristol, and he would therefore be a good deal safer. But Warelwast refused to be dissuaded, leaving Geoffrey unsettled and suspicious.

'I am tempted to stay, too,' said Maude. 'I enjoyed our tryst and would like to know you better. But Barcwit is waiting.'

'So is Rodbert,' said Geoffrey, nodding to where the deputy moneyer was scowling at them. 'You had better go, before he tells Barcwit some tale about us, just to be nasty.'

'He would not dare,' said Maude. 'Barcwit would want to know why he had not prevented it, and then it would not just be you chopped into pieces and fed to the dogs.'

'Dear, gentle Barcwit,' said Geoffrey wryly. 'A kindly soul, much loved by good men.'

Maude gave him one of her mocking smiles. 'Do not tell

me you are a good man, Geoffrey. That would be most disappointing.'

The travellers clattered away, and Geoffrey began the first of several long and tedious days at the side of his ailing friend. He borrowed a scroll from the abbey, which listed plants and their medicinal uses, and read that neither yew leaves nor bryony roots should have worsened Helbye's condition. He even rubbed some on his own leg to check for adverse reactions. Nothing happened, other than a slight tingling sensation that was not unpleasant.

'You think Clarembald poisoned him?' whispered Roger, while Helbye slept.

Geoffrey rubbed his eyes, which ached from deciphering the tiny writing. 'Several attempts on my life have failed, so someone might be trying an alternative way of keeping me from Bristol.'

Roger stared at him. 'By harming Helbye? That would be a sly thing to do.'

Geoffrey agreed. 'But it worked. Who knows how long we may have to wait until he is well enough to ride? It is frustrating, because I wanted to watch the moneyers when they arrive home, to see whether they meet anyone or go anywhere that might give me some clue as to who is lying and who is telling the truth.'

'I do not like any of them,' declared Roger vehemently. 'If I learn that one has fed Helbye something to make him sick, I will run him through.'

'No,' said Geoffrey, watching the old man shift fitfully in his sleep, 'because I will do it first.'

By the next day, however, Helbye had improved. He urged the others to leave without him, but he had been with them through many awkward situations, and they declined to abandon him. While he rested, Geoffrey amused himself by reading more of the abbey's medical scrolls, learning that wild thyme was a good cure for the headaches associated with too much wine, and that hemp juice in the ears was good for getting rid of worms in the stomach.

On the evening of the third day, Durand slipped into the sickroom. 'I have been visiting shops with Bishop John,' he said. He shook his head in admiration. 'That man certainly knows his way around a market! I needed some silk to make myself new braes, and he knew where to find just what I wanted. We had a most enjoyable afternoon.'

'I see,' said Geoffrey. He had not known his squire's undergarments were silk, nor that he made them himself. Sewing with costly materials was not a skill most knights bothered to learn.

'We bought some for you, too,' Durand went on. 'Two new tunics and more braes. You can pay me back when I collect them tomorrow. They were such a bargain that I could not resist them, and you really do need more. I had not realized your old ones were in such a state until I saw them in the bathhouse the other night. They are rather foul, if you want the truth.'

Geoffrey was aghast. 'You bought me silk underclothes?'

Durand smothered a smile. 'Of course not: silk would be wasted on you! Yours will be made from durable linen from Ireland. That is one of the advantages of being near the sea – imported goods are readily available. Bristol does a brisk trade with Ireland, which is why Bloet thinks the missing silver is no longer in the country, if you recall. But I did not come to regale you with details of my afternoon, delightful though it was. I came to say that I visited the apothecary's shop with John – I wanted to buy a salve for this spot on my nose, and John wanted to know what Clarembald had purchased. The spot is becoming unsightly, and I must be rid of it before I meet Bloet again.'

'Did this apothecary know anything about dishonest moneyers?' asked Geoffrey hopefully.

'No, but he told John that Clarembald bought every last grain of his bryony.'

'Yes,' said Geoffrey, wondering what the squire was getting at. 'He slathered it thickly on Helbye's hip, so I am not surprised he needed a lot of it.'

'The apothecary said large doses are dangerous for women – they bring on bleeding, cause babies to abort, that kind of thing.' Durand saw Geoffrey was bemused and tried to make himself clear. 'It is a strong herb, and not only for women, I wager. Helbye is better now you are the only one tending him.'

Geoffrey frowned. 'You think Clarembald used too much bryony in his poultice?'

Helbye winced as he eased himself into a sitting position. 'But you tried it on yourself and it caused you no problems.'

Geoffrey rubbed his chin. 'But Clarembald said that a thief had been in his bags and stolen the items he had bought in Bath . . .'

'Precisely!' said Durand. 'The thief did not steal the rare and expensive items Clarembald has been guarding ever since we left Westminster, but the common potions bought here – bryony, which will not kill, but may lay a man low and prevent him from travelling.'

'You think this potion was intended for Sir Geoffrey?' asked Helbye.

Durand shrugged. 'It does not matter who was dosed with it. The point is that Sir Geoffrey was prevented from going to Bristol when he intended, thus giving his suspects ample time to hide things, prepare witnesses for his interrogations, and God knows what else. Clarembald *may* be the culprit, and he claimed the bryony was stolen to throw us off his scent. Or he may be innocent, and someone else took advantage of his purchases.'

'In other words, anyone could have done it,' said Geoffrey in disgust. 'Just like everything else in this wretched case.'

'Or no one,' said Durand. 'I know it was me who brought all this up, but there is always the possibility that everything is exactly as it seems: Clarembald was robbed by thieves who just happened to steal the bag containing bryony, and poor Helbye is simply ill after a night in the rain. There is no way to tell without more evidence.'

'No,' said Helbye firmly. 'I know my own body, and the agonies in my hip are nothing like the twinges I have had before. I have been poisoned: there is no doubt about it.'

Seven

Three more days passed before Geoffrey deemed Helbye fit enough to travel. The old soldier had become fastidious about what he ate or drank, and refused to touch anything that had not been tried by the others first. John provided him with a syrup of poppy juice to ease the discomfort of the journey ahead, but Helbye declined to touch even that until Durand had taken a healthy swig. It was therefore a pleasant trip, with Helbye free from pain, Durand sleepy and mercifully silent, and Geoffrey feeling fresh and clean in his new underclothes. John and Warelwast accompanied them – John because he wanted to see whether any new or interesting goods had found their way to Bristol since he had last visited, and Warelwast because he seemed glued to Geoffrey's side.

It was an unusually bright morning, which was one of the reasons why Geoffrey had elected to travel, even though it was Sunday – a day normally reserved for rest and religious activities. He wanted to reach Bristol and settle Helbye somewhere warm and dry before the rain started again. They left at first light and, even with Helbye's infirmity, went far more quickly than they had with the Saxons and their baggage trains. It was not ten o'clock before they breasted a hill and looked down on the settlement that nestled at the confluence of two rivers. The mighty Avon curled and twisted to the south, while the smaller Frome lay to the north; the town and castle stood between them.

Bristol Castle, like many others in England, had been raised by the Conqueror's vassals to subdue the local population with a show of Norman might. The motte was surmounted by a wooden watch tower, and a moat encircled the bailey,

139

formed by channels dug from the rivers. The moat was fringed by a wooden fence, which was currently being strengthened in stone at its more vulnerable points. To the west lay the town. Like Bath, it had been a Saxon burgh, so its main streets were enclosed within walls, although the settlement was expanding and some houses lay outside. There were several bridges across the Frome, but only one across the stronger, powerfully tidal Avon.

'What will you do first, Geoff?' asked Roger, as they rode towards it. 'Will you see Barcwit, and tell him what he is accused of?'

'Maude and Rodbert will already have informed him. That was one reason why I wanted to be with them when they arrived back – to gauge his reaction.'

'How about Sendi, then?' asked Roger. 'Will you demand to see his records – this so-called evidence he has amassed that will prove Barcwit's guilt beyond the shadow of a doubt?'

'Barcwit is the one accused, so we should start with him. Now, in fact, while he still feels holy from his Sunday devotions and so less likely to lie.'

Warelwast gave a snort of derision. 'Barcwit does not go to church – unless it is at the witching hour and he is carrying satanic regalia. You will waste your time if you scour the churches for him.'

'How do you know?' asked Roger curiously. 'Have you seen him dabbling in sorcery?'

'I spend a good deal of time here,' replied Warelwast. 'But I have never observed him entering a church.'

'Have you ever seen him in person?' asked Geoffrey. 'Clarembald told me he has not, despite his frequent visits to Bristol.'

Warelwast ignored John's disdainful grunt when his rival was mentioned. 'He and I often travel together, since we live in Exeter. But I *have* seen Barcwit. He has a habit of standing and watching.'

'Standing and watching what?'

'Public hangings mostly,' replied Warelwast. 'He can see the gibbet from his mint, and I have often spied him observing the proceedings from his window.'

Geoffrey knew some men enjoyed that sort of entertainment, although he was not among them. 'What does he look like?'

'He always dresses in black and his face is white. It gleams palely underneath his hood, because he never goes out in the sun. Only at night.'

'He wears a hood inside his house?' asked Geoffrey, thinking Barcwit sounded a little mad. 'While he watches executions?'

'He *is* an odd man,' acknowledged John. 'I have invested with him for years, and a good deal of money has changed hands. I must be one of his better customers – all *strictly* legal, as you will discover when you inspect his records – but he has never once greeted me in person. I see him at his window occasionally, watching me leave, but we have never spoken.'

'He is savage as well as strange,' added Warelwast. 'You should take care when you meet him. He bites the heads off pigeons to amuse himself, and I have heard he would like to do the same to a man.'

Geoffrey could not stop himself from laughing. 'That would require either some very large teeth or a good deal of hard chewing. Human heads do not come off so easily.'

Both clerics regarded him askance. 'How do you know?' asked John.

'We have been to the Holy Land,' said Roger, by way of explanation. The mysteriously evasive answer only served to increase their unease, and neither churchman spoke for some time.

They rode across the bridge, which spanned the river at a point where the Avon was relatively narrow, although the silky coating of mud on its steep banks indicated a substantial tide. Once across, they passed through a gate and found themselves on one of the town's main thoroughfares. It was lined by shops that had John's eyes alight with gleeful anticipation.

'There is an inn,' said Helbye, pointing to a seedy-looking building called the Raven. The journey had tired him more than he was prepared to admit. 'We can discuss how to approach Barcwit over a cup of ale.'

141

'I will see him alone,' said Geoffrey. 'I do not want him on his guard because he thinks I have brought half the King's army with me.'

Roger objected, but Geoffrey did not want to lose what small element of surprise he had left by sitting in a tavern while he waited for Helbye to recover. He handed the reins of his horse to Durand, and strode up the high street to where John told him Barcwit's mint was located. It was not difficult to find, particularly having visited a similar place in Bath. He smelled it before he saw it, identifiable by the sharp stink of hot metal, the coals that were needed to melt the silver, and the dirty aroma of dust and burning, even though it was Sunday and the furnaces were supposedly banked.

Barcwit's domain comprised an elongated building, which stood just north of the crossroads that marked the town's centre. Geoffrey glanced up at the upper window that overlooked the street, and saw it was empty of spectators that morning. He knocked sharply on the door and waited for someone to answer. Eventually, he heard footsteps on the other side, and a grille clicked open.

'What do you want?'

'Who are you?' Geoffrey demanded in his turn.

'Colblac, chief clerk to Master Barcwit.'

'Open the door,' ordered Geoffrey. 'I am here to see Barcwit – in the name of the King.'

'I will fetch Rodbert,' said Colblac, and the grille snapped shut. Geoffrey sighed, suspecting it was going to be as difficult to extract information in Bristol as it had been on the journey west. It was some time before the grille cracked open a second time, and Rodbert's blue eyes appeared on the other side.

'Barcwit is busy,' said Rodbert rudely.

'It is Sunday,' Geoffrey pointed out. 'His mint is closed – unless he ignores the Church's rules about working on Sundays. Now, let me in, before I tell the King you refused to co-operate.'

The grille closed a second time and, for a moment, Geoffrey thought the deputy had ignored his threat and gone away, but there was a scraping sound as bolts were drawn back and the door was tugged open. Geoffrey stepped into a thin corridor, with an open door to the left, and a closed one at the far end. Clanks and knocks emanated from behind it, indicating some sort of labour was in progress, Sabbath or no. Geoffrey also noticed that someone had recently washed the floor, perhaps in an attempt to hide the fact that work was going on. Footprints of all shapes and sizes had trampled the wet flagstones, suggesting they had seen a good deal of traffic that morning.

Rodbert led the way to the open door, and preceded Geoffrey into an airy room, where tables and benches were set to catch the light. Documents were stacked on shelves that covered almost every inch of wall. Colblac sat at a desk with a scroll in front of him; it was a devotional tract with religious motifs in the margins. It was upside-down and, since any clerk would be able to read, Geoffrey assumed the man had grabbed it in a hasty attempt to conceal what he had really been doing. He pushed the scroll to one side, revealing a list of accounts, the ink on which was still wet.

'Prayers,' said Colblac defiantly, not anticipating that a Crusader knight would be literate.

'Prayers about the price of silver?' asked Geoffrey, gratified to see the man start in surprise.

'Barcwit is not here,' said Rodbert rudely. 'And he would refuse to deal with you on the Sabbath, anyway, because he is a very religious man.'

'Which church did he attend?' asked Geoffrey, thinking he would speak to the priest, to find out once and for all whether Barcwit was devout or a pagan.

'St Ewen's,' said Rodbert. His expression was smug. 'But it was a private mass, so no one saw him.' He walked to the door and indicated Geoffrey should leave. 'I will tell him you called.'

'Sir Geoffrey,' said Maude, sweeping into the office. Her amber eyes were mischievous, and she looked as though she was pleased to see him. 'How is Helbye? Has he recovered?'

'Frail old men and squires who wish they were women,' said Rodbert in disdain. 'And dirty knights with gaudy surcoats. What was the King thinking of, to appoint such people to investigate us?'

143

'Actually,' said Maude, walking in a circle around Geoffrey, 'he is not as dirty as I recall. Has the rain washed him clean? And do I see a new tunic under his armour?'

Geoffrey was disconcerted she had noticed, and supposed he had allowed himself to become grimier than he had appreciated. 'If Barcwit is not in, then what about your *cambium*?' he asked, determined not to allow her to deflect him from his purpose. 'If he is sober, then at least one of Sendi's claims against you will be deemed void.'

'He is visiting his mother,' said Rodbert, in a way that suggested he was lying.

'Where does she live?'

'I am not sure,' said Maude, before Rodbert could answer. More intelligent than the deputy, she knew it was unwise to antagonize the King's agent. 'But perhaps you would care to take a cup of wine? Tasso will be home soon, and I am sure he will be delighted to see you.'

'When will the *cambium* be back?' asked Geoffrey, equally sure he would not.

'Later,' she replied vaguely. 'But he will be tired and will retire directly to bed, as he always does of a Sunday evening. Come tomorrow, and I will ask if he is willing to speak to you.'

'*Willing* to speak to me?' Geoffrey was amused by her audacity. 'He must, or the King will assume you have something to hide, and find in Sendi's favour. I am sure you do not want to lose everything because your *cambium* cannot take a few moments to answer my questions.'

Maude's face lost its playful expression. 'Our *cambium* is a contrary fellow and pleases himself what he will do. I will tell him it is imperative he speaks to you, but he may decline. He is not Lifwine, who does everything he is told. Our *cambium* is independent and free to do what he likes.'

'I see,' said Geoffrey, wondering whether 'independent' was a euphemism for 'drunk'. 'However, he is not free of the King, and it is in Henry's name that I ask these questions.'

'*We* will answer,' said Maude. She gestured around the chamber. 'All our records are here, and we can spend as long as you like going over them. The King will prefer documentary evidence to rumours and unsubstantiated accusations, so he will want you to start by assessing our accounts.'

'Meanwhile, I will try to persuade our *cambium* to co-operate,' said Rodbert, resentment dripping from every word. 'But he will decide for himself whether he obliges.'

'And Barcwit?' asked Geoffrey. 'Will you persuade him to speak to me, too? Or will I have to wait until Giffard arrives and conduct my interview in the castle dungeons?'

Maude squeezed his arm. 'My husband is a proud man. He lives for his mint and for his King, and he will resent being interrogated by a minor knight. Please be patient.'

'It is not me you must worry about,' said Geoffrey. 'It is Henry.'

With nothing else to do, he selected scrolls at random and inspected them, hunting for irregularities that might indicate there was truth in Sendi's accusations. But he was not surprised when he found nothing untoward. Barcwit would have stored incriminating documents elsewhere, and Geoffrey did not seriously expect to discover anything amiss.

Eventually, when he felt he had aggravated Rodbert enough, he took his leave. As he returned to the Raven tavern, he glanced back, and his eyes were drawn to Barcwit's upper window. The shutters were partly closed, but he was certain someone lurked behind them. The person was tall and swathed in a dark cloak, and Geoffrey thought he glimpsed a flash of something pale under a hood. He blinked, to look more carefully, but the figure had gone and the window was empty.

Geoffrey had not taken many steps from Barcwit's mint before he saw someone he recognized. It was Bloet, wrapped in a thick cloak and with a hat pulled over his head, although not far enough to hide the distinctive nose or the red hair that poked from under it. Geoffrey noticed something else, too – that although there were a fair number of folk strolling Bristol's streets, no one lingered around Barcwit's property. When people reached a certain point, they lowered their heads and hurried.

'You have noticed, too,' said Geoffrey, walking behind Bloet and making him jump. 'You are watching the way people are afraid to linger. They are everywhere else – standing in the sun and chatting – but the street outside Barcwit's mint is deserted.'

Bloet was clearly annoyed that his 'disguise' was not as good as he had thought. 'People have not lingered around here for years – not since a whole family once stopped to exchange pleasantries and disappeared. But I was looking at something else, as it happens.'

'A whole family?' Geoffrey was sceptical.

'Mother, father, three children, grandmother and dog,' elaborated Bloet. 'Last spotted outside Barcwit's home and never seen or heard of again. Some folk believe he killed them because they dared to laugh on the Sabbath, while others think he was merely hungry.'

'That is outrageous,' said Geoffrey, amused by the unlikely tale.

'Yes,' agreed Bloet fervently. 'But Barcwit is an outrageous man. You should be careful when you visit him; always make sure someone knows where you are.'

'I mean it is an outrageous story. Even Barcwit cannot murder an entire family and expect to get away with it. Nor is it easy to dispose of six bodies – whether he was hungry or not.'

'Who will prevent him from doing what he wants?' demanded Bloet. 'No one in this town, I can tell you! And he has plenty of furnaces in his mint. It is easy to ram a body in one of those – if there was enough left after he had finished feeding.'

'These are fairy tales,' said Geoffrey, surprised that a worldly man like Bloet should believe them. He could see from the stubborn expression on the courtier's face that he would not change his mind, so he turned his attention to an earlier comment he had made. 'You said you were not watching Barcwit, but doing something else. What?'

Bloet pointed. 'Observing Sendi and his household. They lead uncommonly dull lives. They work from dawn to dusk, eat and go to bed. Then it starts all over again the next day. Adelise is lucky: she goes to the market to buy fish and flour. But today was the most exciting of all: they went to church!'

146

'What did you expect them to be doing?'

'I thought one might have had the grace to go and inspect his stolen silver,' said Bloet unhappily. 'To make sure it is all present and correct. But no, not them!'

'You have been watching them ever since you arrived?' asked Geoffrey, wondering whether Bloet might have seen anything pertinent to his own case.

Bloet nodded. 'They do not even visit taverns. I have been lurking for days now, and have learnt nothing about the ingots. I am beginning to think Rodbert is mistaken, and they do not have them.'

'Is that why you are concentrating on Sendi? Because Rodbert said you should?'

'He made a convincing case,' said Bloet. 'And in the absence of any other theories, it seemed as good a place to start as any. But I suspect Sendi knows I am watching him, and that is why he has done nothing incriminating.'

'Do not discount the possibility that Barcwit's own men might have robbed him,' recommended Geoffrey. 'Rodbert is not exactly devoted to the truth: he lied to me only moments ago.'

Bloet was disheartened. 'I thought his explanation was too simple: Barcwit's treasure stolen by his rival.'

'What else have you seen?' Geoffrey peered around the corner and saw Adelise and Sendi in their Sunday best, talking to a priest. Lifwine and others who had accompanied them to Westminster were also there, plus more, so they numbered about thirty in all. It was a large enterprise, and Sendi was clearly a rich man with a prosperous business, despite his complaints that Barcwit was damaging it.

'Nothing. Sendi barely sets foot outside his door.'

Geoffrey found that hard to believe. 'It must be difficult for you to watch all the entrances and exits at the same time. How do you manage?'

Bloet regarded him aghast. '*All* the exits? Are you saying there might be a back door?'

Geoffrey saw he would learn nothing from Bloet, so left him to ponder his misfortunes. He thought the King had made a grave mistake by appointing him to locate the silver: Bloet was the last person *he* would have charged with such a mission, not only because the fellow was incompetent, but because he seemed the type who might make off with the hoard if, by some remote chance, he was successful.

When he reached the Raven tavern, Geoffrey found the others ready to leave. He glanced at Helbye, who sat straight and tall in his saddle, although there was a knot in his jaw where his teeth were clenched. The journey had taken its toll, and it was time for the old soldier to rest in a bed. Geoffrey scratched around for a way to suggest it without offending his dignity.

'Where shall we go?' asked Roger energetically. 'To see Sendi? To interview Lifwine about how he assays his coins?'

'Did you know that Lifwine's shoes cost him more than six months' pay?' asked John conversationally. 'He has them specially made, with thick, hard heels. He says it is because they are more durable, but I think it is to make him look taller.'

'They may cost more than normal shoes,' said Helbye, 'but he says they last for years. Perhaps I should invest in a pair. These boots are so thin that I may as well be barefoot.'

Geoffrey saw he was right, and wondered whether leaking footwear was compounding the problem of Helbye's aching bones. He decided to buy him a new pair the next day. The lines of weariness and pain etched around the old man's mouth prompted him to break into Roger's unrealistically ambitious plans for the rest of the day.

'First, I want to find somewhere to stay. Does anyone know of a good inn?'

'The one I favour – the Swan – is small, and I have reserved the only decent chamber for myself,' replied John. 'You would be better going elsewhere. I like the Swan, because it is conveniently situated for the market, and it is also close to Barcwit.'

'Why would you want to be near him?' asked Geoffrey, recalling the unspoken menace that had pervaded the area around the mint, and the tales of eaten families.

John pursed his lips. 'Because that is where I invest my money. I hope you resolve this business quickly, because I dislike being under a cloud of suspicion, and want to be exonerated as soon as possible. Of course, you will find Clarembald is guilty, and—'

'The inn,' pressed Geoffrey, not wanting to hear more accusations when Helbye needed to rest.

'Do not bother with those places,' said Warelwast. 'I will arrange for us to reside in the castle.'

Geoffrey was startled. The castle would certainly be the best place to stay, given that they were usually secure places where access to casual visitors was denied. Since neither side in the moneyers' dispute wanted him to investigate, it would be good to have a base where murderous nocturnal invasions would be difficult to stage. However, castles were not hostelries, and it was not for any travellers to arrive and demand accommodation in them.

'How will you manage that?' he asked.

Warelwast shrugged. 'I will tell the constable, Sir Peter de la Mare, that that is what I want. You can do that sort of thing when you are a nephew of the Conqueror and a cousin of the King. Leave it to me. It is the least I can do.'

But Geoffrey did not want to be beholden to the man. 'We can—'

Warelwast raised one hand to indicate he would hear no more. 'Sir Peter's wife keeps the garrison in reasonable order, so we shall be able to sleep in safety. She even owns a couple of feather mattresses, if comfort is what you desire. I shall certainly requisition one for myself.'

'Do you intend to come with us?' asked Roger uneasily. He, like Geoffrey, wanted to be rid of the man. 'Surely, a tavern would be a better place for the likes of you?'

Warelwast raised his eyebrows. 'I am not sure what you imply by that remark, but I shall let it pass. We shall *all* stay in the castle.'

'Sir Peter's *wife* keeps the garrison in order?' asked Helbye. 'Why does he not do it himself?'

'You will see,' replied Warelwast enigmatically.

They rode up the high street, then turned right at the crossroads, where the fragrant scent from a spicer's storehouse battled valiantly with the ever-present odour of waterlogged sewage and horse manure. The castle stood at the end of the road, its looming motte and watchtower casting a menacing shadow over the town, declaring to all that the Norman castle and its Norman overlords were in charge and there to stay.

From a distance, the castle had looked unremarkable, but when they came closer Geoffrey saw it was actually a formidable structure. Its moats were broad and deep, with the kind of steep-sloping banks that would be difficult to scale. The timber palisade was topped with sharpened spikes, while the tower was larger and stronger than he had first thought. The enormous bailey was full of the buildings always associated with keeping law and order in a conquered land – stables, storerooms, barracks for the soldiers and a large hall.

Warelwast told the gatehouse guard that he had business with the constable, and Geoffrey and the others followed him inside. When Sir Peter was informed that he had visitors, he hurried to meet them. He had nondescript features, iron-grey hair and the kind of clipped beard now only worn by older, unfashionable men. He smiled when he recognized Warelwast.

'My Lord Bishop! You did not tell us you were coming, or I would have had the latrines cleaned.'

'Why?' asked Roger, intrigued by the curious greeting. 'Is that where he usually sleeps when he visits Bristol?' He roared with laughter, greatly amused by his own wit.

'He complained about the smell last time,' explained Peter. 'But it was summer, so perhaps he will not find them so bad now it is cooler.'

'We will see,' said Warelwast. 'But do not call me Bishop yet, Peter. Exeter's present incumbent still lives, and I cannot take his post until he dies – which will not be for years yet, God willing.'

Geoffrey shot him a surreptitious glance, trying to tell whether he was being sincere, but could make out nothing from the man's bland features. Warelwast began his introductions.

'This is my friend Sir Geoffrey Mappestone, trusted agent of the King. And Sir Roger is the son of the Bishop of Durham.'

Geoffrey winced: the mantle of King's agent did not sit easily on his shoulders, and he would certainly rather Roger's patronage were kept quiet. He bowed to Peter, who reached out to touch his surcoat, taking the material between finger and thumb and feeling it with an awe akin to reverence, although Geoffrey noticed him wiping his hand on his tunic afterwards.

'*Jerosolimitani*,' he said wistfully. 'I wanted to go on the Crusade, but my wife would not let me.'

'You did not miss much,' said Geoffrey, thinking that Peter would not have lasted long if he was the kind to be bullied by a woman. 'Too many men did not return.'

'That is what she said,' replied the constable. 'But I would have liked to have seen Jerusalem. I hear its streets are paved in gold, and that holiness drips from every stone of its sacred buildings.'

'Its streets are paved in donkey dung and the only thing dripping from its "sacred buildings" is the blood of the innocents we slaughtered,' said Geoffrey bluntly. 'You would have been disappointed.'

Warelwast was aghast at the heresy. 'You speak against the Holy Crusade? But it was God's will – that is why He let us win.'

'Warelwast is right,' added Roger, regarding his friend coolly. 'God *was* pleased with what we did, which is why He granted us so much loot afterwards.'

Geoffrey did not think it was worth arguing with them.

'I am Peter de la Mare,' said the constable. 'You are welcome to stay – as agents of the King, as *Jerosolimitani* and as friends of the bishop-elect. But space is short at the moment, and I can only offer one small chamber. You should all be able to lie down, though, if you organize yourselves logically. Of course, you can always sleep in the hall with the servants, if you want more space.'

'The private chamber will suit us nicely,' said Warelwast, before Geoffrey could say he would prefer the hall. He did not like cramped chambers. 'There have been attacks on our lives of late, and we will be safer in a room where we can lock the door.'

'No one will attack you in *my* castle,' said Peter boastfully. 'I pride myself on my security – or rather, my wife does. She is good at that sort of thing.'

151

'A woman organizes your defences?' Roger was shocked.

Peter shrugged. 'She is very skilful – better than you, I warrant – and it makes sense to use our strengths. That is what the Conqueror once said, and his advice has always stood me in good stead.'

'You mentioned tight space,' said Warelwast, before Roger could argue. 'Who else is here?'

'Just an old friend from my youth. He would be more than happy to change chambers with you, because he is an obliging sort of fellow. But I am not so sure about his wife.'

'A shrew?' asked Warelwast sympathetically.

'A terrible woman,' confided Peter. 'I swear she could defend this castle single-handed if it were attacked, and she is three times the size of her husband. Needless to say, she and my own wife Idonea have a good deal in common. You should hear them exchanging theories of warfare around the hearth of an evening. It would make your hair curl!'

'This is beginning to sound unappealing,' said Warelwast distastefully. 'I do not want to discuss battles all night. I like to chat about art and music before I retire to bed.'

'Give me the warfare,' declared Roger. 'These ladies will enjoy discussing military tactics with *me*.'

'They probably will,' agreed Peter unhappily. 'We seem to be horribly afflicted by strident women in this town. Besides those two, there is Barcwit's wife Maude, who is the cleverest lady I have ever encountered; and there is Sendi's Adelise, whose angelic innocence conceals a spiteful mind.'

'We travelled from Westminster with Maude and Adelise,' said Roger. 'We know exactly what they are like. I did not even bother to seduce them! They would not have been worth the effort.'

'Maude would,' said Peter. 'But you would never seduce *her*, because she would get you first. If she decides to have you, then you are doomed, because she will succeed, come what may.'

'Do you speak from experience?' asked Geoffrey, supposing he should have held out after all, just to prove he was no woman's easy prey.

Peter glanced furtively behind him before nodding. 'And

she has been demanding favours for her silence ever since. I pay, of course, because I do not want Barcwit *or* Idonea to find out. I would be dead within hours. It was the most expensive romp of my life!'

'I should say,' admonished Warelwast. 'You should choose your lasses with more care, man!'

Just then, a shout came from the hall and two people started to walk towards them, one considerably bigger than the other. Peter looked around rather desperately, as if he was considering a bolt for safety, but a woman bawled his name in a manner that suggested she was not to be denied.

'Hold on to your wedding tackle, gentlemen,' he advised, seeing there was no escape. 'I am sure this particular lady rips them off the unwary and eats them for breakfast.'

'She does look ferocious,' agreed Warelwast as the woman approached, dragging a diminutive man in her wake. 'I thought St George had vanquished all the dragons, but here is one alive and well.'

'A thwarted whore,' said Roger knowledgeably. 'They all go like that when their advances have been repelled too often. Of course, it only ever happens to very ugly women.'

Geoffrey stepped away from them and his face broke into a beam of genuine pleasure. 'It is Joan!' he exclaimed. 'My sister!'

Joan stopped dead in her tracks when she saw Geoffrey and her jaw fell open in astonishment. There was a family resemblance of sorts between them. Both had thick, light-brown hair, but Joan's was flecked with grey and mostly hidden under a matronly veil. They were also sturdy and tall, although Joan was inclining to fat around her stomach and hips, while Geoffrey led a sufficiently active life to remain lean. Joan's eyes were dark and slightly beady, whereas Geoffrey's were green.

Next to her, dwarfed by her powerful body, was her husband, Sir Olivier d'Alençon. Olivier was about as far from Geoffrey's idea of a knight as it was possible to be. He had never seen a battle, let alone taken part in one, although he had a number of war stories he was fond of telling. Most people knew they were fictitious, but he was a pleasant man, so they tended to tolerate his flights of fancy. He had black hair and a moustache with no beard, which was an odd fashion in Henry's England when everyone else did it the other way around. The sword at his side was bright, shiny and ornate, and Geoffrey doubted it would be of much use in a real fight.

While Joan was still gazing in disbelief, Geoffrey ran towards her and swept her off her feet in a hug. It was mostly affection for the one living member of his family he liked, but also mischief, because he knew she would be mortified by such an unseemly display in front of strangers. When he eventually set her down, she continued to stare at him, so he followed the embrace with a smacking kiss that made her eyes water.

'What are you doing here?' she demanded. 'You said you were going back to the Holy Land. I thought I would never see you again.'

Her gruff words were punctuated by a catch in her throat, which told Geoffrey she was glad to see him, and that she had been sorry when she thought they would never meet again. He was surprised to find he was both touched and pleased: it was good to have someone who cared.

'King Henry ordered me to stay,' he replied, deliberately vague. His pleasure at meeting her was tempered by the fact that he was there to investigate crimes in which she was alleged to be involved. Since he had not imagined for a moment that she might be in Bristol, he had not considered how to broach the subject. She would be furious, and Joan in a temper was not something to be taken lightly.

'I see,' she said, and he saw she was immediately suspicious. 'For how long?'

'I do not know. But Tancred released me from his service, so I have nowhere else to be.'

She raised her eyebrows. 'I was under the impression he liked you. Have you done something dreadful? It had better not bring shame on our family!'

Geoffrey sighed, having forgotten her tendency to assume the worst of him. 'I have done nothing wrong, except perhaps to dally too long in the service of another man.'

'And he did that for *you*,' said Olivier. He flinched when Joan rounded on him, but pressed on with what he wanted to say. 'He could have escaped to the Holy Land last March, but stayed all summer to make sure Henry sent troops to help *you* against the evil Robert de Bellême.'

'Those were dangerous times,' agreed Peter, smiling sycophantically at Geoffrey and obviously chagrined about insulting his sister. 'The Welsh were massed all along the English borders, waiting for Bellême to pass the order to attack. Treacherous people, the Welsh.'

'Not all of them,' argued Joan. 'We are on good terms with *our* Welsh neighbours, because I sent them corn when their harvests failed last year. It cost us a great deal of hardship, because it was before our fortunes turned, but they gave it all back – with interest. Our Welsh are a generous, honourable people, so do not confuse them with Bellême's mercenaries.'

'Well,' said Roger, regarding Joan with considerable interest in the awkward silence that followed the reprimand. 'This is your sister, is it, Geoff? She is not nearly as fat as you said she was.'

Joan glared at her brother, who could not remember ever calling her fat. He supposed, from Helbye's sheepish expression, that the description had come from him. He hoped Roger would not make any more tactless remarks, because Joan was not a very forgiving sort of person, and he did not want her angry with him, making his investigation even more difficult by refusing to co-operate.

'This is Roger,' he said, gesturing to his friend. 'He—'

'The Bishop of Durham's bastard,' said Joan, immediately seizing the opportunity to trade insult for insult. 'The stupid one. Yes, I remember you writing to us about him.'

'My father is not stupid,' said Roger indignantly. 'He is intelligent, full of goodness, and honest.'

Joan regarded him intently, trying to assess whether he was mocking her. She apparently realized he was in earnest. 'Flambard is intelligent, certainly. No one would argue with that, although it is not something he seems to have passed on to his offspring.'

Roger's hand dropped to his dagger. 'I do not think I like

your sister, Geoff. She is too eager to insult honourable knights.'

'I have insulted no honourable knights,' countered Joan.

Geoffrey hunted desperately for a way to end the conversation, not wanting his friend and his sister to fall out over the very first words they exchanged. Roger was a brave man and a fearsome fighter, but Joan would slice him into pieces with her tongue. Warelwast came to his rescue.

'Let us go inside and drink a cup of wine, to celebrate the unexpected meeting of my dear friend Geoffrey and his pretty sister.'

'Who are you?' demanded Joan. She was seldom moved by flattery, and Warelwast would have to be a good deal more circumspect if he wanted to charm her. 'Some court cockerel, no doubt, with silver words and feathers in his brain.'

'He is the Bishop-Elect of Exeter!' breathed Peter, aghast at her words. 'And a cousin of the King. I am fortunate to count him among my friends, just as I am honoured to claim your husband.'

'Peter and I have fought many battles together,' said Olivier, bowing to Warelwast.

'Have we?' asked Peter, startled. 'I do not remember any. I am not a battling sort of fellow.'

'Wine is a good idea,' said Roger, smacking his lips. He was never a man to decline a drink, especially when he would not be asked to pay for it. He grinned at Olivier in a comradely fashion. 'And then you and I shall exchange a few tales of glorious victory.'

Olivier was delighted by the prospect of a new victim for his dishonest stories, and led the large knight to a stone building at the far end of the bailey. Warelwast grabbed Geoffrey as soon as Joan was out of earshot.

'I did not mean to offend you with my comment about dragons,' he muttered, embarrassed. 'I was speaking in general terms about formidable ladies, not about your sister specifically.'

'So was I,' said Peter, less convincingly. 'It is just that she has only been here three days, but she has already reorganized my siege supplies.'

'For the better?' asked Geoffrey. 'Or has she imposed a system that does not work?'

'It *is* rather clever,' admitted Peter reluctantly. 'She and Idonea worked it out between them. However, it is one thing having a wife who excels at warfare, but another altogether for my friends' women to come and tell me what to do. What will my soldiers think?'

'I have learnt to take good advice from any quarter,' said Geoffrey. 'Regardless of the sex of the person who offers it.'

'You men!' said Joan, overhearing. 'You only ever think of one thing. Here is your sister, whom you never thought to see again, and all you do is chat about sex. Do you remember none of the manners I so patiently taught you when you were a boy?'

'You were not patient, and most of what you taught me was not polite,' said Geoffrey, recalling what his mother had done to him when he had acted out one of Joan's little gems of etiquette in a misguided attempt to impress her.

'The vegetable incident!' she said with a sudden, uncharacteristic giggle as the memory came back to her, although Geoffrey did not remember it as particularly amusing. Their mother had been every bit as formidable as Joan, and definitely not someone to cross. 'Do not look so surly, Geoff! It was a long time ago. Surely you have forgiven me by now?'

He pushed the unpleasant memory away and dropped behind Peter and Warelwast to walk with her. 'How is Goodrich?'

'Thriving, as Olivier and I said in our last letter. Do you still read them?'

'Of course,' he replied, bemused she should think he did not. He realized their relationship was one based on uncertainty, and that two decades during which their only contact had been by written communication meant that neither was confident of the regard of the other. It was a pity, and he wondered whether there would be time to set it on a more secure footing before he left again. 'I like hearing from you.'

She took his arm, surprising him with the small gesture of sisterly affection; their mother would never have indulged in any such sentimental nonsense. 'You must think me unkind not to be more friendly in my greeting, but you startled me.

157

I had steeled myself to the fact that you were gone for ever. But why are you really here? Have you taken an oath of allegiance to that usurper Henry? I hope not: you deserve better than to serve a conniving, wicked, greedy, unscrupulous miser like him.'

'You do not like him, then?' asked Geoffrey mildly.

'I do not! The throne of England belongs to the Duke of Normandy, not him. And I do not like the way he forced you to help him this summer, either. It was not the act of an honourable man.'

'No,' agreed Geoffrey, although he was taken aback to find her still angry about it.

She sighed. 'But we should not spoil our reunion with talk of that snake. We can discuss him tomorrow, when we have tired of each other's company and will be ready for a quarrel. So, answer my question: why *are* you here?'

Joan was not a woman to be fobbed off with untruths, and Geoffrey knew better than to try. Besides, he would have to question her about her involvement with Barcwit sooner or later. 'There is a moneyer in Bristol who has been accused of corrupt practices. Henry ordered me to look into the matter. I did not want to do it, but he said he would spare you if I did as he asked.'

'Spare me?' asked Joan sharply. 'What do you mean?'

'There is a list of people who invest money with Barcwit, and Henry wants to know whether they do so because they are offered a higher – perhaps illegal – rate of interest, or because they are involved in a plot to debase the coinage and topple him from his throne. Your name is on that list.'

Joan's hands flew to her mouth. 'I am accused of treason?'

Geoffrey shrugged. 'It depends on what I find. Henry has not discounted the possibility that the accusations may amount to nothing.'

Joan clutched his elbow so strongly that it hurt, then shoved him in the direction of the stables. 'Go. Collect your horse and your stupid friend, and leave.'

He disengaged his arm. 'I cannot. Henry will assume the worst about you.'

He was astonished to see the sparkle of tears in her eyes.

'I do not want you involved in this, Geoff. If you have even a modicum of affection for me, then you will do as I ask. Go back to Tancred. He will accept you again, if you put your request nicely.'

Geoffrey was bewildered, not used to seeing his strong, determined sister in a state of distress. 'If I leave, Henry will charge you with treason for certain.'

A tear rolled down her leathery cheek. 'I am already doomed, and it would break my heart if you were to fall with me. Go now, while you can. Please.'

Eight

'I am not leaving,' repeated Geoffrey the following morning. It was the first opportunity he and Joan had had to be alone, because Peter and Idonea – a dignified woman in her fifties who was older than her husband – had insisted on entertaining them the previous night. He had tried several times to corner his sister on her own, but it had proved impossible. As the evening wore on, Olivier, Roger, Warelwast and Peter became more rambunctious from the amount of wine they had downed, while Geoffrey, Joan and Idonea became quieter. Joan was withdrawn and contemplative; Geoffrey worried about her; and Idonea was disgusted that men who imbibed less than she were far more drunk.

Seeing he would not be able to talk privately to Joan, Geoffrey had abandoned the noisy revelry early, and had gone to the tiny chamber he had been allotted to share with Roger, Helbye, Ulfrith and Durand. Fortunately, Warelwast had taken one look at the cramped quarters and declared he would sleep with Peter and Idonea instead. Neither seemed surprised by his decision, indicating he had shared their bed on previous occasions when space had been at a premium.

Geoffrey woke early the next morning, and went to check the horses; only careless knights neglected the animals needed to carry them into battle. Roger's was looking well, but he was concerned for his own. It seemed listless and its coat was lacklustre. He hoped it was not ill, because he did not have the money to buy another. Next, he walked to the kitchens, where he begged a bone for his dog. But the beast wanted something with more meat, and had its teeth in a haunch of venison before he could stop it. When he paid an irate cook for the theft, Geoffrey realized his funds were lower than he had thought; he doubted there was enough to see him and his men to the Holy Land.

The opportunity to speak to Joan came at breakfast. The hall had been converted into a refectory, with benches for the soldiers, and tables and chairs on a dais for the constable and his guests. There was no sign of Warelwast and Roger, although Peter and Olivier arrived puffy-eyed and pale-faced, prodded from their drunken slumbers by wives who had scant patience for men who had overindulged. Peter rested his head in his hands, wincing when the servants made too much noise. Idonea perched next to him in stony silence, and Geoffrey had the impression they had argued about his fragile state. Olivier sat rigidly bolt upright, as if he was afraid he might be sick if he slouched.

'You must leave this morning,' said Joan to Geoffrey. He could see from the shadows under her eyes that she had slept poorly. 'Take a ship from Exeter. Do not leave from Bristol, because Henry may be able to trace you. Warelwast will help. He is indebted to you for saving his life.'

'So he says,' said Geoffrey. 'But he is also a servant of the King – and what better way to monitor a reluctant agent than to claim undying friendship? His accident in the river had its advantages.'

Joan was horrified. 'You think he is a spy? But why would Henry order him to watch a man who has already agreed to do what he was told?'

'Henry trusts no one. Meanwhile, Warelwast has been promised the post of Bishop of Exeter, but perhaps it is a conditional offer and he is obliged to prove his loyalty first.'

'You have grown suspicious, Geoff. Is it because of that business at Goodrich last year?'

'It is because I have had too many dealings with powerful men – the King, Bellême, their followers. It is hard to know who to trust.'

'I know,' she said bitterly. 'Olivier and I have been drawn into nasty affairs, even while we live quietly at Goodrich. The arms of these men are longer than you think.'

'What do you mean?' he asked uneasily. 'Has someone threatened you?'

She sighed and the eyes that met his were bleak. 'There is something I must tell you. It is about our brother Henry – the only one of us who thought his namesake had a right to the English throne. You once had two sisters and three brothers. I am the only one of your siblings left now.'

Geoffrey stared at her. He knew about the deaths of one sister and two brothers, but the last he had heard, Henry was alive and making a nuisance of himself with his fiery temper and brutish manners. He was a year older than Geoffrey and they had never been friends, although a truce of sorts had been reached after their most recent encounter. He recalled what Edric had said at Westminster: a man called Henry had accompanied Joan on her first visit to Barcwit, but not on subsequent occasions.

'What happened?'

'We found him one morning with a dagger in his stomach. Olivier thinks he did it himself – he was often bitter and lonely when in his cups – but I believe someone murdered him. He made so many enemies over the years that it was difficult to know where to begin looking for a killer. You may have been up to the task, but Olivier and I were not.'

'When did this happen?'

'At the end of September. It seemed such a dreadful thing that I could not bring myself to put it in a letter. I remember how distressed you were when Father wrote so bluntly about our sister's death, and I was afraid I would not find the right words to tell you about Henry.'

'That was different,' said Geoffrey. He had loved his sister Enide, but had never felt much for Henry. He put his hand on her arm, concerned for her. 'I am sorry. Is there anything I can do?'

She smiled. 'I see it has not occurred to you that you are now the heir to Goodrich and its estates. Olivier and I can only stay there with your blessing.'

'Please do,' said Geoffrey fervently. She was right: it had not crossed his mind that Henry's demise meant he was now lord of Goodrich. It was not an inheritance he intended to claim and, as far as he was concerned, Joan and Olivier were welcome to it. 'I do not want to become a farmer, especially in England, where its king would constantly be after me to do his dirty work.'

'In that case, you must leave today. You are the only family I have, and I do not want to lose you.'

'You will not lose me. Why do you think you might? What are you not telling me?'

'Barcwit,' said Joan. 'He will not like you prying into his affairs.'

'If he is innocent, he has nothing to worry about; if he is guilty, then he only has himself to blame. Besides, Bishop Giffard will arrive soon, and if I have not uncovered the truth, then he will – and he is likely to be a lot harsher than me.'

'Then let Giffard do his work,' pleaded Joan. 'You cannot help me. No one can, not now.'

Geoffrey was bewildered. 'But the King is ready to be lenient towards you. If I discover what is really happening here, and present him with the truth, you will be spared.'

'So, you are here for me,' she said bitterly. 'The King has used me a second time to secure your services. If I had thought for one moment that it would come to this, I would never have embarked on this business. It turned dangerous in a matter of weeks. And now I am a burden to you.'

'You are not,' said Geoffrey gently. 'Whatever has happened, we can find a way through it.'

'Not this time. I am well and truly ensnared.'

Geoffrey sat back. 'Then we must see what we can do to untangle you, but you will need to answer my questions first. Sendi claims you have invested money with Barcwit. Is it true?'

'We made our first payment in March. Olivier and I often visit Bristol, because he buys horses from a village near here. Peter told us Barcwit is a safe and reliable merchant – that his investors make handsome profits, which are always paid on time. We had some spare funds, because Olivier had sold a valuable horse, so we decided to test Barcwit. Our investment doubled in weeks, and money has continued to flood to us ever since. It has transformed Goodrich.'

It sounded unlikely to Geoffrey. He knew little about economics, but he was aware that profits tended to be slow in accumulating and did not materialize into grand sums all of a sudden. There was something odd about the whole affair. 'Did Barcwit offer you a higher rate of interest than that set by the Exchequer?' he asked.

'No, that would be illegal, and I am not a lunatic, whatever you might think. Barcwit's clerks told us this is just a good time to invest in coins, because there is a demand for them.'

'Barcwit's clerks? You do not deal with Barcwit himself?'

Joan allowed herself a grim smile. 'Barcwit only deals with important customers, which we are not. I have never met him, although I saw him once and he deigned to nod at me. He made me shudder. He is not a good man, and I wish we had never heard of him or his mint.'

Geoffrey was bemused. 'So, you were presented with what appeared to be a legal investment scheme that provided huge returns. Surely you were suspicious?'

'No,' said Joan, gazing down the hall. Geoffrey wondered if she would not meet his eyes because she was lying. 'Not then.'

'And now?' Geoffrey sighed when she did not reply. 'You must tell me, or I will be fighting with one hand tied behind my back, and that might harm both of us. What happened to make you realize Barcwit's business is not all it seems, and why are you so distressed? It is not like you to be afraid.'

She sighed in resignation. 'Very well, I will tell you. But do not come crying to me when you are mixed up with something dark and dangerous, and can see no way out.'

'I can look after myself.'

She gave a snort of disdain. 'Your Holy Land experiences will not help you here, and neither will the strong arm of your dim-witted friend or the crafty mind of your squire.'

'Henry thinks Barcwit may be debasing his coinage. That is tantamount to treason. How much worse can it be?'

She gazed at him sadly. 'I would not be so concerned if it was mere economics that drives Barcwit. But he has ambitions on a far grander scale.'

'What are they?' pressed Geoffrey, when she did not elaborate.

'He is accruing funds to have Henry murdered and the Duke of Normandy placed on the throne.'

Geoffrey listened in horror as Joan confessed how she had been delighted with the returns on her first investment and, like the gullible men Roger cheated with his loaded dice, was soon giving Barcwit all she had in the expectation of even greater dividends. It was only later that she learnt some profits were being channelled into a fund 'to serve England'. When she had finished, he sat in silence, deeply unsettled. It was not the notion of someone raising money to kill a king that upset him – removing Henry by murder and ousting him through his economy were both treason – but the fact that he had never seen Joan in such low spirits. Even when Goodrich was at its poorest, she was indomitable and ready to battle on. Now she was cowed and resigned to her fate. She tried again to make Geoffrey leave, and even asked if he would take Olivier with him, claiming it was her fault that they were embroiled in a plot to kill Henry, and that she should take the consequences alone.

Geoffrey escaped from breakfast and left the castle on foot, wanting time alone to think about what she had said. He walked through the gate that led to the town, but stopped when someone called his name. Durand was hurrying to catch up, to ascertain what was required of him that day. Geoffrey sent him to tell Sendi he would visit later that morning, then assessed the street, to decide which way would afford him some peace. To his left lay the River Avon, alive with the sounds of a busy port, so he turned right, towards the smaller, quieter Frome.

It started to rain, lightly at first, then in a drenching down-pour, so he trotted to some stalls at the foot of the town wall, intending to take cover until the shower was over. Others had the same idea and, because the shops offered the only public shelter in a fairly large area, they were packed. Bloet slouched in one that sold ribbons, while Barcwit's clerk Colblac poked around another that specialized in pots. Given Bishop John's predilection for markets, Geoffrey was not surprised to see him there, but he was mystified to see Warelwast hurrying through the deluge to join them. John greeted the bishop-elect loudly, making him wince; Warelwast's head was evidently still sore after his night of debauchery, and Geoffrey wondered why he should be out dodging showers when he would have done better to remain in bed. It was odd to encounter him in a cobbler's shop so early in the morning, and Geoffrey had the uneasy sense that he had been followed.

'Wild thyme,' he said coolly, recalling what he had read in Bath while waiting for Helbye to recover. 'It is supposed to be good for your condition.'

'Do you have any with you?' asked Warelwast weakly.

'If you learnt that from Clarembald, it will not work,' predicted John loftily. 'However, *I* shall say a prayer for you, and by this evening you will be well again.'

Geoffrey was unimpressed. 'He will have recovered by then, anyway. Wine-induced headaches seldom last beyond noon.'

But John did not want to argue about medicine when there were more interesting matters to discuss. He gestured around him gleefully. 'This is Bristol's best cobbler, and you will not find a finer pair of shoes in the county. Take my advice and buy these.' He held up a pair that had been dyed a lurid pink, and which boasted pointed toes, highly decorated straps and ostentatious silver buckles.

'They would not look right with my armour,' replied Geoffrey.

John regarded him wearily. 'I was thinking of your sister, man! She is sure to be irked when she finds out you are here to investigate her business transactions with Barcwit. These will appease her.' He pushed them into Geoffrey's hands.

Geoffrey tucked them under his arm and smiled at him, thinking it was as good a time as any to ask a few questions. 'When you made your payments to Barcwit, did he tell you some of your profits were being kept in a fund to be used for something else?'

John seemed surprised. 'Of course not! Supposing I did not agree with the purpose of that fund?'

'My sister was given no choice.'

John was unimpressed. 'Then she must learn to be firm. The customer is always right, and if any tradesman – no matter

166

how influential – tries to tell *me* otherwise, I withdraw my patronage.'

'Even from Barcwit? The man whom everyone fears?'

'The issue has not arisen with Barcwit,' replied John shortly.

'Why do you ask?' Warelwast regarded Geoffrey curiously. 'Has Barcwit been using his ill-gotten gains to invest in matters better left alone? Like sending money to fund an invasion by Bellême or the Duke of Normandy, for example?'

'Not that I am aware,' said Geoffrey, not wanting to tell Warelwast there was a plan afoot to murder his royal cousin.

'Look at that!' exclaimed John suddenly, gazing outside. 'I have never seen a rainbow so bright!'

'Not one, but three,' said Warelwast, squinting as the light hurt his eyes. 'Three rainbows, one on top of the other. It is a sign from God!'

'Another one,' muttered Geoffrey, thinking it meant that either God had a lot to say or people kept misunderstanding, so He was obliged to repeat Himself.

'It is a sign that God will protect Barcwit from these accusations,' said Colblac, as he pushed past to see better. 'And it is a warning for you, too: I saw the way you looked at his wife yesterday and he has killed men for less. And be warned about finding him guilty of anything, too. He will not like it.'

Geoffrey was amused. 'Most felons object when they are caught, but that is a risk they take when they commit their crimes.'

Colblac sighed. 'Barcwit is no felon – you must look to Sendi for that sort of thing. He is occasionally hard on wicked men, but those charges of dishonest coining are a nonsense.'

'I will bear it in mind. If you are right, then Barcwit has nothing to fear.'

Colblac seemed satisfied. He looked at the shoes in Geoffrey's hand. 'Those will clash with the red in your surcoat and you will look like *that*.' He pointed to the shimmering rainbows.

They had intensified since Geoffrey had last looked, and he was amazed by their brightness and clarity. He had often seen two, but never three, and certainly not so vividly. They blazed like celestial bridges, and people in the street were shouting to each other and running, foolishly trying to locate the ends, where treasure was believed to lie. Warelwast and Colblac were among those who joined them.

'How is your hunt for the silver?' Geoffrey asked of Bloet, who was staring at the arches in dismay.

Bloet's face was haggard and his breath was sweet with the scent of the previous night's ale. He indicated the rainbows with an unsteady hand. 'Is that a good sign, or one that foretells disaster?'

'It means the clouds are dark, the sun is at an unusual angle, and it is raining.'

Bloet shook his head. 'You are a strange man. You risk your life on God's holy Crusade, but you refuse to recognize His omens.'

'Did Barcwit ever tell you he was using his profits to invest in something else?' asked Geoffrey, wanting to know whether Bloet had been caught in the same mire as Joan. 'Something treasonous?'

'If he did, I would not tell you,' said Bloet, not unreasonably. 'That would be stupid.'

'You have a royal pardon,' said Geoffrey. 'You can tell me what you like.'

Bloet laughed mirthlessly. 'It is not that simple, as well you know – and I will not be pardoned for anything if I do not locate this silver. But I have been listening to rumours, and there is something odd going on with these moneyers and their clients. You should speak to some of the other investors, not just me and the physicians. There are important Bristol officials who are more deeply involved with Barcwit than is wise.'

'Who?'

Bloet looked shifty. 'I could not say. But, I have just given you a clue, so how about you helping me? Have you heard any whispers about the silver since you arrived?'

'Nothing,' said Geoffrey. He wondered whether to mention Alwold's final words about 'the secret' being known by the King, Warelwast, the priest of St John's and Bloet himself, but decided against it. Clearly, the secret was not the location of the silver, or Bloet would not be looking for it, and

Geoffrey did not want to compound the man's misery by giving him a riddle that was irrelevant and perhaps insoluble. He held up the pink shoes. 'But there is a lot of silver in these buckles.'

It was unfortunate that Bloet had no sense of humour, because he immediately started an ugly argument with the cobbler about the source of the metal used in his shoes. Insults and curses flew back and forth, where they were overheard by John, who declared he would never again buy shoes from a man who knew such foul language. Bloet, not wanting similar censure, slunk away, heading for another vigil at Sendi's workshop. When the cobbler wailed that he would starve without the bishop's patronage, Geoffrey felt so guilty that he bought the pink shoes, waving away the man's concerns that one did not purchase display footwear: one usually had them specially made so they would be the right size. Geoffrey did not care, suspecting Joan was unlikely to wear the things anyway. Durand arrived soon after, to say Sendi was expecting him.

'Did you see the Three Rainbows?' the squire asked excitedly. 'God is definitely trying to tell us something. I was dragged from my monastery against my will, so perhaps He is suggesting that I take the cowl again. I *am* someone He would want in His service, after all.' He noticed the pink shoes and fingered them admiringly. 'Those are nice.'

'They are for Roger,' said Geoffrey. 'Do you think he will like them?'

Durand's jaw fell open in shock, and Geoffrey started to laugh. Durand pulled a face when he saw he was being teased, and snatched the shoes from Geoffrey to inspect them more closely, running covetous fingers across them. Geoffrey indicated he was to lead the way to Sendi's mint, then listened with half an ear as Durand told him in embarrassing detail about the loving relationship he enjoyed with Bloet, and how deeply he would miss the man when their paths diverged. He did not sound at all like the kind of man who was worthy of a celestial phenomenon created to entice him to a monastery.

Sendi's mint did not occupy a prime position like Barcwit's, and it was located in the northern part of the town, near the Church of St John the Baptist. It was something of a backwater, and Geoffrey suspected Barcwit's central location had a good deal to do with why he had the lion's share of investors. His premises were convenient and visible, and exuded an aura of permanence and strength. Sendi's, on the other hand, comprised a sprawling complex of sheds and outbuildings, all enclosed by a fence of sharpened spikes. They looked seedy and uninviting, and Geoffrey would not have felt compelled to leave *his* money there.

Sendi was waiting for them and, as he ushered them inside, both he and Durand turned to wave to a shadow that lurked in a doorway opposite. Durand's greeting was friendly, Sendi's insulting. The object of their attention was Bloet, who had gone straight from the stalls to his observation point. He returned their greeting, then slipped deeper into the shadows, as if he hoped Sendi might forget he was there if he concealed himself more carefully.

Once inside, Geoffrey detected the same sharp, metallic odour he had noticed in Barcwit's mint – hot silver and the fierce fires that were required to melt it. Like Barcwit, Sendi had an office where records were kept. Lifwine the *cambium* was in it, but he leapt to his feet and followed when he saw Sendi conducting the King's agent past him, muttering that they needed as many watchful eyes as possible when such men invaded their property.

The centre of Sendi's operations was much the same as the one in Bath. It was a large room built entirely of stone – to reduce the risk of fire – and was full of benches where men hammered, pounded, clipped and swore. The noise abated when Sendi entered, and Geoffrey had the impression that his workforce was keen to hear what was being said. Adelise emerged from another room, where she had been sewing leather aprons, and she, Lifwine and the man called Edric stood close behind Geoffrey, determined to watch his every move. Durand edged away, giving the impression that if the Saxons united to attack the knight, then he did not want to be in the way when it happened.

'It looks busy,' said Geoffrey politely, when Sendi seemed to be waiting for a favourable comment.

170

'We are striking coins with the new dies from London,' said Adelise, cutting across her husband's more pleasant reply. 'Of course we are busy. And you are interrupting us. Why?'

'The King told me to look into your affairs, as well as Barcwit's.'

'That is unnecessary,' said Sendi. 'You can see for yourself that this is an honest operation.'

Geoffrey smiled. 'You know it is not possible to tell just by looking.'

'Well, it is not *our* fault Henry appointed a stupid agent,' said Adelise nastily. 'And we should not have to suffer for it. So, say what you must, and leave us to our work.'

Geoffrey recalled what he had learnt from Osmaer and turned to Lifwine. 'Show me how you assess the coins that are produced here.'

Lifwine grimaced in annoyance, but led the knight to a table where an array of equipment stood. There were guidelines for examining both blanks and finished coins, and methods to assay the quality of the silver from which they were made. Geoffrey was shown scroll after scroll of records, all of which 'proved' Sendi's coins were uniform and the appropriate quality. Then he was presented with details of sales and accounts, which were gleefully piled high in front of him, so he suspected they intended to overwhelm him with parchment as a way to drive him off. He shoved the documents away and began an inspection of his own devising, picking up coins randomly and weighing them in his hand – although any shortcomings would be far too subtle for him to discern. Edric and Adelise studied him intently, as if they thought he might steal some, while Lifwine tottered behind, his heeled shoes tapping the floor like a horse on cobbles.

It was not long before he noticed he was not the only one under scrutiny. Sendi watched the workmen, and the workmen watched each other, and it was clear that although they had presented a united front to Henry, the reality was that they did not trust each other at all. He wondered whether the charges levelled against Barcwit had created an atmosphere of suspicion, or whether working in an environment that dripped silver – literally – brought out the worst in people. Eventually, his

171

aimless wanderings led him to a cupboard that was secured by several bulky locks.

'What is this?'

'It is where we keep our old dies,' replied Sendi. He opened the door, revealing a row of cylindrical trussels on an upper shelf, and a line of spiked piles below. 'We always keep them safe. Even old dies are valuable – and vulnerable.'

'The ones on the top shelf look more worn than those underneath,' remarked Geoffrey.

Sendi's expression was smugly amused, while the workmen sniggered that anyone should make such a stupid observation. Geoffrey sometimes took the same attitude when people made silly comments about weapons or battle tactics, and resolved to be more understanding in the future. It was annoying to be mocked for not having specialist knowledge.

'The trussel always wears more quickly than the pile, because that is the part that is hammered,' explained Sendi with forced patience. 'You can see that all these trussels are mushroom-shaped. But, by the time they reach this stage, the new dies have usually arrived from London and we are no longer obliged to use them.'

'The trussel is the part with the name of the moneyer and the mint on it,' said Geoffrey, recalling what he had learnt in Bath. 'But why do you keep them, if they can no longer be used?'

'They are waiting to go to the blacksmith, where they will be destroyed,' explained Sendi. 'We have been tardy of late, because we have had so much else to think about. However, these old stamps are just as important as new ones, because they can still be used to produce coins – albeit poor copies.'

'But you are already using your new dies,' said Geoffrey, sensing a contradiction. 'Those have a different design from the old ones. Surely, people will notice if you revert to an obsolete style?'

'Do *you* know when a mint changes its dies, or which coins are current and which are not?' demanded Adelise. She saw Geoffrey's frown and nodded. 'I thought not. And neither does anyone else. We are required by law to buy new dies when the old ones become worn – or when the King decides

172

it is time for a new type – but not everyone obeys. Barcwit does not.'

Geoffrey saw there was no escape from an analysis of Barcwit's transgressions. 'He mints new coins using old dies?' he asked tiredly.

'You know he does,' snapped Sendi. 'You saw some in Westminster – you even held one in your hand. But there is another reason for keeping my old dies safe: if Barcwit gets hold of them, he will mint inferior coins bearing *my* name and I will suffer the consequences.'

'Then get rid of them,' suggested Geoffrey. 'Having them here is a risk you do not need to take.'

He started to wander around the workshop again, amused by the way everyone followed him. It made him feel like an Eastern bride at her wedding ceremony. He inspected the various benches and saw a trussel that was cleaner than the others. He picked it up and held it in his hand. It was heavy, with a cross etched into its head and letters around the edge.

'That is one of the dies we collected from London,' said Sendi, running a loving finger over it. 'It has what we call a "fleury cross", rather than the annulet of the older type.'

'So it does,' said Durand, inspecting it closely. 'The new cross has delicate ends, like lily petals.'

Lifwine took it from him. 'That is why it is called a "fleury" cross. But these are expensive pieces of equipment, and not for just anyone to handle. Not even the King's creatures.'

Geoffrey spent a good part of the morning with Sendi, but did not know enough about minting to ascertain whether the moneyer was honest or the biggest criminal in Christendom. He lingered long enough to make sure the man was thoroughly disconcerted by the inspection, then took his leave, walking quickly through streets that were alive with talk of the Three Rainbows. He entered the curiously empty area around Barcwit's mint, and knocked on the door.

'It is no good doing that,' said Durand. 'I saw Barcwit leaving this morning on a big grey horse. Perhaps that is why the Three Rainbows appeared. God is pleased to have him gone from here.'

Tasso answered the door and stood with his hands on his hips, so Geoffrey would not push past him and get inside. 'Barcwit has gone to Dundreg. He will not be back until tomorrow at the earliest.'

'Where is Dundreg?' asked Geoffrey, prepared to ride there if it meant cornering the man.

Tasso pointed in a vaguely westerly direction. 'He has gone to inspect some stone in the quarry, for when we rebuild our house. You can chase after him if you like, but he seldom uses the main road. A rich man is an attractive target for robbers, so he uses small, little-known paths. If you try to meet him en route, you will have a wasted journey.'

'I thought he was a force to be reckoned with,' said Geoffrey. 'So, why does he skulk on deserted footpaths, rather than riding proudly along the King's highways? And why are you not with him? I thought you were responsible for his safety.'

'He always travels alone,' said Tasso. A brief frown of concern crossed his face. 'I do not approve, actually, and have warned him against it. Especially now.'

'Why especially now?'

'Because there are cunning outlaws at large, such as the ones who took our silver and made it vanish without trace. If they can steal that, then they can certainly harm a lone man, no matter how prodigious his fighting skills. But he tells me he will have no trouble eluding robbers.'

'He has no trouble eluding King's agents, too,' remarked Geoffrey dryly. 'But he will not succeed for ever, because I *will* meet him eventually.'

'He is not avoiding you,' said Tasso. 'He is just a busy man, and cannot wait around for the likes of you to visit. Come tomorrow evening, or the day after. Perhaps you will have better luck then.'

'Let us hope so,' said Geoffrey sincerely. 'However, I am quite happy to tell the King that Barcwit is uncooperative. But perhaps that is what he wants?'

'What do you mean?' asked Tasso warily.

'I mean there are rumours of a plan to kill the King and place the Duke of Normandy on the throne instead – and that Barcwit is providing the funds to make it happen. It may be that Barcwit *wants* the King to descend on Bristol in a fury, because it will give him an opportunity to strike.'

Tasso gazed at him, then burst out laughing. 'That is nonsense! It does not matter to Barcwit who sits on some distant throne, only that the kingdom is stable and in need of coins. Barcwit would not waste his time – or his money – on such foolishness.'

'We shall see,' said Geoffrey, aware that Tasso would naturally deny such a charge. Or perhaps he was ignorant of the plot, because it was reserved for an elite inner circle of traitors.

He left, knowing he had unsettled Tasso. He hoped the man would persuade Barcwit to agree to an interview, because he desperately needed to talk to the moneyer if he was to help Joan. Henry would hardly agree to turn a blind eye to her transgressions if Geoffrey had nothing to give in return. He returned to the castle with Durand at his side, deep in thought.

'Tasso is telling the truth,' said Durand, tucking the pink shoes more firmly under his arm. 'Barcwit *did* go to Dundreg. The priest of St Ewen told Bloet this morning, and I saw Barcwit ride off with my own eyes – alone and swathed in a black cloak. He looked like Death itself.' He shuddered.

'If he is as terrible as everyone says, then he is asking for trouble by going out alone, where people could unite and wreak revenge – or simply rob him of some of his considerable fortune.'

'People have tried, according to the gossip Bloet has heard, but Barcwit is difficult to find once he has left the town. Some say he is a wraith, and dissolves into mist when he is outside it.'

'Then we should pray for some strong winds,' said Geoffrey. 'That should sort him out.'

That evening Geoffrey went with Joan to feed the carp in the castle moat. She walked carefully, so as not to soil her new pink shoes. He had been surprised at her pleasure when he had given them to her, because he thought she would consider them ugly. While she absently bombarded the terrified fish with lumps of heavy bread, she talked more about Barcwit's

plans to kill the King, but he could tell it was mostly speculation on her part, and she had no real idea of how the moneyer
intended to proceed. She was a very small and insignificant
part of a much larger operation. The dog sat with them, and
when it growled, Geoffrey glanced up to see Peter and Idonea
coming towards them.

'I trust you are enjoying your visit to Bristol,' said Idonea,
giving the impression she might strike him if he said he was
not.

'Tell him he cannot stay,' Joan burst out, before Geoffrey
could phrase a polite response. 'He has come to investigate
Barcwit, but if you force him to leave, he will not be able to
do it.'

Idonea was appalled. 'You plan to investigate Barcwit? Are
you *insane*? Do you *want* to die?'

'Warelwast told me that was why he is here,' said Peter.
'But Joan and Idonea are right, Sir Geoffrey – you do not
want to become involved in this. Barcwit's rage is terrible
when he is crossed.'

'So is the King's,' said Geoffrey wryly. 'I cannot leave
without doing what he ordered.'

Peter and Idonea exchanged an agonized glance that immediately told Geoffrey that here were two more people who
had invested with the moneyer and been drawn into a plot
beyond their control. Bloet had been correct when he had told
Geoffrey to explore the finances of certain Bristol officials.

'Do you have proof of Barcwit's treachery?' he asked hopefully. 'Because, if you do, I can present it to Giffard, and the
whole thing can be stopped.'

Peter's face was white. 'You will never stop Barcwit and,
even if you did, *we* are doomed. We have conspired to commit
regicide. Do you think Henry will smile, and tell us to go
about our business, as though nothing had happened?'

Geoffrey felt sorry for them; their future was bleak. 'Then
you have two choices. You can allow Barcwit to carry out
his plan and continue his hold over you for the rest of your
lives. Or you can help me stop him and trust that Henry will
reward your courage with clemency.'

'Henry will not pardon us: we have donated funds towards

his execution,' said Idonea bitterly. 'We were unwitting participants, but *he* will not care about such details. Nor is there any point in denying our involvement, when half the town knows exactly who Barcwit has corrupted.'

Peter explained further. 'When it was just a simple business arrangement, there was no need to disguise our visits, and by the time we realized he had trapped us in something sinister, it was too late for secrecy. But perhaps it will come out all right in the end.' He did not look convinced.

Idonea scowled at him. 'Peter believes Barcwit will succeed and that the King will die, but I am not so sure. It will be very difficult to kill Henry, and I think he will come here and wreak revenge when Barcwit fails. Why do you think I am replacing the wooden palisade with stone walls and laying in siege supplies? We must put up some show of resistance when he arrives to crush us.'

'I hope it will not come to that,' said Peter, looking as though he might be sick. 'What a dreadful position we are in – trapped between the King and Barcwit. I do not know who is more terrible.'

'The King,' said Joan immediately. 'Barcwit I understand; Henry I do not.'

Peter continued. 'If I am wrong, and Barcwit fails, then we are dead for certain. We all saw what happened to Bellême last summer, and Henry will not care that our hearts are not in this rebellion. I rue the day I met Barcwit, and I am sorry we dragged Joan into this mess, too.'

Geoffrey was bemused. 'I can see how you invested in all innocence at the beginning, but why did you not simply withdraw when Barcwit made his traitorous intentions clear? If you had told the King *then* what Barcwit was planning, you would not be in this situation now.'

'We tried,' said Peter miserably. 'But Barcwit said we would be sorry if we betrayed him – and we were. He killed Sir Nauntel de Caen, my dearest friend. He shot him in a village called Beiminstre.'

'How do you know Barcwit did it?' asked Geoffrey doubtfully, 'and not outlaws?'

'Because Nauntel was killed the day after I told Barcwit I

wanted no part in his plot,' said Peter unsteadily. The memory was painful to him. 'He summoned me that same evening and said Nauntel would not be the last to die if I defied him again.'

'I was told the same,' said Joan miserably. She looked away and would not meet Geoffrey's eyes, so he sensed she was hiding something from him. 'Olivier was threatened.'

'Barcwit killed Nauntel in front of me,' continued Peter in an agonized whisper. 'We were riding to Beiminstre to look at a horse he wanted to buy.'

'Then why did you not arrest him?' asked Geoffrey practically. 'You are the constable – you have the authority to imprison those who threaten the King's peace.'

Peter gaped at the notion. 'My men would never tackle Barcwit, and I could not do it alone.'

'Then contact the King and ask for reinforcements,' suggested Geoffrey.

'I considered that,' said Peter, closing his eyes and rubbing them hard. 'But Barcwit anticipated me. He said he would give the King "evidence" that *I* conspired to kill him. He showed it to me: forged letters bearing my seal. Sendi had the courage to take his complaints to the King, and look what happened to him: Fardin murdered and the King's agent poking into *his* business.'

'If you have any sense, you will leave now, before it is too late,' said Idonea to Geoffrey. 'Let us stew in our own mess.'

But Geoffrey was not a man to give up a fight, especially if it meant abandoning his sister. 'It is time Barcwit's tyranny was brought to an end. Henry *will* find out what is happening – if not from me, then from other agents – so you may as well take the opportunity to redeem yourselves.'

'But I do not want to help you,' said Peter, clearly frightened by the prospect. 'I do not trust you to overcome Barcwit, and I certainly do not trust the King to be forgiving. He will encourage me to confess, then execute me anyway. I have seen the way "justice" works for people like me – minor nobles who are dispensable, and good to be made examples of.'

Geoffrey could think of nothing to say, because Peter was right. He did not trust Henry himself, and saw no reason to encourage others to do so.

'My brother will not listen,' said Joan bitterly. 'He has set his heart on exposing Barcwit, and there is nothing any of us can do to stop him.'

Peter gave a low cry and put his hands to his mouth, while even the formidable Idonea was pale. 'Please,' she whispered, fixing haunted eyes on Geoffrey. 'Do not do this.'

'Bishop Giffard will be here soon,' Geoffrey pointed out. 'His remit will be to crush anyone remotely connected with any sort of wrongdoing, regardless of whether they embraced the plot willingly or not. But I am prepared to listen to you, so it stands to reason that I offer you the best chance of acquittal. Help me, and I will help you.'

'It is hopeless,' said Peter gloomily, not bothering to answer Geoffrey's appeal. 'If Henry wins, we die a traitors' death, and if Barcwit wins, we will live the rest of our lives under his terror. We are trapped between two kinds of hell.'

Geoffrey was dissatisfied with the conversation by the moat, and wanted to press Joan for more details about Barcwit and his plans for England's future. There was something she was not telling him and he wanted to know what, feeling that only having partial information in a case involving men like Barcwit might be dangerous. But she spent the rest of the day discussing siege tactics with Idonea, and it was not until the following morning that he managed to tell her he wanted to talk again.

He had encouraged his companions to amuse themselves that day, knowing Helbye would use the time to rest his hip, Ulfrith would eat a lot, and Durand would go to Bloet. Roger was less easy to dispense with, however, and declared himself ready for a jaunt. Meanwhile, Olivier was determined to be with his wife if Barcwit was the subject of any discussion, and Warelwast hovered in a way that suggested he fully intended to go wherever Geoffrey went.

'What shall we do?' asked Roger keenly. 'Make enquiries about Barcwit in the brothels?' He sounded hopeful, always ready to sample local offerings.

'Is *he* coming with us?' asked Joan regarding Roger with distaste. 'I thought we would be alone.'

'I am his friend,' said Roger loftily. 'He never does anything without consulting me first.'

'Then it is no wonder he lands himself in so many scrapes,' retorted Joan. 'But today he is mine, so be off with you. I do not want your company.'

'I go where I please,' said Roger coolly. 'It is not for some shrew to direct me!'

'I think it would be better if—' began Olivier tentatively, attempting to mediate.

'*She* can stay here, while Geoff and I go about our business,' said Roger, overriding him. 'And do not glower at *me*, madam. I am not some serf to order about. I am a son of the Bishop of Durham!'

'Yes, and it shows,' snapped Joan in return.

'Walk with me, Roger,' pleaded Olivier, desperate to avert a row. 'I enjoyed your account of the Siege of Antioch and want to hear more. Then I will tell you how I comported myself at Hastings.'

'You were at Hastings?' asked Roger eagerly, oblivious to the fact that Olivier would have been an infant during that particular campaign. Joan was already forgotten. 'Tell me about it.'

Olivier obliged, and Geoffrey was impressed by the amount of detail the small knight had accrued from second-hand sources. He knew the lie of the land, the movements of different troops, and even the names of minor commanders. He painted a vivid picture, and it was hard to believe he had not been there. He held Roger spellbound, which left Geoffrey free to talk to Joan. Meanwhile, Warelwast had been cornered by Idonea, who was complaining about something he had done in the bed they shared with Peter the previous night. Geoffrey did not like to imagine what.

'I do not know how you put up with that oaf,' said Joan, stalking across the bailey towards the gate.

'Warelwast? He is a clever man. Too clever, I suspect.'

'Roger. He would drive me mad with his inanities.'

'He has saved my life more times than I can remember.' Geoffrey told her about the incident in Bath, when Roger's timely arrival and the dog's barking had driven off his attackers.

'I imagine they were Barcwit's men, determined to stop you from asking your questions here.'

'Or Sendi's, who think I will not be impartial because you are one of Barcwit's investors.'

They crossed the bridge that spanned the moat and eventually turned right along the high street. The roads were busy, choked with carts and animals being driven to the slaughterhouses near the river. Joan almost ran in her haste to be past Barcwit's mint, but Geoffrey refused to be intimidated. He glanced at the window in the upper room as he ambled by, and saw a shadow move away quickly, as if it did not want to be seen. He could only assume it was Barcwit. Moments later, the door opened, and Colblac emerged, carrying an empty basket. Geoffrey strode across to him, while Joan gasped in alarm and did not wait to see what would happen. She fled, and only stopped when she was some distance away. Roger did not notice: he was more interested in Olivier's analysis of the Battle of Actium, where he had captained one of Mark Antony's ships.

'I want to see Barcwit,' said Geoffrey to Colblac. 'I know he is in, because I have just seen him.'

The clerk was puzzled. 'You did not, because he is not due back from Dundreg until this evening.'

Geoffrey was in no mood for games and was determined to have his answers. He shoved past the protesting clerk and strode along the corridor. He was aware of Rodbert glancing up in astonishment as he passed the office, but did not stop to explain himself. He opened the door at the end of the hall and found himself in a vestibule. To his left was a gate laden with locks and bolts; to his right was a flight of stairs; and ahead was a door that, judging from the sounds of hammering and thumping that came from behind it, was the mint itself.

He aimed for the steps and ascended to a landing, which had four doors leading from it. The floor was thick with dust from the mint, and a servant was on his hands and knees, scrubbing lethargically. Footprints were pressed into the dirt, some large and some small, indicating that a fair number of people had access to the upper chambers. Geoffrey slammed open each door as he passed, but all the rooms were empty

181

except the last one. Here he discovered a maid shaking bedclothes out of a window – and Maude. Her eyebrows shot up in surprise when Geoffrey burst in.

'Most men knock,' she said, recovering quickly and donning her usual expression of flirtatious amusement. 'You might have found me naked.'

'I would have killed him if he had,' said Rodbert breathlessly, arriving at Geoffrey's heels. Tasso was not far behind, sword drawn. 'What do you mean by this unmannerly intrusion, man?'

'I am looking for Barcwit,' said Geoffrey, going to inspect a closet. The moneyer was not there, and he realized it had not been Barcwit's shadow at the window after all. Maude wore a dark dress and he supposed it had been her, ducking back when she saw him glance up. He wondered why.

'I told him Barcwit is in Dundreg,' explained Colblac resentfully. 'But he pushed past me before I could stop him.'

'I told him, too,' said Tasso. He glanced at Rodbert. 'Do you want me to kill him? He invaded our house wearing a sword, so we would be within our rights. Even the King could not dispute that.'

'Not true,' said Maude, although Rodbert looked ready to agree. 'Henry will assume we have something to hide if we dispatch Geoffrey. And we do not.'

'What about the coercion of investors and a plan to murder the King?' asked Geoffrey archly.

Maude started to laugh. Rodbert joined in, although his amusement did not sound genuine. Tasso merely looked angry.

'Not this again,' he said irritably. 'I suppose Peter has been putting ideas into your head, because his friend Nauntel was killed. He just cannot accept it that was a random attack by outlaws. Nauntel's death had nothing to do with us.'

'Others have been threatened, too,' said Geoffrey, thinking about Joan.

'We all become impatient with people who are keen to do business with us one moment, but who withdraw the next,' said Maude. 'Harsh words *have* been exchanged, but who has not lost his temper and said things he later regretted?' She glanced at Rodbert to indicate he was the culprit for this particular offence, and he made no attempt to deny the charge.

'If Barcwit is not here, then I will speak to your *cambium*,' said Geoffrey. It was still early, and the clerk should not be inebriated yet – unless Sendi's claims about his drinking habits were true.

'He is not here, either,' said Maude smoothly. 'His mother is unwell, and he is looking after her.'

'Then I shall go to her home and see him,' said Geoffrey.

'He has agreed to meet you next week,' replied Maude, unruffled. 'Surely you can wait until then, and not foist your menacing presence on frail old ladies in their sickbeds?'

'Next week?' asked Geoffrey. He suspected it would take her that long to train a man to take the *cambium*'s place; Durand had predicted as much back in Westminster. Or did she simply need a few days to render the clerk sober and able to answer questions?

'Monday morning,' she replied with a bright smile. 'As early as you please.'

It was odd that the end of the old lady's illness should be predicted with such accuracy, but Geoffrey did not feel inclined to debate the matter. He simply made a mental note to include Maude's odd reaction, and his interpretation of it, in his report for Giffard. 'Very well, but you can tell Barcwit I will see *him* the moment he returns from Dundreg.'

'Do visit again, Sir Geoffrey,' said Maude, giving him one of her knowing smiles. 'But come earlier in the morning if you want to be *certain* of catching me in a state of undress.'

Rodbert made a furious growling sound, so Maude beckoned him inside her chamber with one of her promising leers. As Geoffrey left, with Tasso close behind him to ensure he did not linger, he heard her crooning, and thought they were insane to indulge in such brazen behaviour in Barcwit's own house. He supposed they felt safe in the knowledge that he was away.

The door slammed as soon as he was in the street, making a loud crack that had a number of passers-by scurrying away in terror. No one liked unusual noises emanating from the mint of the dreaded Barcwit. Exasperated and confused, Geoffrey walked to where Joan waited.

Nine

Joan was angry when Geoffrey met her outside a busy tavern called the Greene Lattis, and claimed he was a fool to have invaded Barcwit's domain like a Saracen after Christian virgins. She added, rather tearfully, that she had not expected him to emerge alive.

'I am a *Jerosolimitanus*,' said Geoffrey patiently. 'I have been fighting all my life. I am not Olivier, who needs a woman to watch out for him.'

'Leave Olivier out of this,' snapped Joan, eyes flashing as she leapt to defend her husband. 'He may not be a Crusader, but he has virtues you can only dream of. He is the kindest man in the world, and I would sooner die than be without him. Is there a lady who would say the same about you?'

Geoffrey admitted there was not, and doubted there ever would be, if he continued to meet women like Maude, for whom he was just one in a string of lovers, or like Adelise, who wanted him dead. He was also unlikely to encounter suitable partners if Henry and Tancred kept him busy, and he was not sufficiently important in the eyes of either to warrant being rewarded with a good marriage.

Joan said no more, but led the way along a handsome street lined with magnificent houses, then turned right when she reached the town walls. At the corner was a church dedicated to St John the Baptist. Joan opened a wooden door that creaked, and tugged Geoffrey inside, ignoring his questions about what she thought she was doing. She was in one of her determined moods, and he knew there was no point in trying to force her to answer him. She headed for the high altar, dropped to her knees and hauled on his arm to indicate he should do the same. Meanwhile, Roger and Olivier lurked at the back of the nave, exchanging increasingly unrealistic tales of heroism and chivalry.

'What are we doing?' asked Geoffrey. He glanced around him. The church was poor, with a roof that needed replacing and walls that were devoid of even the merest splash of colour. The plaster had been painted white, which made the interior oddly bright and bare. Geoffrey did not like it, preferring the cosy intimacy of a chapel with proper murals.

'We are here to thank God for allowing us to meet again,' she said crisply. 'And to—'

The door rattled as someone else opened it, and Joan swore as Warelwast approached. He was slightly breathless, as though he had been running. He beamed at Geoffrey, who regarded him thoughtfully, and wondered why the man seemed so determined not to let him out of his sight.

'What do you want?' asked Joan coldly.

'To pray,' said Warelwast, taking no offence at her hostile greeting. 'May I join you?'

'You may not,' said Joan firmly. 'I have arranged to hear a private mass with my brother, and there is no room for interlopers. Here comes the priest now.'

She looked towards the door as a tall, thin man entered. He carried a baby in his arms, while a toddler clutched his leg, making it difficult for him to walk. Two more children trailed behind him.

'This is Father Feoc,' said Joan, smiling as one infant ran towards her. Children liked Joan and were seldom intimidated by the ferocious demeanour that so unnerved adults. 'Do not worry about his little ones; they are always quiet when he says his masses.'

'That is something the Archbishop of Canterbury will soon eradicate,' said Warelwast distastefully. 'This Saxon habit of allowing priests to marry and produce offspring.'

'He may ban priestly marriages,' said Joan tartly. 'But he will never eliminate their children – not as long as his bishops lead by example. Every one has sired an army of bastards.'

'I confine *my* passions to my wife,' said Feoc piously. 'And *my* children are born in holy wedlock.'

'You do not want a married priest to pray for you,' said

185

Warelwast, not acknowledging that Joan was probably right. 'So, let me say your mass. I have no illegitimate brats in tow.'

'None you know about,' corrected Joan. 'But I will hear Feoc. This is his church, and I pray here regularly. Alone,' she added meaningfully.

'Very well,' said Warelwast, fingering the rope he still wore around his neck. 'I shall wait outside.'

'Do you?' asked Geoffrey, when the bishop-elect had gone. 'Pray here regularly?'

'When I remember,' said Joan. 'But I brought you here to meet Feoc. Since you have refused to leave, I feel obliged to help you, and there is no one who knows more about Bristol than Feoc. I hope he will be able to answer some of your questions.'

Feoc fixed Geoffrey with a stern glare. 'But there is one condition: never visit me at home. I do not want Barcwit to arrange for *my* children to have accidents – like the priest of St Leonard's.' He hugged his smallest offspring protectively.

'What do you mean?' asked Geoffrey.

'A cat sat on his son and he suffocated,' explained Feoc. 'It looked like a mishap, but for two things. First, the priest had condemned Barcwit in a sermon delivered two days before. And second, the baby's face had been smeared in fish – to encourage the cat. That is what happens to folk who confront Barcwit. Ask Peter about Nauntel, too.'

'He knows about Nauntel.' Joan nudged Geoffrey with her elbow. 'Ask what you want to know.'

'Is there a man called Piers who lives in Bristol?' asked Geoffrey, thinking he would test the quality of the man's local knowledge by starting with the missing ingots. If Feoc knew as much as Joan claimed, then he would be able to identify the man Alwold had mentioned at Westminster.

Feoc shook his head. 'You are not the first to ask about this. Alwold spoke Piers' name as he died, I understand, in connection with Barcwit's lost silver. However, there is no Piers in Bristol.'

'How about in the past?' pressed Geoffrey. 'Especially someone who might have worked for Barcwit, and whom Alwold could have befriended.'

186

'Alwold had no friends, and there has never been a Piers in Bristol.' Feoc sounded very sure of himself. 'Barcwit is vexed about the loss of his silver, so I would stay away from that matter, if I were you.'

'Geoffrey is not afraid of Barcwit,' said Joan unhappily. 'I wish he were.'

Feoc handed the baby to his eldest child, and indicated they were to play behind the altar. 'Then perhaps he will end Barcwit's reign of terror. Someone must, because the situation cannot be allowed to continue. Ask your questions, Sir Geoffrey, and I will answer if I can. I have lived here all my life, and I know a great deal about Barcwit and his wicked ways.'

'Tell me about his *cambium*.'

'His mother brews strong ale – and she does a man's work at the slaughterhouses.'

'How often is he sober?' The *cambium*'s 'frail and ailing' mother sounded unlikely to be terrified by Geoffrey's 'menacing presence': Maude had lied to him.

'Rarely. Wine is killing him, although Barcwit claims it does not prevent him from working. Perhaps he is right. I knew a priest once, who only gave good sermons when he was drunk.'

Geoffrey decided to take Feoc with him the following Monday; the priest would know whether the *cambium* Maude presented was the real one or an impostor. He changed the subject.

'How many people does Barcwit hold under his sway in this town?'

'Dozens. He sends Rodbert, Maude and Tasso to tell people it is an excellent time for investing in coinage, and they argue their case well. The arrangements offered are safe and lucrative. But then, when it is too late to withdraw, they learn they are involved in sinister business.'

'Why do they not tell him to go to the Devil when they see what is happening?'

'First, Barcwit tells them he has "evidence" to prove their guilt in any enquiry that might take place. And second, people who defy him have accidents – not necessarily fatal ones, like

Nauntel, but nasty, nonetheless. Their cattle become sick or fires break out in their homes.'

'Barcwit has slunk off to Dundreg, and refuses to see me. He is all wind and no substance.'

'He is not, and you must not underestimate him. Joan did, and look what happened to her.'

'She told me,' said Geoffrey. 'He threatened Olivier.'

'That came later,' said Feoc, when Joan said nothing. 'Barcwit has an uncanny ability to sense what his victims would most hate to lose, and for Joan that is Olivier. So, he did not *start* by attacking Olivier: he killed someone else, so she would know he was in earnest. When that person was dead, all he needed to do was hint that Olivier would be next and she was rendered powerless.'

'Whom did he kill?' asked Geoffrey. Joan had no children, and he was her only surviving relative. Suddenly, the answer snapped into his mind and he felt his stomach begin to churn. She had already told him who had died recently, and whose death was a mystery. 'Our brother? Henry?'

Joan nodded. 'So, *now* do you understand why I want you to leave? Henry and I were never close, but I would hate to lose *you* to Barcwit.'

Feoc said little more after Joan admitted she believed Barcwit had had their brother killed, and Warelwast entered the church shortly after anyway, demanding to know why the mass was taking so long. Joan wanted Geoffrey to hide in the castle, Warelwast was clamouring to show him the town, and Roger was keen to sample the taverns. Geoffrey offended them all with his sharp insistence that he did not want to do any of it, and that he intended to exercise his warhorse – alone.

He ordered Durand to saddle his horse, and then rendered the squire even more inept at the task than usual by looming over him and making him nervous. The horse seemed listless, although Durand claimed there was nothing wrong, and they argued about it. By the time the job was finished, Durand was sweating and resentful, and Geoffrey was exasperated with his incompetence.

'You should let me go,' said Durand in a low voice. 'Tancred has released you from his service, so you should release me from yours.'

'And what would you do?' asked Geoffrey, still annoyed with him. 'Live with Bloet?'

Durand glared at him. 'I will re-enter the Church. Life as a soldier does not suit me – look at my hands! They are rough from the work you make me do, and my nails are broken.'

'God's teeth!' breathed Geoffrey. 'I make few demands of you, and those tasks I do set, you perform poorly.'

'Then let me go,' insisted Durand. 'It is clear we have no more to learn from each other. You despise me for my gentleness, while I abhor your barbaric manners and the way you court danger. I do not want to die because you have a penchant for looking into matters that should be left alone.'

'Barbaric manners?' asked Geoffrey, who had always considered himself polite compared to most knights. It was a shock to learn it was not a view shared by everyone.

'I know you promised Tancred you would make me a soldier, but you will never succeed.' Durand sounded defiant. 'So, you may as well concede defeat before one of us does the other some harm.'

'Are you threatening me?' Geoffrey was aghast at the man's effrontery.

'I am telling you how things are,' said Durand, standing his ground. 'We hate each other, and it would be better for us both if we spent no more of our lives in each other's company.'

'I do not hate you,' said Geoffrey tiredly, sorry the feeling was not mutual. He disliked Durand, but hatred was a different thing altogether. 'Has Bloet been putting these ideas into your head?'

'He thinks I should find myself a lifestyle more worthy of my talents,' acknowledged Durand. 'And when I am with him, I realize how unhappy I am with you.'

'You want happiness?' asked Geoffrey, thinking it an odd aspiration when most folk were content with a meal, a roof over their heads and a cup of warm ale. 'That is beyond the reach of most of us.'

'I disagree,' said Durand, his blue eyes filling with tears. 'Bloet is happy.'

'He is miserable,' contradicted Geoffrey. 'He is terrified he will not find the stolen silver.'

'I am not talking about that sort of happiness,' said Durand. 'I am talking about the kind of pleasure one derives from the presence of another human being. Bloet is very content when he is with *me*. He told me so. And he is making the best of this silver business, anyway. As a case in point, take his visit to Barcwit the other evening. They dined together, and he said it was an enjoyable occasion. However, with you, meetings like that always end in something dangerous.'

Geoffrey regarded his squire thoughtfully. 'Bloet dined with Barcwit?'

'That is what I said,' snapped Durand, scrubbing his face with his hand. He was on the verge of weeping again. 'Barcwit invited *him*, but he evades *you*. What does that suggest?'

'That he prefers the company of his investors to men who threaten to expose his corruption?'

'You are missing my point,' said Durand, frustrated. 'Like everyone, Bloet is afraid of Barcwit. However, he went to the man exuding charm and good manners, and was granted an audience – he was even guest of honour at Barcwit's table. But does Barcwit do the same for you? No! He rides to Dundreg instead. My point is that Bloet succeeds where you do not. You are crude and brutal – and *that* is why I do not want to be with you any more.'

'I see,' said Geoffrey tiredly. He supposed he should have anticipated that Durand would want to leave him, now he was no longer bound to Tancred. Should he let him go? It would be one fewer mouth to feed with his rapidly dwindling resources, and he could hardly be expected to continue with Durand's training now Tancred had dismissed him.

'I apologize,' said Durand miserably. 'I should not have said that, but I am out of sorts today. Surely you have met someone who stole your heart, and made you realize life can be so much better?'

Geoffrey nodded slowly. 'There was a woman once . . .' He

did not know how to continue, so he led his horse out to the bailey to mask his discomfort.

'Who?' asked Durand, following him. 'Maude? You certainly enjoyed her company in Bath.'

'It was not Maude,' said Geoffrey. 'It was a lady who . . .' He trailed off a second time, unused to discussing matters that were still painful, even after several years.

Durand sensed his reticence and did not press the matter. 'All I ask is that you think about my request. But do not go riding now. It looks like rain.' He gestured to the dark clouds above.

His comment drew a reluctant smile from Geoffrey, who saw he had taught Durand nothing he had not wanted to learn. Durand still believed in remaining indoors each time a cloud appeared and, if anything, was even less of a warrior than when they had first been forced together.

Geoffrey climbed into his saddle and rode away, thinking about what Durand had said – that Barcwit had not only granted Bloet an interview, but had entertained him, too. Was it because Bloet was more charming? Or was there another reason Barcwit was willing to entertain the courtier? Geoffrey clattered out of the bailey, but was not so preoccupied that he did not notice Clarembald watching him from the shadows of an archway. He reined in and stared at the physician until he emerged.

'Going out?' said Clarembald. 'You should ride to Dundreg, where there are splendid views.'

'That is where Barcwit has gone,' said Geoffrey. 'Why were you watching me?'

The physician's ginger brows waved. 'I wanted to talk, but I believe in assessing men's moods before launching into delicate discussions. I gauged yours to be preoccupied and uneasy, so I decided to wait. That is why I hid.'

Geoffrey was not sure whether to believe him. 'What did you want to talk about?'

'Your investigation, especially the part that involves me. Has Barcwit said anything about me? I assure you it will not be true. However, I guarantee you will find the "Shopping Bishop" is involved in something sinister.'

191

'Barcwit declines to speak to me about you, John or anyone else.'

Clarembald rubbed his chin. 'That is interesting. He is usually eager to meet men he perceives to be a threat, because he is keen to bully them into submission. Have you heard what people are saying about the Three Rainbows? They believe they were a sign from God that Barcwit's reign will soon end – and that you, the King's agent, will be their deliverer.'

Geoffrey shook his head. 'Giffard will do that. However, he will achieve it by executing half the town – including my sister – if I do not find answers soon.'

'People are frightened, and need the hope such omens offer,' said Clarembald. 'They were cheered by the fact that Sendi had the courage to go to the King about Barcwit, but were appalled when His Majesty failed to act on the accusations. And now look at what has happened to poor Sendi.'

'What?' asked Geoffrey uneasily. 'He was well enough yesterday. Is he dead?'

'One of his new dies has been stolen. If Barcwit has it, then he will use it to make bad coins in Sendi's name and ruin him. It is a disaster of enormous proportions.'

'How did it happen?' asked Geoffrey, recalling the heavy palisade around Sendi's insalubrious premises and the thick doors. 'His mint is very secure.'

'Not secure enough, apparently.' Clarembald touched a hand to his hat. 'But you have told me all I wanted to know, so I shall leave you to your ride. If you go to Dundreg, watch out for the marshes near Estune. Barcwit might know his way through them, but you will become bogged down, and your horse is not in the best of conditions.'

Geoffrey ignored Clarembald's advice for the simple reason that he had come to assume everyone was lying to him, or following some personal agenda. But he had not gone far before he discovered the physician was right, and that the boggy wasteland near Estune was a maze of twisting paths, smelly marshes and impenetrable undergrowth, none of which his horse appreciated. It balked and sulked, and was reluctant to gallop, even when the road was firm.

192

But it was pleasant to be alone, and he stood for a long time watching the Avon ooze through a deep, rocky canyon as he considered the few facts he had accumulated. He returned to the castle as the sun was beginning to set, and spent the evening listening to more of Warelwast's grand plans for Exeter cathedral. Olivier and Roger sat near the fire, heads close together as they continued to regale each other with their litanies of lies. Joan watched them fondly.

'I am beginning to like your friend,' she said. 'He is dirty and rude, but I have not seen Olivier so animated for years.' Her gaze settled on Warelwast, who was gathering his belongings in preparation for bed. 'But I do not like *him*. Why does he wear that doll around his neck?'

'He thinks it is a sign from God.'

Joan snorted her disdain. 'He has fastened himself to you like a leech to a festering wound.'

Geoffrey raised his eyebrows. 'You compare me to a festering wound?'

'It is an acceptable analogy,' she said, unrepentant. 'Trouble always follows you, and you attract the attention of some very unsavoury characters. Your squire is a case in point. There are a hundred good men you could recruit, but you choose one with a devious mind and dishonest fingers, who rails against God every night for not making him a woman.'

'How do you know?'

'I heard him. He wants to wear silken—'

'I mean, how do you know Durand is dishonest? You should tell me if he has done something wrong. It would not be the first time. I am certain he accepted payment from King Henry to spy on me this summer.'

'He does have a lot of gold,' agreed Joan. 'Far more than you; you are all but penniless.'

Geoffrey regarded her warily. 'And you know that because . . . ?'

'Olivier and I searched your bags today,' she replied matter-of-factly. 'Just before we looked in Durand's. I wanted to know whether you came here because you are short of funds – if helping me elude the King's clutches would end in a demand for money.'

'God's teeth!' exclaimed Geoffrey, appalled. 'Is that what you think?'

She shrugged. 'Our brothers often claimed that no Mappestone would pee on a burning house unless he was paid first. I do not know you well enough to say whether you are the same. But we are drifting away from Durand. I am not surprised the King set him to spy on you.'

'You think he is still Henry's spy?' asked Geoffrey, trying not to show he was hurt by her comments. He forced himself to think about Durand instead. It was possible the King had continued to pay him after the summer; the squire always had plenty of money to spend.

'I am sure of it.'

Geoffrey studied her, and again had the sense that she was hiding something from him. Her eyes were uncharacteristically shifty, and she fiddled with the pendulous sleeves on her gown. 'There is something you are not telling me. What is it?'

'Nothing.'

Geoffrey sighed. 'Giffard will arrive in a few days and I have nothing to tell him. He will respond by closing both mints and stripping every one of Barcwit's investors of their property – or worse.'

'Then you should be pleased,' said Joan harshly. 'The family estates will be empty, and you can claim them without the bother of ousting me first.'

'I do not want Goodrich,' said Geoffrey, trying to be patient. 'Besides, the King will take it as forfeit if I do not give him his answers.'

'You should not have come,' said Joan softly. 'Peter and Idonea believe we could have brazened it out, but we cannot now you are here, asking awkward questions. They are right: you *will* destroy us.'

'Silence will destroy you,' argued Geoffrey. 'So, tell me what you are hiding. Is it about Sendi's accusations? Or the plot to murder the King? Or this missing silver of Barcwit's?'

'Missing silver?'

Geoffrey saw he had touched a nerve. He grabbed her shoulders and forced her to look at him. 'You have no idea how dangerous it is to keep these things hidden – not just for me, but for you, too.'

'Are you threatening me?' asked Joan, shocked.

'Of course not. I am warning you that—'

'You *are* threatening me,' said Joan, regarding him with a stricken expression. 'You profess to come here on my behalf, encouraging me to co-operate, but when I keep secrets you become angry. You are not here for me, but for yourself!'

'You should know me better than that.'

'But I do *not* know you!' cried Joan. 'We write, but we have not been together for more than a month in twenty years. But I am learning. You are just like our brothers, thinking only of yourself.'

'Believe that, if you will,' said Geoffrey, sensing he would not make her change her mind, no matter how eloquently he put his case. He had known it was only a matter of time before they quarrelled, because they always did, despite his affection for her. 'But I will prove you wrong. However, I need you to help me. Your life may depend on it – Olivier's, too.'

'Olivier!' said Joan, tears in her eyes. 'You know he is the only man I care about, so he is the one you choose to threaten. I wish you had never come back from the Holy Land!'

'Joan,' said Geoffrey with quiet reason, thinking their row had gone too far, and it was time to bring it back to a civilized level. 'Just tell me what you know about the silver. It may be important, because it relates to Barcwit. I have been inclined to dismiss it, but now I am not sure that is wise.'

'You will not find it. Men have been looking ever since it was stolen, but not a trace has been found. Ask Bloet: he is here to get it for the King, but he will no more succeed than the rest of us.'

'You looked for it, too?'

'With Peter and Idonea.'

'You are not the kind of person to race off blindly with a spade,' said Geoffrey. 'And that means you must have known something that told you how to narrow your search. What?'

She grimaced. 'You are too astute for your own good. Peter heard a rumour that it had been dumped in the river near the village of Beiminstre, and that the thieves intended to retrieve it later, when the hue and cry had died down. We hired men to dive for it, intending to offer it to the King in exchange for our pardon. But the rumour was no more true than the one that said God had taken it to punish Barcwit for his greed. So, now you know everything. Are you satisfied?'

Her confession had told him nothing helpful, and he was simultaneously disappointed and worried. She mistook his silence for something else entirely.

'You will die if you try to find Barcwit's silver and keep it for yourself. Someone will kill you.'

'Who?' asked Geoffrey, not liking the fact that her voice carried the hint of a threat. He was unable to keep the disdain from his voice when he glanced at her husband. 'Olivier?'

His tone was not lost on Joan, and when she spoke she was furious. 'Olivier is worth ten of you. You have no friends here, Geoffrey. You are alone, and surrounded by folk who want you dead.'

'I know,' said Geoffrey with a sigh. 'I seem to spend my whole life in this situation.'

Geoffrey woke early the next day. It was November grey, with fine drizzle in the air and fog around the river. He felt confined and restless in the castle, and Joan was still angry with him, so he decided to take his horse for another ride outside the town. Since Durand was asleep, he saddled it himself, noting the straps were becoming worn in places, and that the squire should have replaced them.

When he had finished, he stroked his horse's nose. The animal was showing signs of age: there were grey flecks on its muzzle, and its coat was coarser than he remembered. There was also a dull look in its eyes that he did not like. He had not ridden it in a proper battle for two years, and he wondered how well it would perform when he did it again. Selling it in favour of a younger mount was not a prospect he relished. It took a long time to train them, and he liked the one he had.

He led it outside, climbed into the saddle, then headed towards the Avon, where a road called Wortheslupe ran towards the Bristol Bridge. He paid his toll and clattered

196

across it, riding until he reached a junction. Ahead was a knoll of red cliffs topped by a church, so he took the road to the right, not knowing where it went, but not really caring as long as it did not lead to Estune's bogs.

The track was not in good repair, and had flooded during the recent rains. He let his horse find its own pace, not surprised that it chose a leisurely amble, as opposed to the energetic gallop it might have enjoyed a couple of years before. He was used to seeing its ears pricked forward when he rode, and was unsettled by the fact that now they flicked back and forth listlessly.

His dog trotted at his side, stopping occasionally to sniff the undergrowth and leave its mark behind. Geoffrey's mood was gloomy as he reviewed his situation. He was a knight whose lord had dismissed him, with an ageing warhorse, a dog that stole, and a family comprising one sister who was suspicious of his honourable intentions. He had no wife, nor any prospect of one, and the Mappestone clan had neglected to produce any heirs to succeed them; his brother Henry's sons had died of an ague the previous year.

It was a depressing state of affairs, so he turned his thoughts to what Joan had told him the previous day – that Barcwit had killed their brother as a way to keep her in line. Henry had been found dead one morning with a knife in his stomach. Geoffrey had asked whether the death of his children had unhinged him, but Olivier claimed he had not been very fond of them anyway, because they were too similar to himself. There were no witnesses to Henry's death, and Joan was adamant that Barcwit had sent a silent-footed killer who had done his work quickly and left no clues.

He turned his thoughts to Alwold. Perhaps Joan had been wise to hunt for the silver in order to bribe Henry – and the same would work for Geoffrey himself when Giffard arrived and learnt he had uncovered nothing of importance. He considered the mysterious Piers, then recalled something else Alwold had said. He had claimed that the 'priest of St John's' was party to 'the secret'. Feoc was the priest of St John the Baptist's. Did that mean Feoc knew the whereabouts of the silver? And if so, then had the man befriended Joan as part of a plot to keep the ingots hidden, by leading the King's agent astray with false information? Feoc seemed honest, but Geoffrey had encountered some very skilled liars, and knew better than to trust someone on the basis of a single meeting.

The sounds of the town were soon behind him – the yells of traders, the clatter of carts, the clang of bells, and the metallic thump of the masons at work on the castle walls. The sounds of the country took their place, and Geoffrey could hear the sharp, sweet trill of larks, the wind hissing in the trees and the gurgle of the river to his right. It was pleasant, and his spirits began to rise. Soon he reached a crossroads overlooked by a hillock. The mound was surmounted by a substantial church, and the houses that clustered around it were affluent and well tended. It was a pretty place, with its gurgling brook and grassy meadows. The only odd thing was that it was wholly devoid of people.

Suddenly, there was a hissing sound that he recognized instantly: an arrow being loosed. He hauled his shield from its clip on his saddle, but he had not anticipated an attack and it was too firmly set to be hoisted fast. Fortunately, the quarrel sailed over his head, but the next one went through his saddle, causing his horse to scream in agony. He jabbed his heels into its sides, intending to thunder through the settlement and away from the ambush, but the animal was in trouble. It took one or two unsteady steps, then another arrow scorched across its flank.

It whinnied in pain, flailing with its front hoofs and almost dislodging him. Another quarrel struck his helmet, and when it glanced off he felt it scour a line down his cheek. His horse was not going to save him, and he knew he would be shot like a cornered stag if he stayed where he was. He hurled himself out of the saddle, rolling across the ground to let the momentum help him to his feet. Instinct told him that the arrows were coming from the house next to the church, and that he would be shot if he tried to run away. There was only one option. Holding his shield in front of him, he powered towards his attackers.

The hail of arrows petered out as he drew nearer, but he did not stop. When he reached the door he lowered his shield and used it as a battering ram. The whole frame tore clean from the wall and toppled inwards. With a bloodcurdling battle cry, he followed it, hauling his broadsword from his belt and preparing to fight whoever was inside. His blood was up, and he felt nothing but blind fury that the horse which had carried him to Jerusalem should be slaughtered so meanly.

But when he exploded into the dark interior of the house, he stopped in confusion. Cowering in front of him were at least forty people, all clutching each other in terror. Two of the window shutters were ajar, and a couple of men, white-faced and trembling, stood near them with bows. A boy of eleven or twelve stood at a third window, holding a smaller weapon that had evidently been intended as a toy. A priest began to recite a final absolution in a voice that shook, and a baby started to cry. Geoffrey could tell from the expressions on their faces that they all thought they were going to die.

The room Geoffrey had invaded exuded an odour he recognized only too well: the rank stench of fear. The priest continued his prayers, and the familiar Latin, far from having a comforting effect on his people, served to frighten them all the more. Mothers hugged their babies, and one began to sob.

'What in God's name are you doing?' Geoffrey demanded, unnerved by the way they looked at him. He was sharply reminded of people who had huddled in their houses after the Fall of Jerusalem, before they had been massacred. It was not a pleasant memory, and he was unsettled by the fact that the faces in the village near Bristol brought it so vividly to his mind.

'We were only trying to protect ourselves,' whispered the priest. 'We almost succeeded.'

'You did not!' snapped Geoffrey, unwilling to admit it had been a close shave. He waved his sword at the two men and the boy with bows. 'And put those down, before I chop off your bloody hands!'

'Do not swear!' admonished the priest. 'There are women and children here.'

'I shall swear all I like,' shouted Geoffrey, still furious. 'Look what you have done to my horse!'

'We were aiming at you; we did not mean to hurt the horse,' said the boy apologetically, before a woman – his mother judging by the resemblance between them – poked him sharply.

'Well, that is all right, then,' said Geoffrey sarcastically. 'All is forgiven.'

'Really?' asked the boy brightly. 'That is good. I like it here in Beiminstre, and Father Wido says I am not ready for Heaven just yet.'

'Is that so?' Geoffrey glanced out of the door to see his horse standing with its head down and its flanks quivering in a way that alarmed him. 'Then that is too damned bad, because I am tempted to run the lot of you through right now. You have injured my horse.'

He was not very proud of himself when several children started to cry. He closed his eyes and lowered his sword, feeling the anger drain away from him, leaving only a sick disgust.

'If you spare us, I will see to your mount,' offered the boy. 'I will have him right in no time.'

'Stay away from him,' ordered Geoffrey. 'You have done enough damage, and he is too valuable to be tampered with by the likes of you.'

'But this is Beiminstre,' said Father Wido, sounding surprised that Geoffrey should make such a comment. 'Men travel for miles to have their horses tended by us, and Kea here has a rare talent.'

'You can have anything you want, if you let us live,' said Kea's mother. She glanced at the others, and received desperate nods of encouragement. 'The pick of ponies in our stables – as many as you like. We had a good harvest, too, and you can have some grain. We only ask for our lives.'

'I have a doll,' said a small child tearfully. 'You can have her, too – and she has real hair.'

'God's teeth!' muttered Geoffrey, discomfited. He had little experience in dealing with peasants, especially children, and felt himself hopelessly out of his depth. 'I am not going to kill anyone.'

'You said you were,' said Kea accusingly. He put a comforting arm around the smaller child, and Geoffrey supposed they were brother and sister.

'I have changed my mind,' replied Geoffrey shortly. 'But what were you thinking of, opening fire on harmless passers-by? If the King catches you doing it, he will not be so merciful.'

'We would not shoot the *King*,' said Kea scornfully. 'We would never ambush anyone wearing a crown. But we thought you came from *him*, and we were trying to protect ourselves. We do not want to be slaughtered without putting up a bit of a fight.'

'Who?' asked Geoffrey. He recalled Peter saying that Nauntel had been murdered in a place called Beiminstre. 'Sir Peter de la Mare, to avenge the death of his friend?'

'Sir Peter would not harm us,' said Kea. 'His wife might, though. She is quite a warrior.'

'We thought you were from Barcwit,' explained Kea's mother. Her voice dropped to a whisper when she spoke the name, and several villagers crossed themselves.

'We have been anticipating a visit from his henchmen ever since Nauntel was killed,' added Wido. 'Nauntel was one of his investors, and he was said to have been vexed when he was murdered here.'

Geoffrey was confused. 'I was under the impression Barcwit ordered Nauntel's death himself. How can he be angry with you, when Nauntel was attacked on his own command?' He regarded them uneasily. 'Or did he hire you to frighten him, and you killed him by mistake?'

'Of course not,' said Kea's mother indignantly. 'Barcwit has his own louts for that sort of thing and, besides, we are not very good with bows.'

'My horse would not agree,' Geoffrey pointed out, glancing at it again.

'There is no understanding Barcwit,' said Wido, hastily leading the discussion away from the subject of Geoffrey's stricken mount. 'He is not sane, and often issues contradictory orders. Poor Sir Peter. He wept for hours when Nauntel was shot, claiming *he* should have been the one to die.'

'Is that what Barcwit intended, and the archer hit the wrong man?' asked Geoffrey. He knew such things could happen; knights were often difficult to tell apart when they wore cloaks and armour.

'I doubt it,' said Wido. 'Peter is worth more to Barcwit than Nauntel, because he is the constable.'

'I still do not understand what Nauntel's death has to do with you,' said Geoffrey. 'Or why you should think Barcwit wants to punish you for it.'

'Nor do we, but you cannot be too careful where Barcwit is concerned,' replied Wido. 'Nauntel died here, in Beiminstre, and Barcwit is the kind of man to say that is more than enough to have us all slaughtered. He ate a family once, just because they happened to be standing outside his house.'

Kea had been gazing through the shattered door at Geoffrey's horse. He pushed past the knight and started to walk towards it; Geoffrey followed, not sure what the boy intended to do, but unwilling to leave him alone to do it. The rest of the villagers stood in a silent circle as Kea ran gentle hands over the horse's flanks, assessing the extent of its injuries.

'Back to your post, Ned,' said Father Wido to a man with long teeth, while they awaited Kea's verdict. 'You, too, Theordic. It would be a shame to escape death at the hands of one man, only to allow others to catch us unawares.'

The designated lookouts collected their bows before disappearing in opposite directions. Geoffrey watched them go, wondering how many more travellers would fall victim to their nervous weapons before Barcwit's empire crumbled. He removed his helmet and touched the scratch on his face. It stung, and Roger would be sure to ask how he had come by it. He did not relish the prospect of telling him he had been ambushed by forty frightened peasants, all of whom seemed to take orders from an eleven-year-old boy. He hoped he would be able to fabricate a story that did not make him sound too foolish before he arrived back in Bristol.

'You cannot blame us for shooting,' said Kea as he worked. 'You look dangerous with that funny mark on your surcoat.'

'It is a Crusader's cross,' explained Geoffrey. It was unusual to find folk who did not recognize the distinctive garb of a *Jerosolimitanus*. 'I was at the Fall of Jerusalem.'

'Did it do much damage?' asked Kea politely.

Geoffrey regarded him warily. 'Did what do much damage?'

'Jerusalem,' said Kea patiently. 'When it fell. I hope it did not land on any horses.'

'No,' said Geoffrey, fighting not to smile. 'It did not.'

Kea straightened up. 'This poor animal has been very badly used.'

'I know,' said Geoffrey dryly. 'Someone shot him.'

'I do not mean the arrow wounds,' said Kea. 'Those will heal without lasting damage. I am talking about his general care. He needs warmed barley mash and a good daily combing, sweet hay—'

'I have a squire,' interrupted Geoffrey. 'He takes care of those things.'

'Then he does not do it very well,' said Kea disdainfully. Geoffrey studied the animal, again noting its lustreless eyes and the slight discharge around its nostrils. Was Durand's poor care the reason it had aged so suddenly, and why it walked rather than galloped? 'But leave this beast with me, and in a week I will have him better than new.'

'Leave him?' echoed Geoffrey, aghast. 'What am I supposed to ride in the meantime? My dog?'

Several of the children burst out laughing, oblivious to the irritation in his voice. As if it knew it was being talked about, the dog released a low, piteous whine, which made several adults smile, too. Geoffrey was becoming exasperated, thinking he had better things to do than be a source of entertainment for half-witted villagers who had not even heard of the Crusade.

'You can borrow one of our horses,' offered Kea's mother. 'We have some very fine ones, and in a week, you can come back and collect your own. That is what we agreed, back there in the priest's house. The people of Beiminstre never go back on what they say.'

There was a murmur of assent, and several of them stood a little taller.

'But first, you must visit our church,' offered Wido, obviously out to impress now the danger was over. 'It is the finest in the county. You cannot leave without seeing it, because we do not want it said that the people of Beiminstre have no manners.'

'Then you should refrain from shooting at your visitors,' retorted Geoffrey, but no one was listening. People were delighted by an opportunity to show off their assets, and he found himself manhandled in the direction of the church on its little hill. It took a long time for him to be shown round. The building was scrupulously clean: its windowsills were swept and adorned with fresh greenery, and there was not a cobweb in sight. Many of the carvings were of a very high standard, and he was genuinely impressed by the beautiful chancel and its impressive Saxon arches. Eventually, he followed them to a large stable that was well endowed with horses, some of which were far better than his own. He was astonished, but then recalled that Olivier bought horses from a village near Bristol, and he was a good judge of such matters.

'Olivier d'Alençon,' he said. 'He comes here.'

Kea nodded. 'Did he recommend us to you? Is that why you rode this way?'

'He is my brother by marriage.'

Kea's face split into a grin. 'Then you know Dame Joanie. She is good with my little sister, who is simple-minded. The Dame is a beautiful lady.'

'Joan?' asked Geoffrey, bemused by the unfamiliar name, and certainly by the description. He had never heard anyone call Joan 'beautiful', not even Olivier when deep in his cups. He regarded the boy carefully, not sure whether he was jesting. 'Do you not find her a little . . . intimidating?'

'Joan?' asked Wido, startled. 'Of course not! She is the kindest and gentlest woman in the world, and she is greatly loved here.'

'Joan?' echoed Geoffrey again, not sure they were talking about the same woman.

'Dame Joanie,' said Kea firmly. 'And do not think to slander that good lady's name, or we shall begin to wish we had killed you after all.'

Ten

Geoffrey took leave of the people of Beiminstre, and rode towards Bristol on a vigorous, jet-black horse that Kea claimed was the best they had. Geoffrey concurred. It was a magnificent animal, and he decided that if Kea was unable to heal his own, he would keep it. He gave it its head along the path by the river, exhilarated by its raw power. His dog was hard-pressed to keep up.

When they approached Bristol and he was obliged to share the road with others, he reined in and forced it to walk, although it did so reluctantly; it was an excellent horse, but needed training. His dog panted in an odd way as they slowed, as if through gritted teeth, and Geoffrey was concerned until he saw it held something in its mouth. At first, he thought it was a ferret, but with a sigh of annoyance, he saw it was a doll. He realized the animal had taken it from Kea's simple sister, probably by force.

He dismounted and tried to pull it away, but the dog's eyes took on the opaque, slightly manic look that usually preceded a bite. He took a piece of dried meat from his scrip and waved it until he was sure he had its interest. It dropped the doll and raised one paw in the air, but he knew it too well to give it the food and expect to be able to retrieve the toy, too: the dog fully intended to have both. He threw the meat a short distance away and the dog saw it would have to make a choice. Eventually, its stomach won the contest and Geoffrey rescued the doll.

It was not attractive, comprising a piece of wood that was twice as long as his hand, and a little wider than his palm. Its head was topped with a mass of matted fibre, probably horse-hair, and it wore a kirtle of filthy grey cloth. It was clearly loved, though, and it was with some dismay that Geoffrey saw it was peppered with tooth marks. He considered flinging it in the river, but it seemed a callous thing to do, so he shoved it in his saddlebag, and decided to ask Durand's advice. The squire was useless with horses, but might know how to repair toys. He might even be persuaded to sew it new clothes.

Geoffrey remounted and crossed the bridge into the town, intending to see whether Barcwit had returned from Dundreg. He was riding along the high street when he spotted Durand emerging from a tavern with Bloet. Bloet whispered something that made the squire emit a high-pitched giggle, accompanying his words with an obscene gesture that amused both of them. Their mirth was raucous enough to attract a disapproving stare from Clarembald.

'People still recall the excesses of William Rufus and his love for other men,' said the physician sternly, as the two men walked away. 'Your squire is a fool to flaunt his womanliness so openly.'

'I will speak to him,' said Geoffrey, supposing the physician might be right.

The *medicus* stared at the scratch on Geoffrey's face, where the arrow had grazed him. 'Since I am in the business of dispensing advice, heed this: abandon these solitary rides and concentrate on what you have been ordered to do. You do not want more arrows flying your way.'

Geoffrey gazed at him, wondering whether he had just been threatened or counselled. How did Clarembald know the scratch was caused by an arrow? Or was he a sufficiently good physician to tell just by looking? But surely Clarembald had nothing to do with the ambush in Beiminstre? He could not have known Geoffrey intended to ride that way, so could not have arranged for the villagers to shoot at him. Or had he? Geoffrey recalled it was Clarembald who had recommended against riding to Estune the previous day – advice he had ignored and suffered the muddy consequences. Had his real intention been to point him towards Beiminstre?

'I saw Helbye this morning,' Clarembald went on, when Geoffrey did not reply. His voice was suddenly gentle. 'His hip will never heal. He is an old man, and his bones are crusted

206

and lumpy with age. He rallied to ride from Bath, but it would be cruel to take him to the Holy Land. Can you not see the pain in his face as he tries to keep up with you?'

Geoffrey had, and did not need Clarembald to lecture him about it. 'He does not want to retire from my service, and I will not force him. It is his decision to make.'

'That is a coward's answer. But, if you will not take pity on him, there is a potion I can give to ease the agony when it becomes too hard to bear.'

'Like it did in Bath?' asked Geoffrey shortly.

'My poultice worked,' said Clarembald indignantly. 'I told him not to chase that pig, but he would not listen. He would have been ill a good deal longer if I had not treated him.'

'That was the night your bryony was stolen,' said Geoffrey flatly

Clarembald looked startled, then smiled craftily. 'Nothing was stolen. That was just something I made up, to annoy John. I have the bryony here.' He pulled a pot from his scrip, and Geoffrey could see it was full except for what had been used to make Helbye's poultice.

'None of it was taken?' he asked, to be sure.

'Not a speck,' confirmed Clarembald with a wolfish grin. 'Although my tale had the desired effect of embarrassing John and his beloved Bath. But remember what I say about Helbye. Any physician – with the exception of John, who does not know his arse from his elbow – will say the same. The incident in Bath was the first of many, and they will become more frequent and painful if you drag him around as though he was an agile youth.'

He turned and walked away, leaving Geoffrey with one less problem to solve, but another to worry about. He believed Clarembald's tale about fabricating the theft to annoy John, and he had seen that no bryony was missing – at least, not enough to lay Helbye low for five days. No one had harmed the old man to prevent Geoffrey from arriving in Bristol at the same time as his suspects, only Geoffrey himself with his carelessness. Helbye was understandably more willing to believe he had been poisoned than that he was suffering from a debilitating illness, but he was wrong. It had doubtless been excellent news to the moneyers that Geoffrey could not travel with them on the last leg of the journey, but they were innocent of bringing it about.

'What was he saying about me?' came a voice from Geoffrey's other side. It was Bishop John.

'That it looks like rain,' lied Geoffrey, not wanting to become involved in their feud.

John regarded him coolly. 'You should choose your friends with more care. The King will not be pleased to hear his agent has been seduced by the likes of Clarembald.'

Geoffrey sighed. 'Are you threatening me, too?'

'I am warning you.'

'Everyone is warning me these days. All I want is to learn the truth about Sendi and Barcwit, and leave. The rest is for Giffard to decide.'

'You are a fool if you think it is that simple. Everything that involves the King is complex and dangerous. So, I shall tell you once more: trust no one. Not even your family.'

Geoffrey stared at the bishop as he hurried away after his rival. Was he saying Joan might have a bigger role in the business than he had been led to believe, and that she would betray him? She had not mentioned their brother's death in her letters, even though it meant Geoffrey was now the heir to a considerable fortune. Was she telling the truth when she claimed she had not known how to break the news gently? Or had she remained quiet so she and Olivier could keep the estates for themselves while Geoffrey rode East, never to return? He closed his eyes and wondered what he had let himself in for when he had rallied so willingly to her rescue.

Geoffrey was in another world as he rode up the high street, worrying about Helbye and about the fact that the two physicians were now adding their voices to the clamour of warnings about his enquiry. He did not see Durand wave at him, and came out of his reverie only when he heard the squire's indignant squeal; he had almost ridden him down. Although the road was wide, nearly trampling Durand made him see that taking a large, untrained horse along it was unwise, especially when there were so many people waiting for him to make a mistake. He did not want someone pushed under its hoofs, so he could be accused of reckless riding. He dismounted and handed Durand the reins.

'Where did you get that?' Durand asked warily. 'It looks fierce – too fierce for me to look after.'

'You will manage,' said Geoffrey, hoping the squire did not treat it as poorly as he had the other one. He did not want to return it to Beiminstre in a shabby condition.

'Did you steal it?' asked Durand nervously. 'Should we anticipate furious owners after us? I am growing tired of people coming out of nowhere to warn me about this and about that.'

'You as well?' asked Geoffrey. 'Who?'

'The two physicians. Sendi and Rodbert. Even Bloet, although that was kindly meant.'

'You have not mentioned any of this before.'

'You would not have listened. You never pay attention to such things, and I did not think passing them on was worth the risk of you venting your temper on me.'

Geoffrey stared at him in surprise. He was sometimes angry with Durand, but it was invariably over something the squire had done himself, and he had never blamed him for things other people had said. Then it occurred to him that Durand had a very good reason for not passing on the messages: he had not wanted his master to be on his guard against attack.

'You want me dead,' he said, regarding him in distaste. 'You see that as the best way to escape from me. Bishop John was right: I *do* need to be careful of treachery from someone close.'

'Not true,' said Durand. 'I do not want you dead *here*, in this town. Who would protect me?'

'Go,' said Geoffrey, suddenly tired of the whole business. Durand regarded him uneasily. 'Go where?'

'Take the horse to the castle and ask Ulfrith to look after it. Take my dog, too; it is of a mind to steal today, and I do not want any more enemies. Then collect your belongings and leave.'

'But I do not want my freedom in Bristol,' objected Durand. 'I want it near the abbey of my choice, so I will not be forced to make dangerous journeys on my own.'

209

'Bloet will look after you,' said Geoffrey, continuing up the high street on foot. 'You will be safer with him than with me, especially here.' And, he thought, *he* might be safer without Durand. Their argument the previous day underlined how much Durand detested him, but he had not known the squire might try to bring about his death by remaining silent about the dangers he faced.

He passed the town centre, and headed for Barcwit's mint. Lessons had been learnt from his invasion the previous day, and a guard was outside, causing even more consternation among the townspeople than ever, with his surly, unsmiling presence. He demanded Geoffrey's business, then tapped on the door with his dagger. Colblac the clerk answered it, and showed Geoffrey into the office. It was oddly empty for a work day, with only Rodbert and Maude present.

Rodbert sighed when Geoffrey entered. 'I said we would send word when Barcwit agreed to see you.'

'He is back from Dundreg, then?' asked Geoffrey.

Maude glared at the deputy for admitting as much. 'He is busy with our annual accounts. They are complex, and he cannot be interrupted once he has started. They will take him at least three days.'

'I presume he is interrupted when he eats or sleeps?' asked Geoffrey, thinking that if Barcwit was indeed poring over figures, then it was strange he was not in the room that contained all his records. 'No one can keep at his sums for three days without stopping.'

'Barcwit is a remarkable man,' said Rodbert smugly.

'Why are the accounts so complex?' asked Geoffrey, finally riled into rudeness by their obstructive behaviour. 'Is it because there is so much tampering to do?'

Maude stared at him frostily. 'That is not a polite thing to say.'

Geoffrey shrugged. 'The charges against Barcwit are serious, and he would be wise to tell his side of the story while the King is still prepared to listen. Four charges were levelled against him – having a drunken *cambium*, making underweight coins, encouraging illegal investors and bullying the locals. So far, I have uncovered plenty of evidence to prove the last charge, and nothing to indicate the others are not true, too. Barcwit is in trouble, and he is not making matters any easier for himself.'

'Who says we bully the locals?' sneered Rodbert.

'He had Nauntel killed.' There was Geoffrey's own brother, too, according to Joan.

'You need *proof* to make these allegations,' said Maude scathingly. 'And you have none.'

Geoffrey's temper was beginning to wear thin. 'Tell Barcwit I will return tomorrow, when I *will* see him. If he knows what is good for him he will make no more excuses.'

'They are not excuses,' said Rodbert sulkily. 'They are reasons.'

Geoffrey left abruptly and walked to St Ewen's Church, which stood next door. He waited in its porch for a long time, still and watchful. Eventually, the guard trotted across the road and disappeared into the cemetery, fumbling with his underclothes. Geoffrey waited until he was out of sight, then strode to the door, opened it and slipped inside. He heard Maude and Rodbert talking in the office, and they were sufficiently engrossed with each other that they did not notice him slip past, heading for the vestibule at the end of the corridor. He cracked open the door and saw that Barcwit had taken his previous intrusion very much to heart, because there was a guard there, too.

The room to the left was still secured with heavy locks, while the stairs to the right had not been swept properly, and were thick with dusty footprints. But it was the door straight ahead that Geoffrey was interested in that day, the one that led to the mint. It was evidently not an afternoon for coin-making, because the hammering he had heard on previous occasions was stilled. There was a murmur of voices, and it sounded as if some sort of lecture was in progress. Hopeful that Barcwit might be the speaker, and that he would have the man at last, Geoffrey considered the problem of the guard.

He could have had a knife between the man's ribs before he had so much as turned around, but he did not want to kill a man for doing his job. Instead, he took his dagger from his belt and used it to scratch on the door. When the guard came to investigate, Geoffrey struck him on the head and caught him as he fell. Then he unlocked the room to the left with the guard's own keys, and hauled him inside. He glanced around curiously before re-locking the door, seeing piles of silver ingots and pots of blanks. There was a fortune in precious metal, and he was not surprised that Barcwit was careful with it.

As softly as he could, he pushed open the mint door and peered around it, expecting to see the moneyer giving instructions to his men. However, it was not Barcwit who was addressing his thirty or so labourers, but Tasso. Standing next to Tasso were two others Geoffrey recognized, neither of them folk he would have expected to see there. One was the silversmith in Sendi's retinue who was called Edric, and the other was Clarembald.

Standing to one side, simultaneously dominating the proceedings and remaining aloof, was a tall figure wearing a peculiar hooded cloak. The garment was unusually black, and the way it shielded its wearer's face was unsettling. All that could be seen under the cowl was the merest hint of a visage that was unnaturally pale. Geoffrey saw all the workmen, including Clarembald and Edric, glance uneasily at it from time to time, and knew there was only one man who could exude such a sinister aura just by standing with his hands in his sleeves. Barcwit. Geoffrey's attention was taken so completely by his first sight of the elusive coiner that he almost failed to notice what else was happening. Tasso finished speaking, and Clarembald took over.

'This curse will see us all in our graves,' the physician said, as if in conclusion to points made earlier. His orange brows beetled over his eyes to underline the fact that he was in earnest. 'I cannot stress too much the care you should take. But I will not belabour the point, since I see you appreciate the seriousness of the situation, so I shall bid you a good afternoon.'

Geoffrey only just managed to dart up the stairs before Clarembald bustled through the hallway. Only when the front door eventually closed behind him, did the knight emerge from his hiding place. Tasso was reiterating what Clarembald had said, but in far more colourful terms and peppered with a good many threats. The men nodded keenly, muttering that they understood, although their eyes were on Barcwit when they spoke. Edric seemed particularly willing to please, and smiled and bowed in eager supplication. Then everything happened very quickly.

Without any warning, Tasso drew his sword and, in one single motion, lifted it into the air and brought it down with all his might on to Edric's skull, splitting it in half to the neck.

For a moment, Geoffrey was too stunned to do anything more than watch as Edric fell to the ground in a fountain of blood. The workmen jumped in alarm, although none protested Tasso's action. Barcwit did not react at all. He simply stood and watched.

It was not the violence of the execution that unsettled Geoffrey – he had witnessed more than his share of bloody death – but Barcwit's composure. Tasso wiped his sword and put it away, while the workmen were utterly silent, as if they were afraid they might be next. Geoffrey had seen enough, and did not feel like interviewing the moneyer when he was of a mind to order gruesome murders. He turned to walk back the way he had come.

He had almost reached the front door when he saw the latch begin to rise. Someone was coming in. Since he did not want to be caught trying to leave, suspecting that Barcwit would try to kill any outside witnesses to Edric's murder, he strode into the office instead. He did so confidently, in the hope that Rodbert and Maude would not realize he had come from the back of the house, rather than the front.

Rodbert looked up when he burst in. 'I did not hear you knock.'

'The noise from your mint must have drowned it,' said Geoffrey, wondering whether Rodbert would admit that work had ground to a halt while one of his rivals was killed. He could not imagine what Edric was doing there in the first place, since Alwold and Fardin had already been murdered as part of the ongoing feud, and even the most stupid of men should have known to be careful.

Maude cocked her head and listened. 'They have stopped for their afternoon bread and ale.'

Geoffrey studied them both, trying to assess whether they knew what had happened to Edric, but could read nothing pertinent in the expression of either. Either they did not know about Edric's fate, or they were exceptionally cool and cunning. He had a bad feeling that the latter was true, and that he was facing some particularly ruthless criminals.

'I saw Barcwit at the upstairs window,' he lied, as Colblac bustled in carrying new supplies of ink. It had been him opening the front door. 'If he has time to stare into the street, then he has time to spend a few moments with me.'

'He has just slipped out for a while – to pray for success with his accounting,' said Maude, moving towards him and standing needlessly close. 'He is a devout man, and I do not know when he might be back. Would you like to come upstairs with me, and see for yourself that he is not here?'

'Which church?' asked Geoffrey. The sinister man in black did not look like a Christian to him, and he was surprised Maude should fabricate such an excuse.

'A man's prayers are between him and God,' said Rodbert firmly. 'We will not be the ones responsible for interrupting them.'

'I was thinking of claiming that honour myself,' said Geoffrey. 'Giffard will be here soon, and if I have not spoken to Barcwit by then, the case will be decided in Sendi's favour.'

Maude gave one of her secret smiles. 'I doubt that.'

'Why?'

'Because of the way matters will be resolved,' she said enigmatically. 'But Barcwit is not here, and it is no use scouring churches for him. He prays like he does everything else – privately.'

Geoffrey had had enough of Barcwit's mint and the liars and killers who inhabited it. He bowed to Maude, nodded to Rodbert, and stalked out. Once outside, he closed his eyes, took a deep breath and congratulated himself on his escape, although he was under no illusion that his invasion would remain undetected for long. They would find the stunned guard, recall Geoffrey's sudden appearance, and draw the obvious conclusion. Would they also guess he had witnessed Edric's murder?

He thought about what he had seen. Was Clarembald more than an investor, and why was he lecturing about the 'dangers of the situation' to Barcwit's workforce? What was Edric doing there? He had not seemed alarmed by the fact that he was in the heart of his enemy's empire, nor had he flinched when Tasso had drawn his sword: he had not expected the attack.

Questions clamoured at Geoffrey as he headed for St Ewen's Church, the closest refuge for some quiet thinking. The building was simple: aisleless with a thatched roof. An altar provided the only furniture and two men knelt at it. Bishop John started guiltily when he saw Geoffrey, although Bloet seemed sanguine about the intrusion.

'We are praying for Alwold,' said John. Geoffrey noticed the startled look Bloet shot him.

'Alwold,' mused Geoffrey. 'He died mumbling about the silver Bloet is charged to find.'

Bloet's voice was bitter. 'I wish the man had held his tongue. His deathbed confession was what started Henry thinking there was a chance of retrieving the stuff, and it is obvious there is none.'

'Is that what you are doing here?' asked Geoffrey. 'Discussing silver?'

John opened his mouth to deny it, but Bloet spoke first. 'What else? John tells me Clarembald knows more than he is telling. I hope to God he is right, because I have damned all else to go on.'

'How have you reached that conclusion?' Geoffrey asked of John.

The bishop looked shifty. 'Clarembald was near Alwold when he died, and I believe he overheard something no one else did. That is why he is everywhere – a supporter of Barcwit, a friend of Sendi, a comrade of Warelwast . . .'

Geoffrey agreed there was something suspicious about Clarembald, particularly given what he had just witnessed, but knew for a fact that it was nothing to do with hearing Alwold. Only Geoffrey knew that 'the secret' lay with the priest of St John's, and that the King, Bloet and Warelwast were party to it. Except, of course, that they were not. Assuming that 'the secret' and the missing silver were one and the same, the King did not know where it was, or he would not have commissioned Bloet to find it, and Bloet did not know, or he would not still be looking. That left Warelwast. Could he have unravelled the mystery? Geoffrey would not have been surprised.

'So, we have been discussing ways to make Clarembald confide in us,' said Bloet. 'All I want is the silver, and all John wants is Clarembald disgraced. But we cannot agree on a strategy.'

'What about Piers?' asked Geoffrey, while John winced at Bloet's bald revelations. 'Have you found him yet? He may be able to help you.'

'Piers is dead,' said Bloet miserably. 'He was an anchorite who lived near Dundreg, but he recently drowned in the marshes. Feoc told me today.'

Geoffrey stared at him. Dundreg was one of Barcwit's haunts. Was it coincidence or had Piers been murdered by him? And why had Feoc not mentioned the hermit when Geoffrey had asked?

'All roads lead to Barcwit,' he mused. 'You are even in his church.'

John barked a bitter laugh. 'Barcwit prays to no God of ours! Surely you have seen him at night, stalking the streets in that billowing black cloak as he goes to meet his friend the Devil?'

'I wish I had. He is a difficult man to pin down and I need to talk to him.'

'If only I could say the same,' said Bloet unhappily. 'He is everywhere *I* look. He is probably hoping I will find the silver, so he can get it back before I can give it to the King.'

'You dined with him recently,' said Geoffrey. 'Durand told me.'

'I most certainly did not! I drank a cup of wine at his house, but that was at Rodbert's invitation and Barcwit did not appear, thank God!'

'But Durand said—'

'I lied to impress him,' said Bloet impatiently. 'It does not do to tell your new lover that you are afraid of men in black cloaks. Have you heard about Sendi's stolen die? Clarembald has charged Bishop John with taking it; everyone else thinks Barcwit is responsible.'

'Clarembald accuses me of everything,' said John angrily. 'And I am growing sick of it. It is time we stopped the man's mouth once and for all, by proving to everyone that he is not to be trusted.'

Geoffrey wondered what John would say if he knew about Clarembald's role in Edric's death.

'I hate this place,' said Bloet feelingly. 'All corruption and nastiness. And no silver.'

John brightened. 'We are all miserable and in need of something to put the smiles back on our faces. I know just the thing to reduce our excesses of choler and black bile.'

'What?' asked Bloet glumly. 'Ale? Wine? I have tried them, and they only work temporarily. My problems are even greater when their effects wear off, because I have a sore head to contend with, too.'

'Better than even the best of wines,' declared John grandly. 'We shall go shopping.'

It was not easy to persuade the Bishop of Bath that he detested exploring markets – John did not believe such a thing was possible – and it was some time before Geoffrey managed to escape. Bloet was less fortunate, and was dragged away to spend the rest of the day inspecting trinkets. Geoffrey was frustrated, feeling his investigation was no further along than it had been when he had arrived three days before, but did not know what to do about it. There was no point in returning to Barcwit's mint, and he could think of nothing new to ask Sendi. He wandered aimlessly until he found himself at the Church of St John the Baptist, which reminded him that Feoc had lied to him about Piers.

The chapel was empty, so he went to the ramshackle house that stood behind it. Feoc and his wife were in the garden, digging their vegetable patch, while their children picked stones from the soil and set them in piles to use against marauding birds the following spring. When she saw Geoffrey, Feoc's wife shrieked. Feoc's face darkened when he saw the cause of her concern. He stormed across his cabbages, grabbed

Geoffrey by the arm, and hustled him back to the church in a way that made the knight consider drawing his sword. He did not like being manhandled, even by priests.

'I told you never to come to my home,' Feoc snapped, glancing both ways down the street before slamming the door. 'You have too many enemies: Barcwit *and* Sendi; Maude, Rodbert and Tasso; Adelise and Lifwine; the two physicians. Meanwhile, Warelwast dogs your every move; Bloet suspects you are after the silver he has been charged to find; Peter de la Mare and Idonea believe your investigation will destroy them; Joan and Olivier—'

'Enough!' shouted Geoffrey. 'I can keep a tally of whom I have offended myself, thank you. Am I to assume that your name should be added to it? Or will you answer my questions?'

Feoc glared. 'Ask them, then.'

Geoffrey was suspicious. 'You are oddly helpful. Has someone ordered you to co-operate?'

'No.' Feoc's expression was furious. 'Now look what you have done! You made me lie in church.'

'You lied of your own volition.' Geoffrey would have been amused by the childish abrogation of responsibility if he had not been so angry. 'Who ordered you to help me? Joan? What did she do? Threaten you? Bribe you?'

'She promised to take my two oldest children into her service,' admitted Feoc, evidently unwilling to compound the sin of false witness any further. 'I cannot afford to look after them all, so it is a generous offer. She is a good woman; they will be safe with her.'

'Help me, then,' said Geoffrey. It did not sound like a particularly sinister arrangement, although he could not be sure whether Joan – or Feoc for that matter – had made it to help or hinder him. 'Let us start with this missing silver. Your name – "the priest of St John's" – was on Alwold's lips as he died. How do you explain that?'

'He must have been talking about the previous incumbent – or about another St John's. How do you know what Alwold said anyway? And why has no one mentioned these "last words" before?'

218

'How many years have you been here?' asked Geoffrey, ignoring his questions.

'Twenty-six.'

'Then Alwold was unlikely to have meant your predecessor. Is there another St John's in Bristol?'

'No,' admitted Feoc. 'But you know how rumours distort with the telling. Alwold must have said something else – the priest of St Mary's, perhaps, or St Peter's.'

'What about Piers?' asked Geoffrey, who knew what he had heard. 'Who is he?'

'I have already told you – and Bloet and Warelwast and Clarembald and just about everyone else in the town. I do not know a man called Piers who lives in Bristol.'

'What about one who lives in Dundreg?'

'Piers the anchorite?' asked Feoc. 'He would have nothing to do with silver. Besides, he is dead.'

'Did Barcwit kill him?'

'He recited himself a requiem mass, and walked to his death because he said an angel told him to do so. Even Piers could not mistake Barcwit for an angel. The anchorite was not your man.'

Geoffrey studied the priest carefully, and sensed he was telling the truth about the hermit – or, at least, the truth as he saw it – and it was impossible to say whether there was anything sinister about the anchorite's death without more information. He apologized for invading Feoc's house, and left. He had only taken a few steps when he became aware that he was being followed. Nonchalantly, he strolled back to the church, closed the door and stood behind it. Within moments, it opened slightly, and someone tried to peer through the gap. Geoffrey jumped forward, grabbed the spy and hauled him inside. It was Warelwast.

'There are rumours that you were attacked in Beiminstre earlier today,' said Warelwast, his alarm evaporating when he recognized his assailant. 'You returned with a different horse, so I assume it is true. I would be a poor friend if I did not reassure myself that you are unharmed.'

'By sneaking around after me?' Geoffrey was not convinced.

'You send me away if I escort you openly.'

That was true, at least. 'How did you find out about the ambush?'

'It is difficult to keep such things quiet for long, and Beiminstre is a village of forty people.'

Geoffrey did not believe him. 'Did you follow me? My own horse is slow, and it would not have been difficult to pursue me on foot – although not so easy coming back, when you would have been left behind.' It would explain why Warelwast had only just managed to track him down.

The bishop-elect sighed. 'You are overly suspicious; your sister says you have even accused *her* of shady dealings. I am only here in case you need a friend.' He gazed meaningfully at the scratch on the knight's face.

'Your logic is flawed, My Lord Bishop. On the one hand you say I am overly suspicious, and on the other you claim I need your protection. Which is it?'

Warelwast considered carefully before replying. 'Your investigation has made you unpopular, and you need all the friends you can get, so do not be so ready to distrust those who mean you well.'

'That is the problem,' said Geoffrey, thinking about Durand and his failure to pass on warnings, and about Joan's predictions that he would die. 'It is difficult to tell them apart. But if you want to help, you can find some way to appease Joan for me.'

Warelwast was thoughtful. 'That is a challenging task. Still, I will do it, if that is what you want. I shall have her all smiles and simpers by this evening.'

'God's teeth!' muttered Geoffrey as he left. 'What have I done to deserve this?'

'Talking to yourself?'

Geoffrey spun around in alarm when Maude emerged from behind a pillar. She moved sinuously, like a cat, and he wondered how long she had been there. It was clear she had overheard his discussion with Warelwast, but had she also heard what he had said to Feoc? If so, had he put the priest in danger? He was furious with himself for not searching the church before they had started talking.

'Have you been here long?' he asked, trying to sound casual.

She walked towards him, hips swaying provocatively. 'Long enough. I like this church. Too many are gaudily painted these days, and I like the clean whiteness of the walls in here.'

Geoffrey disagreed. 'They look bald. And plain plaster shows up the cracks.'

'Is that a bad thing? Do you think it is better to disguise rot and decay with bright colours, rather than to expose them, so they can be treated?'

Geoffrey was not sure whether they were now discussing architecture or something entirely different. 'It depends,' he replied cautiously.

'On what? The colours used? The skill of the artist? They are irrelevant if the building crumbles.'

'Did you want something from me?' he asked, wanting an end to the ambiguous discussion.

She smiled seductively. 'I thought we could . . . talk.'

'Good,' said Geoffrey. 'Then answer me this: did your husband have anything to do with the murder of my brother? My sister believes he did.'

Maude's eyebrows rose in amusement. 'How could Barcwit harm a member of your family when they live so far away? My husband is a determined man, but he has limitations, and racing across the country to commit murder is most definitely well past them. So, now we have resolved that, shall we talk about something else?'

'Willingly,' said Geoffrey, not sure whether to believe her, 'if Barcwit joins us. I have been in Bristol for three days now, and I still have not spoken to him.'

'No,' said Maude. 'Just you and me, tomorrow night. This is a pleasant place, and its doors are always open. Come at midnight.'

'And what will we talk about?' asked Geoffrey warily. 'The benefits of murals over plain walls?'

'If you like. Or we could find other ways to occupy ourselves. I have missed you since our encounter in Bath.'

'So has your dagger, I imagine,' said Geoffrey dryly.

'Do not be resentful. If you come to meet me, I will give you something worth your while, something that will help you in the investigation that is at a complete standstill.'

'What?'

She smiled again. 'You must wait and see,' she said, before opening the door and slipping outside.

Geoffrey thought about Maude's invitation as he left the church, noting that there was already no sign of her, even though he was no more than a moment behind. It was almost as if she travelled using different streets to the ones he knew. He stared carefully in both directions, and even explored the churchyard, but she had gone.

Her comment about his lack of progress had annoyed him, because it was true. Should he meet her, in the hope that he would learn something to start him moving again? Why was she unwilling to talk during the day? Was it because she had had enough of Barcwit, and wanted to break away from him? Or was her intention to lure Geoffrey somewhere he could be quietly dispatched and the murder blamed on Sendi? He suspected she had a multitude of lovers, and was not so vain as to imagine she wanted him for a repeat of their pleasures in Bath.

The sun was setting, and there was no more than an hour of daylight left. He was tired after his exertions, but did not feel like returning to the castle. He removed his helmet, which was chafing the scratch on his cheek, and tucked it under his arm. As he walked, he became aware of a familiar hammering sound, and realized he was near Sendi's mint. He decided to pay him a visit, because he had nothing else to do, and there was always the chance that an unexpected invasion might reveal something incriminating – as it had done with Barcwit.

Sendi's workshop was busy. Geoffrey could smell the metallic odour of hot silver, and the ground shook with the fury of industry. He thought about Edric, suspecting they would not yet know what had happened to him, and wondered how long it would be before they were worried. He rapped loudly on the door, which was answered by Adelise.

'It is the King's ferret,' she said coldly. 'Come to twist our honest words into lies again.'

'I have come to ask whether you have spoken to Barcwit

since you returned from Westminster,' he said, refusing to let her annoy him.

She gestured that he was to enter, then repeated his question to Sendi, who was bending over a bench laden with newly minted pennies. Lifwine sat next to him, tossing them carelessly in one hand while writing with the other. Geoffrey did not think the *cambium* was doing a particularly assiduous job with his assaying, and he wondered whether Barcwit's drunkard was any better.

Sendi did not look up when he replied. 'No. Why should I?'

'Neither have I,' said Geoffrey. 'Although it is not from want of trying. The man is elusive.'

Sendi gave a snort of disgust. 'He is visible when it suits him. He just does not want to see *you*.'

'What does he look like?' asked Geoffrey, wondering whether he might have passed him on the street and not known it. Barcwit was large and favoured dark clothes, but Geoffrey had not seen his face when he had presided over Edric's murder. For all he knew, the moneyer disguised himself with bright colours and blended in with the crowd when he did not feel like being noticed.

Adelise replied. 'Tall and bony. Nasty face, full of scars from where hot silver once splashed him.'

'That happened when his apprentices dashed burning coals in his eyes,' said Sendi. 'In revenge, he killed them with his bare hands and melted their bodies in his furnaces.'

'His furnaces are not large enough to consume human corpses,' said Geoffrey, recalling what he had seen when he had spied.

Sendi regarded him with renewed interest. 'You have been inside his mint? You did well: he does not normally let strangers in. What was he doing? Did you speak to his *cambium*?'

'Have *you* seen his *cambium*?' countered Geoffrey.

'Not since we returned from Westminster,' said Sendi. 'I imagine he is in some cellar, constantly supplied with wine. That's how they keep him quiet. Do not believe any tales they tell you about him visiting his ailing mother. She is in better health than all of us put together.'

'Edric,' said Geoffrey, watching Sendi and Adelise carefully. 'Where is he?'

'Gone,' replied Sendi. 'We discovered this morning that he has been betraying us, so we dismissed him. He has gone to Bath, to try his luck with Osmaer, although I doubt he will be taken on. We refused to write testaments to his honesty.'

'What did he do?' asked Geoffrey, not hiding his surprise. He recalled the atmosphere of suspicion and mistrust he had sensed on his first visit; they had known then there was a traitor in their midst.

'He passed secrets to Barcwit and stole one of our dies,' said Sendi angrily. 'Do you know what will happen if that falls into Barcwit's hands? He will use it to make bad coins with *my* name on.'

'Then he will be caught,' said Geoffrey. 'Even he cannot expect to get away with forgery while the King and his agents are watching.'

'*You* will stop him, will you?' sneered Sendi. 'You cannot even engineer a meeting with the man.'

'How do you know Edric stole the die?' asked Geoffrey, puzzled by the accusation in the light of what he had seen at Barcwit's mint. Why would Tasso kill a man who had brought them such a prize? Was it because he had outlived his usefulness? Edric would not be able to steal other dies if Sendi had dismissed him.

'It could not have been anyone else,' said Adelise. 'Unless it was you.'

'It *could* have been him,' said Lifwine, regarding Geoffrey appraisingly. 'He is the only stranger to have visited our premises for weeks, and it *did* go missing the day he came here.'

'I did not take it,' said Geoffrey, who had known it was only a matter of time before that particular accusation was levelled. 'Why would I?'

'Because you want Barcwit to win this case,' said Adelise scornfully. 'And it is an excellent way to ensure he does – he will produce forged coins bearing Sendi's name, and claim *we* are the ones who have been defrauding the King.'

'That is right,' agreed Lifwine. 'Geoffrey stole the die for two reasons: to let Barcwit destroy us with counterfeit coins, and to make us look inefficient and stupid in the King's eyes.'

Sendi drew his knife, and Adelise gestured to the listening workmen that they should do likewise. Within moments, Geoffrey was surrounded by at least twenty people, all wielding blades or heavy tools grabbed from the benches. And every man looked ready – eager, even – to use them.

Usually, Geoffrey would not have been concerned by the undisciplined mob that pressed around him, but Sendi's men were angry and sullen, and willing to defend the honour of their mint with their lives. Despite the fact that it had been Sendi's journey to Westminster that had precipitated the investigation, it was Geoffrey they held responsible, and he could see from the resentful expressions on their faces that they did not believe he would be fair. They were only too happy to vent their ire on the man they thought would support Barcwit and denounce them to the King.

'Put down your weapons,' he ordered, aware that they were behind him as well as in front, and that he was not wearing his helmet. One blow from a hammer would see the fight over in a moment. 'Attacking the King's agent is not a sensible thing to do.'

'You sealed our fate when you stole that die,' said Lifwine. 'There is nothing left for us now.'

Someone jabbed at Geoffrey with a dagger, so he hauled his sword from his belt and swung it in an arc that had men leaping back in alarm. He did not hit anyone, although he could have done, but it was enough to warn them that he was not about to go quietly.

'You said Edric stole it,' he said, turning in a circle, so he could watch as many of them as possible. When one, braver than the rest, came at him with a saw, Geoffrey stabbed his leg. The man howled, and some of his friends edged away, not wanting to be next. 'Both of us cannot be responsible.'

'He took it and gave it to you,' said Adelise immediately. 'It is obvious.'

'I have not seen Edric since I last visited you.' Other than when Tasso had sliced his head in half, Geoffrey thought, although it did not seem an appropriate moment to mention that particular incident. 'And you were watching me the whole time.'

'He is right, Mistress,' said a workman with a bald head and sad eyes. 'Edric has not been out of our sight for four days now – since we first began to suspect his treachery – so he could not have met Sir Geoffrey without our knowing.'

'Then that means Geoffrey stole it without his help,' said Lifwine. 'As I said, it went missing the day he came to see us.'

'But I do not want your dies,' said Geoffrey, not sure what he could say to make them believe him. 'Which one was it? One of the old things that I recommended you destroy?'

'A new one,' snapped Sendi. 'With the fleury cross. As well you know.'

'But you watched me like hawks that day,' said Geoffrey, lunging at someone who wielded a poker. 'Surely, you would have noticed me picking up a die and shoving it in my purse?'

'He could not get a die in that purse,' said the bald man, assessing the bag on Geoffrey's belt critically. 'It is not big enough.'

'He hid it inside his armour, Ceorl,' snapped Adelise irritably. 'Do not speak in his defence.'

'But I would have noticed that, and so would you,' said Ceorl. 'He is right: we watched him the whole time he was here. He could not have stolen the die.'

'We have another traitor in our house,' said Adelise coldly. 'Ceorl, who sides with our enemies.'

Ceorl was comfortable in his innocence. 'Everyone knows I speak as I find. Sir Geoffrey cannot be the thief, because he could not have removed the die without us seeing.'

'It must be someone else, then,' said the man with the poker, lowering his weapon as he considered. 'Clarembald and John have accused each other, although my money is on Warelwast.'

'It was *him*,' asserted Lifwine, pointing at Geoffrey. 'He wants us accused of forgery, so Barcwit will be exonerated and his sister freed from the accusations we brought against her. The King should never have appointed him.'

Geoffrey could not have agreed more with the last part.

'Listen to Ceorl,' he urged, seeing one or two of the workmen begin to waver when presented with the facts. 'He seems a sensible man.'

'He is a traitor,' hissed Adelise. 'And we do not tolerate those.'

Geoffrey was not sure what happened next, only that Ceorl toppled forward with a dagger embedded in his chest. It had come from the direction of Sendi, Adelise and Lifwine, although Geoffrey had seen none of them throw it. For a moment, no one did or said anything, and there was a stunned silence as the man fell to the ground. Then pandemonium erupted.

Knives and hammers flailed at Geoffrey, who fought back hard, feeling his sword strike home a number of times. He had not wanted to spill blood, but he was not prepared to let a mob slaughter him without putting up some kind of defence. Sendi had a shovel that he was waving with deadly precision, while Lifwine was in the midst of the affray, prodding at everyone with a dagger. His terrified eyes suggested it was not where he had intended to be, and that he was more interested in escaping the melee than in attacking the knight. Geoffrey grabbed him around the neck, then cleared a path with his sword until his back was against the wall and no one could assault him from behind.

'Stop!' he yelled, waving his sword at his captive – not an easy task when the blade was long and Lifwine was short. 'Or I will kill the *cambium*.'

He hoped no one would challenge him, on the grounds that it would actually be quite difficult to kill anyone from the awkward position in which he held Lifwine. But the Saxons were inexperienced fighters, and the sight of their *cambium* in his clutches was enough to make them fall back, confused and unsure what to do next. One person was not so easily thwarted, however.

'Let him go,' ordered Adelise coldly. 'Or you will be sorry.'

She nodded to where one of her men stood in a window, aiming an arrow at something outside. Geoffrey was nonplussed. He would have understood if the bowman had pointed the missile at him, although then Lifwine would have died for certain – if not by Geoffrey's own hand, then by the archer's when Geoffrey used him as a shield.

Sendi understood, though, and his face broke into a savage grin when he saw what his clever wife had done. 'Look,' he invited, ordering his friends away, so the knight would have an unimpeded view.

Holding Lifwine firmly, Geoffrey edged along the wall and glanced out of the window. There was a tavern opposite, and its shutters were thrown open to catch the evening light. There, sitting perfectly framed in the largest one was Roger, with Helbye on one side and Ulfrith on the next, oblivious to the danger they were in. Even a mediocre bowman could not fail to hit them, and Geoffrey could tell by the archer's steady hands and unwavering eyes that he was probably a good deal better than average.

'Release Lifwine, or your friends die,' said Adelise, with an expression of gratified malice.

'Alfred is an excellent archer,' said Sendi gleefully. 'He will shoot them before they even know they are under attack. So? What will it be?'

Geoffrey stared down at Lifwine and considered. If the archer hit Roger first, then the others were doomed. Helbye's hip now prevented him from moving quickly, while Ulfrith was slow on the uptake and would sit with his mouth hanging open in astonishment before he thought to jump out of the way. There was nothing for it but to give himself up and hope Alfred did not shoot them anyway.

Once he had made his decision, he began to notice irrelevant things, as he always did when he thought he might be about to die: there was a red line around Lifwine's neck, where his shirt had chafed, and Roger's surcoat was so filthy that its Crusader's cross was almost invisible. Then he looked at Adelise's pretty face, which was twisted into a triumphant, gloating mask, and wondered whether they would be the last things he would ever see.

Eleven

Slowly, Geoffrey eased his sword away from Lifwine's throat. 'How do I know you will not shoot Roger anyway?' he asked, ready to kill not only Lifwine, but the nearest workmen, too, if the archer made a wrong move.

'You do not,' said Adelise. 'But you are not in a position to negotiate. Drop your sword, then turn around and put your hands on the wall where we can see them – or Roger dies.'

There was no point in arguing; Adelise knew his weaknesses. 'Lower the bow first,' he insisted.

The archer did as he was told, so Geoffrey released Lifwine, who scuttled away with a bleat of relief. When the bowman started to raise his weapon again, Geoffrey dropped his sword with a resounding clang and turned to face the wall. The Saxons were on him in moments, searching for hidden weapons with hands that were none too gentle. Lifwine was among them, determined to avenge himself for the fright he had been given, and his small fists packed a considerable punch.

Eventually, Geoffrey was wrestled to the floor, where so many Saxons clambered on top of him that it was difficult to breathe, and there followed an argument about what to do next. Lifwine was all for taking a leaf out of Barcwit's book and disposing of the knight in a furnace, but Sendi demurred, claiming that the smell would draw complaints from the neighbours. He added that it would be foolish to murder the King's agent in their own mint, and that they should do it elsewhere. His suggestion met with general agreement, and Geoffrey was bundled unceremoniously down some stairs and shoved into what he supposed was a cellar.

There was no light, and the walls dripped moisture. Geoffrey detested underground places – they reminded him of a tunnel under a castle he had besieged for Tancred some years before, which had collapsed with him inside it – and it took a good deal of willpower not to hammer on the door and beg to be released. He stood with clenched fists and took deep breaths until he had his irrational panic under some semblance of control. Then he explored, running his hands over the walls in the darkness.

He was in a storeroom with a door so thick that it barely made a sound when he thumped it. There were no windows and, no matter how hard he listened, he could hear nothing of the outside world. It was like being in a tomb, and he hoped it would not become one when they decided the easiest thing to do would be to forget about him. That prospect unsettled him more than any other fate they might have had in mind.

He sat on one of the wooden boxes that were scattered here and there, and forced himself to think about what had happened, as a way to take his mind off his predicament. Had Edric stolen the die, or was Ceorl right, and Edric could not be the culprit because he had been under surveillance at the time? Then why had Edric been at Barcwit's mint? Because he had been unfairly dismissed, and had decided to turn to Sendi's rival out of spite? If so, then his plan for revenge had misfired dismally.

He thought about Ceorl, who had questioned the 'facts', and wondered whether it had been Sendi, Lifwine or Adelise – or someone else – who had thrown the knife that had killed him. Whoever it was had wanted Geoffrey blamed for the theft, and for all the workmen to believe it, although he could not imagine why. Then the answer came to him: Ceorl was probably right to draw the conclusion that Edric could not have stolen the die while he was being watched, which meant someone else had done it – not an outsider, who would find theft impossible with so many watchful eyes on him, but another of Sendi's men. There was a second rotten apple in the moneyer's barrel.

Geoffrey had no idea how long he had been sitting in the dark before he heard the door being unbarred. He was on his feet in an instant, struggling to keep his eyes open in the sudden blaze of light. What he saw did not inspire him with confidence. The cellar had rock-hewn walls that oozed slime, while the ceiling was lacy with cobwebs. There were more crates than he had thought, and they were all well made: obviously their contents were valuable and, taking into account the fact that they were stored in a secure room, he was able to draw only one conclusion.

'Is this the missing silver that was stolen from Barcwit?'

'Certainly not,' said Sendi archly. 'This is our reserve stock, stored so our mint will continue to operate if Barcwit tries to disrupt our supply from the mines.'

Sendi, armed with a long knife, was accompanied by Adelise and Alfred the archer, who had an arrow nocked into his bow and looked more than ready to use it. He indicated Geoffrey should move to the back of the cellar, from where it would be impossible to escape; the knight would be shot before he had covered half the distance to the door, and mail was no defence against steel-tipped arrows.

'I have brought you some ale,' said Adelise, shaking a leather flask so Geoffrey could hear the liquid slopping about inside it. 'You must be thirsty. But first, you must tell us what you did with the die.'

'We know you have it,' added Sendi. 'It is the only possible explanation. Barcwit is not the thief, because there has been no sign of forced entry, and he would not have contented himself with one die anyway: he would have stolen the lot. Besides, we would have heard by now, if he was the culprit.'

'You have a spy in his mint,' deduced Geoffrey. The King had mentioned weeks ago that it was common practice among merchants to tempt a member of a rival's workforce to turn traitor. 'Who?'

Adelise grimaced. 'He will die if that information leaks out, and he is far too valuable.'

'And Edric was in Barcwit's pay,' said Geoffrey. 'You began to suspect him after Westminster, when your rivalry became more bitter and intense than ever.' The circumstances of Edric's death were finally becoming clear. The man had been comfortable in Barcwit's mint, because he had been there before. When Sendi had dismissed him, he had gone to Barcwit, confident in the knowledge that he would be paid for his sacrifice. But no one liked a traitor, and Barcwit did not want one who had outlived his usefulness.

Adelise inclined her head. 'But we now know that Edric could not have stolen the die, because we were watching him day and night. So, that only leaves one other suspect. You.'

'Well, you are wrong,' said Geoffrey. 'Do you think me a fool, to steal from the people I am investigating for the King? Besides, what would I do with a die? I do not have a mint.'

'It can be sold to any dishonest coiner,' said Sendi. 'Tell us where it is, and we will let you go.'

'If you do not, we will kill you,' said Adelise. 'It is a simple choice.'

'Very well,' said Geoffrey, knowing he would never convince them of his innocence. 'It is in a small recess near the top of the castle well. Now release me.'

Adelise gave a diabolical smile, and indicated that the archer should shoot.

'No!' exclaimed Sendi in alarm, pushing Alfred so he staggered.

'Why not?' demanded Adelise. 'He told us what we want to know, and we cannot let him out.'

'Now he has confessed to stealing our die, he is discredited,' said Sendi. 'None of his "evidence" against us will count. We will use him to prove our honesty and Barcwit's corruption.'

'We put our faith in the King's justice once, but it made matters worse,' said Adelise harshly. 'Besides, now we have forced him to confess to theft, he will be even more determined to destroy us, so we must make an end of him.'

While they argued, Geoffrey took a surreptitious step towards Alfred, who acted instantly and without hesitation. He aimed at Geoffrey's legs and released his quarrel, so it snapped into the floor. He had a second one nocked to his bow while the knight was still staggering out of the way. He was watchful and cautious, and the distance was simply too great to allow Geoffrey to reach him before he was shot. Geoffrey would never escape as long as Alfred was present.

'If you kill me, you will need to kill Giffard, too,' he said to Sendi, hoping to appeal to his sense of reason. Alfred had a manic glint in his eye that Geoffrey recognized all too well: it was bloodlust, and he suspected the man would side with Adelise, just because he wanted to shoot someone. 'All we want is the truth – to find out what is really going on under all these accusations and counterclaims.'

'Truth is like molten silver,' said Adelise. 'It can be shaped to how you want it. But we have no time to debate. Roger is already sniffing around because he thinks you are here, and I doubt we will get away with killing two knights. Shoot him, Alfred.'

Alfred raised his bow with obvious pleasure, but Sendi pushed him a second time. 'We should not do anything we may later regret. Roger says he heard the distinctive rattle of a broadsword dropped on a flagstone floor when he was in his tavern, and we need to make sure he does not tell the King that his agent disappeared while he was in our mint. That would cause problems for certain.'

'Not as many as Geoffrey would cause alive,' argued Adelise.

This time Alfred did not wait for Adelise's order before he raised his bow. Geoffrey tensed.

'No,' objected Sendi. 'I—'

'No is a good response,' came a familiar voice, as Alfred crumpled into a heap, bow clattering as it fell. Geoffrey kicked it from his hand, while Roger grinned a smug greeting, knowing the rescue had been in the nick of time and pleased with himself. Helbye and Ulfrith were in the shadows beyond the door, their weapons drawn. There was no sign of Sendi's vengeful workforce, and Geoffrey wondered what Roger had done with them.

'We were only trying to frighten him,' gabbled Adelise, regarding Roger in alarm. 'Geoffrey stole our die, and we wanted to show him what thieves can expect in Bristol. He has learnt his lesson, so you can have him back.'

'Thank you, lass,' said Roger dryly.

'We should lock up these villains and throw away the key,' said Helbye in disdain. 'I would suggest taking them to the castle, but Sir Peter will not keep them.'

Geoffrey glanced at him in surprise, since holding Sendi

and his men in a castle cellar until Giffard arrived was exactly what he intended to do. 'Why not?'

'Because every chamber is full of supplies for when the King comes to besiege him,' explained Roger, amused that the constable should think he stood any chance of withstanding well-trained royal troops. 'There is nowhere to put prisoners.'

'It does not matter,' said Geoffrey, reconsidering. 'They can stay free until Giffard comes.'

Despite his lack of progress, the net was still closing around the moneyers, and they were showing clear signs of unease. If securing them in the castle was not an option, then he was just as happy to grant them temporary liberty. They were unsettled, and he sensed he would learn more from them free than if they were incarcerated – and if they turned on each other in their fear, then so much the better.

Roger took the flask Adelise held and lifted it to his lips for a celebratory drink. Geoffrey saw malicious satisfaction flit across her face. He snatched the vessel from Roger and shoved it at her.

'You first.'

'I am not thirsty. You have it.'

Roger took it back and sniffed it, before flinging it to the other side of the room. They all watched the liquid pooling on the floor – amber, but with a milky hue that would have gone unnoticed by anyone drinking from the container. It was probably ale, but something had definitely been added.

'Poison?' whispered Sendi, regarding his wife in horror. 'You were going to give him poison?'

She shrugged, putting on a brave face. 'We have a lot to lose.'

'Yes,' agreed Roger grimly, pulling out his sword and advancing on her. 'You do, lass.'

It was only with difficulty that Geoffrey convinced Roger not to cleave Adelise's head from her shoulders – the big knight was incensed that she had been so determined to kill his friend. But Geoffrey was confused by the twist the investigation had taken, and wanted his suspects alive so they would be able to answer his questions. Adelise fled when Geoffrey stepped between her and the enraged Roger, wisely opting to hide until the danger was over. Meanwhile, Sendi followed Geoffrey out of the mint, wringing his hands and insisting, not very convincingly, that the whole incident was a misunderstanding. Lifwine appeared, too, and added his voice to the claims of innocence, while Roger told Geoffrey the rest of the men had gone home for the night, which was why the rescue had been delayed: he had known better than to take on a score of angry workmen.

Geoffrey was relieved to be in the clean, frosty air, away from the stink of damp underground chambers and molten silver. He breathed in deeply and glanced up at the starry sky. It was not as late as he had thought, and he had probably been in the cellar for no more than two hours. He started to walk back to the castle, but Sendi and his *cambium* had not finished with him.

'At least let us have our die,' begged Sendi. 'You may think it is safe with you, but you do not know Barcwit. He will find it and use it to destroy us.'

'It is already too late for Ceorl,' said Geoffrey quietly.

'That was unfortunate,' said Lifwine, running to keep up with the rapid pace Geoffrey was setting. 'We do not know who knifed him, but when we find out, the culprit will lose his post.'

'The die,' prompted Sendi. 'I will pay you in newly minted pennies if you give it back.'

Roger regarded his friend in wonderment. '*You* took it? I believed you when you said you did not – you were very convincing. Where is it? Your funds are low, and it would be good to replenish them by selling the thing.'

'The King would not agree,' said Geoffrey dryly. 'But I do not have it anyway.'

'You have already admitted that you do,' said Sendi, bewildered.

'I lied. Ask the man who turned traitor – Barcwit's spy.'

'Edric?' asked Sendi, bemused. 'That is impossible: we would have seen him.'

'Not Edric,' said Geoffrey. 'There is another villain in your midst. He is the man who killed Ceorl when he started to

235

convince the others that I was innocent, because it was in *his* interests to have the King's agent blamed for something *he* did.'

Leaving Sendi and his *cambium* staring at each other in alarm, Geoffrey strode down the dark streets to the castle. Angry voices followed him, Lifwine's saying that Geoffrey's claim was a nonsense, and Sendi's arguing that it was a possibility they should consider. It occurred to Geoffrey that the moneyers might turn on each other sooner than he had anticipated.

'You are wrong to let them stay free when they came so close to killing you,' said Roger, breaking into his reverie. 'They may have another go, and there are too many others tempted to do the same – Barcwit, Rodbert, Tasso, the physicians. I do not like the way Warelwast has fixed himself to you, either. He says he wants to be your friend, but I am your friend, and *I* do not dog your every move.'

'You do sometimes,' said Geoffrey. Roger had been concerned just because he thought he had heard a sword fall on a stone floor. 'Thank God.'

Roger was angry. 'Warelwast trails after you like a lovesick virgin, but the one time he can be of use, he is nowhere to be found. Is that suspicious, or what?'

'I do not know what to think about Warelwast – or anyone else. There is hardly a soul here who has not threatened to kill me. Even my own sister seems intent on misleading me with lies.'

'Joan?' asked Roger. 'She loves you dearly. Olivier told me, and he is an honourable man, not given to falsehoods. He has fought in more battles than any man I know, and is a great warrior.'

Geoffrey did not reply. He had enough to worry about, without Roger accusing Olivier of being a fraud. Joan would leap to her husband's defence, and there would be blood for certain – none of it hers.

'She is angry with me,' he said instead.

'She is none too enamoured of me, either,' said Roger unhappily. 'I invited Olivier to practise his swordplay today, and she was afraid he would be hurt.' He gave a snort of laughter. 'Can you imagine! A man like *him* being hurt!'

'How did he fare?' asked Geoffrey curiously.

'The hilt of his sword was loose, and he declined to spar with me in case it slipped and inadvertently did me harm. But we will go another day, and he can demonstrate some of the moves he used against those Saxon kings. I can learn a great deal from him.'

'Hmm,' said Geoffrey, hoping the case would soon be resolved and Roger would never know the sorry truth about Sir Olivier d'Alençon.

'Still, at least we no longer have to worry about Durand,' said Roger, broaching another subject. 'He says you dismissed him, and was furious, which surprised me. I thought he wanted to go.'

'He did,' said Geoffrey. 'Just not here, where he says it is dangerous. However, if Joan is to be believed, he has plenty of money, which means he can buy himself some suitable protection. I am inclined to believe he earned it last summer, by spying on me for the King.'

'Yes and no,' said Roger. 'Some of his wealth is from Henry; the rest came from someone else.'

Geoffrey stared at him. 'How do you know?'

'I have always been wary of the man, so I followed him when we were at Westminster. I saw Henry pay him a purse of silver, which I presume was to make sure you did not run off to the Holy Land without doing your duty. It was exactly the same amount as Henry gave him to spy on you at Easter, during the Bellême campaign. But Durand owns a lot more than two bags of silver.'

Geoffrey was astonished that he should have spent hours speculating about his squire's loyalty when Roger had had the answers at his fingertips all along. 'Then where did the rest come from?'

Roger shrugged. 'All I know is that whoever paid him must have been pleased with what he did. I suspect he was paid by Bellême's clan, as well as by the King. Durand is the kind of man to accept payment from both sides in a war. He definitely became very much richer after August.'

'You searched his bags?' Geoffrey wondered whether he was the only one with a sense of privacy.

Roger regarded him as though he was insane. 'Of course I did. How else would I know what he is up to? Do not tell me you have never done the same! I look through yours all the time.'

Geoffrey was aghast. 'I had always assumed that a man's property was his own business.'

'Not when we are travelling through hostile territory,' argued Roger. 'How can I protect your worldly goods, unless I know what there is to look after? Besides, if you were to die, they would come to me, as your closest friend, and I like to know where I stand as far as inheritance is concerned.'

'God's teeth! Now even *you* are waiting for my death. Is no one interested in my being alive?'

'What I stand to inherit from you will not compensate me for the loss of a good friend. Besides, I do not want books and grimy shirts.' Roger threw a heavy arm around Geoffrey's shoulders. 'We stand together, you and I. The men of Bristol will not defeat two *Jerosolimitani*.'

Warelwast had been unable to work his charm on Joan, and was astonished to learn there was a woman he could not seduce with honeyed words. While he laboured in vain, Geoffrey spent what was left of the evening with Peter and Idonea, listening to their plans for the siege they were certain was imminent. He asked about Nauntel, but learnt no more about the man's death, other than that the people of Beiminstre had been frightened when they had learnt what had happened in their village, and that they were probably not involved in the murder.

The following day dawned dark and wet, and even Geoffrey, who seldom bothered about the weather, declined to go riding. The rain was hard and persistent, and he did not want his borrowed horse to slip in mud and harm itself. The weather was sufficiently foul that he did not fancy trudging around streets that were ankle-deep in water-logged filth, either, so he found a table in the hall and prepared a report on his findings: if Giffard arrived unexpectedly, there would be at least something written down for him. So far, all Geoffrey knew for certain was that Barcwit did indeed terrorize the people of Bristol, and that he killed those who crossed him. He used Nauntel and Edric as the best examples, but could not bring himself to include his brother's name, too.

The rest of Sendi's accusations were more difficult to assess, given that Barcwit had declined to speak to him – something he ensured was prominent in his letter, because it was indicative of the man's attitude to the King. He sat for hours writing and rewriting his meagre conclusions, and then, just to break the monotony, he went to inspect the castle's provision-stuffed cellars. He returned to the table in the evening, determined to complete his report, but Joan scowled at him until, unnerved by the brevity of what he had composed and unable to come up with more as long as she distracted him with her icy disapproval, he went to sit with her. She was sewing by the dim light of a brazier; Olivier tentatively petted Geoffrey's dog.

'I met some people you know yesterday,' said Geoffrey, in an attempt to start a non-contentious conversation. 'Kea and his family, from Beiminstre.'

Joan's hard features softened. 'They are good folk. Little Rowise is slow in the mind, but even she is excellent with horses. Olivier never buys his from anywhere else.'

'Kea has great talent,' agreed Olivier. 'Warelwast tells me you left your mount with him. It will be money well spent, and you will find him a different animal. What did you think of Beiminstre?'

'It is under the shadow of Barcwit, just like everything else. Kea and his kin will be glad when the matter is resolved, even if no one else will.'

Joan sighed. 'Not this again! If you know what is good for you, you will confine your conversation to other matters tonight. I am in no mood to be interrogated.'

'I am only trying to help,' said Geoffrey, wishing she was not so prickly. 'Giffard will be here soon, and the case will be "resolved" regardless of whether or not I have discovered the truth.'

'You will never succeed,' insisted Joan. 'It is too complex and there are too many strands. You cannot unravel the dangerous mess Barcwit has created here, because you are not clever enough.'

'I know what you are doing,' said Geoffrey. 'You asked nicely and I refused to go, so now you are trying rudeness. It will not work: the days when you could force me to do what you want are long past, and I have no choice, anyway. Henry will not be sympathetic if I tell him I disobeyed his orders because my sister told me to.'

Joan's eyes shone with tears. 'Henry will rob me of all I hold dear: Olivier, Goodrich *and* you.'

The discussion had done more harm than good, because Joan was now distressed as well as angry, although Geoffrey was pleased to be included on her list of loves, even if he was in last place. He had begun to think she cared nothing for him, and was relieved to learn that at least some of her hostility resulted from fears for his safety.

It was not long before Roger, eager to be away from the oppressive atmosphere in the hall, invited Olivier for a jug of ale in the town's taverns. Joan informed Olivier he could not go, so he demurely followed her up the stairs to their chamber for an early night. Roger winked meaningfully as they left.

'Show her what you are made of,' he bawled. 'Show her what a veteran of Hastings can do for a woman.' He turned to Geoffrey. 'It is not surprising she wants him to service her. Men of action are always in demand from their wives and lovers.'

'Are they?' asked Geoffrey, thinking he was a man of action, but there were no queues of lovers awaiting *his* masculine attentions – with the exception of Maude, who seemed to consider any male fair game. 'Then let us go and find some. I am tired of being cooped up in here.'

'Peter!' yelled Roger, so every person in the hall turned to look at him. 'Where is Bristol's best brothel? Me and Geoff feel like relaxing with a whore.'

Geoffrey saw Joan had not gone as far up the stairs as he had thought, and she turned to gape at the question. He laughed when he heard her berating Olivier for thinking he could engage in that sort of activity and expect to get away with it, ignoring her husband's protestations that Roger's invitation had involved ale and military chit-chat only. Peter approached to reply a little more privately to Roger's top-volume query;

Idonea was with him, evidently interested to learn how much her spouse knew about such institutions. But Geoffrey's mind had already strayed back to his investigation.

'How much silver did Barcwit lose when it was stolen?' he asked, ignoring Roger's moue of impatience. The big knight was ready for a brothel, and did not want to talk about the elusive treasure.

'A lot,' said Peter shortly. 'And do not ask me any more about it, or I shall order you to leave. I would have ejected you already – to find lodgings in the town – but Joan would not let me. For some reason, she is fond of you and wants you here, where you will be safe. I thought you intended to conduct a *discreet* investigation, but you have antagonized everyone you have met.'

'Giffard will be here soon. You will find him a good deal less discreet with his questions than I have been – and a lot less patient with evasive answers, too.' Geoffrey sighed. 'I do not understand why people refuse to co-operate when I offer a chance to put their side of the story.'

Peter grimaced. 'You think Barcwit will slip away, and never be seen again, once he is found guilty? Well, you are wrong! He will be even more dangerous, because he will be outside the law. I lost Nauntel, and I do not want to lose more because I have babbled to you.' He stood and stalked away.

'Brothels,' announced Idonea in a loud voice when he had gone. 'What kind of women are you looking for? Ones who are quick and cheap, or ones who have more time, but are expensive?'

'Either will do,' replied Roger eagerly. 'We are not fussy.'

'Barcwit's silver,' said Idonea, dropping her voice and leaning close to Geoffrey, so she would not be overheard. She waved her hands, as if she was giving him directions. 'He lost at least fifteen crates. Why? Have you found them?'

Geoffrey thought about the boxes in Sendi's cellar. The rival moneyer was the most obvious culprit for the theft, and a sturdy vault seemed a good place to hide his booty. But would Sendi be quite so brazen, when it was obvious that Barcwit would look to him first?

He answered her question with one of his own. 'Did you

241

hear what happened to Alwold in Westminster? When he was dying, he insisted on speaking to Maude.'

'He muttered something about the silver, but it was nothing she understood – or at least, nothing that has allowed Barcwit to retrieve it. She is not a loyal wife.' There was a wry gleam in Idonea's eye as she spoke. 'But I imagine you already know that. Barcwit is strong and dominant in the way he runs his affairs, but he is unable to satisfy his woman.'

Geoffrey thought about Maude's invitation to meet him that very night. He still had not decided whether to oblige. 'Rodbert seems to step in for that,' he said absently.

'I doubt it!' said Idonea, shocked. 'But Rodbert is slippery and cunning, and it would not surprise me to learn that *he* had this silver.'

Geoffrey conceded it was possible. He remembered Alwold vehemently refusing to confide in Rodbert as he breathed his last. Was that an indication that he suspected the deputy of the theft?

'Alwold said someone called Piers had it,' he said. 'But there is no Piers in Bristol, and the Piers in Dundreg – the anchorite – died recently.'

Idonea nodded. 'He was mad, and certainly not someone to entrust with a large quantity of silver. There is a man in Beiminstre called Piers, but half the town raced out to see him when Alwold's dying words became common knowledge – Peter and I were among them.'

Joan had told Geoffrey that Peter and Idonea had hunted for the silver in the hope that its discovery might appease the King. He also recalled that Feoc had denied knowing any other men called Piers, which meant that either the priest was concealing information or his local knowledge was not as complete as he claimed. Or perhaps he had simply answered the question he had been asked: did he know a man called Piers in Bristol? Beiminstre was not Bristol, and neither was Dundreg.

'What did this Beiminstre Piers say?'

'That he had no idea what Alwold was talking about. Immediately after, he disappeared into the hills with his sheep, afraid Barcwit would come and ask his questions a little more persuasively. I am sure he is not Alwold's Piers. But who stabbed Alwold? Was it one of Sendi's men?'

'Probably. Fardin had been murdered the same morning, and they seem the kind of people to indulge in tit-for-tat killings. I wish I could speak to Barcwit about all this, but he refuses to see me.'

'He would not deal with you honestly if he did. At least, *I* would not trust anything he said. Have you seen him, so sinister in his dark clothes and horrible hood? But I have been here too long, and people are beginning to wonder how many brothels I know about. Go to the inn called the Mermaid, which is near the bridge. That has clean women.'

The Mermaid was the kind of tavern that needed two burly men to guard its doors, so that those unable to pay the high prices charged by the women within, or those too drunk to behave, could not gain access. Roger almost had them barred instantly, with his stubbly chin, filthy clothes and leering grin, and the dog did not help by growling and baring its fangs. It was Roger's coins that won the day, and Geoffrey was glad his friend had funds for bribery, because he did not. They found an empty table, ordered ale and took in their surroundings – surprisingly pleasant, with a roaring fire in the hearth.

Geoffrey was glad to be away from the castle. His disagreement with Joan still rankled, and he decided to think twice about doing what was right next time, because such behaviour nearly always led him into trouble and he was becoming tired of it. He wished he was more like Roger, who saw everything in black and white, and was seldom confounded by moral quandaries.

Roger leaned against the wall and began to assess which women would receive his advances that night. His eyes lit on a lady near the hearth. She was fair-haired and slender, and dressed in a kirtle made from some silken fabric that accentuated the elegant lines of her slim-hipped body. She held court with a heavily cloaked man, who was clearly relishing her company. Geoffrey was amused to note it was Clarembald, orange eyebrows poking from under his hood, and giving away his identity as openly as if his name had been chalked on to his back.

'Not her,' said Geoffrey to Roger, not wanting an altercation with the physician when there were plenty of other prostitutes available. 'She is spoken for, so choose another.'

'I would not have *her* if she was the last man in Christendom,' breathed Roger. 'That is Durand!'

With an uneasy pang, Geoffrey saw he was right, and was appalled by the completeness of Durand's transformation. It was only the familiar golden curls that gave him away, because everything else was different. His cheeks were reddened with pigment, the charcoal around his eyes made them larger and darker, and the mincing walk was magnified. Uncomfortably, Geoffrey wondered whether his odd skills were the source of some of his money, and recalled how handsomely Bishop Maurice had paid for the services of Angel Locks.

'I do not like this,' he said to Roger. Clarembald had warned him to curb Durand's more colourful behaviour, and he suspected the physician would not be pleased when he discovered his beautiful woman was not all she appeared. 'Durand can risk execution for unnatural acts if he is so inclined, but I do not want to be accused with him. We are leaving.'

'Now?' asked Roger, dismayed. 'But we have only just arrived!'

'I do not care. Besides, Maude asked me to meet her in St John's Church tonight, and I want to inspect it before she arrives.'

'Maude?' asked Roger doubtfully. 'I would not go meeting *her* in dark places if I were you. It will be a trap, and you will end up in Barcwit's cellar while he interrogates you about his missing silver. I do not think I will be able to rescue you from him as I did from Sendi.' He shuddered.

'Barcwit has *you* unnerved?' asked Geoffrey, surprised. 'You, Roger of Durham?'

'We all have our limitations,' said Roger crossly. 'And Barcwit is among mine. He makes me uneasy, because he cannot be seen. He is like Satan: you cannot see him, either, and yet he is all around us. I saw him yesterday, though. Barcwit, I mean, not Satan, unless they are one and the same . . .'

'Where?'

'Standing in the window above his mint, staring down into the street. I felt the hairs on the back of my neck stand up, and all I wanted to do was hurry away. He unsettled others who were passing, too. Have you noticed how no one loiters in that part of the street?'

'When was this?' asked Geoffrey.

'Yesterday afternoon. I was following Warelwast, who was following you. Later, I followed Maude, who was following Warelwast, who was following you.'

Geoffrey nodded, and it occurred to him that Maude had been on his tail because she knew he had witnessed Edric's murder. He wondered how long it would be before she tried to silence him, and supposed she intended to put some sort of plan into action at midnight. 'Was anyone following you?'

'Ulfrith and Helbye, but they are confident they were the last. But Barcwit stood in the window like a demon, eyes boring into folk who passed.'

'You saw his face?'

'Gleaming under his hood. I do not want to see it again! What do you say to leaving tomorrow? Joan does not like you here, and there is no other reason for us to stay. We have made too many enemies, and I am tired of being watchful all the time.'

'I agree,' said Geoffrey, to Roger's relief. 'Joan refuses my help, and I can do no more, anyway. I will leave my report for Giffard, and he can unravel the rest. Joan was right: it is too complex for me.'

'No: it is not complex enough,' said Roger consolingly. 'There is no cunning plot, just several simple ones intertwined. Barcwit wants to kill the King, and is amassing a fortune and followers to help. Those who refuse are coerced. Meanwhile, Sendi is jealous of Barcwit's success. The two sides will do anything to hinder each other – stealing dies, committing murder, issuing threats – and everyone we have met has been sucked into the mess, including the physicians, Peter and Idonea, Joan and Olivier, the folk of Beiminstre, Bloet and even Warelwast, although he pretends he has not.'

'You are probably right.' Geoffrey noticed Clarembald and

245

Durand had gone, so decided to leave, too, sure it would not take Clarembald long to discover the truth. The man was a physician, after all.

Outside, he took a deep breath and gazed up at the sky, where stars blazed like a sheet of diamonds. The air smelled of wood smoke and spilled ale, overlain unpleasantly by the rubbish that lay in the street. He became aware at the same time as Roger that someone was moving behind them. They glanced at each other, and a silent exchange of information took place. They separated, with Roger walking towards the quays and Geoffrey and his dog moving towards the high street.

The shadow chose to follow Roger, so Geoffrey doubled back on himself, padding stealthily along deserted streets until he caught up with the silent figure. He made his move when they reached the wharves, silent and abandoned now work had stopped for the day. He slipped an arm around the person's neck and pressed a dagger to his throat, while Roger spun around, ready to add his strength to subduing the fellow if necessary. It was not. The man immediately began to beg for his life in a high, terrified whine, and Geoffrey released him in disgust.

'Durand! What are you doing here?'

'What are *you* doing here?' asked the squire in turn. 'I thought you were going to meet Maude. It is not midnight yet, but you always go early to such assignations, to assess any possible dangers.'

Geoffrey regarded him warily. 'How do you know about Maude?'

'Clarembald overheard her talking about it with Rodbert. He was giving a lecture on the pox at their mint yesterday, and he heard them discussing you as he left. They were so engrossed with each other, that they did not notice him listen for a moment or two.'

Geoffrey recalled how he had been obliged to hide on the stairs when Clarembald had left the mint, and also remembered that it had taken the physician longer than it should have done to walk up the corridor and open the door.

Clarembald had told Durand the truth about that, at least.

'What is Clarembald's relationship with Barcwit?' demanded Roger. 'Exactly.'

'Investor and physician,' replied Durand promptly. 'I pumped him for information in that horrible tavern, enduring his pawing hands, so I would have something to tell you when I made my approach. That is why I am here: to pass information to Sir Geoffrey.'

'Then why did you follow Roger?' asked Geoffrey. 'He and I were walking in opposite directions.'

'Because I thought Roger might listen to me, and I knew you would not. I have learnt things from Clarembald that I am prepared to share. However, I am no longer in your service, so there is a price.'

Geoffrey was inclined to walk away and have no more to do with him, but Roger was not. The insult of being charged for things that should have been freely shared was too much to bear. 'Will this information help Geoff with his investigation?' he asked softly, fingering his dagger.

Durand nodded, clearly terrified, but remained firm. 'I have worked hard to collect it, and it was done at considerable risk to myself. I will not give it for no return.'

'Oh, there will be a return,' promised Roger menacingly. 'Tell him all you know, and I will let you live to flaunt your wares tomorrow night.'

'No!' cried Durand, almost in tears. 'I do not want to flaunt them tomorrow. That is my price: I want to come back into his service until we leave this place. And then we can rethink our positions.'

Geoffrey laughed in disbelief. 'Why? You have already earned a fortune spying, and I thought you intended to buy a post in some decadent abbey. What changed your mind?'

'Bloet,' said Durand miserably. 'He robbed me last night.'

Roger was astonished. 'But we taught you how to avoid that sort of thing happening. It was the only lesson you took any interest in.'

'I lowered my guard, because I thought he was a friend. My money was in my saddlebags when I went to bed, and it was all gone this morning. Then he asked me to pay my share of the wine we consumed to celebrate my freedom last night, and of course I could not. In return for paying my "debt", he took everything except these clothes. I am destitute.'

'I could have told you he was treacherous,' said Roger, shaking his head in disgust.

'You could not!' declared Durand. 'It was not possible to tell.'

Geoffrey was unimpressed that Durand had been so trusting. 'The morning we left Westminster, when Sendi began the argument over the missing horse, I read in Bloet's face that your attraction was not wholly reciprocated. He intended to trick you from the start.'

Geoffrey expected Durand to burst into tears or protest that he was mistaken, but he did neither. Anger flashed in his eyes. 'Bastard! I shall repay him, but I will need money.'

'How do you propose to get it?' asked Geoffrey. 'Do you think I should give you the chance to earn more from whoever pays you to spy on me, before you leave me at a time that suits you more?'

'That is a good idea,' said Durand, relieved. 'I am grateful to you for being so understanding.'

'No,' said Geoffrey firmly.

'But you must!' pleaded Durand. His expression became crafty. 'Tancred will be furious if he learns you abandoned me in a strange town, clad only in a kirtle – and I will make sure he knows if you do. I said we should not part company here, but you would not listen and, sure enough, I am robbed within hours and forced to sell my body.'

'You sold yourself to Clarembald?' asked Geoffrey uneasily. It would not matter how Tancred reacted to the news that Geoffrey had left his charge to work in a brothel, if Clarembald made a complaint to the King first.

Durand nodded. 'He paid me well, although not as much as I earn for spying. Once I had him ensnared, he was like clay in my hands. He was eager to indulge my innocent curiosity by answering questions – even ones that should have aroused his suspicions, such as what he had seen and heard at Barcwit's mint.'

Roger was curious. 'He is a physician. Surely he knows the difference between men and ladies?'

Durand sniggered in a way Geoffrey found distasteful. 'I am very skilled in making womanly—'

'No,' interrupted Geoffrey firmly. 'We do not want details.'

'And you claim to have an open mind,' said Durand insolently. 'But now you have agreed to take me back until a mutually acceptable time, I shall keep my end of the bargain. You should meet Maude tonight, because you will learn something important.'

'Such as what?' asked Geoffrey, not sure that particular snippet was enough to warrant him putting up with a self-confessed spy for an indeterminate period.

'She intends to give you evidence that will solve your case. I do not know anything more specific, only that you should go.'

'How do I know it is not a trap?' asked Geoffrey. 'Or that you have not invented this wild story about Bloet robbing you to earn my trust and ensure I go?'

'There will be no ambush,' said Durand confidently. 'And I have invented nothing. Why would I, when I have just persuaded you to hire me again? Everything I have told you is the truth.'

'Then you can tell me a little more truth,' said Geoffrey. 'Who has been paying you to spy on me?'

'The King.' Durand regarded Geoffrey in surprise. 'Surely you guessed? I did not even try to be discreet about it, so we would both know where we stood. He has given me assignments ever since we met on the Bellême campaign. I am sorry: I thought you knew.'

'*All* your money comes from Henry?'

'Half. The rest came from that woman you took a fancy to last Easter – Matilda. I sold her a document, but it was a forgery, so had no bearing on the war between the King and the House of Montgomery–Bellême. But Henry has been generous. He says a good spy is worth good pay.'

'What have you told him about me?' Geoffrey was irked, and tempted to let the squire stew in the mess he had made. The implication was that Durand was a better agent than his

master, who had received nothing for his work for Henry –
not even a pardon for Joan, if he failed to solve the case.

'That you are a man who lives by a code of honour we
both find hard to fathom. I told him you are honest – that he
could give you a chest of gold to guard, and when he returned,
every piece would still be there. I told him he would have to
count it if Sir Roger was around, though . . .'

'Here,' said Roger indignantly. 'I do not steal!'

'You call it "borrowing" or "taking a commission", but it
is stealing nonetheless. I also told him you are fond of Joan.
I hate to admit it, but it is probably that particular nugget that
saw us dragged off the ship in Southampton and taken to
Westminster. He thought you might appreciate an opportunity to help her.'

'I did,' said Geoffrey. 'Unfortunately, she does not feel the
same way.'

'Do not take her coldness to heart. She is afraid of showing
her true feelings, because she does not want to appear weak,'
said Durand, surprisingly insightful. 'Give her time; she will
come round.'

'I do not have time. Giffard will be here soon, and I am
no further along with this enquiry than when we arrived on
Sunday – four days ago.'

'Then go to St John's and see Maude. You will soon have
your solution now *I* am helping you.'

'Is that so?' asked Geoffrey coolly. 'Then answer me this:
how can I go about speaking to Barcwit? Who stole Sendi's
missing die and where is it? Does a shepherd from Beiminstre
know the whereabouts of Barcwit's missing silver? What is
Clarembald's role in all this? And Warelwast's?'

'Clarembald is a *medicus*,' said Durand. 'He knows lots of
people, so do not read too much into the fact that he overheard Maude and Rodbert plotting. I do not know the answers
to your other questions, although I will help you find them,
if I can. But time is passing, and we have talked enough. Sir
Roger and I will return to the castle, where he can find me
some clothes that will not see me raped by half the garrison,
and you can go to St John's Church and meet Maude.'

'I do not want to meet her,' said Geoffrey. 'But you have

declared yourself willing to enter my service again, which means you are obliged to obey orders. *You* can do it.'

Durand was appalled that Geoffrey expected him to put himself in danger, but Geoffrey remained firm: either the squire could meet Maude, or he could consider himself dismissed permanently. Durand nodded reluctant agreement, then sniffed miserably all the way to the church. Geoffrey knew he was crying, but was too disgusted about the spying to feel pity for him.

While Durand fumbled with the latch, Geoffrey and Roger waited in the shadows of the graveyard. Geoffrey had no idea what the time was, but sensed it was nearing midnight. He was alert for suspicious movements and unusual sounds, but all was still and silent until Durand had closed the door, at which point voices started to murmur from within. He poked a hole in one of the rotten window shutters and peered through it. Maude was nowhere to be seen.

Because it was a clear night, and therefore chilly, someone had lit a fire, and five or six unkempt men huddled around it, greedy for warmth. Maude had mentioned that the door was always kept open – presumably Feoc was sympathetic to the plight of the homeless – and was surprised she should choose such a place for her liaison. He watched Durand approach the beggars, wringing his hands in front of him.

'Maude,' said the squire tearfully. 'I have come to meet her. Do you know where she is?'

'Not here,' said a man with a shock of matted black hair and scabs on his face. His accent was so strongly local, that Geoffrey had trouble deciphering it.

'I can see that,' said Durand. 'I have come to—'

'This is one of Barcwit's women,' said Black Hair to his friends, who did not seem to care who Durand was, as long as he did not lay claim to a share of the fire. They closed ranks, to indicate there was no room.

'I most certainly am not,' objected Durand, offended. 'What do you take me for?'

'What you look like,' replied a man who was missing a hand. 'Barcwit used to trawl the taverns for whores, but not any more.'

'He has grown,' said Black Hair. 'He communes with the Devil, and gets bigger every day.'

'I see,' said Durand weakly, while Geoffrey wished he would either break off the conversation, and look for Maude, or ask again whether they had seen her. 'I know nothing of his habits.'

'He used to be all right, but these days he just stands and waits for the hangman to come,' said Black Hair with a shudder. 'He scares me, with that dark cloak and them staring eyes.'

'I am looking for Maude.' Durand sounded desperate. 'Have you seen her?'

'She came earlier,' replied One Hand. 'She said she was expecting a knight later – one of that pair with the funny crosses on their tunics. Both are rough, dirty fellows.'

Geoffrey was horrified, thinking that if beggars thought him unclean, then more polite company must be deeply repelled. He had washed once since his arrival in Bristol, and his new clothes helped, but he saw that both he and Roger had some way to go before they broke their Holy Land habits, and became respectable in the eyes of their peers – and even to poor men dressed in rags.

'She said he would chop off our limbs if we touched what she left for him,' said One Hand. He held up his stump, then gestured to a withered foot. 'And I do not have many left.'

'She was telling the truth,' said Durand, gaining confidence. 'Sir Geoffrey has been known to chop the limbs off men who annoy him, particularly those who tell him lies.'

'If that were true, then *he* would be no more than a torso,' muttered Geoffrey. The alarmed expressions on the beggars' faces told him that the squire's threats were having an effect.

'We have not lied,' bleated Black Hair. 'And we have not touched the package she left, neither. It is on the bench at the back of the nave, just where she put it.'

Durand left the circle of light surrounding the fire and went to where the beggars pointed. Geoffrey saw him pick up a parcel, then look under the bench to make sure there was nothing else. While the men went back to their fire, Durand tucked his findings under his arm and left. When

Geoffrey went to meet him, Durand shoved the package into his hands without a word, and he saw the man was shaking. The beggars had presented no threat, and if Durand was frightened of them, then there was no hope for him as any kind of warrior.

'What is it?' asked Roger, intrigued by the parcel's weight and size. He brightened. 'It might be a bribe, some of that missing silver everyone has been chasing. We can take it, head for the coast, and let Joan and the King finish the battle between them.'

Geoffrey supposed it could be some kind of payment, to ensure he stopped poking in her business. But the discussion Clarembald had overheard indicated the gift would help Geoffrey solve the mystery, not encourage him to abandon it.

'We should unwrap it in the castle,' suggested Durand, glancing around uneasily. 'It is dark here, and we cannot see what we are doing.'

'No,' said Geoffrey, aware that Durand was thinking only of his own comfort.

'No what?' asked Roger. 'No to opening it? Or no to returning to the castle?'

'We do not know what it might contain. I do not want to unwrap it with an audience, only to find it contains a severed head or some such thing.' Edric was on Geoffrey's mind.

'Why should it contain a head?' asked Durand in alarm. 'Where are Helbye and Ulfrith? Are you suggesting one of them has been murdered, like Nauntel? Perhaps I would be better on my own after all. I do not want to be a sacrifice in this dark game.'

'It is your decision,' said Geoffrey, thinking about his diminishing finances and quite happy for Henry's spy to leave him. 'Roger, do you have your tinderbox? Light a candle, so we can see.'

While Roger set about igniting one of the candle stubs he always carried, Geoffrey inspected the package. It was large, comprising a wooden box wrapped in an oiled cloth. It was secured with twine, which he cut with his knife. His dog sniffed it curiously, tail wagging, then lost interest. Geoffrey was relieved, concluding that at least it did not contain any part of the murdered Edric, or the animal would have been far more eager to see it opened.

With Roger, Durand and the dog looking on in various attitudes of hope, fear and boredom, he prised off the lid. The box was full of straw. He rooted through it until his fingers encountered something hard, which he drew out with care.

Twelve

'Is that it?' asked Roger, acutely disappointed as he took the metal object from Geoffrey's hand in the dark graveyard of the Church of St John the Baptist. 'A spike? Is it a weapon?'

'Here is another,' said Durand, drawing a second piece from the box. 'And two more.'

'Dies,' said Geoffrey, bemused. 'Two trussels and two piles, comprising a complete pair of dies.'

Roger frowned. 'Maude sent you her money-making presses? How odd! I was under the impression they were expensive, and can only be bought from London.'

Geoffrey took one and studied it in the unsteady light of the candle. 'They must be the ones that were stolen from Sendi, which he accused me of taking.'

'Sendi said *one* die was stolen,' said Durand. 'If he lost two, he would have been far more agitated.'

Geoffrey recalled the incident in the cellar. 'He was agitated, believe me.'

'Perhaps, but neither of these can be the one Sendi lost,' insisted Durand. 'They are old – you can tell by the mushrooming of the trussels – and he claims the one stolen from him was new, with a fleury cross. Do you remember him explaining all this when we visited his mint, and you made him open that cupboard? It is common knowledge that it is one of his *new* dies that has gone missing, not ancient ones, like these things.'

'True,' said Geoffrey, annoyed with himself for not noticing the damage to the trussel himself.

'But if these are Sendi's old dies,' said Roger, confused, 'then how does Maude come to have them? And why has she given them to you, when Barcwit could use them to make himself a fortune?'

Geoffrey inspected the dies in the candlelight, scrubbing their surfaces with his sleeve to clean them. The writing was backwards, so it would read the right way when punched into the blanks. At first, he could not make out the letters, because they were so badly worn – and it appeared someone had deliberately damaged a few of them – but he gradually worked out what had happened.

'These *are* Sendi's dies. I can just make out the letters S, E and D. But someone has been to considerable trouble to obliterate his name and substitute other letters. The second die is further along the process, and bears the name Sewine.'

'Sewine?' asked Durand.

'He is Exeter's moneyer, mentioned when I visited Osmaer's mint in Bath. You can see SENDI has been changed to SEWINE, by adding a few scratches and some judicious smoothing. However, it is not easy to change BRISTO – how Sendi writes Bristol – to EXCESI for Exeter, so that has been rubbed off altogether, leaving only the B, a T and something that looks vaguely like an N.'

'It is supposed to look like BATHAN,' mused Durand. 'Bath.'

Geoffrey nodded. 'And unless you happen to know that Sewine is located in Exeter, you would happily accept such a coin. But it would be a forgery.'

'And if enough are made, the currency is devalued, just as Henry feared,' said Durand. 'He was right. The plot *is* to oust him from his throne through his economy.'

Geoffrey shook his head. 'We cannot draw that conclusion from these dies alone. All we know for certain is that someone is guilty of forgery. Also, the plot to kill Henry is supposed to originate with Barcwit, not Sendi. I suspect these altered dies are Sendi's work, not Barcwit's.'

'Sendi is the forger?' asked Roger. 'Barcwit did not get hold of Sendi's dies and alter them?'

'No,' said Geoffrey. 'For two reasons. First, Barcwit would not have bothered to change Sendi's name to Sewine – he would just have minted poor-quality coins in Sendi's name. And second, Sendi would have made a terrible fuss if he had discovered any of his old dies missing: so far, he has only complained about the loss of the new one.'

'Perhaps he has not noticed they have gone yet,' suggested Durand.

'You are right: he has not. And he has not, because I suspect they are very recently stolen – perhaps even tonight.'

'How can you tell?' asked Roger doubtfully.

'Because I imagine it takes a lot of time to deface dies – days, perhaps. Sendi would have noticed dies missing for days. But he has not, which suggests they have only just been taken from him. He had a cupboard full of them, and I thought at the time that it was odd he should keep them, when it is safer to destroy them. Now we know why.'

'But how did Maude come by them?' asked Roger, perplexed.

Geoffrey shrugged. 'Each mint has a spy in the other's camp. Barcwit had Edric, and I am fairly certain there is another; he – or she – killed Ceorl when he started to ask awkward questions. So, I imagine this traitor told Maude that Sendi is corrupting his old dies, and was ordered to steal a couple, so they could be given to me. They prove Sendi is a forger. There can be no better evidence, and I do not think he will be able to lie his way out of this. Maude has cornered him.'

'He could claim the blacksmith sold them, instead of destroying them,' said Durand.

Geoffrey disagreed. 'Sendi would not have trusted the smith to burn them, when everyone claims Barcwit has long arms that reach everywhere. He would have seen them inside the furnace himself.'

'There is something else in here,' said Roger, who had been rummaging in the box in the hope that there might be a few examples of counterfeit coins he could steal. He was disappointed when it was empty except for more straw and a scrap of parchment. Geoffrey took it from him and when he unfolded it, a key fell out. He scanned the brief message.

'We were right. Maude says these dies were taken from Sendi this evening, and she hopes they will end the investigation. She also says we should look in Sendi's cellars if we need more evidence against him. This key will unlock the pertinent door.'

257

'Will we find an illegal mint?' mused Durand. 'Or piles of counterfeit coins?'

'Probably the latter,' said Geoffrey. 'It would certainly seal the case against Sendi, because he will not be able to explain away large quantities of forged pennies.' He recalled the ingots in the room where he had been held captive, and now knew exactly how Sendi planned to use them.

'So, you will expose two bad moneyers,' said Durand. 'Sendi the forger and Barcwit the regicide.'

'Stupid Sendi, trying to secure the King's help against Barcwit when he is corrupt himself,' said Roger disdainfully. 'He should have known the truth would come out.'

Geoffrey tossed the dies back in the box and climbed to his feet. 'It is late, and there is no more we can do tonight. But tomorrow, at first light, we will ask Peter for soldiers. We shall visit Sendi and search every last corner of his mint, then do the same to Barcwit. I tried the gentle approach and it did not work, so it is time to see what force can achieve.'

'Good,' said Roger. 'I sense we are almost finished with this case, and then we can leave. I do not like it here.'

Geoffrey entirely agreed.

Peter was horrified when Geoffrey woke him two hours before dawn and informed him he wanted two dozen men for a raid on Sendi's mint. The constable claimed that fighting against Sendi would make the King think he was pro-Barcwit, and then he would never persuade him that he had been dragged into the regicide plot against his will. Geoffrey argued that the same men would later be used against Barcwit, too, and that if Peter wanted Henry to know he was sorry, then lending troops was a good way to start. Peter accepted his logic, but only reluctantly.

'What will you do with Sendi and his forgers?' asked Roger, watching Idonea harry the soldiers into orderly lines. 'The reason you did not arrest them before was because there was nowhere to put them: Peter has every cellar stuffed with provisions. Hah! As if *he* could hold out against Henry.'

'Idonea could,' said Geoffrey. 'For a while, at least.'

'Leave it to me,' said Joan. Her face was pale in the torchlight. 'I shall do some reorganizing while you are gone, and there will be a secure room ready for prisoners by the time you return.'

Geoffrey nodded his thanks, knowing he could trust her. She was good with supplies and their rapid deployment, just as Idonea was good at organizing the castle garrison. Joan left immediately, walking briskly and rubbing her hands together in anticipation of a busy morning.

'You are making a terrible mistake,' said Peter, as he and Idonea approached together. 'It is not Sendi you should raid, but Barcwit. *He* is the one who has broken the law with his forgeries and plots of regicide. There is no need to harry Sendi.'

'There is every need,' said Geoffrey shortly. 'He is just as corrupt as the man he accused.'

'I do not like it,' said Peter worriedly. 'It does not seem fair.'

Idonea agreed. 'Sendi had the courage to go to the King and complain about Barcwit's rule of terror, but look where it has taken him. Your attack tells everyone that the King's "justice" leaves a lot to be desired, and that if Sendi can fall foul of it, then there is no hope for the rest of us.'

'We really did *not* know what Barcwit planned when we first invested with him,' said Peter miserably, reverting yet again to his pitiful claims of innocence. 'We were just pleased by the profits. Then it was too late. It was the same for Joan.'

'Tell Henry that,' suggested Geoffrey, reluctant to begin another such discussion when he needed to plan the attack. 'He said from the beginning that he wanted to know which investors are fools and which are traitors. You must convince him that you fall into the former category.'

'*You* tell him,' said Idonea. 'You intend to save Joan – she told me – so you can save us, too.'

'It does not work like that,' replied Geoffrey. 'I do not—'

'You must!' Idonea's voice had steel in it, and Geoffrey glanced at her in surprise. 'I worked hard for what we have here, and I will not lose it because we have made a mistake.

259

I want Peter to remain constable, and for everything to be as it was before you arrived.'

Peter put his hand on her arm. 'It is too late, dearest. If Geoffrey had not meddled, then Giffard would have done. Our only option now is to run. We should go today, while we are still able.'

'No.' Idonea was adamant. 'I will not abandon all we have built. If Geoffrey will not speak for us, then we will hold our castle against the King. Then, when he comes to fight, we can negotiate a truce that will be more to our advantage than slinking away with nothing. Henry will not waste money on a siege when his coffers are depleted from fighting Bellême, so he will listen to our demands.'

'He is not that poor,' warned Geoffrey, suspecting he would not be poor at all once he had seized the assets of Barcwit and Sendi. He gestured to where the soldiers waited for orders. 'But your troops are about to help expose two corrupt merchants. That will count for something.'

Neither Idonea nor Peter looked convinced, and Geoffrey did not blame them. He was unhappy himself, about what would happen to Joan when the full details of the case were brought to light.

'Very well,' said Peter with a sigh. He glanced at Idonea. 'But I am sure I am right: we should escape, not brazen it out here.'

'I will not leave,' vowed Idonea. 'But Geoffrey's proposal is worth a try, I suppose. We will help him bring down Barcwit, and in return he will tell the King we were unwilling participants in the treachery.'

'But we will tackle Sendi first,' said Geoffrey.

Idonea was distinctly unenthusiastic. 'Very well, then.'

It did not take a genius to see she was far more willing to attack Barcwit. She picked inexperienced or indifferent soldiers for the raid on Sendi and held the best ones in reserve, claiming that Barcwit would be the more formidable opponent. Peter supported her to the hilt, and since Geoffrey could hardly confront Sendi with only Roger for company, he was obliged to accept the sorry squad she selected for him. He left Helbye to impose some semblance of order on them, and went to stand near the motte, thinking about how to deploy them. He needed to be alone, but first Olivier joined him, and then Durand and Ulfrith.

'Peter is terrified,' said Durand gleefully. 'Look! He is trying to slip away, so you will not ask him to go with you when you mount your attack.'

Geoffrey saw the constable making for the gate at a rapid clip, glancing this way and that as he went. 'Fetch him back,' he said tiredly to Ulfrith. 'I do not want his flight to put Sendi on the alert.'

Ulfrith obliged, and Geoffrey winced when the squire launched himself at the fleeing constable in a flying leap that knocked him clean from his feet. Even Olivier, resplendent in spotless armour and a sword that had never seen blood, shook his head at the man's cowardice.

'The man is a fool – and a feeble one at that. We have been friends for years, and fought countless battles together, but I am no longer proud to claim his acquaintance. He does not seem to care that he has dragged his wife into this deadly business, whereas I would give everything I own to turn back time and prevent Joan from becoming embroiled.'

'You could not have stopped her,' said Geoffrey, watching Helbye check that the soldiers had remembered to bring their weapons. He was appalled to see that some had not, and were obliged to borrow from the more elite forces being held in reserve for Barcwit. 'Neither of us could.'

'I should have tried. I am deeply fond of her, Geoffrey, and should have warned her more forcefully not to become involved.'

Geoffrey regarded him uneasily. 'You make it sound as if she knew it was nasty from the start – not that she invested in all innocence, and learnt of the regicide later, like Idonea and Peter.'

'We knew something was amiss, but went ahead anyway.' Olivier's hands flew to his mouth in panic. 'Do not tell me she told you something different? Lord! For God's sake do not tell her I contradicted her! She is determined to safeguard you at all costs – even prepared to drive you away with unkind words, although it hurts her to do it.'

Geoffrey rubbed his head, sorry Joan had not told him the truth because of some misguided attempt to protect him. It made his obligation to the King even more awkward, because Joan being drawn into something against her will, and Joan gleefully leaping to embrace the prospect of Henry's murder were two very different things. He was not sure whether the King would spare her now, no matter what he did, and was faced with the sickening realization that he would lose the last member of his family to a hangman's noose.

'I will not tell her,' he said. He nodded to where Peter was trying to wriggle away from Ulfrith. 'But meanwhile, will you keep your friend here and out of mischief?'

Olivier nodded. 'If that is how I may serve you best today.'

'It is,' said Geoffrey. His request was partly so no one would know about the raid from the terrified constable until the soldiers were on their way, but mostly so the little knight would not feel compelled to join them, either. He would not comport himself well, and Geoffrey did not want Roger to denounce him as a fraud – nor did he want Olivier to get in the way of the fighting.

Olivier sped off obligingly, while Durand handed Geoffrey his shield, sword, helmet and the saddlebag he always carried when he rode, which contained such useful items as a spare dagger, a few strips of linen to use as bandages, a whetting stone and a flask of wine.

'You must be careful on that new horse,' advised Durand. 'It has probably never been in a skirmish before.'

'This is not a raid for mounted soldiers,' said Geoffrey, surprised Durand should think it was. Once again, the squire demonstrated an appalling lack of understanding about military tactics. He pushed the bag back at him, indicating he did not need it, but the squire's hands were shaking in anticipation of violence to come, and it fell from his nerveless fingers to the ground. Something rolled out, and Geoffrey saw it was the doll the dog had stolen from Beiminstre; he recalled guiltily that he had forgotten to ask Durand to mend it. He bent to retrieve it at the same time as Durand, and their heads cracked together. Durand yowled in pain, although Geoffrey felt nothing through his helmet.

'I cannot go with you now,' said Durand, holding both hands to his forehead. 'I am injured, and unable to fight.'

Geoffrey had not wanted him there anyway, just as he did not want Olivier. He tossed the doll up and down in his hand, and saw his medicinal wine had leaked all over it: it was heavy with dampness. He hoped it was not ruined, and decided to rid himself of it before it suffered any more damage.

'Then take this to Beiminstre and give it to the priest,' he said, shoving it into Durand's unwilling hands. 'You can look at my horse at the same time, too, and see if he is getting better.'

The day was becoming lighter, and it was almost time to go. Joan came to report that two storerooms would be cleared by the time he returned, and he was startled when she kissed his cheek.

'I know why you told Olivier to look after Peter,' she whispered. 'You are keeping him out of danger, because you know he is dear to me. I am grateful.'

'Right,' said Geoffrey uncomfortably, hoping she never learnt the truth.

'But you must take care, too,' she added. 'I do not want to lose either of you.'

Before he could reply, she had turned away and was striding to where Peter was arguing furiously with the little knight. Peter's objections faltered when Joan materialized at her husband's shoulder, and he slouched unwillingly towards the chamber where Olivier had decided they would wait. Geoffrey watched with a twinge of anxiety, knowing the investigation was spiralling to its conclusion, and that soon the King's traitors or fools would be exposed to judgement. He had the sickening sense that Olivier's unwitting revelation had just pushed Joan firmly into the former category, and was not sure Henry would be ready to spare her, regardless of what other 'truth' Geoffrey discovered.

He tried to push the matter from his mind while he told the soldiers how to surround Sendi's premises, but it kept coming back to haunt him. He hoped it would not distract him if there was a fight, or make him lose concentration and miss some vital clue. He glanced up at the sky. The first rays of sun were beginning to turn the town from grey to gold. It was going to be a fine day.

'What is wrong?' asked Roger, as he marched next to Geoffrey through the wakening town. The sound of boots and the clank of weapons was loud, and all along the street people pulled open window shutters and doors to see what was happening. 'Your mind is not with us.'

'Joan,' said Geoffrey heavily. 'She is not as innocent as I thought.'

'I am sorry,' said Roger quietly. 'I was beginning to like her, too. She is a fine, strong lass, and one who stands up for what is right.'

'Unfortunately, her idea of what is right amounts to treason, and everything we have done to help her will have been for nothing. Henry will not spare her, and we should never have come here.'

'Think about it later,' advised Roger practically. 'Do not dwell on it now, when we are about to fight. Sendi will not go quietly, and you will need your wits about you. Idonea picked us a poor lot, and you should not rely on them too heavily.'

When they reached the mint, they found Sendi's apprentices already busy. Fires were lit, tools were cleaned and laid out ready for use, and floors were swept clean. The workmen were finishing a breakfast of glutinous oatmeal and salted herrings, and the moneyer, his wife and his *cambium* were in the office inspecting documents. The men jumped up in alarm when Geoffrey forced his way inside with his sword drawn, and several bolted for a back door, where they were met by Helbye. Adelise was furious at the intrusion and came storming towards Geoffrey, Sendi hurrying in her wake.

'What do you mean by bursting into our property?' she demanded.

'I mean to bring an end to your dishonesty,' said Geoffrey, throwing the two altered dies on to a workbench, so everyone could see them. 'These were delivered to me last night. Someone here is in the process of defacing them, so they can be used to produce illegal coins.'

Sendi's face was white. 'Who?' he asked hoarsely. 'Who gave them to you?'

'That is irrelevant. The King will be angry when he learns what you have done. You deceived him on two counts: making bad coins and accusing another moneyer of doing the same.'

'But we were right!' objected Adelise. 'Barcwit has not issued a coin of the correct weight for years. He deserves to be reported to the King.'

Geoffrey shook his head in disbelief. 'Even now, with the evidence of your guilt lying in front of you, you can see no further than your hatred. You should let such feelings go, and concentrate on what you will tell the King instead.'

'Does this mean it is over?' asked Sendi in a low voice. 'Barcwit has won, after all we have been through? I have heard rumours this last week that he plans to murder the King; all I have done is made a little extra money. I may be dishonest, but I am not a traitor.'

'Shut up!' screamed Adelise. 'Geoffrey can prove nothing. The King believed us once; he will do so again.'

'But he did *not* believe us,' said Sendi. 'Why do you think he sent an agent to investigate? It was a stupid idea to try to expose Barcwit. I should never have listened to you.'

'Where is Lifwine?' asked Geoffrey, looking around.

'He escaped through the window,' said Adelise, smirking nastily. 'He will fetch other coiners to speak on our behalf, and will work day and night to see the case against us dismissed. You will not succeed with this travesty of justice.'

'Take them to the castle,' said Geoffrey to Ulfrith. He was disgusted that the *cambium* had been allowed to slip away, and realized he should have paid more attention to Roger's advice as they had walked to the mint: forget Joan and concentrate on what he was doing. It was obvious windows should be guarded as well as doors, but the soldiers had needed to be told and he had neglected to do it.

'No!' Adelise cried, alarmed for the first time. 'You cannot put me in a dungeon.'

'Do not forget to look in the cellar,' whispered Roger, when he saw Geoffrey ready to leave with his prisoners. 'Maude's letter said there was more evidence of Sendi's guilt down there – perhaps forged silver coins.' His eyes gleamed; he intended to help himself to a few.

Geoffrey had forgotten about the letter, because his mind was full of Joan. He rubbed a hand over his face, grateful that at least someone was concentrating on the task at hand.

'Wait!' cried Sendi, sounding desperate. 'I have something to show you. It will prove Barcwit is a far more serious threat than us. We are simple people, who have made silly mistakes, but Barcwit is guilty of far worse. Look in the barrel under the window.'

'Yes,' agreed Adelise triumphantly. 'It will condemn Barcwit once and for all.'

'It is locked,' said Helbye at the same time, rattling the latch on the vault door. 'Shall I force it?'

'I will,' said Geoffrey. He raised his eyebrows. 'Unless someone wants to give us the key?'

'Go to Hell,' snarled Adelise. 'Those chambers are private, and you will never break into them. Our locks are the most expensive money can buy, and . . .'

She trailed off when Geoffrey took his dagger not to the lock, but to the door's leather hinges. When he had hacked through them, it was easy to slide a blade between door and frame and lever it open. Adelise watched the operation in disgust.

'I might have known a Holy Land lout would know how to plunder the houses of innocent people,' she spat. 'It is not the first time you have done this.'

'And hopefully not the last, either,' agreed Roger with a grin.

'Bring them,' said Geoffrey to Helbye and Ulfrith, indicating Sendi and his wife. 'I want them to see what we find, so they cannot later claim to be surprised by it.'

He took the torch Roger had kindled, and led the way down the steps that led to the underground storage rooms, trying to ignore the unpleasant churning in his stomach that always accompanied visits to such places. Ulfrith and Helbye followed with their prisoners, while Roger brought up the rear with a second torch. Geoffrey had not paid much attention when he had last been there, more keen on getting out than exploring, and saw the complex was larger than he had thought. Several doors led off a central chamber, all secured. Adelise's face registered outrage when Geoffrey produced the key Maude had left and began testing it. It slipped easily inside the third lock he tried, turning smoothly.

'Where did you get that?' she demanded.

'Mine is here,' said Sendi, indicating the keys that dangled from his belt. He glared at Geoffrey. 'You made a copy! Was it when I showed you around my mint on Monday?'

Roger pushed past Geoffrey, eager to see what was inside. 'Just as we predicted! Poorly minted coins! They are new and shiny, but the letters are already worn.'

Geoffrey picked up one of the pennies, which sat in piles on a table. A lamp stood next to them, along with ink, pens and parchment, and he had the impression the *cambium* had been in the process of inspecting them, to ensure they were good enough to pass into circulation.

'You think we make a habit of this,' said Sendi in a subdued voice, knowing he was well and truly trapped. 'But what you see there is the sum total of all our attempts, and we were only seeing whether it would work. We started yesterday, and it is the only time we have ever done anything like it, I swear. We were forced into it by Barcwit, because we can no longer compete with him honestly.'

'He is right,' said Adelise, who knew a good defence when she heard one. 'But we thought better of using the coins when we saw the poor results, and planned to over-stamp them today.'

Helbye took the keys from Sendi's belt and opened the other rooms. Besides the boxes of silver in the chamber where Geoffrey had been locked, he found barrels of spices, bales of cloth, and exquisitely tooled leather: Sendi and Adelise supplemented their income by smuggling. Living near the quiet wharves of the Frome, away from the eyes of the more honest merchants on the Avon, dealing in contraband was a good way to make use of cellars that were otherwise empty.

Geoffrey poked around in a half-hearted fashion, suspecting Sendi was telling the truth about the length of time he had been experimenting with those particular forgeries. The dies would have been missed had they been gone too long before he had collected them from St John's Church. He did not expect to discover more counterfeit coins, but neither did he expect to find a body, which had been rolled into a blanket in one of the cellar's dustiest and darkest corners.

'Who is this?' he asked.

Sendi gasped in apparent horror when Geoffrey pulled away the cloth to reveal the corpse's face, while Adelise was startled into blessed silence. The body was fresh and Geoffrey thought the man may even have been alive the previous day. The face was lined and worn, with a network of veins across the cheeks and a purple nose, all indicating a fondness for wine.

'That is Barcwit's *cambium*,' said Sendi in an appalled whisper. 'What is he doing here?'

'Do not look at me,' said Adelise, when Geoffrey turned to her. 'I did not put him there.'

'Well, someone did,' said Geoffrey. 'You claimed earlier that these cellars are private, indicating you are the only ones with access to them. And here is your rival's *cambium*.'

'No!' cried Sendi. 'This is Barcwit's doing. *He* stole our worn dies, along with that key. Therefore, it stands to reason that *he* murdered his *cambium* and left him here.'

Such a solution was not out of the question. Maude's note had said 'conclusive evidence of Sendi's guilt' was in the cellar, which implied she knew not only about the forging room, but about the *cambium*, too. Could she and her friends have killed him and put him there to incriminate Sendi? Geoffrey knew for a fact that Tasso was quite happy to execute people.

'How do you know the *cambium* has been murdered?' he asked Sendi curiously.

'I was making an assumption,' said Sendi, agitated. 'He would hardly come here, roll himself in a blanket and die, would he? Not even for Barcwit.'

'He was a drunkard,' said Adelise. 'Perhaps he was fed more wine than was safe, and he died from a surfeit. Is there a wound?'

Geoffrey pulled the corpse this way and that as he looked

for some sign of violence. 'No, but it is possible he was poisoned.' He regarded her coolly. 'I know someone who is not averse to slipping toxic substances into ale and giving it to people to drink.'

Adelise's anger gave way to desperation. 'We have killed no one! Look in the barrel by the window upstairs before you jump to any more wrong conclusions. It will explain everything.'

'That is what Maude said about what we would find here,' muttered Geoffrey.

'You should have let me kill him,' snarled Adelise to her husband. 'You were stupid to be merciful. Now look where it has landed us.'

'It was not mercy that stayed my hand,' snapped Sendi. 'It was common sense. I did not want Giffard to accuse us of murdering the King's agent, and I needed time to think of a rational solution. It was wild accusations by the River Thames that made Geoffrey our enemy in the first place, and I learnt my lesson. We are in a mire, and hasty, ill-considered decisions will only make it worse.'

'How can it be worse?' shrieked Adelise. 'You never listen to me, and yet I am always right. We should have killed Geoffrey, grabbed all we could carry, and escaped before Giffard arrives.'

They continued to bicker as Ulfrith and Helbye shoved them out of the vault. Geoffrey followed, bounding up the stairs and thankful to be away from the clammy dampness. He left Roger to make a brief inventory of the forged coins, knowing he would slip a few into his own purse as he did so, but not really caring – as long as he had the sense not to spend them in Bristol.

'The barrel,' insisted Sendi, trying to struggle away from Ulfrith. 'Look in the barrel.'

'We were saving it to show Giffard,' said Adelise sullenly. 'He will be more impartial than you. But now you have arrested us, we have no choice but to give it to you.'

'Giffard will not listen to your excuses,' said Roger, surreptitiously fastening his bulging purse as he emerged from the cellars. 'Nor will he care about guilt or innocence – only about fining and arresting as many people as possible.'

269

'Then you must help us,' begged Sendi. 'Look in the barrel.'

Curiosity aroused, Geoffrey walked to the window and saw the cask underneath. It was small, like the kind used to transport expensive wines or valuable spices. He lifted the lid and stared inside.

'Well?' asked Roger. 'Is all explained? Are this pair exonerated from their crimes, and the blame put on Barcwit instead?'

'Not exactly. I do not see how part of Edric's head pickled in brine proves anything.'

'It proves Barcwit murdered him,' insisted Sendi. 'We found his body in the river yesterday – and we lied to you about him. You see, we said we had dismissed him because he had been seduced to Barcwit's side. But he had not. Quite the reverse, in fact.'

'He pretended to spy for Barcwit, but he really remained loyal to you?' asked Geoffrey.

Adelise nodded. 'He sold false secrets, to confuse Barcwit and help our cause. He was a very loyal man. We never genuinely suspected him of stealing our die.'

Sendi's voice was unsteady. 'Edric will serve us in death, just as he did in life. We will use his murder to *prove* that Barcwit is a killer who should not be permitted to walk Bristol's streets.'

'There are a number of folk who should not be allowed to do that,' agreed Roger. 'And I am looking at some of them right now.'

Joan was as good as her word, and had a vault cleared of siege supplies by the time Geoffrey returned to the castle with Sendi, Adelise and their senior workmen. His captives protested vigorously all the way, and Sendi was astonished that Geoffrey did not consider Edric's head sufficient evidence that Barcwit was a cruel tyrant who left him no choice but to commit forgery, smuggling and various other crimes. Their outraged voices followed him as he ensured the cellar doors were locked and guards placed outside, cursing him and swearing vengeance. Then he and Roger returned to the mint.

The remaining labourers were bemused and frightened, but

Geoffrey had no quarrel with them. He took their names, then dismissed them with a warning to choose a more honest master next time. When the last one had gone, he locked the doors, nailed the window shutters closed and instructed one of Peter's captains to ensure it was guarded day and night. He wanted Giffard to see the forging chamber, Edric's pickled head and the mint exactly as it had been found.

However, he took two things with him. The first was Barcwit's *cambium*, because he did not want to present the bishop with a maggoty, rat-eaten corpse in the event of any delay in his arrival. The second was a letter that had been fastened under the lid of the barrel. He slipped it inside his surcoat when no one was looking, while the *cambium* went to Feoc at St John's Church.

'Surely, it cannot be over?' asked Feoc unhappily, fetching two planks and a sheet for his charge. 'I thought you would find Barcwit guilty, and have *him* removed from our town.'

'It is not over yet,' said Geoffrey. 'Sendi made a stupid mistake: he should not have forged coins while I was investigating him. He claims he has only manufactured a few – which I suspect is true, as far as *these* dies are concerned – but the arrangements in his cellar indicate he has done it before.'

The clank of the door opening made them turn uneasily, and the knights' hands moved quickly to the hilts of their swords. It was Warelwast, pale and anxious, and gripping a reluctant Clarembald by the arm. Bloet and Bishop John were behind them, curious to see where the bishop-elect was hauling the physician with such urgency.

'There you are, Geoffrey,' said Warelwast, relieved. 'When I awoke, the whole castle was buzzing with the news that you have arrested Sendi.'

'He does not have faith in your fighting abilities,' explained Clarembald, tugging his arm free. 'He insisted I come with him, in case you needed a physician.'

'That is why I came, too,' added John. 'I did not want you to survive Sendi, only to be killed by the ministrations of this heretic.'

'And I am here to see if you have news of the missing

silver,' said Bloet hopefully. The word 'silver' silenced the argument that was about to erupt between the two medics, and they waited with some interest to hear the answer. Silver was, after all, more important than another spat.

'It is not at Sendi's mint,' replied Roger, who had taken more notice of the moneyer's assets than had Geoffrey. 'He had some secret supplies, but not enough to be Barcwit's hoard.'

Bloet's expression was one of acute disappointment, and he began a detailed discussion with Roger about whether the King could be convinced that the load Alwold had lost to robbers was smaller than everyone had been led to believe. Roger thought such a ploy might work; Bloet did not, on the grounds that he knew Henry rather too well.

'Since you are here, perhaps you can answer a question about this man,' said Geoffrey to the physicians, indicating the dead *cambium*. 'How did he die?'

'He was my patient,' said Clarembald.

'And there you have your answer,' muttered John.

Clarembald ignored him. 'I treated him for a hardening of the liver and other ailments caused by an excess of wine. He was dying when I visited him at Barcwit's mint two days ago, and said then that he would not last another night. His death is no surprise.'

Geoffrey was thoughtful. 'So, rather than simply bury him, Barcwit decided to put the body to good use, and have Sendi placed in a compromising situation.'

'That makes sense,' said Roger. 'Maude's letter did tell us to look in the cellar. How could she have known about the body unless she – or one of her minions – had put it there?'

Geoffrey turned to Clarembald. 'When you treated the *cambium*, was Barcwit present?'

'No, it was Maude who summoned me. Why do you ask?'

'I have a lot to do,' said Geoffrey, not inclined to answer questions when he had so many of his own. He considered tackling Clarembald there and then about his sinister relationship with Barcwit, but suspected the man would have replies at the ready, and any accusations were likely to draw gleeful and unwanted support from Bishop John. It was not the right time to confront Clarembald.

'I will come with you,' offered Warelwast, following Geoffrey outside. 'Now Sendi has gone, Barcwit will feel himself all-powerful, and you will need your friends.'

'He has all the friends he needs,' said Roger shortly. 'Me.'

'One can never have enough friends,' said Warelwast smoothly, ignoring Roger's hostility. 'I have done what you asked, by the way.'

Geoffrey had no idea what he was talking about.

'Joan,' said Warelwast impatiently. 'You must have noticed that a little of her frost towards you has melted. I have some way to go, but I will succeed.'

'Prayers,' said Geoffrey, indicating Warelwast should enter the church again. He could hear the physicians shouting at each other, while Bloet was asking Feoc in a plaintive voice if he was absolutely certain he knew of no man called Piers in Bristol. 'I need prayers to win her around completely.'

'Now?' asked Warelwast, knowing he was being dismissed, but not sure how to avoid it.

Geoffrey nodded, then exchanged a grin of satisfaction with Roger when the bishop-elect reluctantly did as he was asked. Then Geoffrey put the annoying cleric from his mind, and concentrated on what they had learnt from Sendi, and Maude's role in bringing her husband's rival to his knees.

'Her whole plan smacks of something hastily thrown together. We know the *cambium* died naturally, so they probably decided to put his body in the cellar at the very last moment.'

'That sounds reasonable, but you cannot prove it,' Roger pointed out. 'Feoc is right: Barcwit has got away with his crimes, while Sendi has allowed himself to become trapped.'

'Barcwit has made mistakes, too,' said Geoffrey, pulling the letter out of his surcoat. 'This was sealed when I found it, suggesting Sendi has not yet read it. If he had, then he would have presented it to me – or to Giffard – and the case would have been over. Barcwit wrote it.'

'What is it?' asked Roger, without much interest. 'And how do you know who wrote it?'

'It carries Barcwit's seal, and it is written in the same curly hand that I have seen on other documents issued from his mint. It is definitely from him. It was either stolen before he had the chance to send it, or it was taken from its recipient.'

'What does it say?'

'It outlines details of the plot to kill Henry. It will happen at his Christmas Court in Westminster, and will involve an ambush at the stables when he goes to hunt.'

'Then that is that,' said Roger, gratified. 'We shall arrest Barcwit and his people, too.'

'Yes,' said Geoffrey with a sigh. 'As soon as Peter's men have eaten. I suspect they will consider Barcwit rather more daunting than Sendi, and they will feel better with full stomachs.'

Roger glanced at him. 'You do not seem as pleased by this as you should. What is wrong?'

'The letter from Barcwit,' said Geoffrey unhappily. 'It is addressed to Joan.'

When Geoffrey reached the castle, he found Peter in a state of wild panic. Even the sensible Idonea could not calm him, and nor did Olivier's polite entreaties and Joan's gruff demands for his silence. The cause of his terror was twofold: Bishop Giffard was approaching the town gates and would arrive within the hour, and Barcwit had got wind of the fact that he was next on Geoffrey's arrest list and was said to be extremely irritated. From the agonized expression on the constable's face, Geoffrey supposed that Barcwit's irritation was deemed to be a lot more dangerous than it sounded.

'What will we do?' Peter wailed. 'I thought we would have more time!'

Geoffrey did not see what the fuss was about. 'We have Sendi and his forgers, and we will soon have Barcwit and his would-be regicides, too. It is almost over.'

Peter was distraught. 'Poor Sendi was driven to his crimes by necessity – Barcwit gave him no choice. Barcwit is a monster, and I hope he dies at the end of a hangman's noose. But that means I may die with him. He will tell everyone that I gave him money to murder the King.'

'Compose yourself,' snapped Idonea. She turned to Geoffrey. 'Is it possible that Giffard will be so absorbed by

Sendi's crimes that he will forget to look at Barcwit's?'

'No,' said Geoffrey patiently. She was grasping at straws. 'He will consider regicide a far more serious offence than forgery. Besides, he is quite capable of judging two cases at the same time.'

'But you have no evidence against Barcwit,' said Joan in a small voice. She was frightened now the case was so close to its conclusion. 'Not like the case you have against Sendi.'

'I do,' said Geoffrey. He took the letter from his surcoat, but did not open it. 'This outlines Barcwit's plot to murder the King. He will be found guilty of treason.'

'Then you must destroy it,' said Peter, white-faced.

'And then what?' demanded Geoffrey, rounding on him, so the constable took an involuntary step back. 'We allow Barcwit to go free and he carries out his plan? He is unlikely to succeed, because Henry knows there are men who want him dead, and he is careful. Barcwit will die a traitor's death, and so will every man, woman and child remotely connected to him – and you will be deemed doubly guilty because you had a chance to stop him and you failed.'

'We should leave this town,' said Peter shakily. 'As I suggested days ago, when you first arrived and started to meddle. We must flee to Ireland.'

'I am not going anywhere,' said Idonea, although Geoffrey could see her resolve was weakening. Giffard's impending arrival had forced her to confront the fact that holding a castle against royal troops was a rash thing to attempt. 'All we have is here. Do you want to live the life of a pauper in some Irish bog?'

'It is better than choking on a gibbet,' Olivier pointed out. 'I spoke to Bloet this morning, and he says Geoffrey has no influence over the King – that even if he does speak in our defence, Henry will still do as he pleases. Bloet also thinks that Henry will refuse to spare Joan once he learns about the plot to kill him.' His face was waxen, and Joan slipped a comforting hand into his.

Geoffrey was about to reply, when he heard excited voices, and turned to see Bloet, Warelwast and the physicians hurrying towards them, full of the news about Giffard. He was currently in Beiminstre, having a lame horse tended, but would soon appear to dispense justice in the King's name. Warelwast was delighted, and Geoffrey supposed the bishop's arrival had been included in his prayers.

Meanwhile, Idonea had thought hard about her husband's suggestion. 'I have a box of gold in my chamber. It will see us to Ireland, and we can come back after Barcwit kills Henry.'

'Yes,' said Peter desperately. 'But we must go *now*. If we wait for Giffard, it will be too late. We will join Sendi in the dungeons, and that will be the end of us.'

'You are leaving?' asked Bloet. 'If I were in your position, I would have gone days ago.'

'It is probably prudent,' agreed Warelwast. 'But Barcwit will never succeed in killing the King, so I recommend you stay in Ireland for a year, and then write to Henry requesting a pardon. By then, this nasty business will be no more than an unpleasant memory, and he may allow you to buy your way home. Be generous in what you offer to pay, though. Royal justice does not come cheap.'

'Well?' asked Idonea of Geoffrey. 'Will you stop us? I warn you, I will not be easy to subdue.'

Geoffrey was sure she would not. 'You may go, but only if you take Joan.'

'More people will slow us down!' wailed Peter.

'Then you can stay here and meet Giffard,' said Geoffrey uncompromisingly.

'No, Geoff,' said Joan, clutching Olivier's arm for support. 'I will not run.'

'You have no choice,' said Geoffrey, thinking about the letter. 'Henry will not spare you, and I should have known better than to believe he would.'

'But where will I go? I have no funds to live in Ireland. Or will you take me to the Holy Land?'

Geoffrey pushed his purse into her hands; it contained the last of his money. 'Take a ship to Barfleur and wait for me there. No one will notice if you leave now, because everyone's attention will be on Giffard and the raid on Barcwit's mint.'

'I will see her safely on a ship from Exeter,' offered Warelwast.

'She is my sister,' warned Geoffrey. 'If anything happens to her . . .'

Warelwast unfastened the rope he had worn around his neck since Bath. 'Here is my pledge that I will do all in my power to protect her – although, to be frank, she looks like the kind of woman who should be protecting me.'

'Come with us, Geoff,' begged Joan, as the knight took the troth from Warelwast and shoved it inside his surcoat. 'You have uncovered enough to keep Henry happy, and Giffard can deal with Barcwit. He has men trained for that sort of thing, but you only have Peter's rabble. Do not—'

'We have no time to discuss it, and I cannot wait for Giffard, because I suspect Barcwit will try to escape.' Geoffrey turned to Peter. 'Are these troops of yours ready to fight?'

'I do not know,' said Peter backing away. 'And I do not care. I am leaving.'

He turned and fled. Olivier began to pull Joan away, although it took Idonea's strength and Warelwast's encouragement to make her budge. Her face was a mask of distress, but Geoffrey had no time to comfort her. He needed to muster the soldiers and march on Barcwit before either the man barricaded himself in his mint – and Geoffrey was not interested in a siege – or he escaped to kill Henry. He thought about the letter in his surcoat, aware of its ugly presence burning against him.

With weary resignation, he saw the 'elite' soldiers had not even donned their armour properly and, rather than watch them prepare with the slow, fumbling fingers of inexperience, he ran the short distance to Barcwit's mint, wanting to observe it and assess whether a raid was expected. He slipped inside the porch of St Ewen's and waited. The mint was silent, which was suspicious in itself, because it should have been ringing with noise and exuding rank smells. It was not long before the door opened and someone hurried out. He was swathed in a hooded cloak, but Geoffrey recognized him, nonetheless.

'Master Lifwine,' he said, stepping out to intercept Sendi's *cambium* and drag him inside the porch, so they would not be seen by Barcwit. 'What are you doing here?'

*   *   *

'Let me go,' screeched Lifwine, pulling a knife from his belt. 'You have no right to manhandle me.'

Geoffrey jumped back as the *cambium* swiped at him. The lunge was clumsy and, although it missed him, it knocked over a bowl of water that had been left for beggars. Lifwine's wet soles made patterns on the dry stone floor as he dodged this way and that, trying to edge around Geoffrey and escape. Suddenly, something clicked into place in the knight's mind, and he understood exactly why he had noticed dirty footprints every time he had visited Barcwit's house. He glanced at Lifwine's expensively heeled shoes, an odd style that created distinctive marks. Lifwine had been a regular visitor there, taken to the upper chambers, where he could be entertained away from prying eyes.

Geoffrey was angry with himself for not pulling the facts together sooner. 'I should have known.'

'Known what?' Lifwine scowled when Geoffrey evaded his blade a second time.

'That you are Sendi's traitor – because of what happened at Westminster, for a start. It was you who insisted most strongly that Roger and I murdered Fardin, even though we had no reason to do so. Your motive was that you did not want Sendi to kill one of Barcwit's men – your real comrades – in retaliation. But Fardin was probably killed by Rodbert or Tasso.'

'Rodbert,' confirmed Lifwine. His voice was full of disdain. 'To get to Maude, although much good it did him. She even bedded you in her new-found freedom, I am told.'

'Leading folk astray over Fardin was not all you did for Barcwit,' said Geoffrey, stepping away from another clumsy attempt to stab him, but making no move to arm himself. There was no need. 'You stole Sendi's dies and left the dead *cambium* in his cellar. Maude could not have done it, because she would not have been able to get in. But you are Sendi's most trusted colleague, in a position to make copies of his keys. You killed Ceorl, too, who was on the verge of exposing you with his questions. And you betrayed Edric, by telling Barcwit he was only pretending to sell Sendi's secrets.'

'Maybe I did,' said Lifwine, eyes darting towards the door

and freedom. 'Sendi is becoming too dangerous for the likes of me. I am beginning to prefer my chances with Barcwit.'

Geoffrey did not think his chances were much improved, if Edric was anything to go by. 'You attacked me in Bath,' he said, as another mystery became clear. 'My dog ripped a gold pendant from one would-be killer. It was yours.'

'How do you know that?' Lifwine was becoming alarmed by the litany of accusations.

'First, you have recently lost one: when I grabbed you in Sendi's mint, I saw marks on your neck that indicate you have worn jewellery until lately. And second, the pendant itself gave you away.'

'How?' Lifwine stabbed again, stumbling when Geoffrey pushed him away.

'It is old and worn, but clearly a gold coin,' said Geoffrey, taking it from his purse. 'It was *your* ancestor who struck gold coins for King Aethelred. There is no question that this belongs to you.'

Lifwine licked dry lips. 'You misunderstood what I—'

'Rodbert was with you in Bath,' said Geoffrey, now guessing. 'He is the kind of man to drown his victim, rather than engage in a fair fight. What about the ambush in Westminster? Was that you, too?'

'No!' cried Lifwine. He spat suddenly, causing Geoffrey to jump back in surprise; the knight had never seen saliva deployed in a fight before. At the same time, Lifwine abandoned his protestations of innocence, and took a firmer grip on his dagger, hatred burning in his eyes. 'There was no need to attack you then, when we had the entire journey to Bristol ahead of us. I wish we had—'

'Put down the knife,' interrupted Geoffrey, tiring of the situation and wanting to fry some larger fish. 'You cannot escape and you will only make matters worse for yourself if you resist arrest.'

'I will never be taken by you!' shouted Lifwine, although his eyes were wide with terror. He hawked again and, even though he knew it would not hurt him, Geoffrey still twisted out of the way.

Geoffrey had had enough. He disarmed the *cambium* with

ease, and hurled him over his shoulder, to carry him to the castle.

'Please!' Lifwine howled. 'I will do anything you ask, but do not put me in a dungeon with Sendi.'

'Where is the missing silver, then?' asked Geoffrey, not breaking his stride.

Lifwine began to shake. 'I cannot tell you, because I do not know. Ask something else. Let me tell you about Sendi's forgeries. He has been doing it for years, and forcing *me* to pass inferior coins.'

'I know,' said Geoffrey. 'There is evidence aplenty to convict him. Tell me about Barcwit and his plot to kill the King.'

Lifwine began to sob. 'There is no plot; I swear it! I would never associate myself with someone who planned to commit regicide. I have standards, you know.'

'Perhaps,' acknowledged Geoffrey, gripping him tight as the man made a last, frantic effort to escape. 'But not ones I admire. You are the worst kind of traitor – one who betrays his friends.'

Thirteen

When Helbye told Geoffrey that Idonea's 'elite' troops were ready, the knight informed the men that they were going to march against Barcwit in the King's name. Some regarded each other with open horror, others looked distinctly uneasy, and only a few betrayed no emotion. Geoffrey hoped the brave ones would set an example to the cowards and not the other way around, because he did not want to find himself battling single-handed. After that morning's debacle, in which Lifwine had been allowed to escape, he had no faith in any of them. As a measure of his distrust, he had even resorted to including Durand among the fighters. The squire joined the ranks of those who were terrified.

'Is Barcwit expecting us?' asked Roger in a low voice, so as not to be overheard by the jittery troops.

Geoffrey shrugged. 'According to Lifwine, he does not believe we have the courage to confront him. Did you make sure the *cambium* is locked up?'

'In the cellar next to Sendi, although it was tempting to shove him in the same one. I do not approve of men who betray their friends – even when those friends are men like Sendi.'

Then they were off, marching in ragged columns along the same road they had taken at dawn. Fearfully, people watched them pass, and some folk darted into their houses and secured their doors. Others quickly followed suit, and it was not long before the streets were empty, with windows shuttered as if it were night, rather than the middle of the morning.

When they reached Barcwit's mint, Roger escorted a third of the men to the back of the building, while Helbye and Geoffrey divided the remaining soldiers between them. Helbye took the alley that ran along the side, while Geoffrey went to the front, indicating that Ulfrith and Durand were to accompany him. He stepped up to the door and hammered on it with the hilt of his dagger. It was opened by Maude, so quickly he suspected she had been waiting for him.

'I heard you met with success today. Have you come to thank me for my help in catching Sendi?'

'I have come to arrest you,' replied Geoffrey. 'I have written evidence of a plot to kill the King, and you, Barcwit and all your people must answer for it.'

'Surrender?' she asked, her eyes unreadable. 'I do not think so!'

She leaned forward, as if to say something else, but Geoffrey had seen the flash of metal in the sunlight, and jumped away from the dagger intended to disembowel him. She staggered and he pinned her against the wall, yelling for his men to enter the mint as he did so. They hesitated, so he hurled her at Ulfrith and led the charge himself, hoping some of them would follow.

'Barcwit!' he yelled. 'Your game is over, and I advise you to give up now.'

'Do you indeed?' asked Tasso from the scribes' room. Rodbert was with him; both held swords.

'Go into the minting chamber,' Geoffrey ordered the soldiers behind him. 'Lead the way, Durand. Find Barcwit, and kill anyone who tries to escape.'

'Me?' asked Durand in an unsteady voice. 'You want *me* to find Barcwit?'

Tasso lunged at Durand and laughed when the squire gave a yelp of fright.

'Go!' yelled Geoffrey to Durand. 'I will deal with these two.'

'Both of us?' asked Rodbert in a soft, dangerous voice.

Geoffrey was aware of footsteps behind him, followed by a good deal of shouting. He hoped the men were doing as he ordered, and wished he had given Maude to Durand to mind, and told Ulfrith to lead the attack. But it was too late to change anything, so he turned his attention to the pair who moved forward to fight him, waiting to see who would strike first.

It was Tasso, who lunged with an almighty swing that Geoffrey was hard-pressed to parry. Geoffrey pretended to stagger, then gave the man a powerful shove when he moved in to press the advantage he thought he had won. Rodbert attacked while Geoffrey was distracted, but the flashing blade did not penetrate his mail. Geoffrey went after him so fast that he tripped over a low bench and fell awkwardly; it was obvious from the unpleasantly soggy snap that he had broken his arm. While the deputy howled and cursed, Geoffrey spun around to face Tasso.

Tasso was evidently anticipating a more leisurely skirmish, because he was unprepared for the lightning way Geoffrey came for him. While they slashed at each other, Rodbert lurched to the shelves and began to lob whatever he could lay his good hand on – inkpots, writing slates, jars of sand used for drying wet ink. Some were heavy, and Geoffrey was obliged to use one arm to fend them off, fighting Tasso with the other. He began to doubt the wisdom of tackling both at the same time.

'You are going to die,' taunted Rodbert, hurling a block of sealing wax with devastating accuracy. Geoffrey's head jerked forward with the impact and he was glad he was wearing his helmet.

He did not reply, but used both hands to whirl his sword in a circle, so Tasso, leaping back to avoid being cut in half, staggered into the deputy. Rodbert screeched as his colleague smashed into his injured arm. Furious, Tasso attacked with a series of clean, sweeping blows. Geoffrey parried them with no trouble, but was beginning to tire. Broadswords were heavy, and there was only so long a man could wield them – especially when one hand was fending off a potentially lethal aerial bombardment.

'Hurry,' Rodbert snapped, gritting his teeth. 'Giffard will be here at any moment, and we do not want to be fighting the King's agent when he arrives. That would be difficult to explain.'

Geoffrey ducked as the deputy hurled one of the lead weights used for anchoring parchments. It thumped into the wall behind him and cracked the plaster. While he was off balance, Tasso landed a particularly heavy blow that vibrated up his arm and numbed his hand. He felt his sword begin to slip out of his grasp, and only kept hold of it by sheer will power. Tasso sensed his weakness and launched another attack.

'I wish Lifwine and I *had* killed you in Bath,' shouted Rodbert. 'Then we would not be in this ridiculous position. I should have used Maude. She knows how to escape from tight situations – it was her idea to use the false dies and our dead *cambium* to trap Sendi. She is quite a woman.'

'I know,' said Geoffrey, deliberately taunting in the hope that it would provoke the man into doing something other than lobbing heavy objects.

It was a mistake. Rodbert's bombardment intensified, and his anger served to make him more accurate, not less. Meanwhile, Tasso used the distraction to drive Geoffrey into a place where he was even more exposed to Rodbert's volleys. Geoffrey went down on one knee when a wax tablet caught him on the chin, and found himself facing a new danger: Rodbert's feet. As long as Geoffrey was fending off Tasso, it was difficult to protect himself. Rodbert's first kick caught Geoffrey on the knee, and the second in the stomach. Geoffrey staggered to his feet, but he was winded, and could not raise his sword. With a blank, professional expression, Tasso prepared to end the encounter, while Rodbert retrieved his own sword and advanced from the other side. Then Ulfrith was in the room, wielding an axe heavily and clumsily.

'No,' gasped Geoffrey, when Rodbert turned on him. Even one-handed, the deputy would kill Ulfrith, because the lad was not yet properly trained. 'I told you to watch Maude.'

'I killed her,' said Ulfrith apologetically. 'She drew a knife, so I was obliged to stab—'

'You killed her?' demanded Rodbert in disbelief. 'You murdered my sister? I will—'

'Your sister?' echoed Geoffrey, startled. He twisted away from Tasso and ducked behind a table, to put a barrier between them while he caught his breath. 'But you are lovers!'

'I thought she was married to Barcwit,' said Ulfrith, equally bewildered. With horror, Geoffrey saw him lower his axe while he considered the revelation: Ulfrith was not able to think and fight at the same time, and Geoffrey saw Rodbert's face twisted with anger and hatred as he advanced.

'Ulfrith!' Geoffrey yelled. 'Your weapon!'

Ulfrith brought his axe up in front of him, and it was pure luck that it parried the murderous blow Rodbert aimed at his head. Meanwhile, Tasso grabbed the table and hurled it away so he could reach Geoffrey.

'Now we will end this,' said Tasso grimly. 'No more playing.'

'Fight me!' Geoffrey shouted to Rodbert, half his attention still on Ulfrith. The sight of a friend in danger gave him the strength he needed to deal with Tasso. Now free from Rodbert's missiles, he attacked with a series of two-handed swipes that demonstrated why he had survived so many Holy Land battles. 'Or does a man who seduces his sister not have the courage? Ulfrith did not sleep with Maude. *I* did. She said she needed a man, because you were not up to the task.'

'Just like their father, then,' Tasso muttered, his face contorted with effort as he countered Geoffrey's blazing attack. 'Barcwit is said to be poor in the bedchamber, too.'

Geoffrey's thoughts whirled, but it was no time for assessing Maude's peculiar taste in lovers. He saw his taunts had not encouraged Rodbert away from Ulfrith, and the boy was rapidly losing ground under the onslaught, so, while Tasso was still in retreat, he snatched up an inkpot and threw it as hard as he could. There was a crack as it struck Rodbert's skull. For a moment, the deputy continued to walk, but then his knees buckled and he pitched forward. Geoffrey could not see whether he was dead when he fell, but he certainly was once Ulfrith had plunged the axe into him. Tasso's assault faltered, and he gazed at his fallen colleague in disbelief.

'Put up your sword, Tasso,' ordered Geoffrey. 'There is no point in fighting further.'

Tasso closed his eyes, and seemed suddenly weary. 'I fought with honour and can do no more.'

Geoffrey took the proffered sword and indicated that Tasso should precede him to the workshop, where he had seen Edric murdered just two days before. Killing unarmed men was hardly honourable, either, but he did not bother to point that out. Tasso was a hireling, no more. Maude, Rodbert and Barcwit held the real power, and two of them were dead. There was only Barcwit to go.

He pushed open the door of the mint, expecting Roger and Helbye to have done their work and secured the rest of the building. He was startled, therefore, to find it abandoned. He was about to go and see what was happening at the back when he heard a click. Slowly, he turned around.

'That is far enough,' said a familiar voice. 'Let Tasso go. He does not like being at the end of a sword – not the pointed end, at least.'

'I killed her,' said Ulfrith, when Geoffrey glared at him. 'There was blood and everything.'

'A scratch,' said Maude. Geoffrey saw there was a gouge in her arm, although it did not affect her ability to hold a crossbow. He saw three others behind her, similarly armed. 'You should teach your men to inspect their "dead" enemies before jumping to conclusions, Geoffrey.'

Geoffrey said nothing, and Tasso stepped forward to disarm him. He considered resisting, but the expression on Maude's face told him she would not hesitate to shoot, just for the inconvenience he had caused her. Then a door opened, and more of Barcwit's men entered, holding Helbye and Roger at sword point. The big knight was scowling furiously, while Helbye limped and his face was ashen.

'It is these new boots you bought me,' the old soldier declared sullenly. 'They pinch, and I cannot move properly. This rout had nothing to do with my aching hip.'

'I am sorry,' murmured Roger. 'Peter's rabble deserted when Maude said Barcwit was coming.'

'There he is!' said Ulfrith in alarm, pointing to the cloaked figure who stood silent and foreboding at one side of the room. Barcwit looked exactly as he had when he watched Edric's execution, with his face in shadow and his hands tucked in his sleeves. Geoffrey frowned. Then, before anyone could stop him, he darted forward and took a handful of the man's clothing. Tasso screamed in outrage, and sprang forward to pull him away, but it was too late.

With a small squeak the figure slowly toppled and landed with a crash.

'Barcwit does not exist,' said Geoffrey, gesturing to the cloak that lay on the floor. 'He is just rags on a stick. You put him in windows and shadowy corners to frighten people, but he is not real.'

'But I saw him walking,' said Roger in confusion. 'Out in the town.'

'That was Maude,' said Geoffrey. 'She disappeared very quickly the time we met in St John's Church, indicating she has intimate knowledge of Bristol's small alleys and hidden paths. She put that knowledge to good use by donning dark clothes and stalking around at night. Her ability to materialize and slip away again made people think Barcwit was in league with the Devil – an image she is happy to perpetuate.'

'It worked,' said Maude with a smile. 'Today is a good example. All I had to do was shout that Barcwit was coming, and your attack turned into a rout.'

'Has he ever existed?' asked Geoffrey. He answered his own question. 'Of course he has. The beggars in St John's Church said he was once a normal-sized man with an appetite for whores. He had an appetite for his daughter, too, if Tasso is to be believed.'

Maude glared at Tasso, who shrugged. 'I have always found your marriage an unusual one.'

'It has been a very successful partnership,' stated Maude irritably. 'And we were married in name only. I would never lie with my father. What kind of woman do you think I am?'

Geoffrey did not reply, but supposed a chaste marriage explained why she sought comfort elsewhere – with her brother, for example. Tasso cleared his throat, troubled, and Geoffrey knew he was searching for the words to tell her Rodbert was dead. He sensed they would not live long once that news was out and flailed around for questions to ask, in the hope that a delay would give him time to think of a way out of their predicament. All Peter's soldiers had fled, and Durand had evidently gone with them: Geoffrey and his three companions were on their own – unarmed and watchfully guarded.

'Your half-brother is—' began Tasso softly.

'We can talk about dies instead,' Geoffrey interrupted hastily. 'Did you take Sendi's new die, as well as his old ones? Or was that Lifwine?'

'We had nothing to do with that,' replied Maude. 'And neither did Lifwine – although he is a slippery sort of fellow and may be lying.' She looked at the mess they had made: overturned benches, scattered tools and spilled materials. 'All this was quite unnecessary. We have done nothing wrong.'

'Except plot to kill the King,' said Geoffrey.

Maude sighed. 'There *is* no plot. We have no reason to want Henry dead, and distant politics are irrelevant to us. We occasionally make slightly underweight coins, and sometimes we offer rates of interest above what we should, but that is all. Where is Rodbert?' She looked questioningly at Tasso, who cleared his throat again.

'I do not believe you,' said Geoffrey quickly.

'It does not matter what you believe,' said Maude. She indicated 'Barcwit' with her head. 'We cannot let you live now you have discovered he is no more than a cloak and a broom handle. It took a lot of clever rumour-mongering to create him, and I do not want to start all over again.'

'I do not see why you bothered,' said Roger in disgust. 'It is stupid.'

'But so are people,' said Maude. 'And they are always willing to believe the worst. A Barcwit who haunts dark streets and likes to watch hangings is far more interesting than an old man with twinkling eyes who married his daughter to protect her from over-zealous suitors – the daughter of a wealthy merchant was too attractive a target, and ambitious men would not leave me alone.'

'We could not have frightened anyone with the real Barcwit,' elaborated Tasso. 'But the spectre of *our* Barcwit encouraged people not to withdraw their investments at awkward times, and not to look too carefully at what we were doing. Even Sendi was too frightened to come and spy. It is fear that keeps us rich.' He turned to Maude, his face grim. 'Rodbert is—'

'Giffard will demand to meet Barcwit,' interrupted Geoffrey.

'And when you refuse – as you did with me – he will pronounce you all traitors, and that will be the end of you.'

'Rodbert has been practising with face pastes and wigs these last few days,' said Maude. 'You have taught us that, at least – the King's agents need to meet Barcwit if we want them to go away and leave us alone. And Giffard will do exactly that. There is no plot to kill the King, and there never was. I have no idea how your sister and Peter came up with that tale.'

'We are victims of our own success,' said Tasso ruefully. 'That story was fabricated by others, because it seemed the kind of thing our Barcwit would do. The yarn about the priest's child and the cat is untrue, too, and so is the one about the family who stopped outside our mint and were eaten. They are myths invented by fear.'

'What about Peter's friend Nauntel?' asked Roger.

'Not our doing,' replied Maude. 'Nauntel was one of our investors, and is no use to us dead. On the contrary, we wanted him alive.'

'And my brother?' asked Geoffrey quietly.

'Joan thinks we killed him,' said Maude. 'And I did nothing to disabuse her of the notion, because I do not want her to withdraw her investment. But we did not touch your brother. I am telling the truth, Geoffrey: you are going to die, so there is no need for me to lie to you about it.'

Tasso steeled himself. This time, his words were out before Geoffrey could stop him. 'Speaking of brothers, Geoffrey has just murdered yours.' He raised his sword. 'Shall I . . . ?'

Maude's jaw dropped in horror. 'Rodbert?'

'Dashed his brains out with a pot,' elaborated Tasso, waving his sword questioningly.

'Rodbert?' whispered Maude again, blood draining from her face.

Geoffrey knew there would not be another opportunity. While she was stricken with shock, he rushed forward and bowled her from her feet. Immediately, a hail of crossbow bolts snapped into the floor around them, and he heard Tasso yelling to the archers to cease fire, afraid they would hit Maude by mistake. While Geoffrey was still rolling across the floor with Maude in his arms, Tasso rushed at him with his sword. Geoffrey grabbed Maude's bow and raised it to protect himself. Tasso's blade sliced it in two. Then he prepared to do the same to Geoffrey.

With a roar, Roger powered across the room, slamming into Tasso and pinning him against the wall, while several of Barcwit's men leapt on to the big knight's back, trying to pull him away. Geoffrey ducked as more quarrels sliced through the air: not all the archers were obeying Tasso's orders not to shoot. One soldier dropped to the floor with a shriek, and Maude scrabbled furiously at Geoffrey, trying to fasten her hands around his throat. Helbye and Ulfrith grappled with their own opponents, and suddenly, the whole room was a frantic swirl of weapons and struggling bodies.

Geoffrey freed himself from Maude and snatched up another bow. He aimed at Tasso, but someone stumbled into him and his shot went wide. More missiles hissed, followed by shrieks as men were hit. He saw Maude fall, and was aware of Tasso trying to rally his troops into some semblance of order.

Then the door was wrenched open, and more men poured in while others scrambled out. Geoffrey had no idea what was happening, so obeyed his clamouring instincts: he grabbed a sword and fought with every ounce of his strength, determined that if he was to die, then he would take Maude, Tasso and their followers with him. It was some time before he became aware that someone was shouting his name with increasing desperation.

'Geoffrey! Stop!'

He stared at the yelling man in astonishment. It was Giffard, looking bulky in his monastic habit. Then he saw the livery of the soldiers who had burst into the mint, and recognized the King's insignia. Durand hovered behind the bishop, pleased with himself, and Geoffrey supposed possessing a cowardly squire had its advantages: Durand had seen the raid turn into a rout and had run for help, rather than continue to fight for a lost cause, as Roger, Helbye and Ulfrith had done.

Geoffrey looked around him. Helbye leaned against a table with his hand to his hip, while Roger gave him wine and Ulfrith hovered solicitously. The King's soldiers were rounding up Maude's men and a priest moved among the dead. Geoffrey saw with regret that there were many, and that Maude was among them, her eyes wide and sightless, and a crossbow quarrel protruding from her neck.

Numbly, he thought about what she had told him. There *had* been no reason for her to lie, and he believed her when she said her crimes were minor. People were superstitious – as evidenced by their reactions to rainbows and suns, and even clenched muscles around a piece of rope – and he knew it would be easy for someone to turn such beliefs to advantage. It was a pity Maude was shot, because he suspected Henry might have been amused by her deception. He would have levied a hefty fine to warn her not to do it again, but he would have let her live.

But she was dead now, and Rodbert and others with her. Tasso was not, though, and he was not with the prisoners, either. Geoffrey supposed he had slipped away during the chaos, and hoped he would have the sense to leave Bristol. The whole affair seemed so monstrously blown out of proportion that he was glad someone had escaped, even if it was a man who sliced the heads of unarmed enemies.

'It is over,' said Giffard, laying a hand on Geoffrey's shoulder. 'You have exposed the corruption of Maude and Rodbert, and saved Bristol from Barcwit's terror.'

'Not really,' said Geoffrey tiredly. 'I have no idea whether their *cambium* roused himself from his cups long enough to assay their coins, but even he must have been more honest than Lifwine. We have been led astray from the very beginning.'

'By Maude?' asked Giffard. 'Or by Rodbert?'

'By Sendi. Lifwine was right when he identified him as the more dangerous of the two moneyers.'

'Sendi is innocent,' said Giffard, bewildered. He gestured at the wreckage of Barcwit's mint. 'The criminals were all here, which is why they fought so hard when you exposed them.'

'Sendi is worse,' said Geoffrey firmly. 'He has been forging for years, and he is a smuggler.'

Giffard looked alarmed. 'But this cannot be true! I spoke

291

to him in the castle, just before Durand arrived and told me to hurry here.'

Geoffrey regarded him uneasily. 'What have you done?'

'I let him out,' said Giffard. 'I set him and his friends free.'

Geoffrey could not believe Giffard had ordered the release of prisoners without consulting him first. Peter had fled before Geoffrey had left to confront Barcwit, and Idonea, Joan, Olivier and Warelwast had gone with him; Bloet was out in a last, desperate attempt to locate the silver before Giffard asked for it in Henry's name. Even the castle guards had disappeared, and were hiding until the battle was resolved and they knew whom to support. The upshot was that there was no one left to tell the bishop what had really happened.

Seizing the opportunity afforded by the chaos, Sendi had informed Giffard he had been wrongfully imprisoned by Barcwit, who was currently doing battle with Geoffrey. He had urged the bishop to set him free, so he could help fight. Then Durand had arrived with news of the rout, which seemed to confirm his story. Giffard had rushed to Barcwit's mint, leaving a guard to release Sendi on the understanding that he would join the affray as soon as he had armed himself. Needless to say, Sendi and his friends were nowhere to be found. Before they had left, they had cut Lifwine's throat.

'I doubt we will see them again,' said Roger, deeply unimpressed by Giffard's gullibility. 'We had them, and now they have gone.'

Giffard was chagrined that he had been so easily fooled. 'We met Clarembald the physician on our way to Barcwit's mint,' he said, his voice thick with self-recrimination. 'I told him about Sendi, but he gave no indication that we had made a mistake. He must have known, given that Sendi's forgeries are the talk of the town today, so why did he not tell me?'

Geoffrey rubbed his eyes. 'Clarembald. I am not happy with his role in this.'

'We should present *him* to the King as a traitor,' said Roger angrily. 'We need someone – but Maude, Rodbert and Lifwine are dead, Barcwit does not exist, and Sendi has escaped.'

'There is no need to rub it in,' said Giffard sharply. 'We

shall have to think very carefully about how to present this debacle. With some of the criminals dead, the King will be spared the expense of a trial. If we start by saying that, then perhaps he will be a little more forgiving . . .'

'He wanted the truth,' Geoffrey pointed out, unwilling to mislead the King. Giffard was clearly horrified by what he had done, or he would not be contemplating such a rash strategy. 'And now he will not have it – at least, not from real witnesses and culprits.'

'He will have it from you,' said Giffard weakly. 'Perhaps that will suffice.'

'I doubt it,' said Geoffrey. 'As Adelise once said, truth is like molten silver, to be moulded how you want it. Henry will not trust my version of events when they are uncorroborated.'

'The fact that you let your sister escape is not helpful,' said Giffard unhappily. 'It looks as though you hedged your bets, in case anything went wrong.'

'Events *did* go wrong,' said Geoffrey dryly.

He spent the rest of the day in the castle, fretting about Joan and whether he had been wise to send Warelwast with her. Peter was weak, and would be of scant use if the party was attacked, while Olivier certainly would not. Still, he thought, Joan and Idonea could probably look after themselves. He fell into an exhausted sleep early that evening, and when he awoke, it was almost dawn. He stood and stretched, easing the stiffness out of his muscles, and went to feed his dog. The kitchens were deserted, so he found some bread and meat in a pantry, and they shared them alone. Then he walked through the slowly lightening streets to look for Giffard.

Giffard had been working all night, sifting through the mints' documents, while his clerks catalogued every item in every room and packed them in wooden crates. They had already stripped Sendi's property, even removing brass fittings from doors, and were just finishing Barcwit's. Geoffrey had seen a good deal of looting during his career as a soldier, but none as thorough as that committed by the King's commissioners. He wondered whether they planned to take the shutters from the windows, too, and the lead lining from the drains.

'Sendi has been cheating the King for years,' said Giffard

grimly, tapping the parchments with a bony finger. Geoffrey noticed again that he seemed heavier than normal, and it crossed his mind that the bishop might have secreted documents in his habit. 'I was a fool to let him go: the crimes of which he accused Barcwit are nothing compared to the ones he committed himself. Not only that, but there is enough evidence here to prove that *he* made the "mules" he showed us in Westminster – the ones he said were Barcwit's. Do you remember the four charges he levelled then?'

Geoffrey nodded. 'The first was that Barcwit had a drunken *cambium* who did not assay his coins. That is true: the man's mind must have been pickled, judging from the state of his corpse. The second was that Barcwit made underweight coins with too much tin in the silver.'

'Barcwit's coins are on the light side,' acknowledged Giffard. 'But it is Sendi's that are full of tin.'

'The third was Barcwit's list of illegal investors,' said Geoffrey, thinking about Joan.

'Also proven,' said Giffard, resting his hand on the parchments. 'Although only occasionally and fairly discreetly. There is no evidence that higher rates were paid to your sister, Peter de la Mare, Clarembald or John, although Bloet once accepted eleven per cent. Again, Sendi was worse: his profit margins were greater, and he was far more brazen in his illegitimate dealings.'

'Joan told me she never accepted an illegal rate from Barcwit. I should have believed her: she is too sensible to break the law with strangers.'

'You should be pleased,' said Giffard. 'We can now prove Joan is neither a fool nor a traitor. She is innocent.'

Geoffrey said nothing, thinking about the plot to kill the King. Maude and Tasso claimed it was untrue, but Peter and Joan did not concur. It was real to them. But Giffard had found no evidence of intended regicide in Barcwit's documents, or he would have mentioned it. The letter Geoffrey had found in the barrel at Sendi's mint crackled inside his surcoat, and he raised his hand to touch it. Who had written it? And was there a plot or no?

'Bloet's profiteering made him two shillings,' Giffard went

on disdainfully. 'Barely enough to pay a servant for a month, and certainly not enough to risk the King's wrath. He is a fool. But then so is Sendi. It was insane to go to the King with charges against Barcwit when he was committing them himself. God alone knows why he did it.'

'Greed and jealousy can drive men to desperate lengths: he and Adelise were bitterly resentful of Barcwit's success, and wanted to crush him and claim his investors for themselves. So, whose operation was the more profitable? Sendi's, because he was so brazenly corrupt?'

'Not by a long way. Barcwit's established business and good location brought him excellent – and mostly honest – trade. Sendi could not hope to compete against such massive advantages.'

'The fourth charge was that Barcwit frightened people.' Geoffrey shook his head in disgust. 'People were frightened all right, but by someone who does not even exist!'

'The case is solved,' said Giffard. 'The four accusations were true – but two of them apply to Sendi just as much as Barcwit – and we have answers to most of the questions the King may ask.'

Geoffrey perched on the edge of a table. 'I know what Barcwit and Sendi have done is illegal, but is it unusual? I went through Roger's purse last night – he has pennies from all over the country – and a number are mules or made with worn dies. They are easier to identify now I know what to look for.'

'Increasing barbarism in coins is not confined to Bristol,' admitted Giffard. 'I predict it will reach a crisis, which will end in drastic monetary reform, although Henry wants to avoid that, if possible. But, to answer your question, Barcwit and Sendi have bent the rules no more than many others.'

'Then why investigate them specifically?'

'Because Sendi made a complaint against a fellow coiner, which is rare – normally, they stick together. Henry wanted to exploit their rivalry, and explore an aspect of his kingdom that is becoming rotten. When news seeps out that two corrupt moneyers have been exposed, others will improve their standards. Of course, they will slip into bad habits again eventually, and there will have to be another investigation to shake them up.'

'It sounds pointless,' said Geoffrey in disgust. 'I have wasted my time.'

'You have not,' said Giffard sharply, 'because you have served your King. He wants you to go Winchester next month, so we can make our final report together. Such as it is.'

'Yes,' agreed Geoffrey. 'Such as it is.'

Geoffrey and Giffard left Barcwit's mint and went to an inn called the Greene Lattis. Geoffrey had noticed the inn before, because it was always surprisingly full, given that it stood so close to Barcwit's property. It was empty now, however, and Geoffrey assumed the bishop had cleared it, so he and his clerks could enjoy ale and respite from their labours without being pestered by locals for gossip. The pot-boy who brought them wine was unfriendly to the point of hostility. He scowled at them, then disappeared into a back room, slamming a door in the kind of way that indicated that was all the service they were going to get. A cart, heavily laden with Barcwit's property, trundled past the window, dragging Geoffrey's attention away from the surly servant.

'I see the looting is going well.'

'I am hoping it will encourage Henry to be flexible over the misunderstanding with Sendi. And about the fact that you let Joan flee, thus indicating you do not trust him to keep his word about her pardon.' Giffard frowned when a clerk approached and presented him with a list of everything that had been seized from Barcwit. 'This is wrong. There should be five times the amount of silver you have listed.'

'There is no mistake. That is all there is, and we have been over every inch of the property.'

'No,' said Giffard patiently. 'I know *exactly* how much silver Barcwit owns, because I have seen receipts from the mines. You list only a fraction of what should be here. He must have hidden it.'

'That must be the silver that was stolen,' said Geoffrey. He glanced at the document. 'I did not realize it was so much. No wonder so many people want to find it.'

'But no one has?' asked Giffard. He grimaced when Geoffrey shook his head.

'We cannot stay to look for it,' said the clerk. 'Not if we want to reach Bath tonight with all the carts. We must leave now, or we will still be on the road after dark, and that would not be wise.'

Giffard agreed. 'Go. Leave me two soldiers, and take the rest. I will catch up with you later.'

'Why the hurry?' asked Geoffrey, after the scribe had gone.

'This seized property should not stay here, when there are disaffected moneyers at large who might want it back. The sooner it is with Henry, the better.' Giffard sighed unhappily. 'I suppose I shall have to leave Bloet to locate the missing hoard. That is what the King ordered him to do, after all.'

'Poor Bloet. There are rumours that it is in Ireland, which means he will never find it.'

'Have *you* made any enquiries?' asked Giffard hopefully. 'It would be in both our interests to present it to Henry. Do you have any clues we might unravel between us?'

'I heard Alwold mutter something as he died, but that is all.'

'We all know about Piers,' said Giffard dismissively. 'It was the talk of the Court for days afterwards. But no one knows the man, not even Father Feoc, who has lived in Bristol all his life.'

'There was an anchorite called Piers, but he is dead. Idonea told me there is a Beiminstre shepherd of that name, but he is said to know nothing, either.' Geoffrey rubbed his head. 'I thought Feoc was deceiving me when he said there was no Piers, then admitted to knowing the hermit.'

Giffard understood what had happened. 'You asked whether there was a man called Piers in Bristol, but you should have asked whether there was a Piers *anywhere*. That is why Feoc neglected to tell you about the anchorite and the shepherd – he took your question literally. These rural priests are apt to be pedantic. However, it is irrelevant, because it seems Alwold *was* rambling in his delirium, just as Maude claimed. His last words meant nothing, although they caused Bloet a lot of trouble.'

'He said something else, too, which no one else heard.' Geoffrey thought hard: Alwold's death had been weeks ago, and the incident was fading from his mind. 'He said, "the secret lies with the priest at St John's. The King knows about it, and so do Bloet and William de Warel."'

Giffard was thoughtful. 'Alwold *did* tell the King about the stolen silver. There were two other men in the room at the time.'

'Warelwast and Bloet?' Here Giffard nodded. 'So, the "secret" really did mean the lost hoard? It does not sound very secret to me.'

'It was to Alwold. He refused to speak about it to anyone – not even Maude. Henry heard about it from Sendi, and ordered Alwold to give him details, but the man said nothing, other than that the stuff was stolen. Bloet and Warelwast were with Henry at the time, which meant the "secret" was all over Court in hours. So, we have resolved that part of Alwold's statement: he told his "secret" to Henry, Warelwast and Bloet. That leaves the other bit – the priest of St John's. That is Feoc, I presume?'

'There is something odd about this,' said Geoffrey, thinking hard. 'Alwold was Barcwit's faithful steward. When he died, he was very particular about whom he spoke to – Maude, but definitely not Rodbert – and he insisted that *Barcwit* should be given his message.'

'But Barcwit does not exist. And why did he wait until he was about to die before telling Maude? Because *he* stole the silver, and intended to keep it for himself, then recanted on his deathbed?'

'No,' said Geoffrey. 'I think he was devoted to Barcwit, and it was only when he realized he had no choice that he confided in Maude.'

Giffard was impatient. 'We are going in circles here. I shall speak to Feoc myself. It is possible he does not know he has the secret – it may be a document concealed in his church, or some clue given to him during confession. But a good deal of money is involved, so we must do all we can to find it.'

'The answer is obvious now we have all the facts,' said Geoffrey, rubbing his chin. 'We have been misled about

Barcwit. He *does* exist, because Alwold would not have expended his dying breath on a message for a man who does not. He also said, "He will be angry if you betray him. You do not know what he can be like when he is angry." You do not say that about someone who is not real.'

'Perhaps he was perpetuating the myth they had created,' suggested Giffard. 'You say that is how Maude and Rodbert kept people afraid.'

'Then why say Maude did *not* know what Barcwit could be like when angry? He should have said the opposite – that she *did* know. There is only one conclusion: Barcwit does exist. He must, or none of this makes sense. Alwold hid the silver for some reason: it was not stolen. That explains why Barcwit was so remarkably sanguine about its loss – to the point where he even asked Alwold to escort his wife to Westminster. It also explains why Alwold wanted Barcwit – and Barcwit alone – to know where it is. But I think I have unravelled his clues.'

'You have?' asked Giffard, startled. 'Where is it, then?'

'In Beiminstre, which is the last village Alwold would have passed through on his return from the silver mine in Devon. We know he stopped "just outside Bristol". But it was not Feoc he entrusted with his secret. It was the priest of another St John's.'

'Is there a St John's in Beiminstre?'

'Yes. I should have seen this days ago – and I should have guessed the truth about Barcwit.'

'But you did not,' came a voice from the stairs, accompanied by the click of a crossbow. 'And that is very fortunate for me.'

'You are Barcwit?' asked Geoffrey, realizing too late that he should have been more suspicious of an empty tavern in the middle of the day. He had made the assumption that Giffard had cleared it, whereas the disenfranchised moneyer, whose premises were all but stripped, was clearly responsible. It explained the pot-boy's behaviour, too: his display of hostility had been for his old neighbour's benefit. Barcwit and the men who now clustered behind him had been hiding upstairs, and had doubtless been very interested in the discussion between bishop and agent.

'I am Barcwit,' replied the man. Geoffrey saw Tasso behind him, sword at the ready. The knight indicated that Geoffrey was to relinquish his weapons, which he only did when one of the men aimed his bow at Giffard. 'I am sorry we did not meet sooner, but my children thought it unwise.'

Geoffrey could see why. Barcwit was tiny, with twinkling blue eyes and a fluffy white beard that was about as far away from the menacing spectre in black created by Maude and Rodbert as it was possible to be. He looked like a kindly grandfather: no one would be frightened of this Barcwit.

'You have caused me all manner of inconvenience,' Barcwit went on. 'My daughter and son are dead, my mint is dismantled, and most of my workmen are either killed, arrested or have fled for their lives. You have destroyed a lifetime's work.'

'That is what happens when you cheat the King,' admonished Giffard.

Barcwit covered the small distance between him and the bishop in a flash, and hit him with his bow. Giffard yelped in pain, and blood oozed from a cut on his scalp. Geoffrey reassessed Barcwit when he saw the expression on the man's face. It was neither kindly nor twinkling, and there was a distinct malice in the glittering eyes. He interposed himself between them. Barcwit would have to go through him before he struck an unarmed monk again.

'Why did Maude and Rodbert insist you change your appearance?' he asked. 'Were they ashamed of you?' He thought about the beggars in Feoc's church, who had said Barcwit had grown larger and no longer trawled taverns for women. They remembered the old Barcwit, before his transformation.

Barcwit regarded him coldly. 'Why would they be ashamed?'

A number of responses sailed through Geoffrey's mind, most involving derogatory comments about his size and elfin features. 'How did you persuade the people of Bristol to believe you went from a normal man to an enormous black-cloaked monster?' he asked instead.

'People have short memories. Maude suggested I stay out

of sight, because folk are more frightened by things they cannot see, than by something they know. She was right: even my name reduces people to paroxysms of terror these days. It went further than we intended, though. We wanted people in awe, not believing me guilty of dealings with the Devil. But it resulted in us making more profit than any mint in the country, so it seemed a pity to correct the misunderstanding.'

'We know this,' said Giffard, hand to his head. 'And it is time to put matters right. We—'

'Put matters right?' snarled Barcwit. 'Matters will never be right again! You have destroyed all I have. Or do you think Henry will give me another mint, as compensation for the one I have lost?'

'No,' admitted Giffard. 'I do not think he will do that.'

'Sendi was jealous of our honest success,' said Barcwit, blithely ignoring the fact that creating monsters to frighten folk was hardly an ethical business practice. 'He accused me of treason, and then Maude and Rodbert betrayed me.'

'By lying with each other?' asked Giffard sympathetically. 'It was a sinful union.'

But Geoffrey did not think Barcwit was referring to their incestuous relationship. 'They did not give you Alwold's message about the silver?'

'They did not,' said Barcwit sourly. 'Alwold told me – before I sent him to Westminster to keep Rodbert away from his half-sister – that the silver was safe, and we agreed to retrieve it on his return. Unfortunately, he never came home.'

'I knew none of this,' said Tasso, startled. 'Why did you allow him to leave Bristol without telling you where he had put it?'

Barcwit grimaced. 'We were rushed. He only had time to mention that he had hidden the silver and shot the guards to make it look as though outlaws were responsible. He thought Rodbert might try to steal it from me.'

'Rodbert would never betray you in such a way,' said Tasso, shocked.

'Yes, he would,' argued Barcwit sharply.

'He betrayed you more than you know,' said Geoffrey. 'He killed Alwold – to get Maude *and* to silence a man who was

301

apparently suspicious of him. He worked out everything in advance. He murdered Fardin first, so it would look as if Sendi had killed Alwold in revenge.'

Giffard agreed. 'One of my clerks saw Rodbert covered in blood shortly after Fardin's death. He did not tell anyone at the time, because he thought rival Saxons killing each other on deserted riverbanks was none of his concern. He knows now that he was wrong to stay silent.'

'Were you plotting to kill the King?' asked Geoffrey, wanting the answer to the question that affected Joan once and for all. He saw Giffard's start of surprise: it had not been in his report.

Barcwit was dismissive. 'Why would I? I want a stable economy that needs coins, and Henry provides that. I even sent a donation for his war against Bellême, to make sure he won. I have – I *had* no reason to harm Henry.'

'Joan lied to you, Geoffrey,' jeered Tasso. 'She invested in us purely for profit. She had no grand or noble motives. She is simply greedy – like Peter, Idonea, Clarembald and the others.'

'Then what about the letter I found?' pressed Geoffrey, ignoring Giffard's growing horror. 'The one you wrote to Joan outlining the details of King Henry's intended murder?'

'Written by my drunken *cambium* under Colblac's malign influence,' said Barcwit. 'Do you remember Colblac? He was the clerk who answered my door on occasion. We had our spy Lifwine in Sendi's mint – but Sendi had Colblac.'

Geoffrey was surprised. Colblac had not seemed like the kind of man to engage in treachery. But then, neither had Lifwine.

'I killed him this morning,' said Tasso. 'But, before he died, he confessed to what he had done. He forced our dying *cambium* to write the letter to Joan, then he left it in a barrel at Sendi's mint. He thought Sendi would find the letter and use it to destroy Master Barcwit. But you got it first.'

'Why address the thing to Joan?' Geoffrey was disgusted.

'To hurt you,' said Barcwit simply. 'Like everyone else in this town, Colblac had no love for the King's agents. They are greedy, corrupt and seek only to accrue power and wealth for themselves.'

Giffard gave a short bark of laughter. 'Most, perhaps, but not Geoffrey! Look at him in his grimy armour and unwashed clothes. Does he look like a wealthy and powerful man to you?'

'No,' acknowledged Barcwit. 'But it alters nothing. Both of you will die, and I shall collect my silver from Beiminstre. Then I shall start another life with those few of us you have spared.'

Tasso moved forward, sword in his hand, and Geoffrey saw he intended to dispatch them as he had Edric. Barcwit nodded to him, while his bowmen watched in gleeful anticipation of bloody slaughter.

'Wait!' cried Giffard,. 'You cannot send me to meet God while I am steeped in sin. You must give me time to make my confession and cleanse my soul.'

Without waiting for permission, he dropped to his knees and began to pray in a loud, commanding voice. Tasso hesitated, doubtless fearing for his own soul if he killed a bishop at his devotions. Some of Barcwit's men, overwhelmed by the power of Giffard's convictions, removed their hats and lowered their weapons. Others bowed their heads as Giffard's beautifully intoned Latin filled the room. Barcwit's jaw dropped at the spectacle, and Geoffrey seized his chance.

While Tasso's sword wavered uncertainly over Giffard's shoulders, he tore forward and bowled the knight from his feet, snatching a handful of Barcwit's tunic at the same time. Barcwit uttered a shrill scream of outrage as he fell, and began to flail with his fists. Then he was everywhere, making it difficult for his men to come to his aid. Maude had already been killed that day with a friendly arrow, and they had evidently been warned about what would happen if they did it again. The result was that they stood stupidly immobile while Geoffrey fought with Tasso. Meanwhile, Giffard continued to pray, confusing the men still further about what they should do.

Tasso scrabbled for the sword he had dropped, while Geoffrey struggled to stop him from reaching it. Barcwit screeched and scratched, and one or two of his men, with more initiative than their fellows, dodged this way and that with their weapons at the ready while they waited for a clear shot. Geoffrey grabbed Tasso around the waist and rolled, so his opponent was on top when one man started to lay about him with a stave. Tasso cursed foully, and the man backed away in alarm.

Then Giffard abruptly finished his meditations and joined the affray. He grabbed Barcwit in a bear-hug, holding him off the ground so his short legs flailed in fury. Several men caught painful blows on heads and arms as they tried to rescue him. Meanwhile, Tasso had reached his sword, and a triumphant grin crossed his dark features. Someone trod hard on Geoffrey's hand, pinning him to the floor, and the vital moments needed to free it were more than enough for Tasso to scramble to his feet.

Geoffrey expected to be skewered immediately, but Tasso had other ideas. The henchman knew whom he held responsible for the disintegration of the empire he had helped to build, and he wanted revenge. He drew back his foot and kicked Geoffrey in the side. Geoffrey finally wrenched his hand free and tried to roll away, but Tasso's boot found him again. While his senses reeled, he saw Barcwit wriggle out of Giffard's grip and turn to plunge a dagger into the prelate's chest. With a startled expression, Giffard toppled backward and lay still.

'Horses!' shouted Barcwit urgently. 'I hear horses.'

'Just Giffard's thieves,' snarled Tasso. 'Making off with every last item from your house – even the stick you use for poking the fire!' He kicked again, and Geoffrey felt the breath rush from his body.

'No!' said Barcwit urgently. 'I have a feeling we were not the only ones who overheard this pair babbling about Beiminstre. Someone else now knows where Alwold hid my silver. The bishop is dead, so finish the agent, and come with me. Hurry!'

He tore open the door and shot outside, yelling for his men to follow. All obeyed, except Tasso, who drew back his foot for another onslaught. Geoffrey's ribs ached viciously, and it took a good deal of effort to rise to his knees and grab a

304

dagger someone had dropped. Tasso knocked it from his hand, so it went skittering across the floor. Geoffrey knew he could not hold out much longer. He fumbled for the knife in his boot, which Tasso had failed to find when he had disarmed him. He gripped its hilt, and when Tasso moved in for another kick, he thrust upwards with the last of his strength.

Tasso reeled, but then pulled back, and Geoffrey saw that while he was injured, he was far from incapacitated. He advanced on his victim again. Then he stumbled, and Geoffrey reacted instinctively by raising the dagger. Tasso gasped when the blade slid into his stomach, and dropped to his knees. Giffard was behind him, white-faced and unsteady. Then Tasso pitched forward and lay still. A spreading stain underneath him suggested he would not be trying to kick anyone else to death.

'I thought Barcwit had killed you,' said Geoffrey, accepting Giffard's help to climb to his feet.

'He tried,' said Giffard shakily. 'I have never been stabbed before, and I cannot say I enjoyed it.'

'You will not abandon your see and become a warrior, then?' asked Geoffrey, wincing as he took a deep breath and felt a stabbing pain that suggested cracked ribs.

'I will not, although I recommend a change of profession for you. Fighting men like these is far too dangerous. Now I know why Henry insisted I wear this bulky and uncomfortable thing.' He pulled his habit away from his neck to reveal a mail tunic underneath.

'Why did you let him go?' asked Geoffrey, recalling how Giffard had lain still while Barcwit escaped.

Giffard gazed at him in astonishment. 'I did not "let" him do anything. He just went. Besides, I am a monk and cannot raise weapons against other men.'

Geoffrey glanced at Tasso. 'Tell him that.'

'That was not me,' said Giffard firmly. 'All I did was give him a shove. It was *your* dagger that plunged into his vitals, so it was *you* who brought about his death. I do not want his murder staining *my* soul when I stand before God on Judgement Day.'

'Well, it saved my life,' said Geoffrey gratefully, suspecting

God would make up His own mind about what constituted Giffard's sins when his soul was weighed, and that the bishop would not be permitted to present a pre-prepared list.

'You saved mine, too,' said Giffard. 'When Barcwit struck me, you interposed yourself between us without a moment's hesitation. I always sensed you were a good man.'

'Henry will not be pleased when he hears Barcwit escaped with the silver,' said Geoffrey, thinking about why the coiner had left so abruptly. 'Especially since we essentially told him where it was.'

'Him and someone else.' Giffard was rueful. 'He was right: another person *was* listening outside.'

'How do you know?'

'I posted two soldiers there, to guard me while I sat in here with you. But when Barcwit opened the door to leave, I saw them dead. Barcwit did not do it, because he was with us. Someone else killed them *and* heard us unravel the mystery of the silver. He will be on his way to Beiminstre as we speak.'

'Then he will meet Barcwit,' said Geoffrey. 'There will be a fight and the winner will take the ingots.'

'So, what are you going to do about it?' demanded Giffard challengingly. 'Let Barcwit and this other traitor steal what belongs to the King?'

'I was under the impression that it belonged to Barcwit, actually,' said Geoffrey, rubbing his side. 'Besides, I am done fighting for today. I feel as though I have been trampled by a herd of horses.'

'It is *not* Barcwit's,' snapped Giffard. '*He* is now an outlaw, because he cheated the King. Pull yourself together! We *must* find out who is racing him for the silver, and at least try to get to it first.'

'It will be Bloet,' predicted Geoffrey. 'Or Clarembald. He is more deeply embedded in this plot than is proper. Or perhaps Warelwast, the friend who is always trying to help me – except when I really need him. It would not surprise me to learn he had abandoned Joan and returned here.'

'Then come,' shouted Giffard, tugging at his sleeve. 'Hurry!'

Geoffrey resisted. 'How many men do you have? Or did you send them all to Bath?'

'Just the two outside,' said Giffard, agitated by the delay. 'The rest were needed to guard the carts, given that every robber in the county will be after them.'

'But the two outside are dead,' Geoffrey pointed out. 'So you have none.'

'I have you,' insisted Giffard. 'And Peter has soldiers . . .'

'All fled,' said Geoffrey. 'I doubt you and I will be able to do much against Barcwit *and* his men, *plus* this other would-be thief, especially when you decline to use weapons lest murder stains your soul. I cannot fight any more, Giffard. I am spent.'

'You must,' urged Giffard, desperately. 'Barcwit may harm the good people of Beiminstre unless we are there to protect them. We cannot leave them at the mercy of a man like him.'

Geoffrey thought about Kea and his sister. The villagers' paltry defences would be useless in repelling a determined man like Barcwit, who would kill every last one of them in his determination to have what he believed was rightfully his.

'Roger will help,' he said, aiming for the door. 'But you will need to count the silver afterwards.'

'I do not care,' said Giffard, almost dragging him forward in his haste to be underway. 'I will *give* him some, if he lends his sword to thwarting these villains.'

Fourteen

R oger had had enough of Bristol, and had made the decision that he and Geoffrey were leaving that day, aiming
for Barfleur, where they would meet Joan. He had packed
their bags, saddled the horses, and was on the verge of sending
Ulfrith to look for his friend so they could get underway.

'God's blood!' he breathed, when Geoffrey limped into the
stable with Giffard. 'What happened?'

'The missing silver is in Beiminstre, and Barcwit and God
knows who else are on their way to claim it,' replied Geoffrey.
'My Lord Bishop believes that you and I can save a village,
restore the silver to the King, and dispatch a few more traitors in the process.'

'Then let us do it,' declared Roger, undaunted by what
seemed to Geoffrey to be an impossible list of objectives. 'I
am in the mood for a skirmish.'

He was thundering across the bailey before Geoffrey had
time to respond, with Ulfrith whooping at his heels. Helbye
followed more sedately, hand to his hip, while Durand slyly
offered to lend Giffard his horse, in the hope that any fighting
would be over by the time he had travelled the mile or so to
Beiminstre on foot. Geoffrey's new horse shot after Roger's,
and he was hard-pressed to prevent the beast from outstrip-
ping them all. He was in no state to arrive first and take on
the traitors alone; even staying upright required more energy
than he felt he had left.

Bristol was oddly deserted as they rode; almost every
window shutter was closed, and there was not an open door
to be seen. No animals roamed the streets, and the only folk
who were out hurried about their business with their heads
down. Geoffrey and his companions clattered across the bridge,

and found no guard on duty to collect their tolls. Peter's men had abandoned their posts, allowing the likes of Barcwit to go about their business unopposed. Bristol was a town without lawful leaders.

Roger set a cracking pace along the riverside path, with Giffard urging him on every step of the way, and Geoffrey and Helbye following less enthusiastically. It was not long before the first houses of Beiminstre came into sight, silent and serene in the morning sun, with chickens in the gardens and smoke oozing from chimneys. Geoffrey slowed his horse and indicated they should dismount.

'Barcwit is in front of us, and we do not want to rush into his arms.'

'The element of surprise,' explained Roger to Giffard, as if the bishop were witless. 'We shall ambush Barcwit – grab him *and* his silver.'

They tethered the horses, and moved forward on foot, creeping through the trees in an attempt to come as close to the village as possible without being seen. Giffard fretted that they were taking too long, and Roger was all for abandoning stealth in favour of an outright attack, but Geoffrey pointed out that they did not know how many men they might face. It was better to exercise caution.

Geoffrey wracked his brains as they walked, trying to guess the identity of the last traitor. Was it Bloet or Clarembald, both of whom were suspect and dishonest? Was it the Shopping Bishop, who had decided a consignment of silver would be just the thing to finance his favourite pastime? Rodbert, Maude and Tasso were dead, as was the treacherous Lifwine, while Sendi, Adelise and their men had fled for their lives. Who else was left? Someone from Bristol, who had decided Barcwit owed him something for his years of tyranny?

When they reached the main part of the village, he led the way along a track that ran along the backs of the houses and their long gardens. He could see St John the Baptist's Church ahead of him, and wondered where Barcwit would go first. He rubbed his side and thought the ache in his ribs was robbing him of his concentration, because the answer to that question should have been obvious. Barcwit knew the priest held Alwold's secret: he would go to Father Wido.

Like Bristol, Beiminstre was curiously abandoned, and Geoffrey hoped the people had had the sense to run when greedy men had started to arrive. When he reached the priest's house, he crept up the path and opened the back door. A bench lay on its side, and several pots had been smashed near the hearth. A struggle had taken place, although he was heartened by the absence of blood or bodies. He heard his companions checking other houses, too, but they came out shaking their heads.

'In here!' called Giffard in a hoarse whisper.

Stomach twisting uneasily, Geoffrey climbed over the dividing fence and pushed past Giffard to enter the home next door. He was startled to see Clarembald lying on the floor, trussed up and gagged with his own bandages. The *medicus* was furious, and his orange eyebrows quivered frantically, to indicate he should be released.

'No,' said Giffard, when Ulfrith went to oblige. 'When I told him I had released Sendi, he said nothing to stop me, even though he must have known the man was a criminal.'

Clarembald made the kind of noise that suggested he had an explanation, so Geoffrey slipped the gag from his mouth. 'I was acting for the King,' the physician snapped when he could speak. 'Although Bishop John has done all in his power to thwart me.'

'John de Villula is a traitor?' asked Giffard.

Clarembald hesitated, and Geoffrey could see he was dearly tempted to say yes. 'No,' he admitted finally. 'But when I heard you had let Sendi go, I said nothing, because there is another traitor in Bristol. I hoped Sendi's release might flush him out.'

'Who?' demanded Giffard. 'The real Barcwit, small of stature and large of aggression?'

'Barcwit is just another forger,' said Clarembald. 'I am talking about someone far more dangerous.'

'I do not believe you,' said Geoffrey. 'I saw you in Barcwit's mint, lecturing his men about curses and the seriousness of some "situation". You are in Barcwit's pay, which is why you are trying to make light of his crimes.'

'You were there?' asked Clarembald, startled. 'Was it you in that dark cloak, lurking in the shadows and making everyone uneasy?'

'Do not try to change the subject,' said Giffard sternly. 'What were you telling Barcwit's men?'

'There is an outbreak of the pox among them, and I was called to treat it. Obviously, it is a contagious condition, and when I spoke of the "seriousness of the situation" I referred to the fact that that lecherous rabble might infect half of Bristol.'

'The pox was the "curse that would see us all in our graves"?' asked Geoffrey. He supposed it made sense – especially since Durand had mentioned the lecture Clarembald said he had given. 'But why are you here now? To meet Barcwit and help him take the silver?'

'No!' said Clarembald, struggling ineffectually against his bonds. 'I came to see whether I might catch this last traitor – not Sendi, not Barcwit, but someone else. I saw Barcwit heading this way and I followed him, in the hope that the real traitor would show himself, too.'

'Who is it?' asked Geoffrey, not sure whether to believe him.

'I do not know, only that he has sided against Barcwit, and that he has helped Sendi in his crimes. *That* is why I was pleased when you released Sendi, and *that* is why I came here – to trap this man.'

'And did this mythical creature follow Barcwit?' asked Giffard, clearly unconvinced. He was not about to be misled a second time by the Court physician.

'I am not sure,' said Clarembald resentfully. 'When I arrived, the villagers grabbed me and tied me up. So, let me go and we will catch this fellow together.'

'You can stay here,' said Giffard, replacing the gag. 'I do not want you free when we tackle Barcwit. You are right: there *is* someone else after the missing silver, but there is nothing to say it is not you.' He led the others out of the house, ignoring the furious sounds that followed them.

'The church,' said Helbye, pointing at it. 'Perhaps the villagers have barricaded themselves inside, anticipating Clarembald to be the first of many.'

Geoffrey was worried. 'Barcwit had a good start on us, so he must be here already. It is one thing knowing the silver is hidden in Beiminstre, but another altogether to find out precisely where. I think the villagers *will* be in the church. But Barcwit will be there, too, trying to prise answers from them – and I suspect they do not have what he wants.'

'We will save them, then,' said Roger gallantly. 'I do not approve of outlaws bullying peasants. Besides, I would rather they told *me* the location of this silver.'

'We need to approach softly and silently, if we want to retain the element of surprise,' warned Geoffrey. 'Barcwit had at least nine men that I saw, and we are only four.'

'Five,' corrected Giffard, grabbing a spade purposefully. 'A work tool is not a weapon; God cannot blame me if these villains walk into this while I happen to be holding it.'

'Remember,' said Geoffrey, afraid the bishop might swing it into action before they were ready. 'Softly and silently.'

The others nodded, and they were off again, slipping through the trees until they reached the church's main door. It stood ajar, and Geoffrey could hear voices coming from within.

All the villagers were there, their faces white and frightened. They stood against the wall, men on one side, women and children on the other, guarded by five men with crossbows. All eyes were fixed on Barcwit and four hard-looking mercenaries, who stood near the high altar. Father Wido was on his knees before them, making a supplicating gesture, while Barcwit held someone by an ear. Kea.

'If you do not tell me where the silver is, I shall slice it off,' said Barcwit in a voice that was chillingly matter-of-fact. 'And if you still do not speak, I shall claim the other ear. Then there are his fingers and toes . . .'

With a piercing battle cry that had more than one villager screaming in terror, Geoffrey hauled his sword from his belt and plunged inside.

'What happened to "softly and silently"?' he heard Roger ask.

The archers wheeled around at the sudden intrusion, and released badly aimed arrows that snapped harmlessly into the walls. One hit a painting and left a mark, and an elderly lady gave a screech of outrage at the damage, before leaping forward to pummel him with her fists. Then all five were lost as the other villagers surged forward. They had been too frightened to save themselves, but their beloved church was another matter. Barcwit's jaw dropped, while his remaining men took one look at each other and darted towards the door. They met Ulfrith, who dealt two of them stunning blows with his mace, leaving Giffard to disable the remaining pair with a swipe of his spade.

Barcwit acted quickly. He tightened his grip on Kea and raised his dagger. 'I will slit his throat,' he hissed, and Geoffrey could see he meant it. 'You do not want the blood of an innocent on your head, so move back.'

After Barcwit had made his announcement, the silence in the church was absolute. The villagers stopped pummelling the archers, and gazed in horror as Barcwit pressed the knife more firmly into Kea's throat. The boy's eyes were wide with terror, and his little sister started to cry.

'It is over, Barcwit,' said Giffard softly. 'Let him go.'

'Barcwit?' asked one of the villagers, startled. 'That cannot be Barcwit. Barcwit is huge.'

'He was small when I first met him,' said Wido. 'His evil powers must be leaching away, because he is so diminished in size.' He took a step forward, and Kea howled as the knife nicked his neck.

'No!' shouted Geoffrey. Underestimating Barcwit would be fatal for Kea. 'Stay back.'

Barcwit grinned. 'You would be wise to listen to the King's agent, Father. He knows that desperate men resort to desperate measures, and there cannot be a more desperate man than me – with no silver, no mint, no soldiers and no family. So, this is what we are going to do. Kea will lead me to my silver, while you stay here, nice and quiet. I will release the boy when I deem myself safe. If anyone attempts to follow, I will kill him. Is that clear?'

'I know where it is,' wailed Kea's simple sister. 'It is by the river.'

But Barcwit was not about to be hoodwinked by a child of

six, whose thick speech indicated she was slow-witted. She was also transparently determined to save her brother. He ignored her.

'You will have to keep Kea for the rest of your life,' warned Giffard. 'Because you will never be safe. Release him and give yourself up. I will not let you leave here, hostage or no.'

'And I will not let you have the silver,' added Roger, making it clear where his priorities lay.

'I do not know where it is!' Kea wept. 'Honestly, I do not!'

'By the river!' insisted Kea's sister. 'My doll told me, before she was stolen by wicked thieves.'

Geoffrey winced, and wondered if Durand had ever returned the thing.

'None of us know,' said Wido reasonably. 'Or we would have tapped into it by now.'

Barcwit seemed to flag, accepting Wido was right and that the villagers would certainly have taken a share if they had known where it was hidden. But the resignation on his face was quickly replaced by a deep, savage hatred, and Geoffrey knew he would not give himself up to a traitor's death. A trickle of blood oozed down Kea's neck, and the boy screwed up his face as the knife began to bite.

Geoffrey had no time to think. He drew back his arm and hurled his sword as hard as he could. It sailed through the air and landed in Barcwit's chest with a nasty smacking sound. While the old man stared at it in surprise, Kea struggled away from him and dashed to Geoffrey's side. Barcwit's eyes closed, and he slipped to the floor, his blood staining the chancel's beautiful white flagstones.

'That is not what swords are designed to do,' said Roger admonishingly, going to retrieve the weapon and ensure the man was dead. 'You are supposed to use a lance for that sort of manoeuvre.'

'I did not bring one with me,' said Geoffrey tiredly, just grateful his unorthodox move had worked, when it could so very easily have failed. He glanced at Kea. 'Are you all right?'

'It is only a scratch,' said Kea, adding tearfully, 'but it still hurts.'

314

'What if you had missed?' Roger went on, disgusted. 'You might have damaged the blade.'

'Or hit the boy,' said Giffard, shocked. 'It was a risky thing to do.'

'Not really,' said Ulfrith. 'He is good at throwing things. I saw that when he killed Rodbert with the inkpot back at Barcwit's mint.'

'I shall have to re-consecrate this poor church,' said Giffard, inspecting the aftermath a few short moments had wrought. 'I count three dead and seven wounded.'

'You killed two of them,' said Ulfrith admiringly, wanting the bishop to have the credit he felt was his due. 'I only stunned the pair I caught, but your action with the spade was lethal.'

'But they were bad men,' said Kea kindly, seeing Giffard uncomfortable with his role as prime slaughterer. He turned to Geoffrey. 'We caught a physician creeping around, claiming he was looking for silver-thieves, but we overpowered him and hid him in our house. Then we discovered that Barcwit was here, too, and he forced us all to come to the church.'

'There is no need to worry about that now,' said Geoffrey. 'Barcwit is dead and you are safe.'

'But what about the silver?' asked Roger in dismay. 'That is why we came, after all.'

'*I* came to save these people from Barcwit,' said Geoffrey. 'I do not care about silver.'

'Well, I do,' said Giffard firmly. 'Remember what we agreed? That to give Henry the treasure may encourage him to overlook Sendi's release and Joan's escape? And do not forget that Barcwit was not the only one looking for it. The people of Beiminstre will not be safe until we have this other traitor *and* the ingots in our hands.'

'Why does everyone think *we* know where it is?' asked Wido in despair. 'First there was Clarembald, then Barcwit, and now you.'

'Alwold told us,' said Giffard. 'With his dying breath. He said the priest of St John's knows the secret. You are lucky Geoffrey has been discreet with the knowledge, or you would have been pestered a good deal sooner.'

'Me?' asked Wido, horrified. 'I can assure you I do not.'

'The others killed Piers the shepherd when *he* said that,' said Kea's sister, regarding Wido as if she thought he might be next.

Wido shook his head and spoke kindly. 'He was not killed, child. He just ran away.'

'He was killed,' insisted the girl firmly. 'He ran away first, but he came back and they killed him. Those others killed him. They probably stole my doll, too.'

Geoffrey rubbed his head tiredly, then crouched next to her. 'What others?'

She hung her head. 'Bad men. I told them the silver is by the river.'

'Rowise does not know,' said Kea, putting a protective arm around her shoulders. 'She and the doll make up stories together – or they did, before she lost it. She heard the story of how Alwold mislaid his silver, and has been dreaming about it ever since. Children have wild imaginations, especially ones who are simple.' He spoke as if his eleven years put him well into the realm of adulthood.

'Alwold took his cart to the river,' insisted Rowise. 'My doll saw him, but he said he would throw her in the water if she told anyone. When she ignored him and told Kea, she disappeared. Alwold drowned her.' She buried her face in Geoffrey's surcoat and started to cry.

'Now what?' asked Roger, disheartened. 'No one here knows what happened to the treasure, so we may as well give up on it.'

'Perhaps, but we can still catch these remaining traitors,' said Giffard. 'This child told them the silver is by the river – whether or not it is true – so that is where they will be. We may have failed with the ingots, but we shall have them.'

Roger turned soulful eyes on Wido. 'Are you *sure* you do not know where Alwold left it?'

Wido shook his head helplessly. 'All Alwold said to me that day was he had been to visit Piers. But when I asked Piers about it, he said he had not seen Alwold in weeks. Alwold lied about that, and he lied about me knowing this secret.'

'Poor Piers,' said Kea sadly. 'I shall miss him. He taught

316

me how to fish off the old wharves. He liked it there, and sat on them every night to watch the sunset.'

'Wharves?' asked Geoffrey, his thoughts whirling as something occurred to him. 'In Bristol?'

'Here,' said Kea. 'They used to be busy, but the ones in Bristol are bigger, and ships prefer to go there these days.'

'Ours are rotten and unstable,' elaborated Wido.

Suddenly, all was clear to Geoffrey, and he wondered why he had not seen it before. He looked at Giffard. 'When Alwold said the silver was with Piers, he did not mean the shepherd. I think he meant the quay – the piers.'

'Alwold did not expect to be murdered,' mused Giffard. 'So, it is not surprising his clues have been difficult to interpret. He expected to return here and retrieve the silver himself, and did not see the need to take precautions against dying before he could tell Barcwit what he had done.'

'Two people have known all along, though,' said Geoffrey. He nodded at the child who still sobbed into his shoulder. 'One was Rowise, who watched what he did. The other was Wido, whom Alwold told – presumably lest anything went wrong – but who did not understand.'

'Damn!' muttered Wido, angry with himself. 'My one chance to be rich, and I bungle it!'

'We all assumed Rowise was making it up,' said Kea, stunned. 'But she wanders alone in the woods, so I suppose it is possible she saw Alwold with his cart.'

Geoffrey gently prised Rowise away from him. 'Tell me about the men who killed Piers,' he said softly. 'Have you seen them before? What did they look like?'

'He had a big yellow beard,' wept Rowise. 'And a wife and plenty of friends.'

'Sendi!' exclaimed Giffard and Roger at the same time.

Roger and Giffard were keen to begin the search for the silver before Sendi also unravelled the clue left by Alwold, while Ulfrith was never averse to looking for treasure. Helbye was uncharacteristically uninterested, claiming that the hoard had remained hidden for weeks, so a few more moments would not matter. He walked next to Geoffrey, who felt they made

317

a sorry sight as they limped along together. The knight thought about Clarembald's prognosis for Helbye's hip, and wondered when he would muster the courage to tell him his soldiering days were over.

'These damned boots!' Helbye muttered, glowering at the offending footwear. 'I will never see Jerusalem as long as they cripple every step I take.'

'None of us will see Jerusalem unless I have something to give the King,' said Geoffrey, knowing it was a perfect opportunity to break the news to Helbye, but too weary to grasp it.

'All along, we thought Barcwit was the dangerous one,' mused Helbye. 'But we were wrong: it was Sendi who was more corrupt and devious.'

Geoffrey agreed. 'Slow down!' he called to the others, who were forging ahead into the woods. 'Sendi may be nearer than you think.'

Roger made a dismissive gesture, and indicated his sword was at the ready. 'They will be miles away by now. All they know is that the silver is near the river, and will be scouring the banks for a cart. It is only us who know about the piers.'

'We will retrieve the silver first, then go after Sendi,' declared Giffard ambitiously, buoyed up by his recent successes. 'We will appease Henry after all.'

Geoffrey's ribs were aching, and he was not sure how good he would be in another set-to. He felt bruised all over, and all he wanted was to find some quiet spot and rest. Helbye, lurching along next to him, clearly felt the same. He hoped Roger was right, and that Sendi was looking for the silver some distance away. Then, with luck, the moneyer would give up when he saw he was not going to succeed and escape, leaving the King's spies to track him. Geoffrey heard a sound behind him and spun around, sword in his hand. It was Kea.

'I told you to stay at home,' said Geoffrey sharply.

'I would rather be with you. I want to help.'

'Then you can take my horse and put him somewhere safe. I do not want him stolen by the likes of Sendi, if he decides to ransack Beiminstre in lieu of silver.'

'We did that ages ago,' said Kea scornfully. 'As soon as

we heard Barcwit was on the loose. He was not nearly as big as I thought he was, but he was still not nice.'

'No,' agreed Geoffrey, smiling at the understatement. 'He was not nice.'

A sudden yell from Roger made him start in alarm. There followed the sounds of fighting: the clang of metal as swords met, the thump as they pounded shields, and the grunts of men struggling hard against each other. Giffard shouted something Geoffrey did not understand, while Ulfrith made the kind of noise that suggested he had already been over-powered and was struggling to free himself.

'Not again!' groaned Helbye in despair. 'Neither you nor I are in a fit state to fight again today.'

'Take the boy,' said Geoffrey. 'And tell his family to hide in the marshes until it is safe.'

'My place is with you,' said Helbye doggedly. 'I cannot—'

'You can save a village, which is a lot more useful than crossing swords with men who will have us outnumbered.' Geoffrey saw Helbye was not going to do it. 'That is an order!' he barked.

Helbye still hesitated, so Geoffrey pushed him hard, and the older man reluctantly hobbled back the way they had come. When he turned the corner, he raised his hand and saluted Geoffrey in a way that suggested he did not expect them to meet again.

The gesture saved Geoffrey's life. He trusted Helbye, and if Helbye thought he was in no condition to win a fight, then he knew he should try to avoid one. He had intended to rush headlong into the skirmish and do battle at Roger's side, but instead he moved off the path and eased into the undergrowth, edging forward cautiously. The sounds of fighting stopped as quickly as they had started, and he sensed he had been wise not to plunge blindly into the affray.

Within moments, he arrived at the edge of a clearing, where he crouched behind a holly bush to assess what had happened. The green-brown glitter of the River Avon lay in front of him, while an ancient and disused wharf stood to one side. It comprised a platform that jutted into the river, which was held up – but only just – by two crumbling wooden posts that were black with rot. It was obviously on the brink of collapse, and would not survive the winter.

Roger, Giffard and Ulfrith were lying face down in the clearing, while Sendi stood over them with a sword. They seemed unharmed, although Geoffrey suspected they would not be alive for long once the moneyer had his answers. Others milled around them, poking in the undergrowth with sticks and swords, as if they expected the silver to be hidden among the leaf litter.

'Roger was wrong,' said a voice in his ear, making him jump in alarm. 'He said Sendi would be miles away, but he is here.'

'I told you to hide, Kea,' whispered Geoffrey angrily. 'Now go. This is no place for you.'

'Master Helbye will lead the others to safety,' said Kea. 'But this is near where I hid the horses, so I have come to put them somewhere else.' He cringed when one of them released a piercing whinny. 'They will give themselves away!'

'What was that?' demanded Adelise from the far side of the clearing.

'The villagers hid their nags nearby,' replied Sendi. 'It is nothing to worry about.'

'We should not linger, regardless,' said Adelise. 'We escaped by the skin of our teeth last time – thanks to a particularly gullible bishop.' She glanced at Giffard, who winced.

Sendi studied all three prisoners, assessing who was the weakest. He chose Giffard, and came to stand over him, pressing his sword into the back of the prelate's neck. 'Where is the silver?'

'I do not know,' said Giffard, keeping his voice steady, even though Geoffrey could tell by the rigid way he was lying that he was deeply afraid.

'You do,' countered Adelise. 'You were heading somewhere with great purpose when you ran into us, and I think you knew exactly where you were going. Now, either you tell me where it is, or I shall round up the villagers, put them in the church and set it alight. You do not want their blood on your hands, My Lord Bishop.'

'Master Helbye has taken everyone away,' whispered Kea gleefully. 'So she cannot do it.'

'But Giffard does not know that,' Geoffrey muttered back.

'It is on the pier,' said Giffard softly. 'Do not harm those people. It would be a terrible sin.'

'Then tell us the truth,' said Adelise. 'Where on the pier? It looks empty to me.'

'I do not know,' replied Giffard. 'Inside the mooring posts, perhaps, or under the planks. You will have to explore.'

Adelise walked on to the jetty and poked the boards with the toe of her shoe. She moved carefully, but even though she was small and light, the planks still bowed under her weight. Geoffrey thought Alwold was lucky the whole thing had not disintegrated and taken the silver with it.

'I think he is right,' Adelise called. 'A number of the boards are loose, and something may well be stored under them. The whole thing is rotten, which has resulted in a number of hollows.'

'Hurry, then,' ordered Sendi. 'We do not have all day.'

'I cannot do it alone,' snapped Adelise impatiently. 'Some of the holes are deep, and we shall need ropes and axes. Fetch them.'

Sendi sighed at her brusque commands, but did as he was told. He dispatched six men to the village, and they dribbled back in ones and twos, laden down with the items she wanted, muttering resentfully that there were no villagers to use as pack horses. One man was so angry that he hurled his coil of rope near Geoffrey's holly bush before stalking on to the pier.

Geoffrey rubbed his chin and wondered what he could do. There were about ten men including Sendi, and he could not tackle them alone. An archer stood over Roger and the others, and he knew they would be shot the moment he did anything rash. While no one was looking, he reached forward and grabbed the rope, for no other reason than that he thought it might inconvenience them and delay their plans until he could think of something else. He and Kea watched helplessly as Sendi and the others began to lay into the crumbling wood with axes, hammers and even branches torn from nearby trees.

'I see something!' cried Adelise, prodding the hollow she had made. She lay flat on her stomach and inserted her arm, withdrawing it moments later with something clasped in her hand. There were gasps of avaricious delight when a silver ingot was revealed.

'It *is* here!' shouted Sendi, delighted. 'The bishop was telling the truth!'

'Fetch the others,' Adelise ordered one of the men. 'Tell them we have found it, and that we need their help if we are to gather it all and take it with us.'

Dutifully, the man slipped away, leaving Geoffrey horrified. How many more were there? Should he try to do something now, while they were only ten men and Adelise, or wait to see who else came, so he would know exactly what he was facing?

The find had a remarkable effect on the moneyers. They redoubled their efforts, hacking and sawing ferociously at the rotten wood, thrusting their hands into cavities, oblivious to the splinters that tore at their skin. Geoffrey saw it would not be long before they had what they wanted, at which point they would kill his friends. They could not let them live to raise the alarm, and there was nothing to be gained from taking hostages. He did not have long to formulate a plan.

'How did you find it?' asked someone who was striding down the path. Geoffrey gasped in shock. It was Idonea, with Peter behind her. Stomach churning, he tried to see whether Joan was there, too.

'Luck,' said Sendi, breathless from his exertions. 'Come and help us. We should get as much as we can and then leave this place. I do not feel safe here.'

'You are right to be concerned,' said Peter. 'Giffard killed Barcwit and most of his followers after you left, and he will not hesitate to do the same to you. That is the extent of the King's justice.' He almost spat the last word.

'We do not need to worry about Giffard,' said Adelise, nodding at the unhappy bishop. 'We will kill him and toss his body in the river when we have finished here. That is *Saxon* justice.'

'Where is Geoffrey?' demanded Idonea. 'He will not be far, if Roger is here. He was difficult to deceive, and I do not want him at large.'

'We even had to enlist the help of that stupid Feoc to mislead him,' added Peter. 'We told the priest what Barcwit had "forced" us to do in the hope that his terrified babbling would frighten the wretched man off. But it did not work: Geoffrey became even more determined to destroy us, just as his sister predicted.'

'I am going to kill him before we leave here,' vowed Idonea. She grabbed a sword and jabbed it into the hapless Giffard. 'Where is he?'

'He is behind that holly bush,' said Ulfrith, to Geoffrey's horror. 'He is watching every move you make, and will soon come to rescue us.'

Sendi started to laugh. 'That means he is nowhere near. These three villains came to see what they could find without him. They do not want him telling that greedy King about the treasure.'

'We can talk later,' said Adelise. 'But now we must concentrate on retrieving the silver.'

Idonea rolled up her sleeves and moved purposefully on to the pier, which groaned under her weight. 'It would be a pity to miss some, for want of willing labour. Come on, Peter; we do not have all day.'

Peter sighed. 'Very well. But this is the last time I am doing anything like this. You have no idea how difficult it was to persuade Geoffrey that I was under Barcwit's sway. I am no good at lying.'

'On the contrary,' murmured Geoffrey to himself. 'You are very good indeed.'

Geoffrey continued to gaze at the constable and his wife with his thoughts in turmoil. Where was Joan? Was she involved in the conspiracy, too? Was that why she had been so reluctant to answer his questions, and tell him the truth? He knew she had lied to him, because there was no plot to kill the King – by Barcwit, Sendi, Peter or anyone else. He supposed she was waiting somewhere with Olivier and the horses, ready to ride away with her accomplices. But at least he had answers to some of the questions that had been dogging him for the past five days.

First, he knew why Peter and Idonea had tried so hard to persuade him to abandon his investigation. Barcwit had denied killing Nauntel, which implied that Peter had used the death of his friend to further his own ends – to "prove" what happened when people were difficult in Bristol. Joan had done the same, using their brother's stabbing to make her point. And they had all painted a vivid picture of Barcwit's evil ways, simply to deflect Geoffrey's attention away from Sendi. Second, he understood why Idonea had picked such poor troops to fight Sendi. It was not because she was reserving the best ones to bring down Barcwit, but to give her ally a better chance. And third, Peter had not been trying to escape from the castle to avoid fighting the previous day: he had been going to warn his accomplices.

The notion that he had been so completely fooled by their protestations of frightened innocence infuriated Geoffrey, and he was determined they would not escape, even if it meant Joan fell with them. He looked at the rope in his hand, then back to where Idonea hacked viciously at the ancient wood, and a plan began to take form in his mind.

'How far away are these horses?' he asked Kea.

'Too near. They will want to use them to carry this silver away.'

Geoffrey was sure he was right. 'Show me.'

With the stolen rope over his shoulder, he eased away from the clearing and followed the boy through the undergrowth. Kea was right: the horses were uncomfortably close. Geoffrey walked the few paces to the riverbank, which dropped away sharply.

'I am going to tie one end of this rope around the pillars supporting the jetty. I want you to put the other end around my horse, and when I shout, make him pull as hard as he can. Can you do it?'

'Of course,' said Kea. 'I will fashion a harness, and will be ready the moment you yell. Do you think it will work? The whole thing will collapse with all those men on it?'

Geoffrey shrugged. 'If not, then we will both be in trouble.'

He struggled out of his surcoat and armour, tearing impatiently at the buckles and damaging one or two in his haste. A scream of delight from Idonea, quickly followed by a joyous yell from Peter, indicated that another bundle had been found.

Geoffrey did not know how many ingots there were, but he knew he did not have time to speculate. Clad in leggings and tunic, he knotted one end of the rope around his waist and skidded down the muddy bank, wincing as the icy water touched his skin.

The tide was coming in, which meant Geoffrey was obliged to swim upstream in order to reach his objective, and he was appalled by the power of the current. It occurred to him that he might not have the strength to carry out his plan. He began to swim, trying to ignore the ache in his side. The pier was fairly close, and he hoped no one would happen to look into the water and spot him: his clothes were far from clean, but they were still bright against the dark water.

When he saw one man straighten and rub his back, taking a respite from his labours, he ducked under the surface, striking deep and hoping he would not be spotted. When his lungs felt as if they would explode from lack of air, he drifted up again, dismayed to find he had not gone as far as he had hoped. Aware that he was near enough to be seen by even the most casual of glances from the people on the wharf, he took another breath and swam underwater a second time. When he surfaced, he was a little closer to the pillars, but it was still not enough.

He heard a shout and ducked again, hoping he had not been spotted. He surfaced only to snatch quick gulps of air, knowing his best chance of success depended on him being invisible for as long as possible. It was only when he surfaced for the sixth time, so breathless he felt dizzy, that he was finally under the pier. He could hear feet tapping on the timbers above, and saw the rope trailing in the water behind him. People were yelling in a way that made him certain they suspected something was amiss. He wrapped his legs around the closer of the pillars, and untied the rope from his waist.

His cold hands were infuriatingly clumsy as he dragged the rope around the pillar, wrapping it once, then twice. But there were shellfish clinging to the wood, and he saw their sharp edges cut into the twine. He tore off a piece of his tunic and pressed it under the knot, hoping it would protect the fibres for the short time needed to bring about the jetty's collapse.

Then he began to question whether the rope was thick enough – or whether it might simply snap under what would be considerable strain.

'There he is!' He had been spotted, and he recognized the voice as Peter's. 'Bring the archer. I want this man dead, before he does any more harm.'

'I should have guessed,' Geoffrey yelled, struggling to make his last knot. '*You* killed Nauntel, not Barcwit. You murdered your friend, just to divert suspicion from yourself. But Nauntel's death did not make sense. He was one of Barcwit's investors, and Barcwit did not want him dead. It was obvious that someone else had done it.'

'Shut up,' snarled Peter, rattled. 'Nauntel is not your concern.'

'Peter did the right thing,' said Idonea, more for her husband's benefit than for Geoffrey's. 'Nauntel was becoming unstable, and we were afraid he would tell someone what we were doing. We had no choice but to kill him.'

'Here is the archer,' said Adelise. 'Move out of the way, Peter, so he has a clear shot.'

'Willingly,' said Peter icily, and Geoffrey could see the archer's feet directly above him.

'And my sister?' asked Geoffrey. One of his fingers was caught in the rope, and he struggled to free it. 'Is she involved in this, too?'

Peter's voice was maliciously satisfied. 'You will die not knowing.'

Geoffrey yelled to Kea at the top of his voice, still trying to free his hand. 'Now!'

Nothing happened.

'Kea,' he yelled. 'Pull!'

Still nothing.

'Are you speaking to this little fellow?' asked Sendi. Just above him, Geoffrey saw Kea struggling helplessly against one of the workmen. His heart sank and he sagged against the wood in defeat. His plan had failed and there was nothing else he could do.

'We saw the rope trailing in the water, so we went to see

326

what it was attached to,' said Sendi gloatingly. 'It was a clever idea, and it is a pity for you that it will not work.'

'Come *on*,' Adelise urged the archer. 'We do not have all day.'

Geoffrey risked a glance upwards and saw it was the same bowman who had been in Sendi's mint. He recalled thinking then that the man was good – and that he was desperate for a kill – and Geoffrey had no illusions about his fate. Exhausted and overcome with hopelessness, he rested his head against the pier, abandoning his efforts to free his hand. Suddenly, the rope went taut. The pillar protested the sudden tug with a tearing creak, and everyone on the platform jumped in alarm.

'What is happening?' Adelise demanded. 'I thought you brought the horses here.'

'I did,' said Sendi, startled. 'You can see them over there.'

There was another groan, and the quay listed violently to one side. Geoffrey wrenched his hand away from the straining rope and glanced up, seeing the entire structure begin to topple towards him. He kicked out for all he was worth, aware of the heavy, rotten wood tilting slowly just above his head. Its shadow fell over him, and he sensed it dropping faster and faster. The current worked with him, but it would not be enough. It was going to fall right on top of him, and crush him on the river bed.

He swam harder, using the very last ounce of his strength, then was caught in a sudden maelstrom of foam and waves. The pier had missed him by no more than the breadth of a hand. He heard Roger shouting, and suspected the big knight had made short work of the guard while he was distracted. Adelise screamed, and he was aware of men splashing into the water all around him. He saw one head break the surface, and then another by its side: Kea and Adelise. She flailed for a moment, then grabbed the boy.

'Fool!' she snapped at Geoffrey. 'Now we will have to dive for the silver. It will delay our escape!'

Geoffrey was bemused. Who had pulled on the rope, when Kea and the horses were in Sendi's hands? And why did Adelise not see she might have opponents to defeat before she turned her attention to the silver again? He glanced towards

327

the bank, and saw Roger and Ulfrith fighting those few who had not been on the pier when it had collapsed. Meanwhile Giffard was "helping" others out of the water, then dashing them over the head with his boot before they could join the affray.

'You should have left yesterday, while you had the chance,' said Geoffrey, paddling towards Kea. Adelise was pushing him under the surface in an attempt to keep herself afloat, and he did not want her to drown the child. 'You allowed yourself to become blinded by this silver, and now you will not even escape with your life.'

Adelise twisted around, and saw other people hurrying into the clearing, weapons at the ready. Those of her men who were not in the water were quickly overpowered, and Roger was already kneeling next to the silver they had recovered, shoving an ingot or two inside his surcoat before anyone thought to count them. Sendi was floundering wildly, yelling that he could not swim, when Peter, apparently in the same position, grabbed him and used him as a float. Geoffrey knew they would drown each other if no one intervened. Adelise saw all was lost, and, with a blazing glare of hatred, she forced Kea's head under the water and held it there, spite and defiance in every fibre of her being.

Geoffrey punched her lightly on the jaw, not enough to stun her, but enough to make her release the boy. She relinquished her grasp with a screech of shock, so he snatched Kea away from her and struck out for the shore. Then he felt himself seized from behind, and his world turned green and frothy. He realized he should have hit her harder, because she was now trying to drown him, snaking her fingers into his hair and pushing him down with the whole weight of her body. Then, just as abruptly, he was released, and came spluttering to the surface.

Adelise was face-down in the water, where the current was bearing her away in a cloud of red. Kea had a dagger in his hand.

'Did you stab her?' Geoffrey gasped.

'She tried to kill me,' retorted the boy defensively.

Geoffrey was so tired he could barely summon the energy

to flap towards the bank. He saw Peter's body twisting this way and that in the wreckage of the quay, prevented from floating away because his cloak had snagged, while Sendi flapped towards the shore and Giffard's shoe. Idonea, wet and bedraggled, sat with several other captives. Everyone who posed a danger was now dead or caught. Geoffrey felt himself slide under the surface, unable to make his exhausted muscles work any more.

Small hands hauled him up again, and Kea's insistent high-pitched voice urged him to swim. By the time he had struggled to the shore and hauled himself up the slippery bank, he was finished. He lay in the clearing with his eyes closed, and hoped Roger did not need his help, because this time he was certain he could not do it.

'Sit up,' came a soft voice at his side. He recognized it, and was immediately on his guard. 'You will feel better if you sit up.'

'I will feel better when I have the truth,' said Geoffrey, struggling to his knees and pulling his arm away when Joan tried to help him. 'Were you involved in this plot to steal the silver?'

'She was not,' declared Kea, outraged by the accusation. 'And you owe your life to Dame Joanie, so watch what you say.'

'Do I? Why? What did she do?'

'She pulled on the rope after Sendi caught Kea and took the horses away,' explained Warelwast, coming to stand next to them. 'As did I, Olivier and a few of the villagers, although I suspect most of the strength was hers.'

Geoffrey glanced around and saw that Helbye had taken charge of securing the prisoners, ordering Giffard away when he offered to subdue more of them with his boot; Roger had declared himself keeper of the silver. Others were there, too: Clarembald and Bishop John still argued, even as they worked together to tie up Sendi, while Bloet, sword drawn, helped Helbye guard those captives who were not yet bound.

'I do not understand,' said Geoffrey tiredly. Nothing made sense. Joan, Olivier and Warelwast should have been on their way to Exeter, and he had no idea why Bloet and John should be there.

'The villagers hid Joan after she managed to escape from Peter,' explained Helbye, glancing away from his charges to explain. 'But when I told her what was happening here, she insisted on coming to see what she could do for you.'

'If she had not pulled on that rope when she did, we all would be dead,' added Kea. 'And Sir Peter and Sendi would have escaped with the silver.'

'We thought we were heading to Exeter,' elaborated Warelwast. 'But then Peter and Idonea drew weapons and told us we were going back to Bristol. We were as surprised as you to learn that they were in league with Sendi, but we should have guessed. Sendi could not have operated so long without the consent of a powerful town authority: namely the constable. Of course Sir Peter de la Mare was involved. He pretended to be under Barcwit's spell just to confuse you.'

'But we escaped,' said Olivier proudly. 'Joan bit through the ropes that bound us.' He gazed fondly at his wife.

Joan smiled back at him. 'But Olivier and I would never have made it without Warelwast. He risked his life to save ours, by distracting the guard while we fled. I flung a dagger and killed the man, but Warelwast was prepared to sacrifice himself to help us nonetheless.'

'I promised,' said Warelwast, looking steadily at Geoffrey. 'I gave you my rope as a pledge.'

Geoffrey handed it back to him, and watched him secure it around his neck. 'So, that is it?' he asked wearily. 'It is over?'

'Almost,' said Giffard. 'We must retrieve the rest of the silver from the river and take it to the King, but we have a complete set of culprits. Peter and Idonea were late to show their hand, but they are the last. All the others who were on Sendi's list of investors – the physicians, Bloet, Warelwast and your sister – are exonerated.'

'Even Clarembald?' asked Roger. 'He has been acting very oddly.'

'Under the King's orders,' explained Warelwast. 'Please do not look at me in that angry way, Geoffrey. You should have guessed Henry would send more than one agent to sort out this mess. Bloet was sent, too – to find the silver.'

330

'And Warelwast was charged to protect you,' added Giffard.

'To protect me?' asked Geoffrey in astonishment. 'How?'

'By being your friend,' replied Warelwast shyly. 'Henry knew you would make enemies with the task he set you, so he sent me as a man you could trust. Unfortunately, you never did. But remember that I did pull very hard on the rope to destroy the pier.'

'It is true,' said Joan. 'Warelwast is a true friend, and you can never have too many of those.'

It was not long before Giffard became aware that Roger was stealing rather more of the ingots than Henry would want to lose. To distract him, he and the others walked to the river-bank to discuss how best to recover what had been lost during Geoffrey's desperate gamble to thwart the thieves. Meanwhile, Joan removed her cloak and placed it around her brother's shoulders.

'But you cannot have my pink shoes, too,' she said with a smile. 'They are special.'

Geoffrey was not in the mood for humour. 'You were deceived in this business just as much as me. There never was a plot to kill Henry.'

She agreed. 'But I did not know that until yesterday. Peter and Idonea confessed that they made it up, to frighten me and prevent me from co-operating with you. They were afraid that if I did, you would identify them as two of the worst offenders. But I did not invest willingly with Barcwit, not even at the beginning. I lied when I said we had spare funds from Olivier selling a horse.'

Geoffrey pulled the cloak more closely around him. 'I should have known. If you had spare funds, you would not have used them on investments. You would have bought a cow or built a barn.'

'I was forced,' she said. 'I did not want to do it, but I had no choice.'

'By whom?' asked Geoffrey, wondering who would be brave enough to make Joan do something she did not want to do.

'I was told, back in March, that if I did not invest with

331

Barcwit, then Olivier would suffer. Of course I did as I was ordered – what is gold, when compared to the lives of those you love? I was surprised when we started to make substantial profits, then Peter told me Barcwit was saving money to fund an attempt on the King's life. I did not understand what I had been dragged into. Then you arrived, and I saw you were going to be sucked into the mess, too. I did everything I could to drive you away: begging, lies, threats. All I wanted was for you to be gone, away from the danger closing around me.'

'Who did this to you?' asked Geoffrey harshly. 'I swear I will kill him.'

'No,' said Joan in horror. 'Do not vow such things when you do not know what you are saying. The man who forced me to invest with Barcwit is the same man who forced you to come here to defend me. He was testing us, to see whether we are worthy of him.'

Geoffrey stared at her, wondering whether they had passed the test or whether they had been found lacking. Would they be allowed to go about their lives unmolested now? Or would he come after them again?

'Henry?' he asked, to be sure. 'The King?'

'Yes, Henry,' she whispered. 'The King.'

Epilogue

Winter had arrived in earnest by the time Geoffrey made the long, dismal journey from Bristol to Winchester. The roads had degenerated into seas of mud, knee-deep in places, and riding was slow. Geoffrey did not want to meet the King, and dragged his heels, blaming their lack of progress on the fact that his ribs were sore, or that he did not want to tire his horse. This last excuse was a poor one, because the warhorse Kea had returned was a new animal. There was a spring in its step, its coat glistened with health, and it galloped at every opportunity. Durand had been killing it with his careless ministrations, and had been banned from tending it again. The squire sulked at the reprimand, clutching something that looked suspiciously like the doll the dog had stolen from Beiminstre.

'I told you to take that back,' said Geoffrey angrily. 'What is wrong with you?'

'I forgot,' said Durand sullenly, shoving the thing into Geoffrey's bag. 'When Henry pays me for my services, I will hire a messenger to return the damned thing, if it makes you happy.'

Geoffrey was not the only one who did not want to see the King. Joan was not looking forward to the meeting either, and was uncommunicative, speaking only to give her opinion of the inns at which they stayed – usually rude ones – or to ensure her brother wore clean clothes. She declined to discuss anything relating to the mission Henry had devised for her, and forbade Olivier to speak of it, too. Geoffrey did not care. The whole adventure had left a sour taste in his mouth, and

333

he felt he had learnt far more than he needed to know already.

They found a small, clean inn in a quiet alley near the abbey, and Geoffrey was looking forward to an evening by the fire, when a messenger arrived. Henry had learnt of their arrival, and wanted to see them immediately. Geoffrey set out with Roger and Durand in tow, and Joan walking stiffly by his side. She was anxious, and he patted her hand encouragingly.

The messenger conducted them to a small but luxuriously appointed chamber on an upper floor of the palace. The windows were open, and Henry stared out across the chilly, grey countryside, watching the shadows lengthen and the last glimmers of daylight disappear. It would be dark in an hour, and the damp, foggy coldness of a December night would settle in. Geoffrey had a sudden vision of the Holy Land sun in all its parched glory, and longed to feel its dry heat in his bones.

He was not particularly pleased to see others had been summoned, too. Bloet sat near the window, scrubbing at his long nose with the sleeve of his tunic. Durand glowered at him, but was intelligent enough to do no more. Warelwast stood with Clarembald, and smiled in genuine pleasure when Geoffrey entered, while Giffard sat by the embers of a dead fire. Warelwast wore the habit of an Austin Canon, and a plain wooden cross had replaced the piece of rope. He saw Geoffrey notice.

'I gave it to Kea's sister,' he whispered, while the others made their obeisance to the King. 'She was distressed over the loss of a doll, and my rope – with its oddly human features – seemed to comfort her. So I let her have it.'

'You parted with it?' asked Geoffrey, surprised. 'After wearing it for so long?'

'I did not have the heart to take it back,' admitted Warelwast ruefully. 'Besides, I no longer need a reminder to tell me I am God's servant. I have taken the cowl.'

'Right,' said Henry, when the messenger had closed the door. 'We are all here – and Geoffrey has even deigned to clean himself up for the occasion. Is that a *new* tunic I see?'

Geoffrey shot Joan a resentful glare when the others joined Henry in sycophantic laughter. It did not last long. Henry wanted to get down to business.

334

'I have read the reports each of you sent,' he said. 'Bloet.'

Bloet shot to his feet. 'Sire?'

'The missing silver is now in my care, so your task is completed to my satisfaction.'

Bloet started to smile, obviously relieved by the verdict. 'Yes, sire. I—'

'However, its safe delivery had nothing to do with you. You were asleep when Sendi and Peter de la Mare tried to steal it from me.'

'I had had a late night,' objected Bloet. 'And I did my—'

Henry raised an imperious hand and Bloet's words died in his throat. 'You failed. I gave you this chance, because I am fond of your father, but you have proved yourself unreliable. I have no further use for you; return to Lincoln, and resume your duties as dean.'

Bloet opened his mouth to object, but saw the flash in Henry's eyes and decided against it. Durand opened the door for him with smug pleasure, and Geoffrey poked him, to prevent him from gloating too openly. He sensed no one would have cause for celebrating much that evening: Henry was angry.

'Clarembald.' The physician waved his ginger eyebrows in alarm. 'You were partly successful and, if you had not allowed yourself to be trussed up by the people of Beiminstre, you probably would have caught the traitors. But you made mistakes and you are not as quick-witted as my spies need to be. I will not employ you in this capacity again, so you may go back to your medicine.'

'Thank you, sire,' said Clarembald with palpable relief. 'John de Villula is not here. Is he . . .?'

'The Shopping Bishop had no role in this,' said Henry. 'He invested with Barcwit, but there is no evidence of dishonesty. You may go.'

Clarembald bowed his way from the room.

'Warelwast,' said Henry, turning to the bishop-elect. 'You performed your duties adequately, but no more. You were not instrumental in assisting Geoffrey to uncover the plot, nor did you protect him.'

'He would not let me,' objected Warelwast. 'He ordered me away when I offered my help openly, and gave me the slip when I followed him covertly. Besides, how can *I* protect a *Jerosolimitanus*? I probed his skills in Westminster, and learnt he would be a difficult man to harm.'

'*You* attacked me?' asked Geoffrey, startled. He recalled the odd words of one of the assailants – 'we have done all we can' – and supposed they had referred to assessing his talents for self-defence.

'I needed to know the extent of the protection you would require,' said Warelwast curtly. 'I did not want to take soldiers if I did not have to – and I did not. Indeed, you were the one who saved me.'

Geoffrey thought about it. While he did not like the notion that Warelwast had been detailed to protect him, it was scarcely his fault, and the bishop-elect had done his best.

'He saved Joan, sire,' he said, as Henry started to berate the hapless cleric for his failures. 'When I made her go with Peter de la Mare, thinking he intended to head for Exeter, he helped her escape.'

Henry sighed and relented. 'Sir Geoffrey seems to have forgiven you for your shortcomings, Warelwast, so I shall do the same. You are a better ambassador than spy, and I shall use you for diplomatic missions in the future. You may go.'

Warelwast bowed and left, smiling his thanks to Geoffrey as he went. Giffard abandoned his reflections near the empty hearth and went to light a lamp. It was becoming dim in the royal chamber.

'Geoffrey,' said Henry. The knight tensed, preparing himself for a reprimand, like the others. 'Giffard tells me you have read his report. Do you have more to add? Sendi and Barcwit were corrupt moneyers, and Sendi rashly complained to me about his rival, while committing worse crimes himself. And Peter de la Mare was paid to look the other way.'

Geoffrey nodded. 'Peter also told Joan that Barcwit planned to kill you, but it was not true.'

'It was not,' agreed Henry. 'It is a good thing Peter drowned, because otherwise I would have condemned him to death without a moment's hesitation.'

Geoffrey frowned, puzzled. 'You seem angrier with him than the others. Is it because he was a constable, and you expect greater loyalty from him?'

Henry raised his eyebrows. 'I do not like traitors.'

Geoffrey glanced at Joan's unhappy face, and suddenly he understood. He gazed at Henry in astonishment. 'Peter was *your* man? It was he who encouraged Joan to invest with Barcwit, and who kept her too afraid to withdraw, by fabricating this tale of regicide. Is that why you consider him a greater traitor: he was under your direct orders and he turned bad?'

'I am careful who I choose as agents,' said Henry softly. 'So, I was shocked when I learnt Peter was in league with Sendi. And I was even more shocked to learn their arrangement was of several years' duration. He was corrupt long before I trusted him with my business.'

Giffard seemed equally startled by Henry's revelation. 'So, that explains why Peter was so keen to flee and why Idonea was preparing for a siege. They both knew it was only a matter of time before their double-dealing was exposed. Their terror was real.'

'You used them to trap my sister,' said Geoffrey, trying to keep the anger from his voice. He felt Roger's hand on his shoulder, warning him to watch his tongue.

'I did not know if she would agree to do what I asked,' said Henry with a shrug. 'I told her to invest in Barcwit's enterprise, because I predicted I would later need an excuse to ask *you* to investigate the man – and what better reason than to help the last surviving member of your family?'

'That,' said Geoffrey coldly, 'was not necessary.'

'It *was* necessary,' snapped Henry, while Giffard made frantic gestures behind his back to urge Geoffrey to caution. 'You would not have gone to Bristol out of the goodness of your heart, and I want to know whether you are the kind of man I can trust with more delicate missions in the future. Durand tells me you have a way with such matters, but I was determined to judge for myself.'

'But Joan was ordered to invest with Barcwit in March,' said Geoffrey, appalled. 'That means you have been intending to put this scheme into action for months.'

'The idea came to me the day you visited Westminster, before Easter, when we discussed Bellême,' agreed Henry amiably. 'It is always wise to plan ahead, and I knew trouble was brewing with my Bristol moneyers. Sendi's complaint against Barcwit was opportune, because it gave me a good reason to call you back before you vanished into the Holy Land. But do not think any of this makes you special. I have many similar experiments in progress, testing promising men and women, and this little episode is not particularly important or relevant.'

'You used us as pawns?' asked Geoffrey, a little shocked that a man who was supposed to protect his subjects should expose them to such grave dangers for what sounded like gratuitous amusement.

Henry nodded carelessly. 'But it all turned out well, so I do not think you have anything to complain about. I am sure you have not forgotten that you are always eager to please your monarch.'

'I did not know what to do,' said Joan in a low voice. Geoffrey saw that the events of the last few months were not unimportant or irrelevant to her: she was shaken to the core. 'It was suggested that Olivier might be hurt if I did not invest with Barcwit, then our brother was stabbed and. . .' She trailed off miserably.

'Henry's stabbing was nothing to do with me,' said the King firmly. 'It was an unfortunate coincidence. I ordered one of my best agents to investigate the matter, and he assures me that Barcwit had nothing to do with the death. I cannot be blamed because he pretended it did, can I?'

Geoffrey glanced at Joan's pale face and hated Henry for playing his selfish games with her. He felt a burning desire to tell him so, but he had not forgotten the King's ire when he had insulted him in Westminster – nor his promise to hang him if it happened again. With admirable restraint, he suppressed his temper and resumed his analysis instead.

'You told Peter to invent the story about regicide, to prevent Joan from telling me she was acting for you. You knew that was our weakness: I would not leave her when I thought she

338

was in danger; she would never tell me the truth if she thought it might bring me to harm.'

'I am a good judge of character,' said Henry comfortably. 'Most men would sell their kin for the price of a manor, but not you two. You have proved yourselves worthy of my trust.'

'You overestimate us, sire,' said Joan flatly. 'We only did what others would have done.'

Henry disagreed. 'Geoffrey provided me with details of the case that most would have missed or ignored – the fact that Sendi was more corrupt than Barcwit, the fact that Barcwit's children invented a myth and used it to terrify the locals, the fact that they enjoyed an incestuous relationship. And he drove Peter into the open and found my silver. He gave me the truth.'

Geoffrey sincerely hoped it had distressed him – especially the part where he had taken the treacherous Peter into his confidence and had been betrayed. 'The truth can be uncomfortable,' he said, as insolently as he dared.

'You are rebellious, disobedient and unpredictable, but I shall offer you a place in my service nonetheless,' Henry went on, choosing to ignore the barb. 'Durand tells me you are still waiting to hear from Tancred, because you believe I forged his original letter of dismissal, but I am prepared to wait. You will find it was genuine, and that your Holy Land prince no longer wants you.'

Geoffrey glared at Durand, who looked sheepish.

'I would have found out anyway,' said Henry irritably. 'So do not pick on Durand. Visit Goodrich and think about my offer. We can discuss terms when you have made up your mind. You may go.'

'Is that it?' asked Joan, startled.

'Thank you for your help,' said Henry, clapping his hands for his secretary, and thus indicating that they were dismissed. 'Giffard will see you receive compensation for all monies invested with Barcwit on my behalf – assuming you have proof of the transactions, of course.'

'Oh, yes,' said Joan icily, producing a sheaf of parchments. 'I have proof.'

'I thought you might,' said Henry, not altogether pleased. 'Leave it with Giffard on your way out.'

339

They quit the royal chamber with relief. Joan seemed suddenly lighter and happier, and Geoffrey sensed a great weight had been lifted from her shoulders. He was surprised, because he had not imagined an audience with the King would have affected her so deeply.

'I thought I would have to pretend we were enemies again,' she said, taking his arm. 'It is not easy saying I hate you, when I do not.'

'Why would you do that? Henry knows it is not true: it is what allowed him to perpetrate this monstrous test in the first place.'

'I thought I might have to persuade him he was wrong.'

'Why?' pressed Geoffrey. 'Your so-called treachery was on his orders.'

'Yes and no,' said Joan. 'If I thought I could put a knife into Henry's black heart and not bring the fury of his minions down on you and Olivier, I would do it.'

Geoffrey gazed at her in alarm. 'What are you saying?'

'When Peter told me about the plot to kill the King I was pleased – delighted – to learn about it. I embraced it willingly, and made plans, arrangements and even additional payments. Idonea was hanged and Peter drowned, but until now I did not know whether they had told anyone else how eager I was for Henry's death. I *am* a traitor, Geoffrey – and a very committed one.'

Geoffrey regarded her uneasily. 'Is that why you have been so subdued since we left Bristol? You were anticipating that you would be exposed?'

She nodded. 'As God is my witness, I am sorry my plotting came to nothing. I desperately wanted that usurper dead. And, after what he did to you, I want it even more.'

Geoffrey was horrified. 'Then you have had a luckier escape than I realized.'

'I have,' she agreed with a grim smile. 'But it leaves me free to plot against him again, at some point in the future.'

The following day, Durand sat in a church and flexed his aching fingers. He smiled at the priest who had furnished him with pen and ink, and indicated he was almost finished. He read over the two letters he had written with satisfaction, certain that no one could tell the difference between the distinctive script of Tancred's scribe and that which he had forged so carefully. One missive was for Geoffrey. It told him that the earlier communication was indeed a true reflection of his status, and that he was no longer wanted in Tancred's entourage. The other was for Henry, listing Geoffrey's talents and recommending him for employment.

Durand did not want to return to the Holy Land. He felt his future lay in England, but he needed Geoffrey until the King offered him a permanent post. His attempt to inveigle himself a place with Bloet had failed miserably, so his next best option was to remain in Geoffrey's service. The knight courted danger and cared nothing for clean clothes and elegant company, but at least he did not steal his servants' possessions.

So, Durand tore up the affectionate letter in which Tancred expressed concern about Geoffrey's delay, assuring him he would always have a place in his household, and substituted the new one. That was one advantage of being a squire: messages were almost always given to him first. He was confident Tancred would soon forget his absent knight, and Geoffrey would endure working for Henry for a little while – and a little while was all Durand needed. He sealed both letters with the ring he had stolen from Tancred months before, and strolled through the city. He delivered the first missive to Henry, then headed for Geoffrey's lodgings.

'This has just arrived,' he announced, bursting into the knight's chamber and pretending all was urgency and action. He feigned breathlessness, as though he had been running. 'I met the messenger near the abbey, where I have been praying.'

Geoffrey took it from him, but did not open it. He sat at a table with Joan, Olivier and Roger, while Helbye was opposite, and Giffard stood by the fire. It did not seem to be a particularly jolly gathering, and Roger had not touched the wine at his elbow. Something was wrong.

'So,' said Helbye, as if in conclusion. 'These boots have damaged my feet, and I can no longer fight. That was the meaning of the Two Suns: it was a prediction that both my heels would burn in an unnatural manner. The Three Rainbows was a sign telling me to cross the rivers Avon, Severn and Wye and return to Goodrich. I am sorry to leave you, but I must.'

Geoffrey nodded slowly, and Durand found the expression on his face oddly difficult to read. Durand knew the boots were a perfect fit and that Helbye was pleased with them; he also knew that a man limping from sore feet walked differently from a man whose hips were crumbling. He opened his mouth to expose the old man's lies, but Geoffrey was looking at him.

'The King wants to see you,' he said.

Durand grinned. Perhaps he had not needed to forge the letters after all. His reports on Geoffrey had been concise and mostly truthful, and it occurred to him that the King might be grateful.

'I doubt it is anything to smile about,' said Joan. 'I do not think he is very pleased with you.'

'He is not, and when you see him, you can tell him you are no longer my squire,' added Geoffrey. 'I am finished with you.'

'What does he want?' asked Durand, the first snakes of unease beginning to uncoil in his stomach.

'Today, you tried to sell the die you stole from Sendi,' explained Roger. 'You disguised yourself, but your hair is distinctive, and it gave you away. The Winchester moneyer is an honest man – or a wary one – and reported you to the King. Bishop Giffard is waiting to escort you to the palace.'

'It was not me,' squeaked Durand in alarm. 'I stole no stamp.'

'You took it when Sendi showed us his mint,' said Geoffrey. 'He blamed me, because he said I was the only stranger to visit him. But I was not: you were there, too. You concealed it in those pink shoes I bought for Joan, which you were carrying.'

'But that does not prove—' began Durand.

'Here is the doll I told you to return to Kea's sister.' Geoffrey held up the toy, then pulled off its head, revealing a hollow space inside. 'This is where you hid the die. It explains why it was heavy the second time I picked it up – it was not sodden with spilled wine, as I assumed. You did not keep it in your own bag, in case its secret was discovered, so you kept it in mine instead. You were happy for me to take the risk.'

Durand licked lips that were dry. 'I . . .' He could think of nothing to say.

'I knew you were a thief,' said Joan. 'You stole one of my necklaces, and I tried to warn my brother about you. You have no place in the company of honest men.'

'Honest men?' sneered Durand, finding his voice. He glanced contemptuously at Olivier. '*He* cannot open his mouth without speaking a lie, with his tales of battles fought before he was born.'

Geoffrey wanted to defend Olivier, but did not know how. Then Roger came to his feet, making the squire back away in alarm. 'Olivier is a noble veteran,' he snarled. 'His stories show him to be a true and bold warrior, and I will hear no slander of his name.'

Joan smiled at him gratefully, while Olivier blushed in surprise.

'Now go,' said Roger. 'You can tell the King why you tried to cheat him – and saying you were short of funds after you fell foul of Bloet will not soften his heart. You must think of a better excuse.'

Durand smiled maliciously. 'Oh, I shall.' He shook off Giffard's hand, and a confident gleam came into his eyes as a plan began to take form. 'I know exactly what I shall say.'

Geoffrey watched him stalk out. 'I do not like the sound of that. I hope—'

'You worry too much,' interrupted Roger. He nodded to the message that lay untouched on the table. 'Open it. I can tell from the dust that it hails from the Holy Land. Now we shall have the truth from Tancred.'

Geoffrey picked up the letter and broke the seal.

Historical Postscript

Coins were a problem in the reign of Henry I. Matters came to a head in 1108, then in 1125, when a massive survey of all English moneyers was set in motion. Each was summoned to Winchester to give an account of himself, and some contemporary sources say the sentence of mutilation was passed on them all, with the subsequent loss of right hands and testicles.

There was a mint (or mints) in Bristol from about 1020. Barcwit (or Barcuit) was producing pennies from about 1092, and he struck two types in the reign of Henry I. Sendi (whose coins sometimes read Sindi or Snedi) started at the same time, and was probably still going c. 1110–1113. Colblac and Lifwine (Leofwine) were moneyers before 1100, while Alwold (Ailwald) and Rodbert were later.

The location of the Bristol mint in 1100 remains unknown. Some coins were produced next to St Ewen's Church, at the corner of Broad and Corn streets in the mid-twelfth century, and some historians have suggested that others – perhaps from a second mint – were produced inside the castle. However, Bristol was not a royal castle at this time, it was a baronial one – and not all barons were King-friendly. Bishop Geoffrey of Coutances, who died in 1093 and is believed to be the castle's founder, was definitely hostile to William Rufus.

It is difficult to imagine Bristol as a port in the early 1100s. It was an Anglo-Saxon burgh, a walled town built on a grid system, and its four main streets – Corn, Wynche (Wine), High and Broad – still exist. No one knows how many churches were in the burgh at the time; some scholars argue there was only one, while others claim there were more than ten. Since then, rivers have been culverted and diverted, the old walls lost, and many medieval buildings destroyed. Little remains of its once-great fortress, except some wall fragments and a grassy park overlooking the river.

Beiminstre (Bedminster) was a royal manor. The earliest record of St John the Baptist's dates from 1003, and it was rebuilt several times until it was finally destroyed by incendiary bombs in the 1940s. It was an important place, once mother-church to magnificent St Mary Redcliffe. The village we now know as Long Ashton was called Estune in the Domesday survey of the 1080s, while Dundry was called Dundreg. The village of Saltford, between Bristol and Bath, was called Sanford.

Many people in the story were real. John de Villula and Clarembald were physicians known to have worked for King Henry or his family. John (died 1122) was probably at the Conqueror's deathbed, and was Rufus's chaplain before being granted the bishopric of Wells. Wells did not suit John, and he moved his ecclesiastical seat to Bath. Bath had a mint, which, along with its moneyer Osmaer (Osmier), passed into John's care. John died of a heart attack after eating his Christmas dinner.

Clarembald (died c. 1133) is a shadowy figure, although he seems to have been a collector of books and miracle stories. He spent a lot of time in Exeter, perhaps in the service of the colourful William de Warelwast, Bishop of Exeter (died 1137). Warelwast has been called the first professional civil servant, more interested in effective administration than in affairs of the soul. He was said to have had little learning, but plenty of talent, and was the kind of crafty ambassador Henry I liked.

Robert Bloet, Bishop of Lincoln, had a son called Simon. Simon seemed destined for great things in Henry's Court, but fell from grace. He was imprisoned, but escaped and died in poverty and exile. William Giffard (died 1129) was Bishop of Winchester. Giffard would have been known as Bishop William, but so would Warelwast, so I have used their second names to avoid confusion.